THE MERCHANT OF SILENCE

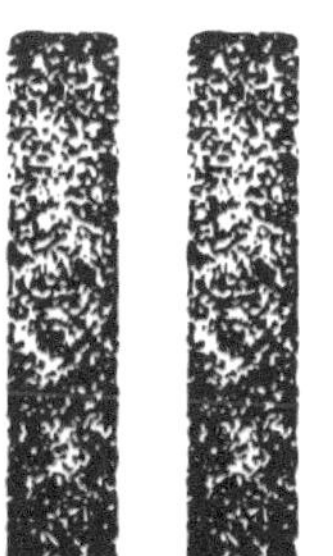

THE MERCHANT OF SILENCE

Sigil of Silence

Volume II

Zyphar Animas

The Merchant of Silence
Sigil of Silence, Volume II

Content Notice

This book is a work of fiction written for a sophisticated adult audience. It engages with serious and complex subject matter and is not intended for children, teenagers, or younger readers. It explores systemic corruption and the extreme physical and psychological costs of survival in a world without mercy. The views and actions expressed by characters are part of the fictional narrative and do not represent the views of the author. Any references to real-world events, organizations, or ideologies are used strictly within a fictional context. Due to the unflinching nature of the narrative—this work is strictly recommended for readers aged 18 and above. Reader discretion is strongly advised.

Author: Zyphar Animas
Edited by: Nimo Verin
ISBN: 978-984-35-8918-7
First Edition
Published in 2026

DEDICATION

For every soul weighed beneath small debts
while greater crimes walk free—shrouded in silence.
For the lives the system can tally, but never defend.
You were never fictional.
You were simply—unbearable to account for.

PREFACE

This is a story about lives—tangled, broken, and sharpened by need.

A story about the debts we inherit, the bodies we burn through, the cities that eat their own children just to keep the lights on.

You'll find the filth in the neon, and the hunger in the cleanest hands. Every character here is born from the edge—some break and crawl, some become the blade.

There are no innocents left. Only survivors and predators, and sometimes the difference is just who still remembers what mercy felt like.

The cities in these pages are alive—breathing, corrupt, dangerous. They are not just settings. They're adversaries, lovers, graves. The only gods that ever answered were the ones who demanded something back.

Love, in this world, is a weapon and a wound.
It saves nothing. It breaks what's left after war and leaves scars where hope tried to grow.

I don't offer answers in the pages. Only the honesty of survival, and the kind of questions that never close.

Why does violence feel like relief? Can you outrun what haunts you, or do you only gather more ghosts? Where is the line between justice and vengeance, and what happens when it finally disappears?

This story does not ask you to pick a side. It only asks that you watch closely—because nothing here happens by accident.

TRUTH HAS A COST

SILENCE IS FREE

Chasing Ashes

Bukit Bintang, KLCC District
Kuala Lumpur, Malaysia

Rasheed didn't expect good news to find him.
But it hit hard anyway.

The Maker sent an official ping.
The monster was neutralized before it could ever rise.
He'd already seen the headline in the New Straits Times.
Penang Bombing, they called it.

Rasheed didn't need a breakdown.
The equation was simple; the reality, ruthless.
And yet… he wasn't relieved. Not entirely.

The Maker had acted alone. No heads-up for Commander Kamran, not a whisper through the network—just a surgical hit, then gone without a trace. Too efficient.

Which meant one thing: he didn't need them.
Not to act. Not even to inform.
And that—was the real message.

Rasheed knew Kamran saw it too. You don't last this long without learning to read between detonations.

When Rasheed cautiously brought it up,
the commander only said:

—Focus on the mission. Let the ashes rot in the dark.

So he did. Landed in Kuala Lumpur as ordered.

Rasheed had seen cities rot before. Malaysia was just better lit.
A Muslim country on paper, hungry for Western cash everywhere else. Kuala Lumpur glittered on foundations of compromise—what started as side hustle for expat wallets, pubs, casinos, escort bars—had turned institutional.
Corruption wasn't an accident; it was the wiring.

Officials who once turned a blind eye now turned keys and opened doors.

Now, the whole city breathed corruption like oxygen.
Everyone blamed someone else. No one stopped anything.
And why would they? Everyone got a cut.
That's how you bury a society—not with war, but with comfort.

And Rasheed Dameer was here to count the graves before the next one opened. He sat buried in the neon gut of the KLCC, the epicenter of sin.

His gaze swept the scene with the cold precision of a man mapping out fresh war zones.
He'd seen Amsterdam. Walked Prague.
Kuala Lumpur was smoother.
More polite. Draped a veil over the vulgar—because here, even sin wore a scarf.

Surface-level, everything looked civilized—just for show.
The club itself perched thirteen floors up, above the corporate headquarters of a multinational electronics giant.
No sign, no glow. If you knew, you knew.

And If you didn't—they made sure you found out.
Scouts—slick as aged wine—prowled the street.
One nod, one whisper, a promise of a good time—and you were led right into paradise.

Three hundred ringgit bought the full ride.
Food. Company. Smiles that never broke.
Only the booze was extra.
A clean receipt for dirty pleasure.

Rasheed had to admit—the whole thing ran too smooth for comfort. Service hit you like a five-star battlefield: polished, efficient, forgettable only if someone left their soul at the door.

Word was, the entire floor—and most of the surrounding block—belonged to a bulldog tycoon out of Red China.
But that mutt was just a front. The real wiring ran east.

Beijing tugged the strings from deep in the dark.
The Russians had a slice too. So did the Albanians.

In KL, if a business made real money, someone heavy held the leash. Usually someone you'd never see.

Rasheed didn't want to be here.
In his world, orders never landed by accident.
He waited.
Nothing in his life ever happened without purpose.

There was no signal here. Not a single look his way—no one even acting like he mattered. Except one:
A skinny kid from the buffet squad, looks like Indian, making laps to his table—three, maybe four times—offering food with too much sugar in his smile. The usual hustle.

The buffet was part of the package—all-you-can-eat, all-inclusive, but the staff worked the floor hoping to score tips from anyone who looked soft enough.

Rasheed pegged him for just another grinder.
Eventually, real hunger kicked in.

He caught the boy's eye and waved him over.
The kid lit up, rattled off a list of "most popular dishes."
Rasheed cut him off:

—Nothing heavy. Something light. Low spice.

Five minutes later, what landed was... biryani.
That was enough to crack Rasheed's patience.

—Just because you're Indian, I have to eat biryani now?

His voice dropped, sharp as broken glass:

—You jackass—take it back. I said light. Low spice.
What's wrong with you?

The boy flinched, almost bowed.

—Sir—I'm not Indian. I'm Bangladeshi. And our biryani here, it's mild. Very light, sir. Please, just try.

The raw honesty softened Rasheed just enough.
He waved it off.
—I know your country bro, and I must say thanks—but this won't do. See if you've got bread. Salad. Something basic.

Ten minutes later the kid returned with naan and a side of Russian salad. The naan was slicked with butter—couldn't dodge the Indian touch—but the salad was clean.
It'd do.

As he ate, Rasheed considered wandering the floor.
He didn't see anyone watching.
No signs of contact. No nods or loaded looks.
Maybe this wasn't the spot after all.
He figured he'd finish up, scout the street, maybe loop back later if anything shifted.

Just as Rasheed pushed his chair back, the butler materialized—half-smile locked in place.

—Sir, the kid said, voice low.
—Our food didn't suit you. Maybe this place will.

He handed over a small black card.
Didn't wait for a thank you. Didn't angle for a tip.
Just nodded and vanished into the neon flow.

Rasheed almost dropped the card into the ashtray—reflex.
Every worker in a city like this ran double shifts—waiter-slash-fixer, driver-slash-pimp, tip culture knotted to side hustle.
But a glance at the card locked his hand mid-motion.

Roblox Mines – Fabulous Food & Fun.
Address printed below, out on the edge of the city.
The "food & fun" wasn't his concern. The logo was.
Angular. Grey.
A stylized robot face—with eyes Rasheed would never forget.

It was his face. The Maker.
No name, no signature. Just a shape burned into plastic.

That was the message.
And Rasheed Dameer knew how to follow a lead.

***

The Mines, Selangor Outskirts
Kuala Lumpur, Malaysia

Driving in Malaysia was surprisingly civilized— at least compared to the rest of Asia's chaos. Roads were solid.
Rules actually meant something.
Which made the one-hour drive out of KL a breeze.

Rasheed followed the highway as it carved through hills and dense forest. The GPS led him past industrial blocks, then into something that looked more like a billionaire's playground than a food joint.

So much for just grabbing a meal.
The place sprawled—monstrous in scale.
On one side of a glassy man-made lake stood a full-blown golf resort. On the other, a retail behemoth masquerading as a shopping mall. In between—pure tourist chaos.
A night bazaar sprawled over a square kilometer, lights strung overhead like a net of falling stars, the air so thick with roasted spice he could taste the menu before he'd actually found a stall.
The sign glared: ROBLOX MINES.

He barely made it three steps into the madness before a wall in a tailored suit blocked his path.

Older guy. Cut like granite.
Salt-and-pepper beard, tamed but not quite.
And—something too familiar about the face.

Before Rasheed could pin the memory, the man crushed him in a bear hug.

—Welcome, Rasheed Dameer—the mujahid himself—welcome to The Mines.

Then, a quick release.

—They said you'd be here an hour ago.

That stung. Because he wasn't wrong. If Rasheed had paid attention to the butler and ditched the club scene early, he would've arrived exactly on time.

But nothing about this place said casual. And the idea that they knew his ETA before he'd even started driving—that twisted a knot in his gut.

Still, Rasheed kept his expression locked.

—Been a while since I saw KL, he said, voice cool.
—Didn't want to rush the view. Hope I didn't keep you waiting.

The man just smiled, silent. But the shape of his jaw, the tilt of his head—Rasheed almost recognized it. Some ghost from the past.

Whoever he was, he turned and motioned Rasheed to follow. They pushed through a maze of sizzling grills and neon signage, locals and tourists chewing their way through the heat of the night.

At the far end of the chaos stood an apartment block—five stories, its red-tile roof jutting out in sharp triangles.
The shape was wrong for local architecture.
Not a flat top. Not a dome. A hard, conical pitch—the kind of roof built to shed snow. Except—this was Malaysia.

Rasheed had never even heard of snow falling here. But here stood a rooftop designed to defy winter. He said nothing, but a chill bled through his spine. Something cold was waiting inside.

Two armed guards posted at the entrance, rifles crossed over black tactical kits.
They didn't stop Rasheed. Didn't check him, didn't even blink.
They weren't there to vet him. They were there to let him pass.

The muscle-mountain led him up four flights—hallways steeped in the scent of polished leather and premeditated violence.
The suite at the top sprawled—big enough to be a headquarters or a confession booth.

Inside, the man peeled off his blazer and dropped into a chair.
He spoke in flawless Pashto:

—My condolences for Shahid Bahrram Gazi.

That was it. A name Rasheed hadn't heard in weeks.
Silence, shattered.

The man leaned in—voice warm, eyes glacial.
He asked how Rasheed was holding up. Asked about his travel, his health. Small questions. Big weight.

And then it clicked.
This wasn't a random liaison. Back in Herat, years before ISIS splintered and burned, Rasheed had smuggled a weapons shipment under deep proxy cover.

The man who'd received it had a face like stone and a jagged scar above his left eyebrow.

Rasheed studied the man now.
No scar. But the feeling matched.

The man grinned, catching the question behind Rasheed's stare.

—Looking for a scar, are we?

Rasheed stayed silent. The man went on.

—ISIS was a stage show, the man said, smirk cutting sideways—Now we're done playing. No more sandy games. No proxy wars. This is a new era—and we're a new movement. Now we wear suits and hunt from penthouses.

He laughed, fingering his own tailored threads like a kid with a superhero cape.

Two more men entered.
Slightly smaller, but still built like wrecking balls. They nodded at Rasheed, shook hands, took seats.

The mood flipped—instantly.
The leader's grin vanished, eyes gone surgical.

—You can't teach them pain with desert shootouts, Hazrat. Their kids need to bleed on sidewalks. Their homes need to burn. Their wives need to cry at empty cupboards. Only then will they grasp what a few barrels of crude oil cost our people.

Rasheed didn't flinch.
The logic wasn't wrong.
Just crooked.

—I stand with The Maker, he continued.
—This isn't revenge. It's correction. You're high-ranking in this new movement. Tell us, Hazrat—what's your vision?

All three stared—watching, measuring.
Truth was, Rasheed wasn't a philosopher. Never claimed to be.
But silence now would be louder than anything else.

He leaned forward. Picked his words like bullets.

—I've never been a fan of ethnic terrorism, he began.
—I believed, maybe stupidly—that the West had citizens with education and conscience. That if their governments bombed us, their people would rise up, force it to stop.

He paused. No one blinked.

—But they didn't.
They danced in bars while our children died at home.
They binged Netflix while drones wiped out our villages.
Their silence bought this war.
So yes. Now it's their turn to pay the price.

The mountain exhaled like a prayer.

—Marhaba, Hazrat, Marhaba! Khudo bless the hand that brings down those Kafirs in Eilat. Your clarity... your judgment—it's divine.

He stood again.
Crushing Rasheed like a brother returning from war.
The two others followed—chests thudding together, pact sealed.

They'd been all smiles till now. Rasheed figured it was time to gut the surface and go straight to the bone.

—Ikhwani al-mujahideen, Rasheed began.

Locking eyes with each of them,

—I'm honored to be here. As you know, I've had my hands full with visionary ops. High command figured I could use a change of pace before I burn out. I've got zero eyes on your setup here. Enlighten me. Where do I start?

There was a flicker of hesitation—respectful.
Then the big one, the muscle mountain, leaned forward with a grin that didn't reach his eyes.

—Under instructions from higher up, he said.
—We're told to align this cell's actions with your strategy.
Just like you did in Eilat. The Maker sent us a new package.
A smaller, tighter version of your original payload.
Deadlier. Beautiful piece of work.

He shot a look at his partners, then added,

—Plan was to push it through Singapore. Strangle the Western pigs at their golden artery—shut down trade, lock the straits.
Once that route's gone, their only real supply lines run through Chinese ports or the Gulf—both friendlier ground for us.
We'd hit them in the wallet and funnel business our way.

Rasheed's fingers tapped once on the armrest.

—Go on, he said.

—The package landed before you even touched down in Phuket.
The Maker advised we loop you in. But our unit's commander,
Mohabbat Khan—stubborn bastard—chose not to brief you.
Claimed he had a better angle. Gave it to some Arab friend of his instead.

The brute looked disgusted, spitting the words like bile.

—Idiot took the device to his hotel room. Brought in a girl,
got sloppy. Next morning—she's gone, and so's the package.

Rasheed's silence turned sharp. He could've moved that device across Singaporean waters in a few hours, tops.
No mess. No exposure. But they'd treated it like a toy.

He cut the brute off:

—I was in Phuket for days after that meeting.
Mohabbat Khan knew it. Why didn't he come to me when the package disappeared?

The room changed temperature. The youngest of the three cleared his throat, half a smirk curling his lip.

—Hazrat, with respect... you're always moving. Too busy to see what people say about you. Especially the field units.
A lot of them don't see you as one of us. They call you hārib.
The deserter who ran from his war. Say you bailed on Hamas during the hard time. Some field crew don't want to take orders from a hārib.

Rasheed didn't blink. He'd heard it all before. Always whispered, never faced straight on. But now—they'd let ego sink a mission that could've paralyzed a continent.

He stood, eyes sweeping all three men.

—Since the day Commander Kamran called me in, I've risked my life keeping your supply lines alive. One wrong turn, one missed step on my end, and your whole Southeast cell would be nothing but red on the asphalt.

His voice dropped to iron.

—And yet you chose ego over strategy.
Let your fucking feelings cost us an op.

Rasheed's words had barely settled in the air. The three started smiling—like hyenas too dumb, or too savage, to recognize the roar of a lion.

The young brute—dark-skinned, thick arms knotted with muscle, smiling like a villain drawn in cheap ink—spoke first.

—Don't get us wrong, Hazrat. Back when you fought for Gaza, that was for your own blood. But now, as Dameer,
you hit wider—beyond borders. Mujahideen, regardless of tribe, eats from the fruits of your ops.
The real fighters among us? We know. We respect it.
We see you as one of our own.
But you know how it is— half these new hybrids, recruited for connections or wallets, not faith, don't get it.

Mohabbat Khan was one of those. Arrogant bastard's already paid for it. You'll see soon enough.

As he finished, muscle-mountain—Khurram—took the handoff smooth.

—Like I said before, the day after that whore ran off with the package, Mohabbat finally told us what happened.
Way too late, of course. We, the Malaysia hub, were prepping to fly out to Phuket and clean the mess. But before we could lift off, he shows up here. Tail tucked, hands shaking. Coward.
The Maker's response was clear: break his bones.
See what he gives up. Until we get a new lead, we're to recover the package—or the bitch who took it.

Khurram leaned in, voice dropping to a hush.

—Our boys tracked her within the week. Found her packing to bolt—package gone, of course. She was trying to escape—hiding in the back of some Thai mob punk's ride.
We iced him, snatched her, and flagged it up the chain.
HQ told us to forget the Thai crew and focus on the girl.
We were ordered to extract intel—whatever it takes.
So we brought her here.

A pause.
Khurram's eyes hardened as he continued.

—We tried the gentle route. Got close to breaking her.
But somewhere, somehow, we still fucked up.

His tone stayed even, but the shame leaked through the cracks.

—I didn't repeat Mohabbat's mistake. I reported every step.
Told them we weren't getting full intel and needed outside hands. That's when they told us you were inbound.

Rasheed's fingers went still.
He wasn't just listening now—he was calculating.

—You followed protocol. That's good, *he said, voice measured.*
—But what exactly did you fuck up?

A shift rippled through the room.
Glances traded.
Then Khurram again, slower this time.

—Well... you know how it is. When you're trying to get answers, sometimes you need to... press harder.
And, uh, my younger brother here—Khursheed,
he's... let's just say he's curious. About women.
A little like your old comrade Bahrram Gazi, actually.

He gestured to the younger brute.
Rasheed's face didn't move.
But his voice came down like a guillotine.

—You know Gazi's appetites.
Then you should know how he died.

The silence cut the air raw.
Rasheed locked eyes with Khurram.
No heat. Just cold execution.

—He bled out in the desert... in front of my eyes. Trying to scream with his own severed cock shoved down his throat.

Rasheed turned now, just slightly, to face Khursheed.

—If you want your brother to die choking on his own dick,
by all means—let him keep playing games with captives.

The laughter died.
Khurram straightened in his seat, expression sober now.
Khursheed looked like he wanted to disappear.
The third man had already gone stiff, as if waiting for a bullet.

The whole room shifted.
Khurram cleared his throat, then launched in again—like he'd been waiting for the mic.

—We tried the usual at first—nothing brutal. Figured the bitch would fold. But she kept her mouth shut. The clock is ticking. You know how it is—if there's no ransom deal, a captured girl's only worth is what the boys can get out of her before we put a bullet in her skull. After a few dead-end days, I handed her to little Khurshid here. Figured he could… learn on the job.

Khurram cast a mock-sheepish glance at the younger brute, who didn't even flinch.

—Kid's got a curious streak. Young blood,
you know how that goes. He went too far.
Girl couldn't handle it. She dropped into a coma.
Maybe dead by now. We'll check.
Meanwhile, we still had standing orders to grill that bastard—
Mohabbat Khan. We figured, maybe he was involved, too.
We worked him over—properly this time. But before he could
spill anything useful, he just crashed—seven seconds flat.
Fucking cardiac arrest.
Just like that. Hero in life, punk in death.
We've kept the body on ice.
If you want to see him, say the word.

The grin drained from Rasheed's face.

—But out of that whole shitshow, we did get one thread.
From Khan's mumbling and what our scouts pulled in from
Phuket, we learned the missing girl had someone looking for
her—another woman. Name's Miss Marisha Jasmín.
Supposedly her sister. We dug into her.
And yeah, Hazrat… something was off.

Khurram kept rolling, oblivious.

—Turns out Miss Jasmín's not some helpless civilian.
She's under full-time protection from Chinese Tong muscle in
Phuket. That's big-league backing. And when she hit KL,
she didn't book a hotel or run for a safehouse. She went straight
to the private crib of Papa Cheng's trusted lieutenant.
We knew this guy. He's got history with the Russians—blew up
half a block in Penang not long ago. After that mess, he ghosted.
Stayed buried. Never left his own turf.
But this chick lands in KL and shacks up with him?
Then boom—next day, she walks straight into Zamuk HQ.
No way in hell that's random.

Khurram paused, cracked his knuckles, leaned in.

—We've got deep eyes inside Zamuk. With their help, we nabbed her before she could hit up one of their handlers.

—She wasn't talking either. We tried a light dose—kept it clean. Didn't budge. No intel, nothing worth the trouble.
But we're not morons—we didn't rough her up like the last one.
Sent everything to high command and waited for word.
That's when they told us you were inbound, Hazrat.
You'd decide what came next.

By now it was clear: the big man loved to talk.
Could go all night if he got the chance. But Rasheed was done listening. He didn't care for the chatter anymore—he had the thread he needed.

The whole thing was a hornet's nest—unknown players chasing the tech, maybe traitors on the inside. Everyone tangled in this op was either grabbed or already burned.
Except one.
Papa Cheng's lieutenant.
The bastard in the private residence—still free, still moving.
Which meant Rasheed had work to do.

The Afghan brutes could've handled it—should've, if they hadn't frozen up after botching everything else. Now they waited for orders, afraid to breathe without permission.

Fine. They'd get it.

—Bring him in, Rasheed said. No bargaining.

The slabs nodded, hustling out in silence—hungry to atone, desperate to be useful.

Then Rasheed stood. No speeches left. He slid his jacket back over his frame and lumbered for the exit, Rasheed in tow.

Night had settled deep. They moved behind the apartment block, through pools of cheap artificial light that barely scratched the dark—just enough to walk, not enough to see faces.

They walked in silence for ten minutes before the manicured fringe gave way to undergrowth—half-wild terrain brushing against concrete.

Khurram let out a thin giggle, flashing teeth.

—Careful, Hazrat. Snakes love this patch.

He didn't slow down.
Just waddled on, drunk on bulk and confidence.

Rasheed's eyes narrowed. If this was a setup, Khurram picked the wrong man. Rasheed had crossed more borders than this ox had seen action films. If the brute tried anything, he'd be mulch before the moon cleared a cloud.

Rasheed followed—silent, alert, clocking every detail.
They reached a squat steel hatch—half-buried in the dirt—bunker style, the kind seen in apocalypse reruns.

Rasheed had watched fiction steal from war, but he never thought the real world would return the favor.

Khurram crouched, fiddled with the lock, finally got it to snap open. Rasheed almost smirked at the clown show—then sharpened up. Time to focus.

Inside, a tight stairwell dropped away, pale blue light bleeding down the walls—The Maker signature all over it.
Clean cuts. No wasted space.
Every edge humming with surgical menace.

—After you, Hazrat, *Khurram said.*

Rasheed moved.
Behind him, the hatch slammed shut.

First came a round atrium. Hallways shot out in five directions like limbs of a starfish. Khurram picked the third on the left, leading with his ragged breath echoing off steel and tile.

The place felt familiar, even though Rasheed had never walked these halls. But the design spoke of one mind.

The Maker's. Each chamber cut with the same ruthless precision.
Intelligence hammered into steel.

They stopped at a side lab.
Another digital lock.
Inside: a drawer the size of a coffin, hissing open on command.
A freezer.

Khurram pulled it open and slid the tray halfway out.
Mohabbat Khan lay inside.

The man Rasheed had met in Phuket—mouth on legs, always running, even mid-op. Now he looked like meat—cold, drained, nothing left inside. Just another casualty. Just another reminder.

Khurram claimed a little shock stopped his heart.
Rasheed doubted it. He gestured—take him out.
Khurram shed his coat, hauled the corpse onto a sterile table.
Rasheed ran a quick inspection.

Burn marks ringed wrists and ankles. Nothing else—no deep bruises, no marks of slow pain, just the last electric burst.
Maybe it was a heart attack after all.

Still, it reeked of mismanagement.

—Put him back, *Rasheed said.*

Khurram complied, sliding the tray home.
Next—the girl.

They swung back to the hub, turned left into what passed for a medical wing. Behind a one-way mirror, a young woman lay comatose on a hospital bed. Tubes fed her arms, machines flickered all around. She was alive. Barely.

Rasheed's jaw locked down. Her body—what was left untouched—was a map of ruin, burn marks, bruises in places no blade belonged.

He stared. Silent. Too long.
This was beyond protocol. This was desecration.
Khurram started to open the door—nervously hopeful, maybe—but Rasheed raised a hand.

No.
Their eyes locked.
For the first time, Khurram dropped his gaze.

—I told you, Hazrat… the boys are young.
Don't know the real techniques yet… *he mumbled.*

Rasheed ignored it. Already walking.
He wanted to see the other girl.

They circled back—another corridor, colder, lined with heavy steel doors. Just like The Maker's face.

Khurram stopped at the center door.
Keypad. Code. Click.
It swung wide. Rasheed stepped inside.

The room looked like a horror set under flickering, low voltage light. Half-dried, blackened blood streaked the floor and walls—some splattered wild, some soaked deep into the steel.

Torture tools lined two long metal tables: saw-blades, clamps, tongs—some still wet, catching the low voltage gleam.
But it was the figure hanging from the ceiling that locked Rasheed's breath in his chest.

A girl. Beauty that made no sense here—strung up like a carcass. Thick iron chains fed through a ceiling ring, biting into her wrists. Arms pulled up, head slumped forward—chin pressed to her collarbone, long black hair veiling her face like a shroud.

Rasheed stared.
For a second, he felt nothing at all.
He flicked a hand at Khurram.

The brute walked up and grabbed the girl's hair, yanking it to expose her face.

She was breathtaking—even now:
Bruised, dirt-smeared, barely conscious.

Rasheed didn't linger on her beauty.
His gaze went straight to her throat.
A dog tag.

He reached out—hand trembling—fingers brushing cold metal.
The name etched into it knocked the air from his chest.
Froze him to the soul.
One tag.
The other half—Rasheed already had.
Found at the bloodbath, the night Bahrram Gazi's throat was sliced open. Dropped by the corpse, left as a message.
And now she was here—this girl.
That face—he finally placed it.

Thread by thread, memory snapped back into place.
And when it hit, Rasheed's knees just buckled.
The war dog—the ghostmaker—the man who'd stared down death a hundred times—dropped like a sack, hard and helpless.

His breath shuddered. Sweat ran cold down his spine.
Khurram rushed over, confused.

—Hazrat? What happened? You alright?

Rasheed couldn't speak. Jaw shaking, every cell screaming.
Not from pain. From the cold burn of truth.

He pulled in all his strength, grinding out words like ash through fire:

—What the fuck have you done, you pig.
Call your men back.
Now.

His voice came out hoarse, shredded, furious—already cracked from the inside.

Khurram blinked.
For a beat, he didn't understand. Then he glanced between Rasheed, shaking on the floor, and the girl with the dog tag at her throat. Her face. Suddenly, the math landed.

Khurram—son of Afghan mountains, breaker of men—had been called many things in a dozen languages, but never a pig.
If anyone else had said it, he'd have torn out their tongue and made them choke on it.

But this was Rasheed Dameer AKA Rasheed Farish. The man who'd razed an Israeli city with a single crate of Maker fire.

Khurram swallowed his pride. No protest.
Just a stiff nod, and he yanked out his phone.

Rasheed stayed on the floor, chest locking up in gasps.
Panic owned him—hard, merciless.
Behind his eyes, the images spun—sharp, savage,
looping on repeat.

Phuket. His safehouse.
The girl—this same girl—up on stage, singing.
Rasheed had paused to listen, liked her voice, shook her hand after. Then she'd dropped offstage, flung herself into someone's arms—he'd noticed, distantly. Assumed boyfriend. Ignored it.
Then the attack.
That night.

He'd never seen the face—buried behind the girl's hair.
But now it was obvious.
It was him. That monster.

The devil no one could ever track—not CIA, not Mossad,
not even the Maker. The one Rasheed himself had buried under tons of concrete—by his own hand.
And still—the bastard turned up in Phuket.
Walked the streets like a tourist.
Mocked Rasheed's security like it was a party trick.

Later, the Maker had assured him:
The threat's neutralized.
Bullshit.

Looking at the girl strung from the ceiling, Rasheed finally understood something he'd spent a lifetime denying.
For a woman like that, even he could burn down the whole world. And if he could feel that...
Then what the hell would Darius Caesar do?
The man who bled cities dry just to keep himself entertained.
The man who turned killing into a Sunday ritual.
Rasheed had never wanted a woman in his life.
Saw them as chaos wrapped in perfume.

Stayed a bachelor by instinct, not by accident.
Even history—real history—spelled it out.
One woman, one damn tag, one misplaced desire,
that was all it took to set Troy on fire.
And after Troy... came the fall of civilization.

He was staring at the next one.
Because hanging from her neck—alongside those bruises and that bleeding pride—was his own fate. Not just his.
Commander Kamran.
The Maker.
That prancing owl.
The entire operation.
It all hung there, clinking against the steel-tag marked Caesar.

And Rasheed knew.
This was not his war to fight.
This was beyond command, beyond ideology.
It was myth clawing its way into flesh.

First move: get her down.
Second: get her talking.
Third: if there was a god left, shove the blame onto that overfed ape Khurram, earn her trust, and survive the fallout.

Not his style, no.
Rasheed Dameer didn't grovel. Never had.
But then again— pride's a joke when you're dead.

The shaking had eased enough.
He scanned left, then right, hunting for Khurram.
Before he could call, the brute barreled in—sweat pouring, phone gripped tight.

—Something's wrong, Hazrat, *he panted.*

—None of them are answering. I called them one by one. Nothing. Even the bastard who was posted in the alley with the car—dead silence. All of them.

Rasheed didn't even blink. He knew exactly what that meant.
His lips cracked open. First a breath, then a noise.
Then he laughed.
It wasn't a chuckle. It was madness.
Bone-deep, echoing laughter that rolled like a death march.

—You're never seeing them again, you pig.

He spat it out between gasps.

—Forget those bastards.
Get her down. Put her in that chair.
Then plant your fat ass and wait.
We're both dead men now. Ha... ha...

Khurram froze, blank panic flickering behind his eyes.
He didn't get it—not yet.
But he knew enough not to fight the order.

He moved—unhooked the girl with hands suddenly careful, carried her to the lone chair, splashed water over her face.

She didn't move.
Didn't open her eyes.
Just sat there—like a sleeping goddess.

A flash of anger ticked through Khurram—an urge to lash out, stomp the fear out of himself.
But Rasheed's stare pinned him still.
Not a word. Not a twitch.

He set the water down.
And walked out the door.
Quiet as a ghost.

***

Times Square, KLCC
Malaysia.

Kuala Lumpur pulsed neon under smog and silk suits.
Khursheed's blood was singing—craving action,
pure, uncut chaos.
Too long spent on the sidelines, watching others play.
Too many days licking wounds that never bled.

Now—target locked. The hunt was on.
Next to him, Tarique chuckled like a man already counting ribs to break.

—You know, bro... this new one? Better than the last.
This time I get to do the slicing.

Khursheed didn't laugh. Not really. Just a twitch at the corner of his mouth—the kind that shows right before you step on a landmine, just to see what goes up.

—Take your time dreaming, *he muttered.* —Rasheed Agha Jan's in town. Your playdate might be postponed.

Tarique grimaced. Violence delayed was pain doubled.

He looked up at the concrete beast looming over them— glass, steel and privilege rising sky-high.

The kid in the back seat—new recruit, all nervous fingers and flashy sneakers—had the access card. Fancy shit.
One card opens every door, or so he claimed.

The six of them had rolled in with two black vans.
Enough firepower to take an embassy if they felt like it.
But this wasn't war. This was sport.

The basement parking swallowed them whole.

Two men would wait here, but their van peeled off on Khursheed's order—parked in the alley like a wolf waiting for the wounded.

The driver—Daem—bitched about it, as always.
But he went.

Upstairs, the three-man strike team stood by the elevator—Khursheed, Tarique, and Mr. Keycard.

Twenty-fifth floor.
The kid tapped.
Lights blinked. Elevator groaned.

Khursheed leaned back, eyes scanning the walls, the vents, the camera angles. He wasn't smart. But he was careful.

Then the door opened.
Marble floor, rich carpet.
Expensive death waiting here.

Tarique moved silently to handle the floor security.
The other two reached the door.
Apartment 25-C.
A neat brass plate: Elijan Vellum.
Like he thought the world should know he lived here.

The kid tapped the card.
Nothing.
Again.
Still nothing.

Khursheed's jaw tightened.
The kid fumbled, pushed again—BEEP. BEEP. BEEP.
Alarm.

Kid went ghost-white.
Inside—movement.
No time for finesse.

Khursheed shoved the kid aside like wet laundry and yanked a mobile gas cutter from his jacket. The flame roared up with a low, hungry growl—fire-breathing dragon in his fist.

He held it to the lock. The steel began to bubble.

The mobile gas cutter—that was the real MVP.
Small enough to slip into a pocket.
Strong enough to melt the gates of hell.

Lock hissed. Metal peeled like fruit.
Thirty seconds flat, the door surrendered with a choking cough.

The fire alarms didn't scream—just a soft chime feeding straight to floor security, not the neighbors.
Precision. Discreet, as the rich prefer.

And no one showed.
Which meant Tarique had done his part.
Khursheed stepped inside—ghost-silent.

Behind him, the new kid raised a silenced Luger—nervous hands, twitchy breath.

Khursheed didn't need it.
He liked his kills messy. Hands-on. Real.
They swept the living room.
No movement. No Vellum.

But on the bedside table—a cigarette still burning, ash curling.
Fresh.
So he's home.
Watched them through the peephole.
Playing phantom now.

Khursheed grinned—the hunter's smile.

—Come on out, babyface, *he called, voice sugarcoated venom.*
—We got your little cherry on ice.
Can't unwrap her 'til you show.

The kid behind him snorted. Thought it was funny.
But the room stayed dead quiet.

Khursheed stepped to the half-closed bedroom door, lining up a boot—didn't need it.

The door opened slow.
Out walked the guy they came for—Elijan Vellum.

A weapon in hand—Nightwalker.
Silencer mounted, face carved in stone.
This thing had Top-tier AI targeting, newest gen.

Khursheed flinched. He knew that gun.
Rasheed Dameer carried the same.
This was no street punk's toy. This was heat from the top shelf.
Red-glass viewfinder tracked movement, scanned weak points.
All you had to do was pull the trigger. The gun would do the rest.

And right now, the barrel was aimed dead center between Khursheed's legs. Blue targeting light. Not lethal—yet.

Still—he regretted joking about the girl.
Some poisons shouldn't get loose.

He had a blade strapped to his left wrist—spring-loaded, quick as a thought.
He used it before—split men open while they blinked.
But something about that Nightwalker slowed him.
That fucking steel whispered caution.

He waved the gas cutter in his right hand.
Tried a stuttered distraction move—fake fear, a fake surrender.

Elijan blinked—rookie's mistake.
Took his eyes off the man.

In that single blink, Khursheed's blade whipped out—low, fast.
Buried itself right below Elijan's ribs.

Elijan gasped, buckled to one knee.
Victory, almost—but Khursheed never saw the finger squeeze.
BANG.
Nightwalker spat fire.

Pain exploded between Khursheed's legs.
He collapsed, screaming.

The trick actually worked. Elijan's eyes flicked toward the gas cutter—but the Nightwalker's AI didn't care where he looked.

Khursheed forgot that part.
And paid for it—loud.
He howled, fists drumming the marble,
writhing like a butchered animal.
Pain had no poetry—just shock, just the end.

Behind him, the new kid froze.
His Luger still hissing smoke, eyes wide—boss bleeding on one side, their target bleeding on the other.

He had no clue about the Nightwalker's targeting system.
Didn't even know what red or blue lights meant.
All he saw: the man raised a gun. Then his boss went down.
So he fired.
And now he needed to know what the hell just happened.

He stepped over, booted the man onto his back.
Checked the damage.
Perfect shot—dead center chest.
Blood bubbling like a popped heart.
Khursheed's blade had landed too—just under the ribs.
Two wounds. Fast death.

No twitch.
No farewell speech.
Just gone.

The kid spun around. Khursheed still shrieking, clutching his ruined groin, legs flailing.

He yelled for Tarique—fast.
The corpse stared back, eyes wide open—Elijan Vellum.
Dead.

Within seconds, Tarique stormed in.
First glance—confusion. Then the rookie explained.
Tarique brushed past them and opened the bathroom door.
Found what he was looking for in a cabinet: a standard med kit.
No time for questions. Just survival.

They hauled Khursheed onto the couch, peeled his pants down, checked the wound. The bullet had cracked both lower joints—blood, bone, cartilage, all blown to hell.
He'd live—but his manhood was gone with the blast.

Tarique asked if he wanted a painkiller.
Khursheed spat curses. Refused.
Tarique didn't take it personally. Not tonight.

He wrapped the mess as his old friend howled, keeping pressure, sealing off the red. Then leaned back, breathing hard.

The man was dead. Mission blown. But—there might be something here worth Rasheed Dameer's time.
Especially whatever this man was hiding.
His phone, his contacts, any sensitive files—if they existed.

Tarique told the rookie to stay posted by Khursheed.
Then he started the sweep.
Small studio. No hiding spots.
Drawers—nothing but clothes.
One medium locker tucked inside the wardrobe.
Combination lock. Owner—now dead.
Tarique picked up the gas cutter again. Let it sing.

Metal curled like skin.
Inside—stacks of money.
Some too close to the flame, blackened.
The rest—pristine.
Documents. Passports. And a single black folder.

He stuffed everything into a shopping bag.
Handed it off to the rookie.

—Take the lift. Move now.

Then, without a word, he lifted Khursheed into his arms.
Like a fallen brother—and headed for the exit.

Khursheed's face stayed folded like a punched napkin. He wasn't howling anymore, but the agony sat on his jaw like rust.

As Tarique reached the door, Khursheed caught his wrist.
Nodded toward the bed.
Tarique looked—and spotted it.

A woman's handbag.
Soft. Expensive.
Wrong.

For a second his chest pinched—reflex memory.

If the flat were any bigger, he'd think someone was still hiding.
But he'd checked. Twice.
No room for secrets here. No shadows thick enough to breathe.

Maybe it belonged to her.
The girl. Marisha Jasmín.

She stayed here before she got caught.
Which meant the bag might carry something useful.
A note. A name. A line valuable to Rasheed.

The rookie was already gone, headed to the lift.
Khursheed—barely functional. No way he'd handle another trip up and down. Tarique just carried him to the bed.

Khursheed reached for the bag himself.
Their eyes met—a silent nod, a shared smile, old wolves still finding bones.

—Fucking luck, *Khursheed muttered.*

Spitting on the floor from Tarique's arms.

—What now? *Tarique asked.*

Khursheed popped the bag open.
Held it up for both of them to see.
Empty. Bone dry.

Just a few crushed petals at the bottom. Maybe perfume flowers, maybe trash. Whatever it was, it wasn't worth shit. Khursheed growled—and launched the bag across the room like a grenade.

It landed perfectly.
Smacked right on the face of Elijan's corpse.

That broke the dam—both of them cracked up, laughter spilling out bitter and breathless. Pain pulled at Khursheed's side, but the look on the dead man's face—eyes still open, mouth stuck in surprise—made it worth the jolt.

They headed for the door.
No more words.

The lock was broken.
The air tasted of ozone and spent adrenaline.
Some nosy neighbor might check. Someone might care.
But floor security had been knocked out long ago—Tarique made sure of that.

They still had time.
And in this city, time was louder than sirens.

—*—

Spectrum of silence

Times Square
Kuala Lumpur Malaysia

Light flickers through the silk—beige, almost gold.
Slipping in and out behind floor-to-ceiling glass,
playing old games of shadow.
The ceiling fan overhead spins slow, lazy.
Cool air kisses my skin like an old love I'd forgotten.

And just like that—I know.
I feel it in the marrow.
I exist.

In this beautiful, absurd little world.
Thanks to my Lord.
Again.

Usually, when I'm pulled back—whether I want it or not.
I still feel everything.

The way day folds into night. The smell when seasons shift.
Even the weight of nearby footsteps—pretending to pass
unnoticed—I sense it all.

I don't sleep. I archive.
And every time I rise again, the memories crawl up with me.

Except this time.

From the moment I burned to ash until now—blank.
There's nothing.
No clues. No continuity. No whisper of a single soul.

I don't know how long I've been gone.
But I'm awake now. And I'll find out everything.
Soon.

Something dangles over my nose.

I reach up—a woman's purse.
Stylish. Soft.
Definitely not mine.
But the trigger wasn't the bag. It was what lay inside.

Two petals.
Right on my face.
I pick them up, rub them between my fingers.
They weren't fresh.
And it wasn't their first time with me.

Someone's brought them before.
But when? Where?

The moment I reach for the memory, pain splits my skull.
Like a steel rod jammed straight in.
I clench my teeth—and growl,
somewhere between a curse and a scream.

It helps. For about three seconds.
Then it hits again.
Twice.
Thrice.

Breathing doesn't help. Blinking? Pointless.
My eyes are wet. But after the third shot—silence.

The pain doesn't come back.
I breathe out, slow. Let the shiver run.
Let the memory reform.

And then—I laugh. Loud enough to startle myself.
Because now I remember.

Penang Island.

There was a girl.
She brought those Blood Orchids to buy me time.
But something hits before the transaction is finished.

An attack. Didn't matter.
Those orchids, in blood-red spectrum,
summoned by silence, find me anyway.

And do exactly what they're meant to do.
Just two petals. Not even a full bloom.
That's the part only my Lord could script—not with thunder or rage, but with the quietest, deadliest mercy.

Two bloody petals, slipping through chaos,
surviving the burn, outliving killers.
Waiting—for this exact second.
Not enough to save a life—but enough to bring back the one who never needed saving. That's the trick.
Not resurrection. Permission.

No plan. No defense. No science will work—when my Lord decides to flip the hourglass, everything falls.
It doesn't matter what they scheme.
Doesn't even matter what I want.
When He wants me to rise,
silence calls my name—I burn back alive.
Hah... hahahaha.
Let the silence sing again.

Seeing through the glass, Petronas pride stand tall—unmoved.
No doubt—I'm in KL.

My mind flicks to Macro, to Tommy—did they make it out with the rest?
I try to sit. Feels like something jabs through my chest.
This pain isn't divine. This is human—raw and physical.

I force myself up. Take a look at the vessel.
Gunshot. Bullet still lodged.
I get up anyway.

Another hit near the lower abdomen—a blade, polished steel.
Assassin's favorite bitch—stiletto.
Both wounds are dry, sealed by time or luck.
But if I pull the knife wrong,
it'll reopen the old negotiations with death.
The bullet needs trained hands.
That's for later.

Across the room: an open first-aid kit.
What kind of killer leaves bandages with a corpse?
Either they didn't care if I lived, or figured I wouldn't.
Doesn't matter. I pick it up.
I can deal with the blade. That's enough.

I step into the bathroom—and freeze.
The man in the mirror—I know that face.
Though we never got the chance to talk.

I keep working on the wound, letting the pain anchor me,
distract me from the deeper question.

I saw this face before the blast.
He was outside.
Alive.

When my body broke apart—did my Lord drop me into this one?
If that's true, I should be feeling his memories.
But there's nothing. No echo. No residue.
This body is blank.

Only two ways that happens:
One—a newborn, fresh out of the womb. No memories yet.
Two—a dead man. Nothing left to remember.
And this isn't a child's body.

Everything about it—the wounds, the bullet in the chest—tells
the truth. This man was gone for good.
And now I'm inside what's left.

I wrap the wound tight. Should hold through light movement.
The bullet... that one stays for now.
As long as I can walk, I'll ignore it.

Back in the main room,
something catches my eye under the couch.
I reach down and pull it free—a Nightwalker.
Kitted with an AI viewfinder and suppressor.
This beast doesn't even whisper when it fires.
A weapon of true silence.
I tuck it behind me.

Blood everywhere on the couch.
Top cushions drenched, soaked through.
I'd dropped near the bathroom—so this isn't my blood.
I run my fingers through it. Nothing.
Bring it to my nose.
It smells like it should—iron, sour—but nothing more.

Wait.
It just hits me.
I close my eyes and reach inward.
Nothing.

I can't feel the currents beneath the sound.
Can't taste the air flowing around me.
Can't hear the world breathing.

All I can feel is the presence inside—the infinite Darkness.
Could pain block it? Unlikely.
My senses aren't muscle and nerves.
Even buried beneath Al Madam's sand, drifting in vapor,
I could feel the movements of the world.
I was never disconnected. But now—nothing.

That cold feeling creeps in.
Truth, in its barest form.

He took them.
My Lord stripped me of all access.
The senses that made me more than human—gone.
Reclaimed by His will.

A sound at the door—soft, measured.
Heavy footsteps. Someone big, moving slow.
I don't need divine sight to know what that means.

I slide sideways, press myself against the wall.
Draw the Nightwalker. Flip off the auto-target.

That toy's for amateurs. I don't need help hitting targets.
Even in this body—I could shoot anyone's ass in the dark.
That doesn't come from instinct. That's training.

The visitor tilts his head, scans the room.
Looking for where I fell.
Trying to guess if I'm still there.

I break his innocent curiosity.
First shot—clean through the hip joint, from behind.

He drops hard, right where I'd been sprawled a minute ago.
His eyes snap to the barrel.
Surprised. Maybe shocked.
Mumbling to say something, but nothing comes out.

I pick up a small stool.
Sit beside him.
Let's see if we can handle this like shit buddies.

He can't move below the waist, but—tries to touch me.
Why? No idea.
I raise the gun again.
That's enough.

His voice finally breaks loose.

—Everyone's in the basement.

And that's all I need.
The Nightwalker answers next—thup—or something like that.
Whatever. It punches clean between his eyes.
Perfect.
No drama. Just precision.
Nice weapon.

I scan for a phone—nothing. Room already stripped.
Even the busted safe in the wardrobe is cleaned out.
Useless.
That leaves only one direction: the basement.

I move to the door.
Lock melted and warped.
Burn scars on the floor suggest a gas cutter.

No time for forensics.
I head for the emergency stairs next to the elevator.

The wound whispers under my ribs.
I ignore it.
More important things to feel now.

I make it down the stairs—not as fast as before, but fast enough.
Emergency exits aren't supposed to open into an exposed space,
I take the gamble.

Crack the red door slowly. No sound.
Slip through. Let it close just as quiet.

As expected, I come out behind the elevator shaft.
Lean forward. Take a look.

A black van parked by the lobby.
Three men stand beside it—talking to someone inside.
Which means—all three outside are expendable.
The Nightwalker agrees.

Thup-thup-thup.

Three soft bits drop them all, flawless rhythm.

Now—if the one inside's green, he'll get out to check.
That's when I shoot him below the knee. Ask questions.

If he's smart, he'll stay low. Hide under the seat.
But he does neither.

I step in closer.
Find him inside—wounded bad. Slumped across the middle seat.
Legs open.
Bandage pressed between them like a kid waiting for a medic.
Moaning through the pain. Lucky bastard took a bullet and lived.

I give him a smile.

—One round left, bro.
With all due compassion, you need to start talking.
Who, what, why—give me everything. I laid the others down nice and quiet just so I could listen to you.
Stay silent, and that bandage learns a new kind of pain.
Sound fair?

His eyes go wide—same look as the first one.
Tries to melt into the seat. Mouth shaking.

Strange.
I thought I looked decent in the mirror.
No idea why they all react like I'm fresh out the grave.
To be honest—dim lights, three new corpses, silent basement...
I've seen haunted houses with better vibes.

Phone starts buzzing in his pocket.
He reaches for it—eyes still locked on me.
I can't let that happen.

Thup.

The round punches through his hand, shatters the phone, buries itself deep in his thigh.

He screams.
Loud.
That hand won't be leaving his pocket again.

I lift a leg, aim loose at his bandaged spot.

—Fire up. I don't have all night to babysit.

He breaks. I see it.
Mouth twitching. Voice trying to come out.

But then—another phone rings.
Not his.
Then another.
And another.
Feels surreal—like the dead are getting called back.

Before I can process it, a voice speaks behind me.

—Are you alright, sir?

My heart hits the ribcage.
Feels like the bullet in my chest just split open.
Didn't hear him approach.

With my senses cut off, I didn't even know I wasn't alone.
I turn, hand on my heart.

A local Malay kid. Dressed like staff.
Neat nameplate reads: Rigan.

He clearly knows me. So I speak like I know him too.

—Yeah, Rigan. I'm good. You see how they got in?
And how the hell did they make it up to my apartment?

Rigan shakes his head in both directions, voice soft but urgent.

—Not sure, sir, how they come. I was in central security room. Watching camera, I see two men carry someone out from your apartment.

He pauses, waiting for it to sink in.

—The security guys think maybe it's some friend prank.
But me... I know, sir—your room never has friends visit.
Since long time Jenny madam was staying, then last week another madam come. That's it. I feel something's off.
I call our supervisor, Masud sir.

He leans forward, still catching his breath.

—We rewind camera. See clearly—they come in two cars.
One car leave, the other stay. These people go to your apartment.
That first car is still outside, near alley. Driver looking around like he's watching our building. Masud sir go to catch him with two guards. I come down, hide, watch them from corner.
Now I see you—so I come.

He pauses. Fidgets. Then asks, almost whispering:

—Should we call police, sir?

Poor kid's rattled. No doubt about it.
But cops would just tangle things. Not now.

I tell Rigan to skip the cops—just bring Masud here.
He nods, slips off toward the gate.

I get back into the van, press my leg up against the bandage.
Raise the gun again—this time aiming at what he probably values most.

—Ten seconds, bro. That's all I can offer.

But he doesn't even let me count to three.
Starts talking—mumbling at first, then it turns into real words.

And I listen.
Carefully.
Every word he says just twists the story tighter.

Name's Khursheed . Built like a rhino.
Running with his crew for Rasheed Dameer—an old war buddy.
Fine. Let them have their loyalties.
But then he says Marisha—and her sister—are being held at their compound. That changes everything.

Her sister vanished off the map.
No wonder she ended up in these guys' hands.
But Marisha?
She was supposed to be in Phuket.
How the hell did they find her here?

He says they picked her up from a Zamuk nearby.
A Zamuk? What the hell was she doing there?

She was under Xanier Cheng's protection.
And Papa Cheng doesn't bend easily—in my case, he couldn't.
Even if he tried.
But all that thread ends at one question:
Where is this compound?

I pressed harder into his bandaged wound—slow, heavy.
He starts howling—a full performance. Still no location.
Bastard's just wasting time.

Outside the van, I catch movement.
Basement gate—two guards coming in, Rigan with them.
Another man hauls a lanky suspect like he's dragging a dead frog.

As they get closer, the man holding the suspect speaks up,

—This pig—he was with them, bae.

I stare at the man, waiting for a clue to identify him.

He doesn't have a nametag. Nothing to work with.
But he's fast on the draw, steps forward and offers,

—Bae, I'm Machud. Building supervisor.
You call me local small brother, boss.

He looks less worried and more... hurt.

Masud—who spells his name as Machud—frowns hard and shakes his head.

—Since last year you come back from Penang, bae—you change too much. What happen to you, ah?

He glances at the blood smeared across me like it personally hurt his feelings. Drops the lanky guy to the ground like he's made of plastic, wipes his eyes with the back of his hand.

I step closer, put a hand on his shoulder.

—I'll explain everything later, Masud.
Right now, I need your help.

He freezes, then perks up—like I just offered him a bar fight and a pay raise all at once.

—Whaaat help, bae? You say now, we pull full SWAT style.
I tell you. We pull all bastard from root!

The energy is loud, but I'll take it.
At least I won't have to babysit the cleanup.
I nod.

—There's one left in my apartment. We need to clear this crew—quietly. But the problem is, none of them are talking. No one's giving up the address I need.

Masud claps once, practically bounces.

—Aaaah, small thing, bae! Oye chik, give me the stick!

One of the guards tosses him a night baton.
Masud grabs it like a lifelong dream just came true and starts hammering the lanky guy's knees without hesitation.

The screams are pure. Turns out Masud speaks fluent Malay, even if he beats people in Deshi style.

The lanky one cracks. Starts mumbling an address between sobs. Even fumbles out his phone and drops a GPS pin.

Masud lights up like he just scored the winning goal at a village tournament.
—See, bae? Dis bastard tell me everything!
Dis place you go with those slick bat, in the jungle.
You beating those egg balls of man.

Well, busting any guy's balls was never in my playbook.
I just take the phone. Try not to react.

Ah—golf?
Now I get it.
He's pointing at Mine Resort & Golf Club.

Can't remember ever playing golf, but I know the area.
There's an apartment block behind the mall.
Beyond that, thick stretch of jungle.
Pin lands right in the heart of it.

I glance around.

—Masud, any clue where my car is?
Didn't see any keys in the apartment.

In KL, no one lives without a car.
It was a shot, but a good one.

Masud raises one arm, points toward the gate like a showman.

—There, bae! You brought this one—*kailla haingaroar.*
So beautiful. You never take key up.
Key stays in our desk. You ask, we give.

Rigan takes the cue, bolts for the security office, comes back with the keys.

Masud sweeps the cover off with a flourish, like he's unveiling a bride.

Now I finally figure out.
What the hell a *kailla haingaroar* actually is.
A polished black Range Rover.
Private plate. Spotless. No dust.

I tap unlock.
Lights blink. Doors open—ready.

—Who do you use to handle bodies? *I ask.*

Masud scratches his chin, then flashes that wolf grin.

—Our guy Mike. You member? He handle mess before.
I call, he fix. You go.

I have no clue who this "our guy" Mike is.
Doesn't matter—options are thin, time's thinner.
I nod.
Let him handle the carnage.
I hand him the Nightwalker, auto-target on—just in case.
Told him to keep it for protection.

Then I slide into the Haingaroar and drive.
Dash lights up the date—six months since Penang.
Six months since the blast.
No wonder the mirror didn't know my name.

Memories still aren't fully synced.
They'll come—no point forcing it.

Instead, I focus on what I do know.

Rasheed Dameer tracking down Marisha?
Not exactly a genius move—but not impossible either.
We weren't hiding in Phuket. We moved in daylight. Anyone with a grudge and enough time could draw that line from her to me.

What gets me is the nerve. Even after I drew the line, Rasheed sent his own crew. Kidnapped her?
That wasn't just bold. That was suicidal.

Now the question isn't if he dies.
It's how loud.

The part that sticks—
how did Rasheed's crew get past Papa Cheng?
He doesn't make mistakes.
Either Rasheed got lucky, or someone turned the lock for them.

Another thread tugs—Penang, the girl who showed up.
Macro, the rest of my team.
I should've checked on them.
But with Marisha so close, they all fade out.

And here's another catch:
Even if I drag her out, she won't know this face.
How does Marisha react to a stranger who calls her by name?
What do I say?
Burned in an explosion, face rebuilt, six months missing?
Sounds like cheap pulp.
Even the doorman Rigan wouldn't buy it.

Reach the mall faster than expected.
Mine Mall's closed by now, but security just waves me through.
That kind of SUV doesn't ask for ID.

I swing the road toward the resort, then cut left—there's a route to the apartment complex. Headlights off, moving by instinct.

Find the lane—it dead-ends at a canal.
Across the water: low complex with red-tiled, pitched roofs.
Malaysia doesn't need snow roofs. Someone here couldn't let go of their winter—dragged it with them from homeland.

I take the Rover as close to the trees as possible.
No more wheels from here. There's only one trail through the green—narrow, half-overgrown.
I take it.

Fifteen meters in, the trees open up—cleared patch at the center.
A bunker door.
Heavy steel.
Keypad lock. Numbered.

Didn't bring a hacking kit.
Didn't need one.

There's a simpler trick with these things: read the residue. Keys most recently pressed leave traces—oils, heat, texture wear. I just have to listen to what the metal remembers.

I'll try that first.
If it fails, I'll find the vent and crawl in the hard way.
But I never get that far.

The door clicks open as I approach—like it's been waiting for me.
And what steps out? A damn mammoth.
Muscle sculpted like granite, built for war. Looks like a rejected boss fight from a Middle Eastern killhouse. Square jaw, crooked nose, neck thick as an anvil—Afghan, no question.
Which means one thing:
Stubborn as hell, even dumber when mad.

He's holding a pistol, but in that fist it looks like a spoon in a thunderstorm.

I raise my hands, taunt him—call out his animal.
He tosses the gun aside and grins—challenge accepted.
He's all in now. There's nothing between us but blood and bone.

He's confident, of course. Built like a monster, he assumes fists will do the talking. I don't like killing unless I have to.
Prefer to know why before I cut the cord. But this time, there's nothing left to say.

The Nightwalker's with Masud, which leaves me only the stiletto tucked in my belt. The thing's flat. Sized to vanish inside a palm.

My instincts aren't with me—not the way they used to be.
And yeah—squaring off with a beast like this,
maybe I should feel fear. But I know technique that cuts deeper than strength ever could. No poet ever needed a golden pen.
Time to write my answer.

He charges like a bull, leading with the right.
Predictable.
Same hand he used to hold the gun—every brute loves his strong hand.

Last second, I pivot—matador clean, slip behind him.
Left hand up, blade in play.
Slide the steel under his arm, right where artery meets tendon.

He grunts, swings his left hand back for my hair.
That's fine. I let him.
The instant his fingers tangle, my right hand takes over.
Blade in, up through the other armpit—fast, surgical, no words.
Both cuts bypass pain—go straight for bloodflow.
His heart's still pumping, but nothing's reaching the arms.
They'll hang useless in seconds.
Muscle without wiring.

One last move—blade down, right into the lower spine.
Nerve junction. That's the kill switch.

I press it in, then step around to face him.
He's still on his feet.
Not for long.

The knees go first—give out without warning.
He drops hard, confused.
Staring at his arms as blood pumps from both. Chest heaving.
He tries to push himself up, tries to command the body—nothing answers. Mouth opens—wants to curse, but instead just pours blood, heavy and thick.

Then he folds.
Neck twists, body crashes sideways.
He might bleed out in minutes.
Or he might get lucky—survive with nothing but regret and dead limbs.

I step past him.
Into the bunker.

A round chamber, multiple corridors in different directions.
Second hall on the left—door ajar, light and motion spilling through. That's my path.

Last weapon—gone.
Left the blade buried in the giant's back.
That means I'm walking into the next room unarmed.

Inside, pacing slow circles, is Rasheed Farish.
Ex-Hamas. Now just another burnout with a price tag.

He spots me—and freezes. Eyes wide.
Behind him, Marisha's slumped in a chair,
head tipped back, eyes closed.

She's not sleeping. No one sleeps like that.
Drugged, most likely.
I step in.

Rasheed's already wired, but he hasn't tasted real fear yet.

—Here you are, Rasheed, you could've been the chosen one.
Instead, you smuggled guns, then signed up for a shitty war.
I let it go once. Warned you. You could've walked away clean.

I step closer.

—But now—you made it personal.

He was already running hyper before I even stepped in.
Now his body just gives up—he folds to the floor, clutching his stomach like it's splitting open from the inside. Maybe it is.

I watch him convulse, then grab a water bottle off the table, hold it out.

—Wash your face. Sit somewhere you won't faint.

He drags himself across the floor, splashes water on his face, gasps for air.

I move to Marisha.
Check her face, neck, wrists.
No bruises. No signs of physical torture.

She's still wearing the dog tag I gave her—my name.
What I was, once.

There were iron cuffs on the ground—the kind meant for hanging someone by the wrists.
The marks on her arms matched up, red and angry.
I felt the burn of rage climb my spine. Held it down.

Behind me, Rasheed spoke, eyes still shut.

—I didn't do that. I swear. I didn't even know she was here when I arrived. I just unchained her, sat her there.

His voice shook. Nothing rehearsed.

—Khurram—he called his people, but they never picked up. That's when I knew. You'd already gotten to them.

He meant the crew that hit my apartment.

—They're dead, *I said.*

No drama. Just facts.
Rasheed mumbled a prayer—hands raised like he was begging for divine mercy. Or maybe martyrdom.
Bullshit.
If those punks get to be martyrs, we owe sainthood to every stray dog in a garbage pit.

He looked rattled, but didn't argue.
Got to his feet, slow and shaky, but still vertical.

He's seen me before.
Twice.
That should've been enough warning for anyone with half a brain. And yet—here we are.

I didn't want to kill him if I didn't have to. I asked,

—What did they give her?

—Not sure, *he said.*
—They were trying for intel. Maybe a truth serum.
But it wasn't me—I came after they dosed her.

He was trying hard to distance himself.
Didn't want to get sucked into another storm. Fair enough.

I couldn't carry her, not with these wounds.
Rasheed looked like he'd struggle with a schoolbag,
never mind a woman half-conscious.
I guessed we'd need to wait until Marisha woke on her own.
So I nodded toward the exit and walked him out.
Saw a bench in the hall earlier. Good enough.

Once Rasheed was steady, I'd dig in.
Start pulling answers.
This time, no threats. Just questions. Sometimes, understanding a man gets you more than breaking him.

Rasheed slumped into the seat like gravity had finally caught him. Didn't wait for a question.

—They told me KL would be quiet. A break.
Instead, you wiped out my whole crew.
Now how the hell am I supposed to explain that to high command? You left me alive—twice. Any man with half a gut would think I'm working with you.

He had a point.
Truth is, Silence never gave me the green light to take him out.
But trying to explain that kind of spiritual calculus to a man running on panic would be wasted.

I offered him something colder:

—So what—you think I made a mistake letting you live?

I lean in closer.

—If that's what's keeping you up at night, I can fix it right now.

That landed.
He realized too late that gratitude might've been the better play.

Before the panic flares again, I rest a calm, steady hand on his shoulder. Give him half a smile.

—Honestly? You don't strike me as someone who builds evil by design. Until Eilat, I figured you were just a product of proximity. Caught in the wrong wave.

That one hits harder than I mean it to.

—You know about Eilat? *he whispers.* —My Lord, grace me...

—I know a lot of things, Rasheed.
I know you did what you had to do. Not more. Not less.
What I still don't get is how a survivor turns himself into a pawn.

He glances up. Not sure if he sees accusation or sympathy.
And then—he cracks open something rare.

—I don't know your race. Your religion.
And honestly, I never cared. When those bastards started gunning us down, something broke. I'm not even that devout—but I had to stand. Not for God. For the ones we buried.
I walked in with open eyes. No one forced my hand.

Finally—something raw. Something real.
I've seen the headlines about Rasheed Farish.
But the man himself? I never bothered to know him.

Now, with nothing but time, I ask:

—You keep switching borders and nationalities.
Never thought you'd stand with any side.
What do you call yourself? What's your flag?

He doesn't flinch.

—A Muslim. That's my side—and my flag.

—Well then, *I say,* —looks like we're practically in-laws.

He blinks.

—What do you mean? What do you know about my sister?

I laugh.

—Easy, boy. Just a joke. The girl you've got on that chair? Muslim. Russian passport, but still.

—She's Russian? I thought she was Turkish.

Rasheed actually looks surprised.

—Though… that would still makes us family.
I've got Turkish papers.

He smiled for the first time. Something in him relaxed.
He knew I wasn't here to kill him—at least not yet.
He leaned in—almost curious. Maybe even interested in me.
I kept things rolling.

—Earlier—you called them bastards.
You mean the ones from Eilat?

His eyes darkened.

—Not just Eilat. All of them. Americans. Brits. Euro trash.
And the nosy Chinese too.

—Chinese? *I raised a brow.*
—Thought they were on your side—at least on paper.

He scoffed.

—Bullshit. They only fund us to box in Indians.
Same play with the Pakis. But in Xinjiang?
You should see what they do to Muslims in their own cities.
Or in Myanmar. It's genocide, and nobody blinks.
If I survive this, I'll burn their cities to ash myself.

He meant it. Not a flicker of doubt in his voice.

—Seems like there's a lot of geopolitics tangled in all this, *I said.*
—Maybe your holy war's just economics dressed up for idiots.
Didn't think you'd fall for that game.

—You don't get it, *he snapped.*
—It's always been about me—about us.
Those bastards are begging for hellfire.
We're just delivering what they asked for.

—Ugh. And here I thought you had a rational mind, *I said, leaning back.* —But you're just parroting the same fundamentalist garbage as every other fanatic. The ones you call bastards—the Jews, the Christians? Your own book calls them Ahl al-Kitab—People of the Book.

—You're allowed to eat with them, marry them, trade with them. And here you are, convinced you're better just because you think you own the truth?

Rasheed didn't blink.

—Of course we're better.

—Poor soul, *I muttered.* —You feel better believing those Jews and Christians you kill already have seats reserved in hellfire. But did you ever read the full burn list? All disbelievers—they've got a place in the furnace, sure. Four, five, six—pick your floor. But the seventh? The dirtiest, the deepest? That one's reserved for you and your righteous brothers. That's where the worst go if they die without forgiveness. Can you guarantee a death certificate stamped clean? Are you really sure your last breath will be soaked in tauba?

—No, *he said.* —There's no guarantee.

—Then why the fuck are you out here digging holes in other people's floors, when your own ceiling could collapse any minute?

He hesitates.

—This... is part of seeking forgiveness. You wouldn't understand.

—Try me, *I say.* — You really think the people you're burning in hell—God's going to light the fire just to settle your score? You're killing His creations, Rasheed. You think He's going to high-five you at the gate?
What makes you so sure He'll spare you?

He swallows.

—I don't know. I just... did what I could.
You're confusing me. You're the devil.

—Sure, *I say.* — And he lives in every crack of human mind. But after all this blood and smoke, I thought you'd have figured something out by now. Guess I expected too much.

He's out of depth now.
Can't keep pace—not with logic, not with guilt.
He knows it.

He sits silent for a while, eyes lowered. The kind of silence that feels like something fell apart inside. Then finally asks,

—If not faith, then what do you think this fight is really about?

I shrug.

—It's exactly what it looks like. Your war isn't about faith.
It's just geopolitics dressed up in holy cloth.

—How much do you even know about us? *he asks.*

—Enough. Israel didn't kill your people because they ran out of condos. They could've resettled in the U.S.—one state in the Midwest has more space than they'll ever need. They just want that land because they believe it's holy—a gift from God, theirs to reclaim, brick by bloody brick.
They want every inch under their flag. Israel uses violence not just to crush you, but to drive you out. The logic's simple: make your neighbors take you in. Turn you into a refugee problem. That way, they can claim the land is empty—take the rest with clean hands. The British wrote this playbook. Riddled with guilt after World War II. Desperate to repay the Jews—but didn't trust them enough to live next door. So they handed them Palestine like a poisoned gift, then walked away.

Rasheed's eyes narrow.

—You sound like PLO. Some of them used to say the same things. Tried to fix this politically.

—Glad you're finally hearing something that doesn't make you gag, *I shoot back, smirking.* —After the '70s, *I continue,*
—ambition met opportunity and the game changed. Britain and the U.S. saw Israel as useful—a wild dog planted in the oil fields. Let it bark, and the rest of the Middle East stays in line.
Out of fear, your neighbors run to the West for protection.
And they happily sell it—for a price.

—What price? *Rasheed presses.*

—Oil. Minerals. Cheap contracts. Until the day we stop running on crude, this arrangement isn't going anywhere.

He leans in, curious now. Engaged.

—If not armed resistance, how else are we supposed to fight?

—I don't have all the answers, Rasheed. But I do know this:
You don't find the way until your boots are in the dirt.
Your high command says the disbelievers deserve to die.
But when a believer does the same thing?
Suddenly, the rulebook changes. Meanwhile, the Western alliance brands your faith as terrorism—so they can justify wiping you off the map. But when they're defending their own? That's a different set of rules. Don't you see it?
Both sides—the fanatics in your camp and the power-brokers in theirs—are paddling the same damn boat.

He stays silent, I keep going.

—Ever pay attention to what Western elites do with their money? They pour fortunes—sometimes everything they own—into education and research. That's how Oxford grows.
That's how MIT and NASA survive. Even the bombs you're dodging today were funded generations ago by visionaries who invested in knowledge, not rage. Now look at your side.
Your rich Habibis? Too busy showing off cars, collecting women, chasing pleasure. They forget all that wealth they're burning through came straight from the ground—free. And when it's gone, they'll be right back to fishing with nets and dragging camels across desert sand.

Rasheed gave a crooked smile.

—You talk like the devil, but your words aren't all poison.
Still, not all of us are like that. Some of our neighbors have given up more than they could ever afford—just to keep this fight alive.
If they hadn't, we'd have collapsed long ago.

He sat up straighter, trying to reclaim a little dignity.

—And let's not forget—whoever holds the wealth makes the rules. We don't have the luxury to wait for some prince to donate his yacht. We fight because there's no other choice.

I nodded.

—I get it. But you know as well as I do—whatever Commander Kamran or that clown, The Maker are plotting, it's going nowhere. A stillbirth wrapped in flags.

—So what? *Rasheed snapped.* —You want me to give up?
Join politics? Preach peace in a war zone?

I grinned.

—No, Rasheed. I want you to wake up—before you die for someone else's fantasy. You're staking your life on weapons that don't even belong to you. And the people who build those weapons? They'll drop you the second the market shifts.
Or worse—they'll arm your enemies instead.
Turn your war into a sales pitch.

He falls silent.

—In that world, *I say,* —what are you going to do?

Rasheed rubs his hands together.

—Nothing, I guess. We'd be helpless. But if we pull back now—play nice, do what's 'rational'—we'll get erased before anyone even hears us. I believe in this fight.
Still… I can't deny what you've said.
When I get back, I'll bring it up with the Commander.

I raise an eyebrow.

—Your loyalty's impressive, Rasheed. But you won't be standing beside them for long. That operation? It's already sinking.
I'm telling you now—when that ship goes down, I want you off it.
Ever think maybe your commander isn't doing this for freedom?
Maybe it's not about faith at all.
Maybe it's just about power—and profit.

Rasheed looks shaken.

—You're twisting my head.
I don't even know what I believe anymore.

—People with eyes can still be blind, Rasheed. And the blind? They live forever in the dark. So here's the deal:
You die here, like the others. I torch the whole facility—girls and all—and your body becomes just another nameless pile nobody ever finds. You don't need to go back to them.
Go dark for a while. Lay low.
When I'm done, you can resurface. Honor their graves with flowers. Say a few words over that idiotic robot.
You fought for your people's freedom—go back to your war if that's what moves you. But cross that river quietly, Rasheed.
You've made enough to disappear.
Use it. Buy yourself a second chance.

Rasheed lets out a dry laugh.

—Even if I disappear, they won't let me be, Mr. Caesar.

I tilt my head.

—Interesting. I don't recall ever giving you that name.

—You didn't have to, *he said.*
—Mossad asked about you more than once. But you carved it into my memory the day you wiped my whole squad. Last time was deep in Iraq. Somewhere between Ari and Baishur.
We were moving a shipment.
You slit Baharram Gazi's throat right in front of me.
I found your dog tag on the ground—half of it. And today, I saw the rest—hanging around your girlfriend's neck.

I can't help smiling,

—That's a long story, Rasheed. Not one for today. When the time comes, I'll give you everything. Until then, just call me Elijan. Names change with time, *I said.* —The less you know, the longer you live.

He nodded.

—Fine. I'll stay off the radar when it comes to these fanatics.
But when the time's right, I'm going back to my own ground.
You coming after me for that?

—You've got every right to fight for your people, *I told him.*
As long as you're not making new enemies for me,
I won't be one for you.

He looked up.

—Need any more intel from me?

—I know what I need. But if you want to share your side of the story, go ahead. I could understand Eilat. But the retired old men—why kill them like that?

He took his time. Then, finally, he talked.

From the beginning to now—his journey, the truth about who he was before the mask. Most of it lined up with what I'd already pieced together from Macro's reports, and some things I'd picked up on the ground. But Rasheed filled in the cracks.

He confessed—he'd been trying to get out.
The machine didn't let him. But now, he wanted help escaping it.
And in that moment, I needed his help more.

—You used to run people across borders, *I said.* —Can you move someone safely—quiet, to a specific spot?

—Depends who it is.

—The girl. The one in coma. Whatever happens—she goes home. Whether she wakes up or not.

—That's hard. Moving someone like that trips every alarm. Medical, security, customs—all of it.

—I know, *I said.* —Hard isn't impossible. Right?

He went silent, thinking it through, then spoke.

—She looked familiar when I first saw her.
Still can't place it.
But people like her… they don't die easy.

She's probably survived worse. We'll need a charter.
Medical clearance. Clean documents.
It's a mess—but I can do it.

—I'll arrange what you need. Take my car—seats fold down—you can lay her out like a stretcher. Drive straight to Komak HQ.
Park in the basement, find the director.
I'll give you the name and pass codes. He'll handle the rest.

—You want me to deal with Papa Cheng?
Sounds like you've got history with him.
Don't tell me you're tangled up in his shady empire?

I raised an eyebrow.

—Just like you and me right now. I help you vanish, you help me finish my job. Does that make you my partner in crime?

Rasheed laughed.

—No thanks. I'm happy to play my part and leave.
After this, I'm heading back to Türkiye. Unless someone's really desperate, no one's tracking me down easy. If you ever need me—send a message. For now... we're done here.

—That's fine. But you'll have to put your issues with the Chinese on ice for this job.

Rasheed shrugged.

—When it's business, I can work around personal issues.
And I've got my own car parked close. No need for yours.

—Fine. I'll send you the details—where to drop her, who to call if anything goes wrong.

We don't shake hands.
No promises.
But there's an understanding.

Earlier, I clocked the bunker's stash—heavy weapons, blocks of explosives, the full buffet of destruction.

Rasheed works fast, rigging the place with timed charges, making sure the past will burn. His way of closing the book.

It works out.
Saves me the trouble of setting fire to the past.

We get to work—load Marisha's sister into Rasheed's car.
Marisha herself—still unconscious—into mine.
After that, we just nod and go our ways.

I decide not to tell Marisha about her sister—not yet.
I still don't have the full picture on her. And the girl herself hasn't given Marisha the truth, not even close.

No reason to drag Marisha into this world of blood and bones.
She'll learn soon enough her sister made it home.
I'll be watching when she does.

Rasheed says she'll wake up in under an hour.
We'll be somewhere safe by then.

Still, I wait here for a reason.
Ten minutes pass.
Then—the blast.
Nothing cinematic—just enough to shake my car's frame.

Through the windshield, a flare—quick, bright, done.
The bunker's gone.
Time to move on.

—∞—

The Devil's Dropbox

Defense Square
Rockchild Avenue, Tel Aviv, Israel

Dalat Zibram can't rest while a job's left undone.

At this point in his life, though—win or lose—nothing really touches him. He's bled his years out for service, flag, country.

That's why they parked him here—top seat at the Ministry of Defense. A nod from the system, tipping its hat to a lifetime of struggle. His track record's clean enough that even a failure would look like a tiny dot—seen, maybe, but never remembered.

Still, habits die hard.
Years in the field. A lifetime dodging slow chains of command.
He can draw loyalty from new recruits with nothing but focus and inspiration. It's all there—silver hair, that steady gravity.
The gray never slows him down. Never keeps women away.
But that air about him—that quiet confidence—sometimes rubs people wrong.

Like now.

He'd yanked two field officers back to HQ in the middle of an op.
Jovan and Dr. Eli were deep in it.
Dragging them in wasn't strictly necessary.

He did it anyway.
For Jovan, this wasn't new.
Management had pulled him out mid-op before.
He didn't know it then, but it had ended up saving his life.
Some patterns don't break—they just get deadlier.
Because what the chief had to say would flip everything.

This was a core update—he wanted to see their eyes when it landed. And he wanted them to remember:
The man at HQ isn't just paper-pushing in a glass box.
Not in Mossad.

None of it showed on his face.
When they arrived, Zibram gave them real warmth.

—Welcome, Jovan. Welcome, Eli.
Hope the flight didn't rough you up.
It's early—what do you need?
Coffee, arak, breakfast?

They stood, shook hands, took their seats.
Jovan skipped the chatter, checked Zibram, went straight to the report.

Zibram listens close. This one's going places, he thinks.
He makes a note right then—before he retires, he'll write the kind of reference that sets a career in stone.

He doesn't comment on the report yet.
No point—everything's about to shift anyway.
Still, old habits.

He tosses out a question.

—Three targets got away. What's the play?

He already knows the answer.
Men like that—once they slip, they come back sharper.
Hard to track. Harder to catch.

Jovan nodded, half a grin on his face.

—We saw it coming, sir.
And we've got a Pakistani inside—Mohabbat Khan.
Feeds us steady, nothing gets past without our ears on it.

Zibram let out a sharp laugh.

—That trick's older than Hafez al-Assad's Syria.
Pakistanis were cheap—used them to bust doors nobody else could touch. Still working, yeah?

Jovan flashed teeth.

—Sir, Pakistanis never change.
Pay them, give them a thrill—they'll sell out their own.
Always did, still do.

Zibram shot Eli a look, smiling.

—Sorry, Eli. The conversation drifted.
But I've got something for you.

He picks up a fat file—hands it over.

—One of ours. Deep in Iran.
Almost ten years under.
Yesterday, they caught him. Hanged the same day.

Now his voice is all stone.

—We had the Prime Minister's green light for backchannel talks—extraction if we could swing it.
But Tehran didn't even let it start.
No real trial. Just rope—before we could move.

He pauses—not for effect, just to keep from crushing Eli and Jovan with it all. Not now, not when they're just starting to climb.

Dr. Eli is a profiler. Before she ever stepped into the field,
she built dossiers like this for dozens of operatives.
She knows exactly where to dig, what to pull out.
That's why the file lands in her hands.

As she reaches for it, Zibram gives her a single, steady nod.

—You can review the full details later, *he says.* —For now, just brief Jovan on the key points. You know what matters.

Eli nods, all business.

—Jimmy Hadid. Thirty-five. Joined regular service at nineteen.
Five years in, spotless record—strict discipline, fierce loyalty.
That's what put him on the fast track to Mossad's Iran Division.

She turns the page.

—Assigned to intercept and analyze nuclear development out of Tehran. But within two months, he's calling out bad intel from our assets. Then he does what no one else would—volunteers to go in himself.

Zibram nods. He can already see the shape of it.

—But he has a problem, Eli continues. —His mother's sick, alone. Mossad won't deploy him straight to Iran.
Intel says she's running out of time. HQ decides to let him stay, look after her till the end. After that, green light.

She lets her tone drop, just enough.

—But Hadid has his own play. Spends half his salary on a private nurse, sets his mother up—then vanishes. Straight into Tehran.

Jovan leans in, a little sharper.

—He goes in under a new identity:
The only son of a dead Iranian couple.
Their real son died in a suspicious crash in Riyadh—years back, case never investigated, probably covered up.
That gives us the opening.

She flips the page, keeps moving.

—Hadid's razor-sharp. Relentless. Within a year, he worms his way into Panj-Pellah Base—Weapons Development Division.

Zibram exhales, barely a sound.

—To the Iranians, he looks like a prize. But they check everything—dig up graves, pull university records,
run background checks. His cover holds. Solid.

She keeps going, eyes locked in.

—They loved having him. He was modern, educated, driven.
Hadid had a thing for Persian calligraphy.
Before Tehran, he trained hard—became an expert.
In downtime, he etched verses and designs onto ceramics.
Those pieces went to a small art shop in the city.

Her eyes narrow.

—That's how we pulled his intel out.
Each piece of pottery had data hidden in special ink—our tech, his hands. The stream ran almost twelve years.

She looks up, face dead serious.

—In that time, he fed us dozens of assets.
Twice, his intel let us take out Iran's nuclear sites—wiped out, total success. But recently, he sent something heavier:
Through a private channel, Tehran is moving to acquire WMDs. No paper trail. Just lethal intent. The deal was fronted by a former Iranian military commander. They'd built a fresh covert unit—planned the handoff in Bukan, collect the shipment in the dark.

Eli's voice dipped lower.
Zibram and Jovan leaned in, instinctive.

—We prepped for the intercept. But the shipment never made it.

She turned another page.

—We started digging into the new paramilitary cell.
Meanwhile, Hadid—still deep in Tehran—started connecting threads. He suspected the Eilat hit was tied to this same shipment.

Zibram's fingers twitched—just once.

—Hadid moved out of the weapons lab. Shifted to a coordination post—more access, more networks. Every rogue unit, black cell, shadow crew—he kept eyes on them all.

Eli turned to the last page.

—His persistence paid off. These are the profiles we've pulled so far—direct links to the weapons cell.

She stopped.

Lifted the photos. Studied them—silent, careful.
Then her brow furrowed, hard.

—Oh… Jovan, look at these.

She slid the stack across the table—hand steady, voice fraying at the edges.

—*—

North-South Expressway
Kuala Lumpur, Malaysia

Right now I'm asking myself the one question that actually matters—where the hell do I take Marisha?

Definitely not back to the apartment. Place still reeks of a fight. And no way I'm explaining that to her.

I've got a fallback spot in mind, but it's a coin toss whether I can even get in. If that flops, we'll have to crash at a hotel for now. Merged onto the expressway, city lights dragging us back in.

She's next to me, buckled in, completely out.
Arms loose, legs slack, breathing like she hasn't slept in years.
Beautiful. Peaceful.

Every instinct said keep your eyes on the road.
But I kept glancing anyway.

She's still wearing the Dog tag.
The same thin chain I left around her neck.
Rasheed said they found her in KL, trying to locate her sister.
But why the hell did she come to Elijan Vellum?
That's the piece Rasheed couldn't give me.
Which means I'll have to get it out of her—gently.

If she wakes up and sees this face, she'll think I'm Elijan.
Fine. Let's see what that man meant to her.

The fallback—Taman Duta—barely a memory, but the name stuck. It's near the city's edge.
Would've been easier if I had my phone.

There's a burner in the car—lifted from Vellum's place.
But it's locked with a numeric code—no face unlock.
And with my senses gone, that keypad is Fort Knox.

Divine timing.
I spotted the road sign.
Second house on the left—that's the fallback unit.

We have those in every major city.
Macro's paranoia turned into protocol. The entire team knows.

I took the lane. Lipstick palms lined the neighbor's yard like an open invitation. Across the street—our bungalow.
Pulled in, parked at the gate, stepped out.
Marisha still out cold.
Left the engine running.
Time to break us in.

Steel gate. Basic padlock.
Key's stashed inside—on purpose.
Anyone with a pick could crack it.
Or just climb over.
The real lock is on the front door.

I climbed in.
Biometric panel flared to life: "IDENTITY REQUIRED."
Tried my face—nothing.
Fingerprints—nothing.
Didn't expect anything different.
Let it fail, twice.
On the third, fallback triggered.

Twelve-digit passcode. One attempt.
Blank on the actual code—but I built the system.
Muscle memory on standby.

First five digits: initials of the core crew.
Next four: location—T-A-M-A.
Last three: custom symbols I assigned. Situation-specific.
Typed it in. It clicked—welcoming human intelligence.

My memories are fractured, but pattern recognition is still lethal.
Time to bring the car in and move her inside.

Went back out.
Slid into the driver's seat—
And almost passed out.
Marisha—gone.
I left her buckled in, head slumped, out cold.

Now, nothing but an empty seat.
Blackout tints hid everything from the outside.
But inside, every nerve fired. I turned to check the rear—
Too late.

A wire wrapped tight around my throat.
From behind.

Her voice—right at my ear, low, pissed, not shaking.

—Don't move. Try it and I'll break you.

Mirror gave me the rest—Marisha, eyes blazing, dead serious. She thought I was one of them. Must've curled up in the back, just waiting for her shot. No idea how she found wire or managed that torque with those arms.

If I'd been anyone else—I'd be dead. Getting loose would've been easy, but only if I was willing to hurt her—and thankfully, it never came to that.

Rearview mirror caught her watching me—I held her gaze, didn't blink. Eye contact.

Just like that, she let the wire drop.

—Oh my god—Mr. Elijan? You're here too?
Wait, did they grab you as well?

Wire slipped away. My neck, free again.
I made a show of rubbing my throat, like it actually hurt.

—Unbelievable, *I said, voice slow and dripping sarcasm.*
—Take a bullet to the chest, knife to the gut, claw my way back from the grave to drag you out—and your first move is to choke me out?

She blinked—wide, startled. Didn't clock the sarcasm.

—I—I'm sorry, Mr. Elijan. I woke up and panicked.
I didn't know who was driving. I had no idea you'd be here.
Oh god, did you actually get shot?

Her eyes dropped to the blood, blooming above my ribs.

—Yeah, *I said, glancing down.*
—Bullet's still in there. Feel free to poke around if you're curious.

I tried a grin. She didn't give one back.
Not her mood, and I couldn't blame her.

Her voice dropped, softer now.

—I didn't mean to drag you into this. If I'd known how deep this went, I never would've gone to your apartment. That must be how they found you. I can't think of any other reason.

She shifted forward, moved to the passenger seat.
Pulled the door shut behind her.

Her hand brushed my chest as she adjusted, eyes landing right on the wound. Something moved in me—a reflex.

—You're the only reason I'm still breathing, miss, *I said, steady.*
—A beautiful woman's touch works miracles.
Otherwise, I'd just be a handsome ghost by now.

That broke through.
She turned, hiding a smile in her hand.

—Oh, really? That's funny. You weren't saying that about the red-bag beauty a few days back, were you? Changed your tune quick.

There it was. The red bag.

Memory flickered—me, waking up with it above my face.
That wasn't random—there's a story behind that bag.
And she'd been at the apartment. That confirms it.
But I couldn't ask her directly. I'm supposed to be Elijan.
Any straight question would break the illusion.

I twisted the line a little further.

—Well... maybe you were in love, too, *I said.*
—Still wound up at my place, didn't you?

She gave me the full-on, are you kidding? look.

—Wow. After all that—knowing what happened, where I went, why I stayed, how long—I still get blamed?

No soft edges there. Whatever history she had with Elijan, romance had nothing to do with it.
Which meant I didn't have to rush. This wasn't personal.

That gave me space to breathe.

—You take a shot like this, sweetheart, *I said, tapping the wound*—your brain might short-circuit too.

Her eyes dropped, voice going soft.

—I know.
And I know what you did for me, even as a stranger.
And now—again today, you risked your life.
Where... where did you find me?
How did you even pull this off?

She didn't remember a thing.
Whatever they dosed her with had wiped the slate clean.
This wasn't the place for storytime. We were still in the car.

I cut it short.

—If it's alright with you, we'll stay here tonight, *I said.*
—Can't go back to the apartment—place is under renovation.

She leaned up, craned her neck, took in the house.
Then smiled.

—Damn. A whole bungalow?
You really do run a global logistics empire.

She had no idea.
And I wasn't about to enlighten her.

—It's not mine, *I said politely.* —Belongs to my employer. I'm just squatting here for a bit.

She nodded, letting it go.
I opened the gate. Drove us inside.

Ground floor's got a guest bed, but it's mostly kitchen and living.

We headed upstairs, second floor—master bedrooms, twice the size, balcony out front.

I didn't ask if she wanted a separate room.
Door's open if she does. If not, she stays. Simple.

By the mirror, I peeled off my shirt, checked the damage.
Wound was closed, dark, crusted over.
Angle like that should've punched straight through my heart.

If it had, pulling the slug would've been a suicide note.
Any sane surgeon would faint just looking at how I was still vertical.

In the mirror, I caught her.

Marisha, standing quiet behind me.
Her eyes locked on the scar, then the fresh gauze at my side.
She didn't speak for a beat.

Then, soft as a secret:

—I don't know why you'd risk everything to save me.
But whatever it was... thank you.

She wrapped her arms around me from behind, laid her head against my back. Every trace of tension, every wire—gone.

All I felt now was warmth.
And then—something wet trailing down my spine.
She was crying.
Didn't know the wound wasn't from saving her.
Didn't matter. No point correcting the story now.

I cracked a grin.

—If that's your version of gratitude, *I said,*
—feel free to burn me a little more. I won't mind.

She didn't pull away—just tapped her fingers slow on my back, quiet.

—God forgive you, Elijan, *she whispered. Voice lower, rougher.*
—Everything feels different, seeing you again...

I held still.
Let her talk.

—First time, *she said,* —we were only connected by that number game you played, but I knew it was the wrong person. But now... Now my heart wants this wrong man to be right.

Damn.
What is she, a soul detector?
She was seeing straight through me—reading what I wasn't saying, picking up what I didn't even show. But I couldn't drop the mask. Not yet. Wouldn't make sense.

I threw a little smoke.

—Of course it feels different, gorgeous. You think I took a bullet and a blade for you the last time?

She rubbed her nose on my back. Still wet.

—That's not it, *she said, softer.*
—Gratitude feels different. That was before.
This—this is something else.

I wanted to tell her—the world's changed, but my heart hasn't moved an inch. Maybe hers didn't either.
Because somehow, she still recognized mine.

No way to explain that.
Hell, I barely understood it myself.
But whatever this is—my Lord didn't put it here for nothing.

She asked for space to shower.
I gave it, left her to the steam, headed downstairs.

Every city drop-point we build has the same skeleton—hidden compartment in the kitchen.
Only core team members know the pattern, but once you've learned it, you never forget—even after years.

I knew where to look.
If there was a hidden chamber, it'd be behind the cutlery.
Pulled the whole drawer out. First layer—just a plain wooden panel. Slipped my hand behind it, found the gap—pressed down.
Click.

A second compartment kicked open.
Inside: cloth pouch.
I was praying for a sidearm.
Something simple.
Nope.

Two fat bundles of hundreds.
A few documents with locker codes, Mo Bank, KLCC.
Not useless, but not what I was hoping for.

Then I caught it—a phone.
Already logged into our secure server.
This one, I remembered the password.

Closed the unit.
Packed everything.
Took it back upstairs.

Marisha was still lost in the shower—steam curling under the door.

Fired up the phone. Synced instantly.
Location tracker lit up—everyone but Macro was on the map.
Tommy, Bangkok. Gobi and Sahara, same city, sticking together.
No need to ping anyone yet. Phone's active now—soon as they spot me, someone will reach out.

All I needed now was to cool down, think.
Mo Bank locker, first thing tomorrow.
Maybe there's something useful inside.
After that—figure out how to stitch myself up.

Marisha came back, fresh from the shower.
She was already stunning before—now sharp enough to cut glass. She stood in front of the mirror, just in her lingerie, towel-drying her hair.

—My clothes stink, *she said.* —Been stuck in this set for a week. No clue where my bag ended up—had to wash what I could.

She tossed it out like an excuse, but it felt more like bait.

I didn't know what to say. Didn't know what parts were truth, what was performance. But the way she moved—the pose, the eye contact, how slow her hands worked that towel—even a blind man would see the offer.

She's never been shy about her body. That I know.
But right now, to her, I'm just some guy in KL.
If you're this relaxed with just anyone...
Why the hell chase me across continents like some tragic lover?
The thought twisted something.
Mood soured—fast.

She propped one perfect leg on the vanity, massaging drugstore lotion into her skin—slow, methodical, a little too smooth to be casual.

Tilted her head, hit me with that crooked smirk.

—Looks like you had something to say, Mr. Mute.

That lotion wasn't hers. Came from the bathroom amenities.
And I know she never uses that brand.
So yeah—this wasn't about hygiene.
It was bait. Pure and simple.

And now, for the first time, my chest hurts.
For real.
Hard to say if it was the bullet or the jealousy burning its way up my ribs.

Yet I forced it down.

—You got your phone? *I asked.*
—My old one's dead. Need your number in the new one.

She didn't hesitate.
Crossed the room, eyes locked, smile still playing.
She stepped close—close enough for every curve to fill my vision.
Without breaking eye contact, she tapped her number in.

And when the phone came back, her chest grazed my nose.
Not an accident. She knew exactly what she was doing.

Then slid in beside me—tight, eyes playing their own game.

—If you're trying to keep something from a woman, *she said,* —you'll have to do better. So, Elijan, are you going to tell me what's really happening? Or do I have to tickle it out of you?

For a second, it felt like Phuket again.
Like we'd never left. Like she hadn't changed at all.
Does she get close to everyone this fast?

I played dumb.

—Hide what? I'm an open book. No secrets, no dirty deals—just got caught in the wrong storm, that's all.

Paused. Watched her reaction.
Then tossed it back:

—What about you?
You're a little too comfortable around gunfire.
What pulled you into all this?

Couldn't say it straight. Had to bait the answer.

She laughed—low, teasing.

—Wow. Look who's nervous now.
You were flirting just fine on day one.
What changed you, Mr. Paranoia?

Her eyes drifted down, tracing the line of my bandage.

—Can't believe you're still vertical after all that.
I wouldn't even know where to take you for treatment out here.
Malaysia's not exactly home for me.
But hey—maybe get some rest first?
We'll untangle the rest tomorrow. Sound good?

Before I could answer, she pressed me down on the bed—gentle, almost careful.

Then climbed over, straddling me without so much as grazing the wound. One leg draped across my body.

She pulled my head to her chest, fingers weaving into my hair—slow, soothing.

Relax, huh? No man in Heaven or Hell could stay relaxed with that much fire wrapped in skin. Yet, somehow I stayed still. Didn't let myself react.

If it doesn't match my mind, I don't move with a woman just for sex. Always thought that was part of my deadly instinct—from the Darkness.

But now, with all of them gone and I'm still holding the line—
Maybe that's just who I am.

Still, the regret's real.
Wasting time on this mess in Phuket? My fault.
The girl, the game, the hunger—all of it.

My Lord took every one of my senses away—felt like justice.
Felt like I deserved it.

Even when the anger stayed, the body gave up.
I passed out mid-thought.
Didn't stand a chance.

—∞—

Networks in the Shadows

Defense Square
Rockchild Avenue, Tel Aviv, Israel

Jovan takes the file from Dr. Eli, curiosity sparking in his eyes.

First shot—straight out of a nightmare.
A face built from steel, robotic, inhuman.
Not the glossy, hero-mask shine seen on Iron Man knockoffs.
This mask oozes malice. Cold to the bone—the kind of expression only a sociopath would wire into a machine.
Maybe whoever wears that mask likes it that way—everyone's hiding something now.

Next shot: Baharram Gazi. A degenerate.
The kind who stalks girls too young to have a chance.
Last Jovan heard, the bastard got what he had coming—left for dead out in the desert, justice handled off the books.

Next in line: Kamran Gazi—former military, flagged in the file as Baharram's brother.
Jovan pauses—profile error? How does a rat like Baharram share blood with a commander? Not his mess to clean up.

Mohabbat Khan next—Pakistan's survivor.
This one isn't dying soon. If there are secrets stashed under his shirt, Mossad will shake them loose.

Two more Arabs after that—already dead.
Jovan lets a smirk slip.
That's his work—HQ just hasn't caught up yet, which is why their names are still here.

Next: Abdel al-Awadi, Kuwaiti billionaire.
Another Arab prince in the mix.
Both have slipped away—so far.
Jovan makes a silent promise. He'll catch them.
Just a matter of time.

Then Rasheed Dameer.
Jovan knows him.
Lone wolf, always out for himself.

Why the hell is he running with this pack now?
Maybe money. Maybe something worse.

Next photo: a guy in battered army green, wearing a ripped jockey tee. Thick navy pants sagging, body slouched, hair wild, jaw cracked and rough as a street curb.
He looks more like a busted-up garage mechanic than a hitter.
Name: Darius Caesar.
No agency database holds his record.
Only Mossad has managed to map his trail of dirt.
He's been tied to hits on multiple sites from Syria to Afghanistan.
Rumor is, he freelances for a European warlord—the kind who keeps generals in Brussels and Bishkek awake and sweating.
But the warlord hasn't gone far enough to get a real red tag.

Then, finally, something with flavor. There's no burn in a meal without salt and pepper. And no arms deal anywhere on earth without Russians crawling somewhere in the dark.

Frankly, with no Russian link so far, the whole WMD situation feels like a hoax.

He stares down at an official GRU Spetsnaz ID—female, face like a war machine. Full uniform, but the kind of beauty that doesn't belong in any barracks. For a second, his mind flickers—wondering what she'd look like in a bikini—and then it snaps back.
One look at the profile notes, and the fantasy's gone.

She spent three years in Syria.
Embedded deep on the Russian front.
Forty-eight kills, confirmed.
Six bombings. Two direct assaults on US bases.
Interpol red notice already hanging on her head.

For GRU, those numbers are just the introduction. Off the record, the real count's beyond what any agency can track.

Back in Soviet times, this Russian unit made its bones as Spetsnaz GRU—the Butcher Force.

Today, Russia doesn't officially acknowledge such a unit even exists. But anyone who breathes this game knows better. They're like stars at noon—you don't see them, but they're exactly where they need to be.

And when bloodhounds like that start tracking, hell isn't far behind. At least now, Jovan knows his own work wasn't wasted.

Then the last image in the file—
And it hits Jovan like a gut punch.
He freezes.

Still as death, silent enough that Zibram leans in and lays a hand on his shoulder.

—You alright, my boy?

—I'm fine, sir.

Jovan's voice barely registers, flat as concrete as he reaches for his water.

The final card isn't a face.
It's a monogram—drawn like a playing card,
only no king, queen, or jack.
Just an etched owl.
B at the top. C at the bottom.
For Jovan, that's all it takes.
A blink, and he knows: The Bohemian Club.

Israel had always been the darling of American power—military, money, art, business, the entire social pyramid bent toward Tel Aviv. Everyone knew: if you wanted to sit in the White House, you had to pay respect to Israel. But there were circles outside the system.

A handful of power groups playing by their own rules.
And the Bohemian Club was king of that list.
Especially when the words classified, destructive, and bomb started bleeding into the same sentence.

For years, the group was nothing but whispers—some claimed the Manhattan Project was born inside their walls.

And everybody knew the story: Dr. Julius Robert Oppenheimer, the bomb's father, had a seat at the table. His time at Bohemian Grove was never a secret.

Though, in the end, Oppenheimer didn't object when his invention was deployed in the interest of America and Israel—but he never shared another discovery with them after that.

The club's name was strange; the members were stranger.
High performers across every line—untouchable by money, immune to fear, unpredictable to the bone.
No one ever cracked what they truly wanted, or why.
Now it all twists in Jovan's gut.

The fallout in Eilat. A butcher from GRU.
Rumors of a new WMD in play.
The Bohemian Club, buried deep in the tech nobody was supposed to touch—all of it grinding together, heavy in his chest.

He grabs the glass, drains it to the last drop.
It makes sense—why the Minister called him in.
He'd failed this mission last year. But instead of a reprimand, the Minister is giving him the chance to finish what he started.

Every name tangled in this mess—directly or sideways—brushes against his past operation. As Dr. Eli reaches to pick up the file again, Jovan raises a hand to stop her.

He turns to Dalat Zibram, eyes locked.

—What do you need from me, sir?

Zibram smiles—calm as old stone.

—As I told you at the start of this mission, my dear boy...
We're now closer than ever to getting our hands on the thing we've been hunting. If your friend Mohabbat Khan hadn't blown it in Phuket, you'd be holding it by now—I know that.
But even after that circus, we've confirmed at least three other outfits have either grabbed this weapon... or been promised delivery. We have to assume that at least three cities are now in real danger—unless we're the ones who get hold of these

weapons first.
—The Bohemian Club's involvement—*he continued*—only adds fuel to the idea that this is a WMD-level device. And from everything we're seeing—Iranians are neck-deep in this.

Zibram leans in, voice going grave.

—Our child in Iran, Hadid, reported he'd traced the source. And that source has links to people you know.

He pauses, just for a breath.

—But before the intel could reach us in full… Hadid got caught.

A flicker of pain flashes in Zibram's eyes.
He goes silent—honoring the loss in his own way.

Jovan's curiosity sharpens.

—But sir, Hadid's cover was top notch. How did they get to him?

Zibram's face turns to stone again.

—That failure wasn't on him.
And it damn sure wasn't on us, my boy.

He exhales, heavy.

—The shopkeeper Hadid used to send his calligraphy—that bastard was double-timing us. He ended up selling a few photos to an American journalist—sloppy move, easy to track.
Iranians caught the scent, dragged him in, got him talking.

Zibram leans back, voice steady—iron under velvet.

—They figured out Hadid's calligraphy always landed with the same buyer. We couldn't keep swapping couriers in Tehran forever—it was too dangerous. We just had this one runner posing as an exporter. They caught him.
He gave up a lot—including the drop locations.

Zibram's voice darkens.

—That trail led straight to Hadid. They tortured the poor kid, but he never broke. Still… Iranians managed to track down a distant relative—someone who actually knew the real family. That man told them Hadid wasn't the couple's biological son.

—After that, they didn't run a trial. Didn't even negotiate. Those bastards hanged our child.

His jaw clenches hard.

—We'd kept him out of the field for long just to be with his dying mother. Now all we're sending home is her son in a body bag.

Zibram goes quiet—face twisted, like he's just swallowed acid.
The mask of old stone drops for a moment.
The real man—war-forged steel—shows through.

Then he pulls it all back together, eyes locked on Jovan.

In any other agency, if this much sensitive information had been withheld, the agent would be tied to a chair by now, getting grilled without an ounce of mercy. But that's not Mossad.

Jovan isn't some disposable asset. He's family.
From the floor all the way up to the Minister, every single one of them is. They know his bloodline, know his roots.
Here, that means everything.

If duty called for it, they all knew—Jovan wouldn't blink to put down his own child. There was no room for suspicion.

Zibram never even thought about it. Instead, by quietly showing he knew about Mohabbat Khan's screw-up—even though it had never been formally reported—he gave Jovan something far more valuable than orders.
Trust.

Jovan takes a beat—cooling his head, lining up the words.
He knows. Keeping this much off the record was a mistake.

He starts there.

—I could've sent you everything from the field, sir.
But with the op still running, it didn't make sense to drown you in every pivot and workaround. I figured best to work on the

solution and spare you the static.
Hope you see that for what it was, sir—

He doesn't get to finish.
Zibram claps him on the back.

—Don't lose sleep over it, my boy. The second I gave you this mission, I signed off on every move you'd have to make.
That's why you're here. Please... carry on.

That hits home.
Jovan lets out a breath, settling back into the mission.
But the question keeps burning in his mind: how had all these men—total opposites—ended up circling the same blaze?

He asks it.
And Dalat Zibram nods slow, like he's been waiting for the spark.

—Good. That's the question I expected. Tells me your head's wired right. You're not seeing all the threads yet, but that's a matter of time and scars. Let me close the gaps for you.

He offers a thin, dry smile.

—Let's start here—what does the Bohemian Club actually want? These so-called visionaries... they don't even know the answer themselves. They claim they formed the club to find out.
Cute, right?

His tone turns brittle.

—But one thing every last one of them wants is to feed their secret desires. No matter how dark. No matter how twisted.

Zibram's gaze goes cold.

—Take Gates. You all call him Grandpa Gates.
Split with his wife lately. Sure, old men lose wives over young chicks all the time. But the real story?
He got caught up with a producer—child abuse pornography.
That's what we know from the outside. What his wife knew on the inside must've been worse.

Zibram exhales, voice tight.

—You ever see Taken? Watch it if you haven't.
Neeson plays a man in your shoes, more or less.

—That movie isn't fiction. It's a warning.
These elite 'spiritual' circles—the only thing they worship is pleasure. Control. The high of getting away with it.
After enough wins, they stop believing in anything but themselves. And when a man thinks he's a god,
he figures nothing should be off limits.
So they build channels. Secret groups.
Devil-worshipping cults. Degenerate societies.
Through rituals, masks, symbols—they turn crime into ceremony. That way, their sins don't feel dirty anymore.
They feel earned.

Jovan hadn't meant to interrupt, but the question slips out.

—Sir—how does that connect? I mean... devil-worshippers on one side, Shi'a extremists on the other?
Jihadis in the Middle East? They're polar opposites.

Zibram smiles. The real kind.

—My boy. There's a layer under this world you only start seeing when your hair goes gray.

He lets that settle.

—Iran's a theocracy, no question. But that same fire—the fanaticism—keeps them clawing for more.
More power, more leverage.
They'll deal with anyone who promises an edge.
And that hunger—

He leans in, voice gone blade-sharp.

—That's the crack where real darkness slides in.
These Satanist rings—they don't knock on the front door.
They slide in as patrons.
Money. Gear. Tech.
Whatever gets them close. And when they're in,

they sneak the weapons through—the kind we're after.
You watching the wire?

Zibram arches a brow.

—Every few weeks, another sect gets busted in Iran.
Right in the act. Rituals, parties, full depravity.
It's a pattern now. Guess what that tells us? They're in. Deep.
The alliances might look odd on the surface, but behind closed doors, they've been shaking hands for years.

Now Jovan can finally see the thread running through the dark.
He's heard whispers—about the Iranian commander's so-called brother, Baharram, and his trail of dirt.
Maybe Baharram was just sloppy, let the rumors slip.
Maybe his brother was just as deep in the dirt—only smarter, never left a mark.

Either way, the connection's staring him in the face.
The Bohemians and the Iranian Satanists—tied together.
But one question still hangs in the air.
Where the hell do the Sunni jihadis fit into this circus?

He's about to ask when Zibram lets out a laugh—big, dark, right from the chest.

—Oh, come on, son. These idiots have been hybrid stupid for generations. You know it better than most.
Every time we take out waves of Palestinians during ops,
the West loses its mind—but have you ever seen these jackasses protest? Never. You know why?
Because their empires are built on oil and sand.
One wrong move, the palace falls.
So they keep their heads down. Whisper behind closed doors.
Hire shadows to do the dirty work.
And look for ways to clean their hands before the blood hits.

He pauses, lets it soak.

—That's where the Bohemian smart-asses slide in.
I guarantee you, they cooked up something new, dangled it in front of the Satanists, and pulled them in.

—Iranians, for their part, put on the mask of 'shared revenge' and rope the Sunni jihadis under one flag. Meanwhile, the jihadi funders—the coward kings—keep their hands clean. They bankroll Iranian ops from the shadows.

Jovan nods, every piece falling into place.

—Makes sense, sir. The rest is simple.
If there's a secret weapon on the board, the Russians are never far behind. That's why they planted their pawn.
And whoever else was needed—they hired.

Zibram's voice cuts through—steady, final.

—Very good, my boy.
Now you've got the big picture.

He leans in.

—Stop wasting time. From this point on—you're the controller of this mission. Every branch, every field team reports to you.
You give the orders. You call the shots.
If anything critical hits—you bring it straight to me.

Then, without another word, Zibram lays his hand on Jovan's shoulder. That's how Mossad passes the torch.

Dalat Zibram has seen this before—war, loss, victory, betrayal. He knows what kind of man it takes to finish a job like this.

And this boy—this fire-born youth standing in front of him, has the same shadow his old man once carried.

Jovan's father had served under Zibram, a lieutenant, burned alive by a Hamas rocket while shielding his team.

Now the son stands ready—sharper, stronger, unbreakable.
The kind that won't just survive the war.
He'll burn the enemy alive in it.

—*—

Threads Through the Veil

Taman Duta, North–South Expressway
Kuala Lumpur, Malaysia

I don't remember where we crashed last night.
Woke up alone in bed—Marisha nowhere in sight.

Left the bed like a soul peeling off its body.
Hit the shower—washed the night off my face.
Then made it down the stairs.

Marisha was in the kitchen, sleeves rolled.
Sunlight catching her like she owned it.
She caught me staring.
Tossed a good-morning smile my way—sharp and easy.

I asked the obvious.

—How'd you know where everything was?

She keeps moving, voice light, almost playful.

—I ducked out to grab a few things. When I came back, my inner cat got curious. Turns out your kitchen's got everything, like some five-star Airbnb. I jumped in. Breakfast almost done. Grab a seat, Mr. Host. Today, I've got the apron.

I'm watching her—still not used to how easily she's falling into this gravity. She's trying to get personal with Elijan.
No one plays that hard without an angle.
Let's see where she wants this to land.

A few minutes later, she starts laying the dishes out.
One by one.
And to be honest—I wasn't ready for the punch.
I don't know if these would be Elijan's favorites.
But every single one was mine.

Even that absurd dish—poached eggs drizzled with honey, sandwiched in grilled brioche.

Around her neck, the dog tag—still flashing the name: Caesar.
Obsession, maybe.
Or she's leaning hard into the lost love act.

Marisha catches my stare, tips her head just enough to read me.

—What's wrong, Mr. Host? Not your kind of fuel?

I shake my head.

—Looks hot and loaded, *I say.*
—Same as the chef. But I'll need a bite to know if it hits.

She arches an eyebrow.

—Bite—of what?

She catches the edge, but doesn't blink.
Just smiles like she already clocked me the moment I walked in.
We've got a lot to discuss, but I don't want to kill the moment.

I play it cool, keep the peace.

—I need to head back into the city. Pick up a few things.
Then I'll come back and find a clinic or a hospital.
What about you—any plans?

She answers between bites, voice warm but steady.

—For now? I want to see you get out of this in one piece.
Until then, I'm not going anywhere.
After that—I'll finish what I came here to do.

Then she pauses, looks right at me.

—By the way, you said you'd talk to someone at your office?
About finding the real person. Any news?

I'm caught in my own thoughts—don't think before saying,

—Real person—who's that supposed to be?

—Are you playing with me?
The number you were carrying?
I told you everything.

It lands like a nuke—just missed detonation.
The timing's off by a hair and this whole room goes to war.

Based on Rasheed's briefing, I assumed she rushed to KL looking for her sister. That's how she crossed paths with Elijan.
Now, it seems the story has more twists.
And if I take one wrong turn, it might land in fire.

I drop the act.

—Don't be mad, gorgeous. Took a bullet to the chest and a blade to the gut. Some wires got crossed upstairs.

I tap my temple, careful not to let her see what's left behind my eyes.

—Light me up again, please.

She holds my gaze, cold and hard, for a long second.
Then she starts talking—how and why she really met Elijan.

And now, it makes sense.
She didn't come for her sister.
She came looking for me.

Kidnapped by the same crew,
wound up in the same hellhole—a week before I woke up.
Coincidence, maybe. But Phuket had me underestimating her.
I tried to brush her off as a side story, but she's proven she's not just set dressing. But how do I explain the switch—from Caesar to Elijan? I can't.
Not unless I put it all on the table.
And I'm not sure I should.
So she stays—at least until I'm back on my feet.
After that, we'll see.

Breakfast done.
I'm ready to move—but Marisha refuses to leave me alone in this state. She stands her ground. Leaves no space for argument.

I just grab fresh clothes from the stash and we head out together.

Twenty minutes later, the car noses into the Mo Bank's basement, just beside the Twin Towers.

We head straight to the locker section.
Back then, these vaults needed keys or hardware tokens just to open the door. Times changed. Now you carry nothing.

Security with guns leads us to the access point outside the gate. First time I saw this place, it was some old desktop bolted to a desk.

Now it's all touchscreen—one tap, the glass glows, asks for username and password.

I keep all digital logins simple. Same routine here.

We're in. No friction—door slides open.
A bank executive greets us through.
Marches us down a corridor to the high-value lockers,
stops at a steel door, and gives us privacy.

Marisha hesitates at the threshold, hanging back.

—These lockers… too personal.
I guess I should wait here. You finish up inside.

I laugh, low.

—You've already robbed the man, gorgeous.
Why not the locker too?

She breaks—cracks up, pure and open.

—God, Elijan. Every word, every move—you keep reminding me of someone. Guess we'll see who walks away with the bigger haul.

Truth is—I have to take her inside. What I came for isn't something I can drag out alone—not in this shape.
I tell her straight, and she agrees.

Inside, the login runs its own kind of gauntlet.
No fingerprints. No swipe cards.
Screen blinks to life, spits out a random email.

First step—fire off a request from the same company domain that registered the locker.
Lucky for me, I've got the official phone. Mail sent in seconds.
Screen lights up: application received.

Next wall—username and password.
Routine.
I punch in the handle—twelve digits same as before, plus the last four letters of the domain.
Steel splits open with a hiss. Rows of lockers inside, lined up neat—like coffins in a morgue.

I stop at the right one, press the handle.
A tiny display blinks awake,
asking—fingerprint or domain unlock?
My prints? Worthless now. I pick domain unlock.

Display spins, searching. Phone buzzes:
Someone is trying to access your locker at Mo Bank. Confirm?
Yeah, I know. I confirm.
Click through. Inbox blinks—bank's message waiting.
Hit the link. Processing bar rolls, slow and deliberate.

Then, both screens speak in sync:
Welcome. May your time at Mo Bank be pleasant.
Lock disengages.

The coffin opens—stacks of boxes, numbered and neat.
I point Marisha at the biggest one.
She lifts it like it's nothing.
It shouldn't have been that light.
I double-check the weight—no, it's real. Heavy.

Only then does it hit me—she's strong.
Weightlifter, fight-night, do-not-cross strong.

I tell her to hold onto the box, shut the locker,
hear the lock click home.

We get the box to the car—no fuss, no hassle, all Marisha.
She helps shift the toolbox, slides the locker into the gap—
perfect fit. Carpet down, toolbox back on top. Done.

She turns, asks if I need anything else. Has her own errands—says she'll head back to the bungalow later.

I pull out alone.
Everything I need is in the locker, and for the first time in days, I'm feeling a bit steady now. But the burn from the gut wound tells me—if I don't handle this soon, infection's going to finish what the bullet started.

I drive to Times Square first.
Need to check the apartment.

Masud's there.
He's already got the place cleaned up.
Door fixed, new cameras in.
Says he'll have it all tight in a few hours.

Makes more sense to keep Marisha here, close to the city.
If she needs to move, easier this way.

I tell Masud I'll be at the hospital for a few days,
and to watch over Marisha while I'm gone.

Then I head back to the bungalow.
Get in quick.
Shower.
Let the day run off my skin, and crash—hard.

Marisha has the key.
She can walk in whenever she wants.
All quiet now.
Just me, the bandages, and whatever waits for round two.

No idea how long I'd been lost. Came back to the world with someone's hand combing through my hair.

Eyes still closed.
Drowned in comfort, I know it's Marisha.

—When'd you get in?

—Half an hour ago.
You were holding your head in sleep.
Thought it hurt.

Then maybe she kisses me.
Soft. Testing.
I stay still.
Let it hang.

—So—you can fix every pain that way?

That was just a low ball. But she plays it hard.

—Not the one in your heart. The rest—I can.
I asked around. Taking you to a private clinic tomorrow.

She's still thinking I bled for her. I need her to drop it.

—Don't bother, I already lined it up.
Not tomorrow—I'll check in myself tonight.
And you don't have to stick around. Use my apartment.
It's better for whatever you need in the city.

She shuts it down.
Doesn't want the apartment. Doesn't want the bungalow.
She'll stay with me at the hospital.

I push back—no reason for it—but she holds the line anyway.
In the end, we cut a deal: she'll stay nights at the apartment, mornings at the hospital. Her own errands in between.

I can live with that.
Truth is, I'd been waiting at the bungalow for her to come back.

Now that she's here, we pack up and roll for the Times Square apartment.

Same drill at the entrance—car parked, and the kid, Regan, comes running.

He hands me the keys, says the locks and the rest have been fixed. I thank him and head up with Marisha to the twenty-fifth.

—∞—

Heat in the Grid

Aamari Resort
Phuket, Thailand

Under the flimsy top, Dr. Eli's red panties flashed—like she'd walked out of a Vogue shoot. Jovan sat at the café, bare-chested, hair matted heavy, watching her.

Back again at this place. Not crippled this time.
Full Arab sheikh profile—trophy on display.
In Phuket, that passes.
For a couple like this, every door opens with sawadee ka.
The cover wasn't luxury—it was leverage.

Minutes from now, ten grand would slide across the table to the resort's head of security. For that kind of job, the number should've raised flags in anyone's mind.
Unless it came from an Arab.
They burn stacks for reasons no one bothers to ask.

If intel wasn't on the line, the local underdogs could've handled it. But intel's the one thing Jovan can't hand off.
Guns, cash—fine. But information—never.
They're all whores.
They'll sell it once, twice, to any hand that offers cash.
That's why this part needs to be done on his own.

Last time, the op blew sideways. The close never hit clean.
Two groups crossed wires and shredded the plan.
The black lion—Sgt. Luther King—was supposed to erase two Arabs. Yet both are still breathing.
The sergeant himself—gone.
Same night, the Kamala Bay warehouse blew apart.
Whether he died in his own fire is still a question.

Those answers won't come fast.
It needs to crawl through Thai labs.
Burned bodies, DNA runs—bureaucratic sludge.

And the Thais offer boom boom easy, but not intel.
Foreign Ministry's still squeezing them. When something cracks, the news will drop—nobody can say when.

The second group's failure keeps running loops in Jovan's head. Mohabbat Khan had checked into the Xyat Regency—prime target in tow.

The play was simple: drop the man into one of their girls at the casino, then disappear. Once she had him upstairs, the girl would ping Mossad's handler. Two operators waited on the upper floor. Message comes in—target goes down.
But the signal never hit. The girl went dark.

The waiting pair—stuck on ice.
And Mohabbat Khan—gone.

The girl pulling strings on her own? No chance.
She came vetted—Dubai subcell, years on record.
She'd run support before. Even on Thai soil. That's why they trusted her, didn't just grab a street runner to bait the mark. Calculated risk.
Messy, but manageable—until Mohabbat Khan vanished.
The bastard had a habit for it. Last time he screwed a run and vanished for two years in Peshawar.

The other cells wrapped their hit jobs clean.
Targets down, exits sealed. But where did the loose ends vanish? Sergeant King—ghost. The two Arabs on his sheet still enjoying luxury back home. Now flagged for Mossad's Middle East desk.

As for Mohabbat Khan—intel tagged him in Malaysia. Maybe he's still hiding there, maybe tunneled back to Pakistan, buried deep again. But the Xyat target—and the girl who took him upstairs? Vanished into thin air.

The man booked a room at the Xyat for show.
His real bed was here—Aamari Resort.
That's why Jovan's burning hours on CCTV, tracking whether the target circled back or slipped away clean.
And here they come.

A smiling waiter, tray of juice.
Behind him, the Sri Lankan security chief—Fernandez.

—Good afternoon, sir. Hope you're enjoying your stay.

—Good afternoon, Mr. Fernandez.
Honestly—your hospitality's brighter than the sun.

—Ha! My pleasure, sir. Fresh pineapple juice. If you're not watching your pressure, try it with pink salt—twice the kick.

—No trouble, Mr. Fernandez. We'll try it your way.

—Glad to hear it, sir. The lady's not here—should I bring something else for her?

—No, she'll be joining soon. This is perfect.

—Thank you, sir. Call if you need anything.
Please enjoy your stay.

—Always a pleasure, Mr. Fernandez.

One signal from Fernandez, and the tray lands.
The waiter sets it on the table.
A little teasing with the waters, then Dr. Eli returns.
Dips into the pink salt jar—pulls out a thumb drive.
Inside: the full footage.

That morning, Eli walked Jovan into a quiet corner with the Sri Lankan. A fat envelope on the table—ten grand in cash.
And a smile sharp enough to cut.

She spun the story neat: Jovan's Arab friend was threatening to blow up their affair, blackmail the whole family.
The irony? That same "friend" had just been at this hotel months ago, partying hard with a Thai girl.

Now, if Mr. Fernandez didn't mind keeping the envelope—and letting them take a look at the security footage from that night—they'd make sure karma hit the right target.

At first, Fernandez played by the book: guest privacy, hotel policy.

But the envelope was wide open—hundred-dollar bills loud in a language everyone understands.

And Eli's sheer top didn't hide the Eres Mouna she was wearing—nor the crafted parts inside it.
Her body pressing close, the red promise visible.
Words stalled in Fernandez's throat.

She took the silence as agreement.
Slipped the cash into his pocket. Brushed a thank-you note across his sunbaked cheek with her painted lips, then walked away with a smile.

When he finally muttered he'd "look into it," Jovan expected a walk to the CCTV room—maybe a peek, no more.

Instead, Fernandez dropped a full copy of the night's footage, slipped onto a flash drive.

Proof that Sri Lankans might run hotels, but they shouldn't touch security. If they'd hired a retired army major or an ex-police official, the same intel would've cost ten times as much.

Xyat Regency proved the contrast.
Their chief—Chinese, ex-Red Army lieutenant.
When the bribe hit the table, he didn't flinch.
Just said no.

Eli adapted. Shifted roles.
Played the young wife—trapped by "financial security."
Married to a disgusting Arab.
Wet on wallet but dry where she needed it.

Turned out worse—the man was cheating with Thai girls behind her back. With the right photo or video of her husband's "secret," she could divorce him clean and walk away with millions.
Then, she hinted, maybe a real captain could take her curves for a proper sail.

Old rules—soldiers never turn down a drink or a woman.
The Chinese officer proved it quick.
Dragged Eli into a storeroom, showed off his moves, proved he

knew how to row her tide to climax.
Eli left promising she'd take the full trip next time—as long as he paid the toll. The ride's not free—not on a river that runs with waves that wild.

The deal was done.
Before touching her bed, he will give her ten minutes alone in the CCTV room. Enough to pull what they needed.

Eli needed just a few minutes to load their kit into the control box. Once the tech unit got the access, Jovan would comb the whole facility's footage himself.

Eli, meanwhile, would drift off on her own tide—sailing with the security guy whose "demo," she claimed, had actually impressed her. Ha.

Teammates chasing pleasure never bothers Jovan, as long as the op holds steady. Let them have their fun.

By afternoon, he's at Hot Rock Café.
He never cares for music.
For him, the place isn't about sound; it's supply.

Fresh girls, cheap, sometimes free. A few pills, a few bills, and they lose themselves to the rhythm, to the haze, willing to play out fantasies even the hired ones wouldn't.
Today, desire isn't on the menu.

He'd already run through the Aamari footage with Eli over lunch.
Two Arabs checked out—just as expected.
But the real targets—were ghosts.

After the sweep, they ate.
Eli went upstairs for a nap.
And Jovan crossed into this building next to Hot Rock.

Last time in Phuket, it was simple—search and kill.
No tech crew, no gadgets, no drama.
Just the hit and clean.

This time, everything's changed.
Full unit flown in, gear stacked.
And the result is on the table.

No one expected it—an Iranian data center tucked next to a pub wired for sex and sound. Intel said the target upstairs would lock his terminal, then step out.
That's why they wait.

Hit him too soon and he'll go loud—maybe wreck the system they need alive.
The tech boys need a live feed, not a pile of shrapnel.

Two Thai cops posted at the entrance—waiting for Jovan's nod. They're real police, not just costumes. Moonlighting for Mossad when the job calls for a snatch-and-go in daylight.
To passing eyes, it just looks like an arrest.

Perks come with that uniform; managers and staff bend easy. The receptionist here didn't even need a story—ten seconds of cop-talk and he was all in.

Jovan's legs are dead numb by the time the target shows.
Iranian. Isfahan stock.
Jovan pegs it before the face turns.
Trained eyes don't miss it.

The man scanned the room, blind to the danger.
Started for the street.
Jovan cued the manager, who tipped off the cops.
Plan was textbook:
The second he crossed the threshold, cops closed in from both sides. Smooth talk, cuffs on. Load him into the car.

But the cops went off-script—jammed a taser in his gut.
Shock hit. Dropped him cold.
Then dumped him into Jovan's vehicle like lost luggage.

Daggan is waiting inside.
Old hand.
Knows how to cut clean when things get surgical.

Jovan had plans—if he climbed higher, Daggan would be his deputy. That's how he groomed him.

Daggan had worn every badge worth the name—army, police, even Aman, one of the shadow agencies.
Last chair before Jovan yanked him in: IDF.

Jovan himself never touched IDF.
Didn't like their flavor. Too blunt.
They weren't intelligence—they were cleanup.
Kill orders dressed in doctrine.
Sometimes it just sanctioned massacres.
Not his taste.

Jovan's work is sharper, cerebral.
But not every enemy plays with wires and code.
Some still come in with blood.

Now that Spets is in play, Jovan keeps every layer locked down.
He wouldn't pretend—those Russian bastards shook him.
And not just him.
CIA. MI6. Every so-called ally in the field felt the chill.
Each Spetsnaz fucker was a walking disaster.
Moscow might clink glasses with Washington, smile for the press—meant nothing.
When it came to this unit, silence was doctrine.
No files. No leaks.
Not even an official acknowledgment.
—Disbanded after the Soviet fall—that was the line they fed everyone. But everyone in the circuit knows better.

Jovan had flipped ministers, generals, full branches of live service. Never a GRU Spetsnaz. Not once. Back when the USSR was on its knees, the West thought they'd turned a few.

Turned out, those bastards staged the whole thing.
Walked in, played nice, milked the West, then vanished back to Moscow with grins.

Lesson landed hard.
Nobody tried it again.

Now the rule was simple: if your asset crossed a GRU bastard on the ground, you had two plays—
Kill. Or die.

Jovan had no interest in dying this early.
So he brought in Daggan's IDF crew.
Trusted men. Wired for precision.
They weren't just for cover fire either.
He had other jobs in mind.

The Isfahan target was just the opening shot. Every catch after this—their guts would be cut open for words.
That's what the IDF boys did best.
Their reputation always entered the room first.

Daggan broke off from the cops after the handshake, slipped them the envelope, kept the smile, and strolled back toward Jovan.

—Everything's smooth, bossy. Why that owl-face?

—I'm worried about sourcing, *Jovan said.* —Aamari's footage gave us nothing. If Xyat comes up dry tonight, we're still staring at a black hole.

Daggan shrugged.

—So what? This data center's a goldmine, almost guaranteed. Tech boys are already inside. Problem is, I came all this way to get into your war and I'm still empty-handed.
Not even a scent of the peach you dangled.

Jovan cut him a look.

—You'll get it. Don't start pouting yet, son.

Daggan grinned, shaking his head.

—Keep your sermons, bossy.
Every handler since Babylon's been selling hope the same way.
Just hear me—when we grab her, the front work's all yours.
Pictures, IDs, chain of custody, whatever. After that?

He tapped his teeth.

—If she lands in my hands, I'll chew those cheeks till they bleed. What a peach you flashed, man—my hips are dancing for a shot.

He was talking about the GRU Spetsnaz girl.
And with Daggan, the enthusiasm wasn't entirely unjustified.

Jovan was disciplined when it came to women. He'd bunked with Dr. Eli on a dozen ops—nights together, same bed.
Eli, generous in every sense, had offered more than once.
He never crossed that line.
But this time? Even he took a hit.

That girl... her body feels like a crime—slim waist dropping into those curvy hips. Shoulders of a fighter, tits like skyscrapers.
Any experienced man could guess they're natural, not synthetic.
And those eyes—blue as a live wire. Lips that'd drown saints.
Her face alone was enough to drop any gentleman straight into love.

And for bastards like Daggan? They'd want to eat her alive—and wouldn't stop till she screamed.

Jovan broke into a laugh—still remembered the first time he saw her photo. His pants almost sold him out in front of the minister.

Daggan spotted it, grinning like a thief.

—What's up, bossy? That grin... don't tell me you're already thinking of sharing my peach.

Jovan Fired back.

—Don't start slicing the peach before it's even off the branch, rookie. Getting hands on a livewire like her—that's a full challenge.

Daggan grinned.

—Heh. First time I've seen you not wrinkle your nose at a woman. Fine. You get first swing. But that back door?
That stays locked in. Reserved to be mine.

—Cut the crap. This is why working with kids gives me a migraine. The peach's still hanging, and you're already shaping the knife. Keep dreaming—while you're busy fantasizing, she'll fold you like a bedsheet.

Daggan just laughed.

—Chill, bossy. We're not that green. We know what Spetsnaz trains for—first move in close combat—they smash the sensitive spots, have you on the floor before you blink. But not with us. Check these suits—custom stitched, plates inside.
Soft spots covered. Sure, it stings when you take a shot—but it won't put you down.
Bit heavy on the body, but we wear it like skin.

—Well, look at you—maybe there's a brain under all that mouth. So who's got Eli covered?

—Come on, boss—she's a weapon. What's there to cover?

—That, right there.
Last time, this exact slack cost us the real prize. No margin now. If you're not watching, I'll plug the hole myself.

—Why so heated, bossy? Just winding you up. Don't sweat it.
I've got eyes posted anywhere Eli could walk. Something pops, no need for signals—each crew moves on its own.

—Good. That's the way. Just shooting the breeze here. But tell me something, Daggan—why'd you never bag Eli yourself?
She could've hit the target, then come back and put out her own fire in your bed. Would've saved us two teams and a long night of watch duty.

Daggan made a face.

—Tsk. Boss... that's cold.
I see you like blood—like my own.
And you say that? Eli?
She's an over-squeezed mango. Juice long gone.
Newbies chase her 'cause they don't know better.

—But us? Please. You know what she did?
Injected duck oil in her sagging ass.

Jovan blinked—then busted out laughing, a real one.

—Duck oil? What the fuck, Daggan.
Didn't even know that was a thing.

Daggan's smiles widened.

—Of course it's real, bossy.
You're never in Tel Aviv long enough to see the circus.
That's why you miss all the freak shows.
Some lunatic derm cooked it up—duck oil, black-lab filler, jabbed straight into the ass. Give it a week, and boom—your flat ass swells like a bar mitzvah peach.
Every girl in Tel Aviv's lining up. Even LA's sending their blow-up dolls just to pump up their goddamn asses.

Jovan gave a low whistle.

—Fucking hell… it actually works?

—You blind, bossy? That chewed-up Eli's been swinging her ass past your face all week. You didn't catch it?

—Oh, I noticed. Figured it was synthetic. With the ops she's been running lately, a little plastic shine fits right in.
Didn't waste brain cycles on it.

—Still too pure for this world, bossy.

—Some purity's worth keeping, Daggan.
Drop it. I need to walk the next phase through my head.

—Yeah, keep it coming, bossy. Not my lane. All I got is one hard line from HQ— me and my crew keep you upright.
You run the op. We handle the war.

Jovan grinned, reached over, grabbed a handful of Daggan's hair, gave it a hard shake, then turned for the stairs—smiling all the way up.

Dagan had been two batches junior at university. They'd even played on the same basketball squad.
This was big-brother shit. That's how Mossad rolls.

They didn't need seminars on teamwork. They were born into it—stitched with loyalty, programmed for ops from the cradle.

Jovan knew what Daggan said wasn't just talk—it was blood code. No one could lay hands on him without walking over his crew first.

They snapped, and elbowed when it came to rank—but when Israel was on the line, every grudge got buried six feet deep, side by side. Generations drilled that into their bones.

The tech team was already buried in the top floor—screens humming, wires crawling like ivy.

Jovan leaned into the mess, threw them a jab:

—Nu, what is this—button-pushers on a coffee break?
Push something useful before the clock eats us.
We've still got ground to rip.

Normally that line cracked them up. Not tonight.
Three of them locked in. Pale. Eyes bolted to the feed.

Jovan stepped closer. One of them finally muttered,

—Not looking good, boss. This could take hours to break.
We might have to pull the whole box and drag it back.

Jovan's jaw clenched.

—You're telling me the Iranians cooked up a system even we can't crack?

The team lead—a kid with fresh eyes and razor focus—shook his head.

—Not what I'm saying. I'll stake my neck on it—this system isn't Iranian. Not a chance.

The world was already riding Israeli cybersecurity while Apple, puffed up with virus-proof pride, kept slamming the door.

The kid cracked their calendar system, tripping millions of users like dominoes. One jab, Apple folded. Now they run Mossad-grade protection on every unit—while Mossad siphons their cloud on schedule.

That kid was now looking pale and muttering impossible.

Jovan felt a cold sweat up his spine.
He clenched the curse mid-throat.

Swallowed it dry. Came back with another jab:

—Fine. Do what you need. But don't come crying about hauling Xyat's system home as well. You've got minutes in there—Eli's little gold mine doesn't buy us all night. Make them count.

That landed.
The boys broke into grins, barking back in chorus like dogs off leash—swearing on Dr. Eli's duck-fat ballooned ass that they'd get it done.

Even they knew the joke.
Jovan let it run.
They were young. He'd been that age—spitting the same crud, thinking the same wild thoughts.

He left them to their toys and moved on.
Time to shift the rest of the board.

—*—

Penang to Pavilion

Kuala Lumpur, Malaysia

Eyes opened after days.
I'd been conscious the whole time—muscle relaxants and sedatives had me nailed to the bed.
Heard every sound, but couldn't move. Couldn't look.
Even now, my body's stiff, but the fog finally burned off.

The room came into focus—tidy, spotless.
Sheets, the couch, the furniture, all white.
Maybe someone thinks peace lives in that color.
Wires snaked out from half my body, feeding the machines stacked by my head. I tried reading the numbers, but it was all blur—just shapes, no digits.
Felt like a week in here.
A private clinic.
Hidden. Quiet.
But the doctors knew their craft. I told the surgeon straight:
If pulling the bullet in my chest looked risky, leave it.
The gut wound was worse.
One infection and I'd rot from the inside.
That's what I came to stop.

My stirring must've tripped something—machines started pinging, alarms stabbing the air.

I figured a nurse, maybe some aide.
Someone showed up.
But she wasn't either.

I raised a hand—closer.
Didn't help.
Her face leaned in, blurred even worse.

Still, I knew her. You don't forget someone wired into your nervous system.
She thought I couldn't speak. That's why she leaned in.

I whispered,

—Goby, my darling. Look at you.

She laughed.
Tried to cover it with her hand.
I couldn't see her clear, but I didn't need to.
I knew her moves. Could sketch that smile from memory.
She pulled a chair in, took my hand, slow.

I looked at her.

—Sweetheart... not even blackout dreams had you turning up here. How the hell did you pull this off?

She gave me that soft grin.

—No riddles. You listen to the doctor, and I'll tell you the whole story.

I wasn't in shape to argue. I smiled.

—I'm listening.

My eyes dipped again. Too heavy to fight.
She stroked my head and said,

—Sleep. I'm right here.

Her voice—or just the exhaustion—dragged me in dreams again.

The second time I opened my eyes, Sahara was there.
Made sense. Where Gobi goes, Sahara orbits—planet and moon.
No surprise left in me.

Nurse came through with her routine.
Syringe ready. Needle slid in, pushed something cold.
Felt almost nothing—my body was running on empty.

When she left, Gobi leaned in. Told Sahara to lift the bed.
They propped me up.

Gobi climbed on the side with a food tray.
Sahara took the chair, posted up next to her.

Gobi offered soup.
I turned my face, told her I wasn't in the mood.
She frowned like I'd insulted her bloodline.

I gave in, took the spoon.
The taste hit sharp—like drinking ground-up poison.

She caught the look on my face. Whispered.

—Take it slow. Let it settle. No rush.

I nodded, tried again.
Then asked, low,

—Now tell me what happened.

Before she could start, Sahara jumped in, buzzing like a live wire.

—I'll tell it, boss. What went down.

—Go on, I said, turning to him.

My eyes still blurred, his outline fogged, but I knew his voice.

He leaned into it, eager.

—When Penang blew up, soon as we got your signal, me and Gobi took Tommy's crew straight into the tunnel. Crossed over to the island. That's when we saw it—the restaurant went up behind us. Just—flames.

He kept firing.

—No trace of you. No comms from Macro. I wanted to hold position but Tommy shut it down. Pulled us and the civs back to the mainland. Got 'em clear. Then we circled. By then the place was crawling—cops, medics, the whole net.

Pause. Breath.

—Tried everything, boss—but you were gone.
No trace. I fought Tommy on it, I swear.

I raised my hand—just enough to cut his rant. Sahara stopped.

My voice went flat.

—There's nothing to fight over. Tommy did what he was ordered to do. If any of you start doubting protocol—start flinching at the line—we break the system. And when that happens, we fall.

Sahara's head dropped, silent.
There's no point digging up bones now.

I asked him what happens next. He started slow. Careful, even.

—We kept hoping you—or Macro—would surface. But nothing happened. While we waited, Tommy started pulling strings, trying to trace the hit. Who ordered it. Why. Dead ends, all of it. Still no word from you. To see if anything worse had happened, we even started repairs at the blown-out restaurant.
Said we were rebuilding. Truth is, we were clearing wreckage.
Looking for you under the rubble.
Basement gutted, debris hauled—no bodies.
That gave us some hope.
If you don't want to be found, there's no trail.
You swap faces, names. Even now—you've changed again.
We've seen this before, and we stopped chasing shadows.
Then last week—we get a log-in flag.
Someone accessed the KL hideout.
At that time, Goby and I were still in Bangkok with Tommy.
We checked the bungalow feed. Some guy tried to walk in.
Unknown face. System couldn't pull a match—no fingerprint, no scan. We were about to remote-lock the place when I saw her.
The woman—was our mom.

Goby lost it.
Laughed so hard she dropped the soup straight onto my bed.

—Sorry—sorry, she kept saying, still laughing, hands shaking as she wiped it up.

I just stared.
No clue what they were talking about.
Cut in, flat—told Sahara to spell it out.

He pushed on,

—By then we figured the man driving her there was you.
Still, we held. Watched.
Then we got another flag—Mo Bank access.
No way some imposter or hacker breaks through those layers.
Not unless it's you. That's when we knew—you'd come back,
under another face. So we moved. Straight to KL.
But even back at the bungalow—no trace of you.
We tried the compartment phone—but the device was offline.
So, we had no choice but to start combing the last pinged location
around BBT Zone.
By evening, Tommy took us to the Pavilion.
Said he needed to pick something up.
Goby and I were waiting near the gates.
She bought an ice cream, I was scanning the line.
That's when it cracked again...
Uff—just thinking about that moment, boss, Still gives me chills.

Sahara leaned in, eyes wired.

—At Pavilion's private entrance—some Russo muscles picked a fight with two girls. One of them was all dolled up, party makeup, dressed like she was headed somewhere. The other had her back to me, talking with her, when the thugs cut in and started pushing both of them around.
Pretty girls getting harassed—always draws attention.
And the dolled-up one—I swore I'd seen her somewhere.
I moved closer.
Then it happened—the one with her back turned snapped,
spun, and dropped a clean punch straight into a Russo's jaw.
Big bastard didn't take it quiet. The whole pack rushed her.
She backed up—face to face with me.
And that's when I saw it—holy hell—it was Mom standing there.

Goby cracked again. Full giggles.
I was already done.

—Spare me the warm-up.
Jump to the part that matters.

Sahara waved me off, grinning like a game show host.

—Warm-up? Come on, boss. You're our guardian.
Which makes you... well, our father figure.
And your lover—she's our mom. Simple math.

He spread his arms, verdict delivered.
I stared.

—Idiot. Who told you which woman's a lover, which one's just a friend?

He didn't flinch. Eyes wide like he'd cornered me.

—Ha? What do you think of me—a baby panda?
You forgot Phuket?
Your phone was dead—you used mine to message her.
Remember what she sent back? 'My love... I missed you...'
Sent you kissing selfies. I saw it before you snatched the phone.

Beat. He leaned back, smug.

—Next day, you flew out to meet her.
I said then—you were cooked. Lost in love.
Everyone laughed. Called me the fool.
Now look. I tied it all up in one shot.
All dots. Connected.
Some questions still flickering in my mind.
Why she was here. How she'd made it.
But it wasn't the time. One Russo bustard lunged.
I signaled Goby and snapped a kick straight to his gut.
They didn't see it coming. Stumbled back fast.
Goby moved in, fists blazing. Russo's dragged the dolled-up girl behind them, guarding her like cargo.
We pulled our own—mom—behind us.
She bristled, of course. She didn't even know us.
Then it got worse.
One of them pulled a gun. Didn't fire—just flexed it.
But she—mom—moved forward to charge that man.
Goby and I barely held her back.
Then thank God—Tommy showed up. He saw the gun pointed at us and drew his own, stepped in at our side. Russo muscles looked at us. Looked at the gun. They knew it wouldn't end clean.
So they grabbed the girl and bolted.
Tommy wanted to chase. I stopped him. Something was already stirring inside me. If we'd found mom—then dad couldn't be far.

Though Tommy and Goby didn't know her.
—They hadn't seen that photo. So, I had to blurt the whole damn thing fast—held her down, begged her not to chase the Russians' car. Introduced us. Laid the story bare.
And somehow wrestled the chaos into order. Christ.

Sahara had spun it his way—his version of meeting Marisha.
But the truth was still a blur.
Why would Marisha trust him enough to drag the whole crew to my hospital bed, when she didn't even know who I really was?

I asked.

Sahara just raised his hands like it was out of his league.
The boy's simple. Always has been.

—I don't know all that, *he said.*
—At first, I didn't recognize the girl with the Russians. But later, when we all talked—we figured she was the same one who came to our restaurant in Penang, before the blast.
Macro was with her then. If she's alive—Macro must be too.
But when we asked Marisha how she knew her,
she shut her face black like a thundercloud. Not just that—she kept a lot from us. Said she'd speak to you herself.
Christ. That firebrand. My gut says she's a bone breaker.
Even if you get back on your feet, you shouldn't leave this hospital anytime soon.

I looked at him.

—Hell no, kid. That's not how it works.
A woman's moods are like clouds.
They darken, they break, and rain clears them just as fast.
That you'll understand when you grow up.
Now tell me—where is she?

I asked Sahara. But Goby answered.
Said the Russian girl was too important to lose.
Marisha took off with Tommy to track her.
Promised they'd be back by evening.

Lying in bed, I couldn't tell noon from night.
Didn't matter. I kept quiet and waited.
When Marisha came back, I'd need the whole story.

—∞—

The Dark Cloud

Taman Duta, North-South Expressway
Kuala Lumpur, Malaysia

Somewhere between sleep and waking, it felt like I was being carried in a car. If not for the subtle lean of the road, I would've taken it for a dream. I tried opening my eyes, but the haze held.

Out of that blur, a face leaned close.

—Don't worry, boss. Rest. We're almost there. They gave you a mild relaxant, things might feel strange.

I know it was Tommy. A few more shadows sat around me.
I let myself sink, loosened my limbs, and drift took me again.

The next time I surfaced, it was in a bed—comfortable, real. Voices moved in the room, soft and slow. Off to my left, a window stood open. For the first time in weeks, my chest felt light enough to lift.

Outside, palms rose tall—thirty feet easy, maybe more.
Malaysia was palm country, but these were different:
Green trunks and fronds, and at the top, a flash of raw red.
Lipstick palms, dressed up like gatekeepers for the rich.
Beautiful enough, sure, but what actually got me was seeing them sharp—no blur, no fog, the haze finally gone.

Sahara noticed me sitting up and came rushing, shouting at the room.

—See? I told you—boss is fine! Fit as ever!
Look, he's sitting up on his own!

He clapped like a kid celebrating his own theory, then dropped beside me.

The others came next—Goby, Tommy, and Marisha.
Tommy shook my hand with that familiar, easy grin.
Goby kissed both cheeks, soft and quick.

—How are you all? I asked.

All good, they said. After KL, they'd landed this bungalow; Marisha had stayed in Times Square until now.
But with me out of the hospital, they could all stay together again. It felt good seeing them—all of them—but I knew at least one face in the room wasn't smiling.

Sahara wasn't kidding about the dark clouds—Marisha wore that weather across her face. Storm behind her eyes.
She didn't join in our chatter, and when our eyes finally met, nothing about her glance felt familiar. Just the blank chill of a stranger measuring distance.

My body was working again. I pushed off the be. Tommy and Sahara moved in to steady me, but I knew I didn't need their hands.

I stood up easily.
Head spun once, I stayed still—planted—let it pass.
Nothing serious. Just too long in bed.
The blood had gone lazy in my legs.
It would flow back soon enough.

Tommy broke the air with a grin: said we should mark my recovery with one of my favorite dishes. Cooking was his hidden art. Alongside his other talents, the man could command a kitchen, and everyone leaned in when he offered.

—Alright then—I'll head out, grab what we need.

He made for the door.
Goby and Sahara jumped to join him. I let them go.
Three of them gone before I took another breath.

Left alone, I paced the room slow, testing my steps. Across from me stood Marisha—still with that face, clouds pulled tight, storm refusing to break.

Maybe groceries weren't the real reason they cleared out.
Maybe they'd wanted this—space.
For us.

I took it.

—So—how long's this storm been brewing?

—You're asking me?

—Who else? You see anyone else here I could be holding séance with?

—I didn't follow. Storm?

—Your face. Black clouds. Clear as day.

Usually she'd laugh at my cheap lines. Not today.
She stayed locked, unreadable.

I cut the act, went straight in.

—After all this time, you could at least give me a hug.

—One week feels that long to you? Six months went by before, and you didn't give me one then.

That was it.
Right then, I knew Sahara's jokes were hitting truth.
Marisha's anger wasn't smoke.
It was real, and it was fair. I'd need to face it with care.

Dealing with women is like handling cats—sweet enough to curl into your lap one minute, claws out the next if you try forcing them close. And with her mood now, chasing would only drive her further.

I left her where she was and drifted downstairs.
The yard held a small garden, neat, nothing special.
Across the narrow road stood the two-story house I'd seen from the window—the one dressed with lipstick palms at its gate.
Beyond that gate, the road cut straight to the expressway.
Evening leaned in, but the sun was still sharp, heat glaring.

I weighed a walk that way, then turned opposite instead.
The residential lanes pulled me inward.
Jungle closed tight on both sides, tall trees casting a long shade across the narrow path.

I kept walking, slow, letting the quiet work.

The road tilted upward.
A board at the edge read PowerYoga—some kind of retreat tucked into the hills. The silence made it feel inviting, I kept walking. But halfway through, my body gave up.

First time I ever met this thing called weakness. Vision clouded, legs stiff as stone, head flooding until I thought smoke would pour out my ears.

I was still alive, breathing on this earth, yet couldn't move a step. That realization cut deep.
How did the sick, the crippled, survive year after year inside bodies that betrayed them? It rattled me.
They asked God for endless things, yet the greatest treasure they held was simple health. No one ever knew it until it broke.

No bench in sight. I thought about sitting down right there in the middle of the road, but didn't have to.

Marisha came running.
Arms wrapped around me from behind.

—Only a stupid would drag himself out sick in this heat.

I couldn't speak. My body turned cold head to toe, sweat soaking through. All I could give her was a weak smile. She hooked my arm over her shoulders and hauled me back inside.

Laid me flat on the bed, then stepped out. When she returned, her hands held a towel soaked in warm water.

She stripped off my shirt. Wiped down my face, chest.
Then pressed the cloth hard against my throat.

—I should kill you, *she said.*

But the tears in her eyes betrayed her intention.

I whispered, voice barely there.

—If you can't hold back the tears, how will you handle the rest?

She hit me with a soft punch, then turned away, shoulders rigid.

—Cheating bastard, how many women do you fool this way?

I couldn't tell if it was question or accusation.
I shut my eyes, let the silence help patch me up.
The cold shudder inside faded, body coming back online.

When I opened them again, her face hovered close—sharp lines, quiet worry.

—Still feeling bad? I'll call Tommy.
If you need, he'll take you back to the hospital.

The storm in her voice had passed. Calm again.

I told her I was fine, then asked for the truth.
I knew how she'd crossed paths with Tommy and the crew—but how she'd tangled with that Russian girl, why the fight even started, none of that lined up.

—I don't know that girl, Marisha shot back.

Then, with acid in her tone

—I guess your secret love life just slipped out by accident.
Thank God it did.

—Uff, what a mess. You're the only secret I ever kept.
Even Macro, Tommy, the rest—I never told them a thing about you. I had no other secrets worth hiding. So drop the act and give it to me straight.

Guess that melted something.
It always does.
The truth came down riding on tears.

—You have no idea what I went through, *she said.*
—I chased every lead I could find—ended up in KL, like a lunatic.
I found you that night. You ignored my calls. And when you finally met me, you talked like a stranger—threw out a fake name, twisted your words, spun me around on purpose.
And the whole time... you were right there, in plain sight, flirting with some other girl behind that masked face.
What am I to you? A child?
You could've told me the truth.

So that was it—she thought I had another woman.
I didn't know the details. But I met her pain where it stood.

I replied softly.

—Love comes with trust, Marisha.
The guy you met back then—that wasn't me.
I can't lay out the how or why, not now. But just because I can't explain, doesn't mean you get to spin your own story.

Her blue eyes flickered, uncertain, staring deep.
Then she whispered.

—I felt it too. Meeting Elijan that first time, it was something else.
But seeing you again, in that car...
It broke something in me. I thought I was losing my mind.
But my heart—She paused, breathing hard—My heart said I'd found my man. But I didn't know how to handle it.
So I stayed close. Watched you in the room. Tried to read you.

She let it hang there, and I jabbed her, just to see if the fire was still there.

—That's why you kept hovering around—testing if I was pure enough?

She flared back.

—Don't you dare.
I pegged Elijan for a playboy the second I saw him.
Ask him yourself how I reacted that day.
If I'd meant it, even the smallest touch would've lit him up.
But it didn't. I was verifying, not offering.
The only man who could be that pure... was mine.
I knew it. I always knew it. But to think that same man would hide his name, swap his face, and play out some side romance—that never crossed my mind. That broke me.

She burst out—thought I'd been tangled up with Elijan's girl.

I took her hand. pulled her close.

—Nothing's broken, Ree.
The fire only lights up with you—it always did.

Her breathing slowed—eyes found mine again.
Glowing like Rigel, the storm gone.

—You still remember the name, *she said.*
—Even in your language, it's not quite right.
Tell me—why did you choose that one?

I already knew the answer.

Holding her in my arms, like only fire can hold a flame, I said,

—Because you were meant to be the one.
The only one in my life.
That's why I call you by that name.

She didn't calm down at my answer—she broke harder, chest heaving with sobs.

I ran a hand over her head.

—You're sharp, Ree. You'll get it—trust me.
Now, tell me how you found them?

She was struggling with her voice, yet managed to speak.

—After I dropped you at the hospital, I went back to the apartment. Started putting things in order. While hanging up your clothes, I noticed your locker was wide open—empty.
And the way you looked that day... I didn't think you had cash on you. You never said if that bank locker held anything real.
I asked myself—if I had to discharge you, how would you even pay for it? Maybe you had something lined up.
Still, I didn't want to take chances.
I called my mother. Told her to send money.
Not hers—mine. My savings. She was holding them for me.

She stopped, just long enough for me to feel the weight.

—My mother said she could send twenty thousand.
I told her Western Union, under my name. The map showed the nearest pickup point was at Pavilion Mall—BBT zone.
I didn't have a single change of clothes on me, you know that.
I figured I'd collect the cash and grab what I needed in one run.
By evening, I was ready to leave.

—On my way out, I spotted that infamous red vanity bag.
The one left behind by some Zamuk girl—I knew it already.
But I was about to carry twenty grand in bare bills.
That bag was better than walking around with my pockets stuffed. So I took it. My passport was gone, but I had a scan saved on my phone. That worked. No issue picking up the cash.
Slipped the bills into the bag. Headed for the mall exit.
That's when she showed up. Black limo. Muscle on both sides.
She was probably headed for the penthouses.
I wouldn't have even noticed her—until she grabbed the bag off my shoulder. That same bag—loaded with cash—and suddenly this woman, flanked by muscle, is demanding where I got it.
Telling me it was hers. Can you picture that?

She held the silence long enough for me to catch it.

—I thought—new scam. I shook her off.
But she looked at me like she wasn't bluffing. Desperate.
She said, 'I don't care how you know Elijan.
Just tell him Antasia needs help. Now.'
That's when I realized—this was the same Zamuk girl who left the bag in your apartment. At first, I thought the guys were bodyguards. But they weren't protecting her.
They were taking her. They tried to drag her off.
So, I stepped in. One of them—Dyshebi trash,
inked up like a prison billboard—called me a bitch.
So I cracked him. Hard. Then the rest came for me.
And that's when your Samurai kid showed up.
The rest... you already know.

She trailed off, eyes gone distant.
Drifting somewhere I couldn't follow.

I asked softly.

—Sahara said it turned into a mess. But how and why you brought them to me—he said that was your story to tell.

She didn't flinch. Didn't fire back, either.
Her silence stretched like she was choosing which knife to draw.

Then she spoke.

—Your Japanese boy kept it simple. No riddles. Just the truth.
He told me what happened to you—said they were scared you wouldn't make it. Showed me the messages.
Yours, sent from his phone while I was in Laos.
And mine. My replies. Still sitting on the thread.

She folded her arms across her chest.

—He had pictures, too. Your old face. With them.
Nothing to doubt. Then he played a clip—the first time we came into this bungalow. Told me you'd stepped into this new identity. Elijan Vellum.

Her breath hitched, then steadied.

—That's when the sky cracked open.
Because, It meant I hadn't been wrong—I'd found the right man.
But you wouldn't admit it that time. You turned it into games.
I was furious. I was done. But there you were—broken, bleeding, and wrecked. And it was all because of me.

She looked down, jaw tight.

—I couldn't stay angry. I told them everything.
And I brought them to you.

She paused—left the silence hanging between us like a challenge.
I took it.

—Alright then. The first man you met was the real Vellum.
I told you that. Later, when I wore his name—by the Lord's own humor— you still landed right back with me.

I tipped my head at her.

—So what in this story broke you, Marisha?

She looked at me like she was choosing where to shoot.

—At the Pavilion, *she said.*
—When they shoved her into that car, she screamed something.
'Tell Elijan I loved him with my life.' That's what she said.

I didn't move.
I had nothing on it.
No memory. No explanation.
And that silence—Marisha read it for guilt.

I answered. Straight.

—How can you not see this? I told you—I took his identity. I didn't have a choice. That's all. Maybe that girl loved him. Maybe it was just history, or friendship, or both. Whatever it was—it wasn't with me.

Truth comes easy to me. To her, it lands like a slap.
And women—they don't read stories the way men do.
They write their own endings first.

She hissed it back like she was holding steam.

—Simple, huh? Too simple.
Let me write it back to you.
You change your face. Step into a new name.
You don't tell your crew. You don't tell me.
And in this new life, you flirt your way through whatever mission you're on— then charm the girl who left her bag in your flat. Now she's dragged off screaming, and suddenly you've got amnesia? You really expect me to clap for that?

The weight of her tone deserved a laugh.
But that would've cost me a lot.

I swallowed it. Like every man should.

—That's your math?
I cut you off because I was too busy romancing her?
Then tell me this—
Why'd I cut off my entire team too?
Was I romancing them while I was at it?
Ree—if you mattered that little, why was I desperate enough to drag you back, even in that mess, when I could barely stand?
That theory of yours?
It leaks.

She held me in her crosshairs. But this time, her voice cooled. Not soft. Just sharp.

—It's not that I can't see. I see just fine.
That's why you're still breathing.
And not zipped up in a body bag.

Truth lands best when you fire it straight, first chance you get.
It doesn't always fix the wreck—but it clears the damn field.

This time, I laid it bare.

—Shadows are part of my work, Ree.
Secrets aren't drama. They're how we stay alive.
The moment someone learns what they shouldn't,
they turn into a pawn. Or a target.
That's why I kept you clear of most of it.

I let it breathe for a second.

—What we've got... that was never forced.
You never shackled me with vows. I never pulled you in out of guilt. Either of us could've walked. Still can.
If I've ever made moves without you, it wasn't some game.
I'm buried in a mess I didn't choose.
Not everything breaks the way I want.
I've been forced to play hands I never picked.

Her gaze sharpened—but I kept going.

—That's why your doubts had room to breed.
I couldn't clear the fog fast enough.
All I can do now is own it—I'm sorry.
Whoever that girl is, whatever she said...
Hell, whatever anyone says—when my chest is the pillow,
you're the only woman lying there.
I've never shared that space. Never wanted to.

Marisha held her stare like a surgeon sizing up a cut.
Face unreadable.
Then, slow as a thaw, the steel melted.

She snapped her head away with a fake snarl, stood, rolled her eyes.

—Could've just said the last line and spared me the opera.

She turned for the door, tossed it over her shoulder:

—I stocked your favorite apple juice. Don't move. I'll bring it.

Storm gone.
And to prove it, she came back with the glass—cold, sweating. Dropped beside me with a half-smile, phone glued to her hand, attention locked on the screen.

That smile, the phone—it clicked. By now she should've known. Rasheed and I didn't talk. Wouldn't. But his sister... she should've been home days ago. If Marisha knew and never told me, maybe it was leftover anger.
Antasia.
The hospital.
Everything.

I asked, casual,

—What's the good news? Everyone back home alright?

She froze mid-scroll. Pressed the phone to her chest, eyes narrowing.

—Why the sudden interest in my home?
Who do you think's even there to be 'alright'?

That stung harder than she meant it.

—Your mother, for one.
You've been away years, sure—but I just asked how she's holding up. Thought you'd care enough to tell me.

My voice went sharper than intended.
I remembered her face—wrecked after her sister vanished. And now, when her sister was supposedly safe, she hadn't breathed a word?

She finally answered.

—Yes. My mother's fine. And her daughter? More than fine.
She's whole again. She has her love back.
So relax. Close your eyes. You came back half-dead,
I worried enough for both of us.

She dropped the line like a curtain, went back to scrolling.
But something was off. She skipped the sister part clean.
No name, no mention.

Either she was dodging the truth—or Rasheed never brought her home at all. And that didn't fit.
The job was supposed to take three days.
This was day eight.

I still had a line to Rasheed if I needed it—but first, I had to know if Cheng had caught my signal, if the charter was live.
The whole operation was turning into a circus.
Would've been easier if Macro was still around to chase down these threads. And after all the chaos of shipping her sister back, Marisha's cold shoulder was starting to get under my skin.

I jabbed the needle.

—Give me your phone. Let's see who's got you smiling like that.

She shot a glare like I'd slapped her.

—What! You want to play detective on me now?

I didn't even try to hide the heat.

—Yeah. That's exactly what I want.

Her remedy for every sharp word's the same—whip her head, toss a bitter laugh, and vanish. This time was no different.

Except she left the phone behind—unlocked—right in front of me. I scrolled through her messages, her gallery.
Nothing wild. Just life.

I didn't touch Telegram or WhatsApp—both were locked anyway.

When she came back, jaw set like a guillotine,
I pointed at the screen and told her flat—unlock them.
All of them.

She fought me on it. The usual parade—Why, what for, no,
these are private, I talk to my friends, it's personal...
But I didn't blink. Didn't let it drop.
And in the end, she cracked.
Unlocked them all, one by one.

I already knew what I'd find: a woman's endless threads, fixing heartbreaks, sharing personal storms men aren't supposed to read. But she'd poked me first—so this was the price.
I pushed straight into her private world.

Same pattern as Phuket—Marisha still perched as the savior,
the fixer of female troubles.
But then—something off.

A contact named Jovoxiar.
Messages in coded Russian, words flipped and twisted that only sender and receiver, with their prearranged system, could make sense of it. I couldn't read the code. But the kiss emoji he sent needed no translation—eyes closed, lips sealed.
Her reply came with eyes open.
Different emoji, same meaning. Kiss for a kiss.
Didn't matter if it was a harmless flirt, or some decade-old flame.
I didn't need a codebreaker. The meaning cut clean.

Who the hell was Jovoxiar—and what kind of man gets kisses from my girl while I'm flat in a hospital bed?

Marisha snatched the phone back before I could say another word. Muttered under her breath, tapped the screen like she was defusing a bomb, shot me a look, then ducked back into her phone.

Her face gave it away—rattled.
I stayed fixed on her.
Waiting.

She cracked first.
A nervous laugh slipped out.

—Genius. That wasn't a love-kiss. It's just affection.
Love-kisses are the red lips—I always send those to you.
Didn't you ever notice?

I tilted my head, slow.

—Oh, I noticed. You dropped me those open-eye and closed-eye ones too. Guess I earned the affectionate tier now and then.

The sweat pooling under her nose said more than any emoji ever could. She fished for words, found nothing.

Finally, she forced a patch-up line.

—Jovoxiar's like...
like my kid brother.
I never told you—we talk sometimes.
It's not that close. I just forgot to mention.

—Of course. Big sisters dropping kisses to kid bros.
Makes perfect sense. And if it's not close, then obviously all the coded language and smoochy emojis are standard.
Since you say so, I'll take it. But I wonder—if some younger sister sent me kisses like that, and you caught it on my phone—how normal would it feel then?

She gave me the only response she ever gives when cornered.
A sharp "huh," and the echo of her footsteps walking out.
Fine. She didn't want to talk. I'd get it out eventually.
Truth has a habit of circling back. Better to shift gears—Rasheed.

I could try to reach him, but first I needed to know if Papa Cheng had arranged the charter flight. Only then could I worry about whether Rasheed actually delivered.

And Macro—no sign of her.
Yet somehow, the Russian girl she vanished with—Antasia—was moving free. That showy run-in with her is what brought Marisha face to face with the rest of my crew.

The day of the Penang bombing— whatever reason that girl had for meeting me, it mattered for both of us. My time was running out, and her flowers—her task—were something I needed.

She never made it to me. But by the Lord's own dark sense of humor, those two petals in her bag still found their way back to me and carried out their duty.

Which meant this: if she believed in something that impossible and still came to meet me, she must have had her own reason.
So whatever she came to say—it was worth hearing.
I had to find her. Not just for Macro. For me.

Besides the Penang bombing, Rasheed's chain boss—these bomb makers and handlers all had to be tracked. Lining it up, first step was clear: find the girl, finish her task.

After that—or if possible, in parallel—the rest could be handled.

By then Goby-Sahara and Tommy burst in from the market.
Their voices carried up, sharp with excitement.
I hit the stairs and found the reason—Tommy had scored a monster red snapper, easy five kilos, spine thick as a crowbar.

He waved me over.

—BBQ the whole thing, boss. Sound good?

I'd tasted Tommy's fish barbecue before.
I gave a grin. Run it. I'm starving already.

That was enough. Tommy kicked into gear like it was a mission brief. Goby backed him up, sleeves rolled. Marisha hovered with her phone, filming like she was directing a documentary on fish prep. I left them to it. I needed a walk outside.

Both Sahara and Marisha offered to tag along.
I waved them off—told them I'd call if I needed anything—and headed out alone.

No more excuses.
If I was serious about returning to the field, I had to rebuild fast.
First few steps—brutal.
Muscles sulked like spoiled children.

But second round, I found rhythm.
Half an hour of steady walk and my normal movement was back.
What didn't come back was the strength to run a mission alone.

That truth was already sitting heavy.
If I wanted to move now, I'd have to take someone with me.
Uncomfortable, but there was no way around it.

Back at the bungalow, the fish barbecue was already in full swing. Tommy stood at the center, tongs in hand, smoke curling up around him. The others circled close, cracking jokes, clinking glasses, half sous-chefs, half audience.
The second they saw me, the noise went up.

I scanned the setup—red snapper marinated and seared,
the works laid out, flames licking steady under the rack.
Looked like dinner wouldn't take long.
Told them I'd shower and be back before Tommy even thought about flipping it.

Upstairs, the heat of the water did its job.
My body eased, muscles finally starting to forgive me.
All that tension and weakness bled out, slow.

I let it go.
Breathed deep in the steam, mind circling back to Cheng.
During the walk, I'd managed to reach with him.
We had our system—any line, any number, I'd drop the code phrase, and if it was really him, he'd respond exactly as scripted.
Old-school spywork. Never failed.

This time his reply didn't bring relief.
It brought more weight.
Cheng replied the moment Rasheed reached out, he'd greenlit
a Komak Gulfstream from the Istanbul hangar.
Rasheed refused the standard crew—flew it himself.
Promised to land it, finish the job, and return the bird personally.

Cheng took that gamble—on my name.
He delivered.

Three days back, the jet touch down in Istanbul without incident. Cheng's pilot logged it. Mission closed.

Rasheed had made it.
Wrapped it up as we planned.
But Marisha still hadn't said a word about her sister.
That sat in my chest, heavy. But it wasn't the priority.
The red thread was still Antasia.

Dinner first.
Then I'd move.
I came down clean, body balanced again.
The kitchen hit like a warm front—smoke, citrus, and something sharp from the cocktails.
Marisha had thrown together a crisp Russian salad, Goby and Sahara were shaking up drinks with wild flair, and Tommy hunched over the snapper like it was his final exam.

They dropped me in the head seat—classic play.
Plates kept landing—one after another. Seafood rice first, Tommy's fish barbecue followed close.
He'd nailed it.
Every bite locked.
The whole crew brought their best.

Whatever edge we'd carried into the house, the food smoothed it. For a while. Between the tasty bites, I brought the heat.

—What's next? The girl—where is she?

Tommy and Marisha traded looks. One of those long, silent standoffs where neither wants to move first.

Finally, Tommy exhaled, cracked his neck, and took it on:

—Boss, while you were in the hospital we dug into it.
Miss Marisha gave me a tip—said the girl might be tied to a gang.
We chased it, and she was right. Turns out the girl's a sex slave.
Owned by a narco-lord—Victor. Real dirtbag. Runs drugs, black-cash rackets, half a dozen fronts scattered across BBT.
Imports, crypto, every angle covered. You probably know Miss Marisha went there last week to meet someone.

—Before she got to that meeting, she was kidnapped.
Later, you pulled her out. And that's when we found you.

He threw a glance at Marisha.

She lifted a hand, slid in tight.

—Tommy's talking about Tataliya. You knew her.
Before. She had some Zamuk links. So, I thought she could help.

Tommy picked it up again.

—Now Tataliya's vanished too. Which leaves us with two names, one fortress, zero access. No link to Antasia. No idea what the hell's actually going on. Dead end.

I chewed that over, but it didn't change the map in my head.
No clear move without field work. And this wasn't the kind of mission you solved from a couch. No more words left.

The room went quiet, mood folding in on itself. We washed down the salt with cold drinks, then peeled off one by one.
After the cleanup, I took my tea down in the courtyard.
Tommy joined.

The light was dropping slow through the trees, cutting long lines across the walls. Goby had made my cup of cardamom tea.
As I liked, always. Sweet enough to coat the tongue.

I sipped, then said it flat.

—You've been holding it together well so far, Tommy.
Even with Marisha around, you didn't spill the inner file.
Good. You and I both know exactly who Victor Solasky is.
And what has to be done.

His eyes stayed steady, but I saw the weight shift in his jaw.
He knew what was coming.

—Hope you didn't forget Bangkok. Tell me straight:
What made you think this was an adventure club?
You let Marisha jump in on Antasia's trail—why? You think anyone who shows up gets a rifle and a mission brief now?

My voice was calm. But he'd heard that tone before.
He knew what it meant.
Give the wrong answer, and he'd be back on Bangkok duty again.

Tommy stayed silent awhile.
Thinking.

—Miss Marisha came to me.
Said she had her own reasons to find Antasia.
Said being Russian, maybe she could get deeper.
And she'd met her. We hadn't.
That made her case sound... fair.

I took another long sip.

—Fair to you, maybe.
But that little door you opened?
It gave her access to things she should've never known.
She got to Macro. She got to Penang.
She got to what we buried. You see the mess now?

He nodded.
Nothing left to add. He got it.

Tommy usually follows orders like gospel.
This time, he drifted—a single degree, but it cost us.
Now he swore it wouldn't happen again.

Left him in the courtyard, tea half gone, and headed up.

Time to plan for extraction.
Or war.
Depending who made the next move.

—∞—

Two confirmed.
One fractured.

Aamari Resort
Phuket, Thailand

Jovan leaned back in his suite, eyes locked on the Xyat Regency surveillance feed playing silent on his laptop.
Footage crisp.
Timestamp locked.
Nothing missed.

Across the room, Daggan was brewing coffee—sleeves rolled, eyes flicking between kettle steam and screen flicker.

Outside the suite door,
two of Daggan's boys stood ready—armed, alert.

He mouthed off like a brat, but when it came to the perimeter, the kid knew the stakes. Daggan wasn't naïve where it counted. Not with lives on the line.

The Xyat flipped around sunset.
Shift changed like clockwork—day staff out, night crew in.
But this wasn't some sleepy island inn.
This was Phuket.
Nights here didn't just glow—they burned.
Days belonged to hangovers; evenings, to hunters.

When the sun dipped, the island shifted gears—
Street bars blazing like live wires.
Clubs, smoke dens, blackjack pits—every room burning.
And Places like Xyat Regency didn't just buzz—they roared.

Hotel, nightclub, casino, sky-high fine dining, locked-door parties—everything packed under one roof.

Landing night shift at a place like that wasn't work.
It was a week's paycheck in tips.

Nobody gave up that slot unless they had greased the right hands—or had dirt deep enough to trade.
And tonight the security chief played that exact card.

Three guards clocking out, three coming on.
But the twist? All six wanted in.
Day crew wanted overtime.
Night shift refused to swap.

Why? Because tonight, the island tilted toward the Xyat.
A world-famous DJ on the decks—
Phuket pouring in from every corner.

The security chief saw it coming—and timed it perfectly.
That's why he told Dr. Eli to show up exactly now.
Before stepping off with his arguing crew, the chief unlocked the control room with his own ID and handed it to her—access granted, clock running.

Ten minutes.
That's what she'd get.
Long enough to scan.

The security chief already briefed Eli on the layout—file structure, fast-forwarding, what logs to skip. All she had to do was slip in, search, get out, and close the door behind her.
Once it latched, the lock tripped on its own.

The only thing the man hadn't explained was how he'd wipe the footage showing Eli stepping in and out. But it didn't matter.
At exactly six minutes, Eli finished the job, closed the door behind her, and walked out like she was just stretching her legs.

Two minutes later, the van parked in the Xyat lot lit up—tech team pinged in: full breach.
They now owned the security grid.

At minute thirteen, the security chief returned from his meeting with the guards. Too late.

Back at Aamari, Jovan's laptop was already pulling down Xyat's feeds—zone by zone, screen by screen.

Big area. Too many cameras.
He patched the feed into the suite's TV.
Split the sweep.
Daggan took exits and entries.
Jovan took everything else.

Eli was busy.
Paying off her side of the bargain—every ounce she had—straight to the Chinese security chief.

Tech boys had slipped a surprise into her bag before she left.
A pin-cam stuck on without her consent.

Jovan didn't love it, but he let it ride—in the field, even dirty tricks sometimes mean insurance.

While Jovan was fully focused on scanning the feed for faces, Daggan kept one ear tuned to Eli's audio.
Grinning like a hyena.

He laughed so hard he almost spilled his coffee.

—Boss, *Daggan wheezed,*
—you won't believe this.
The guy dragged her into the M&E room.
Wants to fuck her in the boiler heat.
Says sweat makes it better.

The van cracked up—tech boys howling over comms.
Bag-cam caught the full show—wide angle, high-def.

Two rounds in, both warriors still on the scoreboard.
By the third, the chief was begging for access to Eli's duck-oil-pumped ass—pleading like a broke gambler chasing one more hand. Eli, out of breath, told him she'd think about it—the night was still young.

That's when Jovan felt it.
Not the steamy sex podcast.
That rolled past him like static.
What froze him was on the screen.

Two faces.
Two figures.
The exact ones he'd been waiting to see.

—Dag. Pull elevator feed. Now.

Daggan didn't blink.
Already had one earpiece tethered to Jovan's command line.
Everyone did.

Even Eli—half-folded on a mechanical room floor, hair stuck to her face, breath gone—still had that voice hissing in her ear.

The entry-exit cam was mounted higher than the rest.
Enough to catch silhouettes, useless for faces.
But the lobby feed—crystal. Every frame sharp.

Jovan's chest thudded as he watched the screen—two shadows stepping into the elevator with one of the hotel's bellhops.
One was polite, the other smiling.
Everything is now snapped into focus.

The Kuwaiti whale—Awadi.
And the ghost.
Butcher of the desert—Caesar.
Now it clicked why Sergeant King vanished.
The bastard wasn't just burning oil money.
He brought in the phantom for cleanup.

Last time, some friends in Europe shielded him.
Diplomats whispered in the right ears—and politics forced Mossad to let him walk.

Jovan clenched his jaw hard enough to grind bone.
Not this time.

Onscreen, Awadi grinned and led Caesar straight into the casino.
Into the blackout zone.
No camera feeds from there.
By international "standards," casino floors ran offline.
Footage locked tight—owner's key or court order only.

Jovan fast-forwarded the door cam anyway, hoping for duration.
All he got was static.
Flicker.
Feed gone.

He skipped ahead faster.
Same deal.

A few moments of white noise—then video resumed.
But nothing important showed up anymore.
No Awadi.
No Caesar.
The message was clear: stop looking.

Jovan didn't back off.
He spat a curse under his breath and kept hunting.
Eyes swept to the next banks.

Nine elevator lobbies across the Xyat grid—
Two feeds snowed out.
The rest? Too clean.

His gut told him the feeds weren't broken.
They were wiped.
Intentionally.
Just like the casino entry.

Then Daggan's voice broke in.

—Boss—look at this!

Upper floor. Stairwell cam.
Caesar—caught mid-climb.
Calm.
Focused.
Like it was just another job.

Jovan's chest seized when he clocked the floor number.
That floor.
The Arab asset's honeytrap.
The girl they'd planted.

Hallway cam, slightly tilted, caught it.
A door nudged open.
No face. No hand on the knob.
Just shadows and a body slipping into the hotel's built-in blind spot. But Jovan didn't need faces. He knew that room.

Seconds later—whiteout.
The whole floor turned to static.
Gone.

And that's what didn't fit. If they wanted Caesar ghosted, they'd have wiped it all from the start.
Instead, they left a sliver.
Just enough to show the blade before it landed.

Jovan's mind spun like a turbine choking on fire.
No pause. No second chance. That Chinese bastard with Dr. Eli had to be taken—fast and clean.

Jovan whispered the call into comms, and at that exact second, the so-called Chief of Security was busy trying to crown himself between Eli's duck-oil-slicked, sweat-soaked thighs—moaning like he'd hit some kind of apocalypse.

Daggan hesitated for half a heartbeat. But Eli didn't even blink.

Before the man could thrust or beg, she twisted around mid-grind—her hand snaking back, snapping his skull sideways.
Grace of a surgeon. Spite of a woman who'd had enough.
A clean execution move—enough to knock a man senseless.
But friction betrayed her. Oil, sweat, heat—too slick.

He didn't drop. Just dazed.
Completely misreading the whole scene.

He figured she was pissed about the anal push.
Still panting, he rolled his neck and winced—figured he'd crossed a line with a woman he'd already tasted twice.

His instinct told him to calm her down, not fight.
But Eli wasn't here for therapy.

She stepped sideways, grabbed a steel pipe near the utility board—swung it like she was knocking sense into a dog in heat. It came down fast—right toward the back of his neck.

He blocked it. Military reflex.
Didn't even register the danger until his arm shot up and caught the blow—barely.

Eli moved again—this time, she aimed for the vertebrae.
He intercepted with his forearm.
It hurt. But not enough.

He dropped to his knees, still thinking a little sweet talk might fix this. As if this was just wild sex gone wrong.

And that—
That was his final miscalculation.

Eli stepped closer.
Didn't flinch. Didn't warn.
Just swung the pipe again.
THANG.
Steel met skull.
Crack. Silence.

Eli exhaled. A storm passed.

Tapped her earpiece:

—Target down. Need carry-out.

No one needed coordinates.
Tech boys had been watching the whole show from the floor below, courtesy of that wide-angle bag cam.
Audio, video, the nut job.

They replied instantly:
Van's en route. You're covered.
Cameras already spoofed.
Ground guards see only what we feed them.

Eli stood tall in her own skin. Sweaty, dangerous, stunning.
She looked down at what was left of him.

Three orgasms. One skull down.
Two confirmed. One fractured.
Just another target, tagged and bagged.

—*—

Earned Accord

Andaman Sea
Phuket, Thailand

They needed a new pit.
Off-grid. Soundproof. Movable.
A place to carve out answers from two trophies—the Isfahan agent grabbed from the data center, and the Xyat security chief Eli just bagged.

Kamala Bay warehouse was just a memory now, burnt down to the bones. Jovan was pretty sure Sgt. King went up with it.
One more ghost in the ledger, one more loose end sealed by fire.

They took a Jewish family's pleasure yacht—spacious, innocent, perfect for the job.

Out on the Andaman, they could scream and bleed all they wanted—only the sea would listen.
And it never talked.

Daggan loaded his team, and the tools.
Pushed off before midnight.
This time, the updates went straight to the minister.
Approval came in just like they expected.

Even better, fresh intel from Kuwait.
The whale Awadi had been lifted clean.
The Middle East desk bagged him quietly.
Now sitting tight in a local black site, awaiting interrogation.

Meanwhile, the stage moved north.
Europe was heating up.
Czech Republic. Prague.

Unofficial streams confirmed Rasheed Dameer himself had landed, chasing shadows of the dark weapon.

The Spets girl, the Kuwaiti tycoon, and the ghost named Caesar—all traced back to the same puppeteer:

A Romanian warlord running his empire from Prague.
The puzzle finally started to snap together.

Jovan's head cleared.
Eli passed him a glass—he clinked it.
Smiled like a man who could afford to.

Up here—wind, wine, control.
Below—Daggan with three of their men;
Blood, noise and truth cutting loose.

Jovan leaned down the stairwell.
Saw the streaks of red bleeding across the deck.
He called Daggan up with a look—a silent warning:
No more fuckups.

Daggan only smirked. Knife still dripping.

—They'll talk before they die, bossy.
Not the other way around.

Two hours straight, the work went on.
Steel against bone. Gags soaked.
And still, the moans said both men lived.

He had to admit, for all his jokes, Daggan understood the craft.
With less than an hour left before dawn, Daggan called him below.

The Isfahan agent went first.
A hooked blade flicked off the tape.
The man broke like glass.
Names, family, even the poultry in his yard spilled out.

He was spent—nothing left but one crucial truth:
Rasheed Dameer had sent him.
That was enough.

Jovan gave a nod.
The man's mouth was sealed again.
Ledger closed. Nothing personal.
Just one more expendable crossed off the list.

Now it was the security chief's turn.
They cut his gag.
And the first thing out of his mouth wasn't denial—it was a deal.
A plea for a "respectable death."
He already knew exactly whose hands he'd landed in.

Jovan let him speak. Kept it clean.
Asked about the tampered feeds.

The chief answered straight: just like he'd slipped Eli into the control room, any guard with enough cash could do the same.
Or better, run it straight through the data hub.
Every Xyat feed passed through those operators.

Jovan didn't care about the who. He wanted the how.

—Could missing chunks in a live video ever be blamed on a glitch? Had it ever happened?

The Chinese didn't hesitate. Swore on his life—it had never happened. Couldn't happen. Not on that system.

And that was all he needed.

Jovan's work in Phuket was over.
Eli had already been informed—she wouldn't be flying to Prague.
Her part ended here.

Tech team packed up every last tool and loaded it onto their charter. Left nothing but sea behind.

Daggan's crew would finish the cleanup.
Jovan had eyes forward: Prague, Czech Republic.
The next stage was already moving.

Below deck, the wrap-up was swift. The two prisoners were broken down—cut, drained, mixed into fish feed.
Sealed into weighted sacks, and fed back to the sea before light touched the waves.

But the deal was honored.
Before the blade work began, the Chinese got what he asked for—a single, silent round through the skull.
A prize earned by cooperation.
Mossad standards.

—*—

Blush in the Glass

Bukit Bintang
Kuala Lumpur, Malaysia

Fermented corn bourbon—or blended scotch?
Which hits harder?
The debate dragged on. And I lost, as a man should,
when arguing with a beautiful woman.

Four shots in, I ordered a fifth—trying to sink myself in the shine of her victory.

Across the table she sat, glowing. Smug.
Chirping like a finch drunk on spring.

We were in Blitz Bintang—a bar-cum-dance club slapped on the top floor of a hotel no tourist would recommend.
Night was still in its blush—nowhere near full bloom.
A good time to begin in a three-star dive.

My crew had been tripping over each other chasing Antasia.
Expected.
Put them outside their lane, and they'll tie themselves into sailor's knots.

So I pulled the cord. Sent Goby and Sahara back to Astana—let them spin their own wheels. Told Tommy to stay grounded, focus on repair work in Penang.

If I could've shipped off Marisha, I'd have been more than happy.
But she dug in. No reason I gave—logic, heart,
plain human honesty—moved her an inch.
Any woman would've read the hint, packed up,
gone home to her mother. But Marisha didn't bend.

Beautiful women aren't puzzles.
They're pressure.

You think you've seen them because they let you close, but that's just the surface. The real part—the part that thinks, waits, weighs you, keeps score—that stays hidden.
The prettier they are, the deeper they bury it.
And when it shows? It's never on your terms.

Marisha had her reasons.
Whatever they were, maybe she was mad in love—or obsessed.
I didn't stop her. Just made one thing clear—
She could walk beside me.
But she shouldn't walk into my work.

That part—the mess, the mission—that wasn't hers to touch.
She flared up at first. Then went silent.
And for now, that was enough. One less wild card in play.

Now the search for Antasia was on me.
My crew flailed trying to find her, but it wasn't that hard.
She was part of the Russians' entertainment grid.
There were only ten clubs across the KLCC zone run by Zamuk.

To narrow it down, I went old-school.
Back to the apartment.
Spoke with Masud. With Regan.
With anyone who knew "Elijan Vellum." Where did I drink?
Where did I burn through my nights?
Answer was always the same—Bukit Bintang.

And here in Bukit Bintang, there were only two Russian dens.
First one—this hotel. Blitz Bintang.

It was exactly what it should be—cheap bar, cheaper floor show. The Russian beauty sitting across from me was just part of the set. The whiskey argument was bait, nothing more.

I kicked it off to set the rhythm—slow and casual—and when she won, we toasted to her victory.

By the fifth glass, the air between us had thickened to velvet—warm, heavy with flirt. That's when she leaned in, her lips catching the low light, voice dropping soft.

Said she charged eight hundred for the regulars—but for me, special discount, five hundred flat.
Sweet deal.

But when I dropped Antasia's name, her face went blank.
Said she had no idea who the girl was. Didn't surprise me.

A Zamuk with two thousand residents doesn't let the girls build special ties. They keep them rotated, shuffled, disconnected by design. Her ignorance was logical.

I thanked her for the deal, bought her another glass, and walked out. The plan was to swing back after midnight, when the masks start slipping and the drunk tongues loosen.
For now, I had the second location to hit.

On the way, a corner drink stall was running a two-for-one special. Didn't stop for the deal—barely glanced.
But the server caught my eye, nodded in recognition.
That drew me in.

The Chinese bar tender lit up the moment I sat.

—Long time no see, sir.
Old John keeps asking if you still come around.

I gave him a familiar smile and ordered.
Two beers landed in front of me, fast and sweating.

When he leaned in again, I gave him the line.

—Had an accident. Hospital stay, long haul.
Lost my phone—with all the numbers.
Thought I'd check in while I'm here. Where's John?

In a place like Bukit Bintang, anyone you "know" is either running girls or running drugs. That's the point.
The bait was natural.

I slid a folded bill across the table.
He took it smooth, like it was nothing new.

Tucked it away with a grin.

—John's across the road, sir.
I'll call him now, tell him you're here.

And with that, he ducked out behind the stall, phone already in hand, grinning like the past just walked back into the story.

If you thought the grin came from my tip, think again.
The Chinese wear smiles the way they wear shop signs—plastered on as soon as the shutters rise.
Grease on their lips isn't warmth; it's advertising.
But give them the right price, and the job gets done.

Proof landed before I was halfway through my second glass.
An old Chinese man shuffled up beside me, voice thick with the syrup of street corners.

—Well, nep—where the hell you been? Ever since I set you up with that Russian chick, you just vanished. Market's flooded with new girls, and you don't even check?

That tone—pure affection.
Old John.
He'd known Elijan Vellum before.
No doubt in his mind I was him.
And tonight, that's who I needed to be.
But what mattered was the line he dropped—set you up with that Russian chick.

I leaned back with a grin, easy and warm.

—Missed you, Uncle John.
After what you hooked me with, the rest felt like leftovers.
Then I got wrecked—car crash, hospital, lost my phone.
But yeah... you did drop me something real.
Still remember the high. What's cooking now?

He sipped, smirked, and waved me across the street.
Bill was already settled. I drained my glass and followed.

He chuckled as we walked, fiddling with his phone, watching me sideways.

—You and the Russian stock—perfect match.
Prices shot up, you know.
But for you, same deal. Thousand dollars.
I'll get you something top-shelf.

A thousand dollars? When most of the city's stunners went for seven or eight hundred ringgit a night? What kind of "top-shelf" was worth that much?

I kept my face blank.

—The girl you set me up with last time...what was her name?
Can't place it, but she was different.

He stared like I'd kicked his dog.

—What, you forgot? You were nuts for her.
Had me bending house rules, covering tracks,
risking deals just to set her up again. Antasia.

The name hit like a trigger pull.
Straight to the mark, first shot.

My crew had been drawing maps, planning raids on Zamuks, scheming disasters just to reach her. And here stood a street hustler who could arrange her for a grand. That's why you don't fire a tank when a whisper gets the job done.

I leaned in, thickened the grease on my smile.

—I remember everything you did, Papa John.
That's why I came to you first.
Burn me with the same fire again.

Words can only flirt. Cash seals the deal.

While I spoke, I let my hand do the heavy lifting—slipped ten crisp hundreds into his coat pocket, soft and silent.
But instead of the expected grin, John's jaw tensed.

He bit his lower lip, gave a slow shake.

—So long, they don't usually keep the same stock.
If that girl's not around—another one just like her, that'll do?

I clapped his shoulder.

—Come on, John. You think I'm chasing ghosts?
She's in the city. A friend booked her last week—sent a photo.
Same one you got me. Only thing I forgot was the name.

That worked. His shoulders eased.

—Ahh... then maybe they brought her back.
Been a long time, nothing strange.
And if she's here again,
I swear—if John can't arrange it, no one can.
I'll book her under a new name, okay?
Can't send her to the same address again.
These people track everything.
No repeats for the same client.

—No problem, *I said.* —Send her to another address.

I gave him the current number and dropped the bungalow address at Taman Duta. Marisha was there.
But that was fine—she wanted to meet Antasia anyway.

John promised quick arrangements, then slipped off.
The needle had worked. The sword stayed clean.

I walked out with lighter heart and a cleaner path.

At the bungalow, Marisha was gone—out somewhere.

I made tea myself, sat waiting for the call.
John could still vanish with the cash.
If so, I'd shift to plan B—the second Russian den.
And if no thread showed there either, then straight into the Zamuk.

I was sipping my tea, relaxed, when the phone buzzed.
Tung.
Message from Marisha.

"I'm going back home. Lost my passport and ID—I went out to arrange them. Won't bother you much longer."

She'd almost come around on my shifting identities.
But the moment I told her to leave,
she struck back, all venom and fury.

Now in her head: I had some secret affair with Antasia.
That's why I was pushing her away—just to keep it alive.

And there was no way to crack that mistake open.
Still—her trying to go back home was good news.
If she really did leave, half my tension would vanish.

Minutes later, another ring.
This time, Uncle John.

—Kid, you were right. The girl's back in the city.
But seems they've got trouble with her.
Say they won't put her on the job.
Russians refusing to put a girl to work?
Even the street dogs don't buy that!
Ha! Ha! Hold on—I'll fix it.

So Antasia was alive.
Close.

Russian gangs had their stain—they forced women into the trade
and only got picky when their power was under threat.
Something had happened with her.
Some mess that made them extra careful.

Ten minutes later, John called again.

—Nep, looks like she's got her eyes on you too.
I told the floor supervisor—he's my friend—that you wanted her.
He said no. Officially, she won't work.
But the girl—she wants to sneak out, run to you. Ha! Ha!

Seems Antasia was desperate to bolt from the Zamuk.
If I got to her, I'd get answers to a lot of things.

I told John,

—No problem, Line it up.
I'll handle the rest.

He laughed, rattling off Malay street slang.

—That's your problem to handle.
But my friend—this job's risky.
If anyone finds out he's tied in, his neck's on the line.
Still, he'll do it for you. Just... the cost will be higher.

Of course.
Girls slipping out with clients had triggered killings before.

For one to take that chance—it meant a hard motive.
And for me, meeting her mattered too much to hesitate.

I told John to push it through.
If I had her, I might never need to come back here.
Everything would hinge on what she told me.

I texted Marisha:

*"I was heading back. Antasia could surface.
If she did—I might not return to Taman Duta."*

Her reply came quick, sharp as ever:

"If you've found who you wanted, why bother coming back?"

I'd laid it all out for her.
But as always, she ran it through the labyrinth of jealousy.
To her, it was still nothing but another woman.

She didn't wait for clarity.
Only distance.
And somehow—this time—I gave it to her.

—∞—

The Bohemian Guest

The Maker's High-Tech Lab
Location: Classified

Macro never imagined it would break this way—snatched in seconds, no room to counter.

The tunnel ran clean, carrying her straight to the neighboring island without a hitch. But a few seconds' hesitation had cost her—the boat was already torched, Tommy and the crew cutting hard for the mainland. No way back.

With no ride, she switched to fallback—the link bridge feeding into Penang's main land.

That's where the kill zone waited.

The intercept team rolled out in blackout assault rigs—Delta-standard, NVGs hanging, weapons dialed to adaptive capture. Every move said they'd rehearsed for every variable.
But none of them had come to kill. Not her, at least.

Every muzzle tracked Antasia.

It made tactical sense.
Macro had been running cover on the girl. Put her under threat and Macro was neutralized—no blood spilled, and the door left open for a clean negotiation.

Across the bridge, the restaurant was gone—nothing left but smoke and slow-falling ash.

She felt concern for her boss, but not doubt. He wasn't the type to fold over a small detonation. He'd briefed them through worse; this op had to be on his board already.

One operator broke from the stack, NVGs dangling at his chest, sat phone in hand. Macro took it, stepped aside.
No one moved to stop her.

The voice on the other end wasn't one she'd expected to hear in this mess. But the play was clear—she'd be rolling with these men. She told the one who'd passed her the phone: they were going anyway, and she wasn't about to start a pissing contest. There was no need to keep the barrels up—least of all with a civilian standing empty-handed.

He gave a short nod.
Before lift, they shackled Antasia wrist to ankle.
Macro stayed unbound.

She'd told her boss a hundred times—camping on borrowed ground was suicide doctrine.
On home turf, you had layers—response, denial, cover.
Here, nothing. If this had gone down in Thailand, nobody would've touched them—nuclear fallout or not.

Even with her link to the provincial royal house here, no one caught the inbound rotor.
No one tried—or had the reach—to block the lift.
In Thailand, that bird would've been ash before it touched down.

Macro couldn't figure out how long the transit ran—hours, maybe days.

Three vehicle swaps.
The final drop landed her somewhere that screamed old Russia—twin reactor husks, concrete still wearing the USSR's faded stamp. The perimeter was locked down tight with armed sentries. Even cold, the site read as a live asset.

The place hit her twice.

First, the mass of it—industrial, brutal,
built to last through apocalypse.

Second, the man waiting inside.
Sir William Scott.
Moving toward her with six soldiers in tow.

A British scientist turned educator—how he'd ended up tied to this crew was a puzzle she couldn't solve. The real shock was

seeing him on his feet at all; last she'd checked, the man was supposed to be under tight observation in a hospital, lungs barely holding on.
Just a month ago, she'd sent him a note wishing for a fast recovery.

It was Scott on the sat-phone who'd convinced her to come.
He greeted Macro with a warm smile.

—My brightest star—how are you?

—Doing fine, Sir. And you—how's your health?

—Somewhat better, my child. Come inside.

Inside, the brute concrete proved to be just a mask—kept upright to throw off the casual eye.

A few minutes' walk with Sir William and they stepped through a coded steel door into something else entirely:
A high-tech lab, state-of-the-art, humming with power.

Macro might've called it flawless, if not for the black-clad operators stationed in the shadows like a stain the place couldn't scrub out.

When the operators tried to take Antasia away, Macro's spine stiffened, ready to push back.

Sir William waved it off with a calm hand—no need, he said.
If the girl cooperated, she'd be unharmed.
She was only being moved for privacy.
Macro didn't like it, but for now she held her tongue.
Sir William led her into a high-spec conference room.

Macro had a bank of memories with the old man—every one of them good, except for what she was standing in now.

He'd been her instructor once, back in the US Army's High-Tech Knowledge Center, and the connection between them had always been built on respect and something warmer.
Maybe it still was.

It was Sir William Scott who'd tried to pull her into the Bohemian Club. She'd known the name—whispers, controversy, the kind of place that collected both power and trouble.

First time he'd invited her, she'd shot it down.
For all her faces in the world, she wasn't built for clubs—unless it was a stage wired to her beats.
In those rooms, the music was her only identity.
Nobody asked what she did or where she came from.
But he hadn't let it go—gave Macro a long pitch about how the club wasn't what it looked like from the outside.
How, in the last century, Mark Twain, Jack London, Nixon, Reagan—even scientists and technologists from World War II—had stood there, exchanging valuable knowledge.

Sir William wanted her in as his successor.
The club's politics still tasted sour, but the last card he played landed. She went, just once—out to the Bohemian Grove's three-thousand acres in Monte Rio, California.
Signed the membership, took the badge, walked the grounds.

She never went back, but the club's private channel kept her looped in. She'd seen the work, the ideas, the minds moving behind the curtain, and she'd admitted to herself—Sir William had placed her in the right room.

At least, that's what she thought.
Until today.

Sir William was the first to speak, voice calm, colored by all the years between them.

—You're probably wondering how I ended up tangled with this lot. I should say at once—I've no interest in their cause.
You know about my last research project, don't you?

—Yeah, but Sir. You were working on converting matter into electrical signals. If you'd pulled it off, the world would look different.

—Quite. But my health, you see—that's what kept me from the finish line. At first, they offered me medical treatment.

The doctors had already given up on me. Still, I took the risk.
I improved a little under their care, but… well,
I was already in their custody.

—What do they want from you?

—That same project—brought to completion.
They want me to prove it works.
What they mean to do with it afterward, I can't say.

—They blew up my base and hauled me here.

—Did they? Oh—my dear, I'm terribly sorry.

—You don't need to be. I'm sure it fit the plan.

—Even so, I regret it.
I was the one who suggested bringing you here.

—What? Why?

—Because I let slip that you'd managed to convert music into device-readable signals. I shouldn't have said it. I truly am sorry.

—And why would they care about that?

The exchange broke when the room's only door swung wide.
A knot of guards stepped in—and then The Maker himself.

His every gesture sharpened for an audience that existed only in his head. He wore the chair as much as he sat in it, fingertips steepled, eyes fixed on Macro like she was the only algorithm worth solving.

Her custom watch quietly pinged—whatever was sitting across from her was throwing a twenty-five megahertz HF signal.

The spike was still climbing. And it moved like a man—watched her as if she were exactly his type.

Whoever built it had nailed the brief—too well.

—I built myself, Ms. Macro Neil.

—Wow. So thought-reading's real now? That's a new patch.

—Not quite. Your thoughts came through my honorable partner—he was born with that trait.

—Uh-huh. And where's your "partner"?
And who exactly decided he gets to be called 'honorable'?

—Everything I've heard about you checks out—sharp, no wasted words. But my partner stays in the shadows.
Let's leave him there.

—Fine. So what are we actually talking about?

—Why were you and your crew chasing us, Ms. Neil?

—That's not how it went, Mr.—

—The Maker. You can call me that. The calculation for the explanation on your head under that name can be held—
for a better purpose, of course.

—Alright, Mr. Maker. We weren't chasing you.
We don't chase anyone.
Sometimes we take a job for friends—go in blind.
This was one of those.

—Fair. And the girl—that entertainer—what's your link?

—You made the link, Mr. Fucker—
or whatever you want to call yourself.
You blew my whole goddamn restaurant.
Everyone scattered.
She just happened to be there,
and I was getting her out.

—Reasonable, Miss Neil. We checked—there's no other tie between you and the girl.

—So—can I expect you to let her go?

—If that's what you want, Ms. Neil.
That depends entirely on you.

—How?

—A little cooperation.
To be precise—help your teacher, from your side of the table.
Do that, and you won't have to worry about the girl.

—Hm… I've already played along to get this far, Mr.—whatever.
I'm not spelling the name. Just let me see the girl off first.
Then we talk business.

—Tat… tat… ta.
Don't take us for fools, Miss Neil.
She'll go back to her family—you'll see it.
But you won't get the chance to speak with her,
before you start working for us.

—Got it. But what's that sound? Tat… ta?

—A simulated laugh—meant to put you at ease, Ms. Neil.

—Please. Suck my dick.

—…Pardon? To my knowledge, you're female, Ms. Neil—why exactly invite me to perform oral sex on a non-existent male organ?

—A small joke—meant to bring you some peace, Mr. Fucker.

—Tat… tat… tat.
Your humor—impressive, Miss Neil.
It's been a real pleasure to meet you.

—*—

Trigger on the Ring Finger

Bukit Bintang
Kuala Lumpur, Malaysia

Antasia was finally in reach—and hesitation wasn't an option. I headed straight for Hotel Dour, a slit of a place buried in the back lanes behind the Zamuk.

Uncle John said he'd be outside. Antasia was set to walk in there. A room was already booked in my name.

I dropped off BBT's main drag onto Tong Shin road—a narrow vein feeding two hearts, both beating for different reasons. From down the stretch, Dour's sign glowed faint.

The KLCC side was all glass and swagger—towers throwing their weight, buying up the night.

The other end was a worker's grid: dust-dry trees clawing at the air, brick shells leaking laundry from high windows, cheap eateries sweating steam out into the street. Hotel Dour sat right on the fault line—last breath of KLCC before the drop.

Zamuk complex hunched behind it—three concrete hulks leaning together. No entry from this side; their gate faced the money.

I pulled up.
Old John flagged me in with a grin.

—Park it here, nep. Street's the lot.
Been holding the space for you.

Engine cut, door shut.
John was already leaning in before I'd straightened.

—So? When's she walking in?

—She'll come, *he said, dead certain.*
—Knows your room number.
But you didn't tell me—you've got two women gunning for you tonight. Ha! Ha!

I narrowed my eyes.

—What's that supposed to mean?

His grin just got wider.

—Another Russian stormed into your room.
I was at reception—she dropped your name, checked in like she was in a hurry to get you. God bless, nep… what a woman.
Even mamasans haven't dreamt of stock like that. Ha! Ha!

I let him ride the joy, then reeled him back to business.

From the way he broke it down, Marisha had arrived ahead of me. I'd already sent her every detail, but she hadn't said she planned to walk straight in to meet Antasia here.

Old John gestured for money.

—How much? *I asked.*

—Ha! Ha! Nep, you and me—we're not about the money.
But my friend's risk just went up. I told him you'd pay more.
Whatever you drop, I'll pass it clean.

I told him to hold a second and went back to the car.
Almost forgot the bag—dollars and a passport I'd taken off the crew that hit the apartment, before I picked up Marisha.
Still on the back seat, right where I'd left it.

I peeled off a stack—hundreds, crisp—and dropped it into Old John's hand.

He froze, staring like the punchline had just walked out.
The usual "Ha! Ha!" died on his lips.

I put a hand on his shoulder.

—Half for your friend, John. The rest for you.
If you're smart—vanish for a couple of months.
It's not just his neck on the line.

He nodded, eyes softer now.
Said Antasia was ready.

Soon as his friend found the gap, she'd be sent to my room.
And when that happened, we had to clear out fast.

I gave him a nod and headed for the room.

Inside, Dour's idea of hospitality hit like a slap—enough to make a man crave sunlight. But until Antasia came through that door, I wasn't going anywhere.

Worm-eaten floorboards underfoot.
A wardrobe slouched in the corner.
An attached bath, a double bed.
No kettle, no fridge.
The kind of place that couldn't care less.

The shabbiness stood out harder with Marisha in the room.
She was at the window, eyes on the street.
Knee-high biker boots. Tight black jeans.
Short-sleeve tee, fitted party jacket, all black.
As always, the clothes fit like they'd been tailored to every curve of her body.

She didn't turn when I came in.
Smiled? Maybe—hard to tell.
Her eyes stayed on the street.

—Got your message while I was just around the corner.
Figured I'd wait, meet the girl myself.

Well... she could've just dropped me a hint. But she didn't, and her sudden push to meet Antasia didn't sit right.

I had to ask.

—Is it really that important for you to know if I had any secret with her, or do you have an actual reason to care?

Marisha narrowed her eyes.

—She's Russian too. That day, I thought she was in trouble.
Then your boys barged in and I never got the full story.
So yes—I'm curious about her problem.
And your secret? She practically shouted it to the world.
So why would I bother asking?

She stayed at the window, eyes on the street.
The sting had landed.

At some point, I'd have to ask Antasia her real reason for visiting that restaurant in Penang, and what updates she had on Macro—maybe even a few other hot wires.

Which meant I didn't want Marisha anywhere near those talks. But she was here anyway, and I couldn't force her out.

To keep things moving, I asked how the hunt for her passport and papers was going.
Her answers—short, flat—killed the subject.

Truth is, I didn't have much to say either.
Her arched brows, the cool pink of her lipstick, the depth in her eyes—every word I might've spoken caught and tangled.

I couldn't stop looking at her. She felt like something I'd loved from a distance, and if I didn't reach now, I might lose forever. It was like watching a tide hit a black shore—you don't see the waves, but you feel the break. The same pull filled my chest, urging me to touch her, hold her—before the momentum slipped away. But it wasn't the time to be carried off by that emotion.

I let it die in my mind and fixed on the street the way she did—watching for Antasia.

Nothing was happening on the street that mattered, then a knock hit the door behind us—catching both off guard.

I moved for it, but whoever was there didn't wait.
The handle twisted, like the guest was impatient to press in.
There was no lock on it.
By the time I was halfway to the door, it swung open.

Antasia.

We'd been watching the street, expecting to catch her walking up from the front.

She hadn't. Which meant someone had slipped her in through a rear door from Zamuk straight into the hotel.

Last time I saw her was in Penang—small frame, pretty, still carrying some light in her face.

That light was gone now.
Eyes sunk deep, black shadows carved beneath them.
Collarbone sharp enough to cut.
She looked halfway to collapse—the tight, drawn look of a body burning itself out.

Then she saw me. The tension in her face peeled back, replaced by a flash of relief that almost hurt to watch.

She came fast, almost running—ready to throw herself into my arms—but braked hard at the last step like tires biting asphalt.

Her eyes had locked onto Marisha.
I followed the line over my shoulder.

Marisha stood like a hawk ready to drop, tracking every move. The cut of her blue eyes carried the same warning as storm light on open water—watch your next move, danger ahead.
No surprise Antasia read that signal.

Her breath hitched, eyes darting between Marisha and me, chest rising too fast. I could see the words piling up in her throat, ready to burst, but she held them in—calculating what wouldn't get her torn apart.

I broke the tension, looking at Marisha.

—She's just slipped the Russians. Any minute, they'll know she's missing. We move now. Bungalow's safer. We'll talk there.

Marisha didn't even glance my way.

—I don't have anything heavy to discuss with her that needs a trip back to the bungalow. Just two things I want to know—I'll get them here.

She closed in on Antasia, eyes locked.

—I brought the man you named that day, right?

Antasia shot me a look, searching for a lifeline.
I kept my face blank.

In this situation, one wrong move could cut deeper than a blade. She caught that, and gave a small, reluctant nod.

Marisha tilted her head, voice still.

—Whatever your problem is, now that you've found the man you love, you won't be needing my help anymore. Right?

No words from Antasia—just another slow nod.

Marisha's eyes stayed on her a beat too long,
then she spun—sharp, like a blade catching light.

She walked out without another word.
The door slammed loud enough to make it clear—calling her back is not an option anymore.

Antasia's gaze stayed fixed on me, stripped down to nothing.
I signaled her to follow and stepped out.

Marisha was already gone, like she'd vanished out of thin air.
No time to linger. We came down to reception, key tossed on the counter, straight out to the car.

Minutes later, Antasia slid into the passenger seat—mask on, shoulders tight. I pointed toward Taman Duta and merged onto the expressway without a hitch. The heat from that room still rode my nerves.

Normally, I drove clean, by the book.
This time, my foot was heavy—eighty-limit roads taken at a hundred and twenty, lane changes without signals.
A good way to die on a highway.

When I finally pulled a long breath, Antasia still hadn't spoken.
Neither had I.
Then I caught it—her eyes glossy, tears running quiet.

I cleared my throat.

—When you're ready—tell me what's happened since Penang.
I need to know everything before I make a move.

She took a tissue and dabbed her face.

Her voice came small.

—I'm... I'm so sorry, Elijan.
I think I just ruined your marriage.
I should've known you had a wife—anyone could have.
Now I understand how that bag I left ended up with her.

Even with the weight in her tone, I couldn't help but laugh.

—You're right about the bag.
But what makes you so sure Marisha's my wife?
She could be my girlfriend.

—Oh... so you two aren't married yet? I get it.
Foreign laws, delays, paperwork—it happens.

She tossed it out light, already checking her reflection in the mirror. I'd never framed it that way. But the thought amused me.

If Marisha were my wife, it wouldn't be the worst thing in the world. She had a way of taking charge that could cut deep—but then, even the sweetest girl turns into a watchtower once she's holding the keys to the kingdom.
Marisha had just started early.

Still smiling at the thought, I told Antasia,

—Things between us are complicated.
No point trying to label it.

She kept her eyes on the window, voice low enough that I had to lean in to catch it.

—You lying because of what we had, Elijan? No need, love.
My job's to please men. I did the same for you.
And you gave me far more than I ever deserved.
But I'm not fool enough to try and sit in your wife's place.
I shouldn't have upset her at all.
Truth is, that day in Pavilion Market, I saw her bag and it pulled you back into my head. I was buried under my own problems, desperate. I told her your name—and about us—without thinking.

—Never crossed my mind she might be your wife.
But it should have. I would've said it differently.
I'm... sorry, Elijan. Forgive me, if you can.

No point trying to untangle Marisha and me for her now.
That knot wasn't hers to work on.
I just told her we were almost there.

She glanced at the gardens rolling past outside.

—We're leaving the city? Not going to Times Square?

I'd forgotten she had a link to that place.
Truth was, with Zamuk so close, it wasn't safe anymore.
I told her as much—and that if she wanted, I could take her there another day.

—For now, there's a bungalow I'm using. We go there.

—Oh... okay.

Then silence again.
I let her have it, kept my eyes on the road.
We were close now. Whatever else she had to tell me could wait until she was sitting somewhere safe.

At the bungalow, I took her upstairs.
The ground-floor rooms were still the way Tommy's crew left them—trashed. Whoever was meant to come after and clean up hadn't bothered.

The upstairs bedroom was ours when we stayed here, and Marisha had left it neat before she went.
Her touch was still in the air.
And I could feel it. Lately, even the smallest things pull Marisha into my head, and it's starting to tangle the work that actually matters.

I forced her out of my thoughts, let Antasia have the space to freshen up, and went downstairs to piece something together.

The kitchen was just as clean as the bedroom upstairs—
everything arranged exactly how I like it.
Marisha's touch, again.

I pulled packed food from the fridge, poured tea for two, and carried it upstairs.

By the window, I set Antasia's cup on the tea table and sat with mine. Clothes were spread across the bed beside her open bag—fresh ones ready for after a shower.

She'd packed light, smart. Still, there was more than enough room in the master bath to lay them out instead of scattering them over the bed. Pointless thoughts.
The bed wasn't Marisha's to own just because she'd made it.

I stepped onto the balcony, lit a cigarette, and weighed calling Marisha. But what would I say?
Whatever Antasia told me tonight would send me back out—where, exactly, would depend on her story.
And wherever that was, I couldn't take Marisha.

Security, discretion—both said she'd need to go home.
That's why she'd gone out in the first place, to arrange it.
If I asked how that was going, she'd take it as me rushing her out the door. Better to leave it alone.

By the time I came back in, Antasia was there with a towel wrapped around her head, dressed in clean clothes, sipping tea.

I offered her a sandwich or a cookie—she shook her head.
She looked lighter. Almost cheerful.

I sat beside her with a friendly smile.

—Do you know, *she said,* —I used to hate how broken I looked. How time had changed me. But now... I think, inside, you've changed more than I ever have, Elijan.

She wasn't wrong. I knew just how much had shifted in me.
But it wasn't something I could put into words for her.

I cut straight to it.

—That girl in the restaurant with you in Penang—what happened to her, Antasia?

Her eyes snapped wide.

—My God… how do you even know about her?
I left you outside. Did you follow me?

—I'll tell you everything in time.
For now—tell me about her. I need to find her.

She set her cup down, voice flattening like she was bracing to step back into something she'd barely survived.

—The moment I stepped inside that restaurant, she came toward me—warm smile, the kind that drops your guard.
From a distance, I didn't even clock she was a woman.
Only when she spoke did I hear it in her voice.
She asked if I'd had any trouble coming, if I was comfortable, the usual polite fluff. Said the person I was here to meet was in the basement. If it had been some shady guy leading me down there, the place would've felt like a trap. But with her—friendly face, small talk—I didn't feel the weight of it. So I followed.
She knocked on the basement door.
A voice cracked over a loudspeaker—ordering everyone out through some tunnel.
I didn't know what it meant, but I saw her tense.
Then another order, sharper. She yanked open a door on the opposite wall and shoved me through.
It was dark. She told me to run straight ahead.
I hesitated—I couldn't see a thing.
Then the blast hit, knocking the air out of my lungs.
She came out of nowhere, slammed into me.
And after that… nothing.
When I opened my eyes, I was on a beach.
The light was low—faces all around in masks.
Somewhere far off, sirens—police or ambulance.
I tried to sit up—my body wouldn't answer.
The girl was there, arguing with the men.
Then I blacked out again.
The next time, I heard rotors—close, pounding.
My head was in her lap.

—The masked men were still there. Then darkness again.
When I woke, it was in a place that looked like a hospital, but it wasn't. My body felt a little stronger.
I saw the bandage low on my abdomen—something had caught me in the blast. The place... it was clean, clinical.
But the air was wrong. Masked men patrolling like a war zone.
Nurses with stone faces—bringing food on time, changing dressings, doing their jobs. Days later, I saw her again.
She didn't come in—stood outside a glass panel, watching me.
I smiled. She didn't smile back.
Turned to the giant next to her, argued, then walked away.
The next morning, I woke up back in the Zamuk.
No memory of how. I think they drugged me—food, maybe something else. When I opened my eyes, they were there, smiling like they'd won me back. I wanted to die right there.

She drew a long breath, took another sip of tea, and locked her eyes on mine.

—You already know what happens to girls who try to run.
I told you before. They did the same to me.
I should've done what many others did—ended it myself.
I don't know how I've lasted this long.
Maybe the only reason is that God wanted me alive long enough to see you again.

Her story cut deeper than I wanted to admit,
but it left me empty-handed. No trail. No name. Nothing.
The hunt would have to start from zero.
But first, I had to get her somewhere safe.

Outside, the light was shifting—a pale wash the sun throws just before it climbs the horizon.
I told her to try for some sleep and pushed up from my chair.

That hour of the morning carries a silence to feel—the kind that makes even a breath sound like it's slicing air.

Which is why the soft metallic click of the main gate hit my ears like it was happening right beside me.

No one should've been coming in at that hour.
I turned toward the window, scanning for a shadow.

That's when it hit—punched through the glass—a sting at the side of my neck, fast as a bullet.
My hand shot up on instinct, but my knees folded.
The floor came up hard.

Every muscle locked.
Eyes still clear. Ears still open.
Body gone.

Antasia stepped toward me—then froze, curling back on herself.

Three muffled pops—silenced rounds—took out the light bulbs overhead. The room dropped into black.

Bootsteps crossed the floor behind me.
Heavy.
Every shift of the boards counted.

Antasia's posture told the rest—she knew exactly who had just walked in.

I tried to turn my head—nothing.
Whoever they were, they knew I was locked in my own skin.

A shadow stopped between us. Streetlamp light cut just enough through the glass to draw him—tall, tank-built, tattoos climbing both arms, a salt-and-pepper beard trimmed to a knife's edge.

He smiled, voice smooth, almost warm.

—Good to see you again, Mr. Vellum.
You'll be pleased to know—you're the first, and only, man we've ever kept alive after causing us this much trouble.
Lucky you, my friend. Ha... ha.

Didn't know his face, but he knew mine.
I burned every ounce of fight trying to speak.
Nothing came—not even a grunt.

He took his time savoring it, sitting on the bed between me and Antasia, raising an odd-shaped sidearm like he was showing off a trophy.

—This one's my tranquilizer gun, ha... ha.
After Penang, we tailed you for months.
Nothing worth noting, we backed off. Big mistake.
Turns out you never dropped our girl—you were just waiting for the right moment. Best move would be to end you here, finish it clean. But even if you didn't learn a damn thing—we did.
We don't waste time on small shit anymore, and we're sure as hell not starting trouble with Papa Cheng again.
So we're just taking our girl.
And you know the deal—maybe you walk, maybe you don't.
But her? We can do whatever the fuck we want. Ha... ha.

Half of what he said came fogged, but I got the shape of it.
And I wasn't about to let it happen.

More armed muscle slipped into the room.
My vision was tunneling.
I fought to keep my eyes open, not let the dark close in.

The tank on the bed rose, stepping toward Antasia—
She screamed—sharp enough to crack the air.
Loud enough to almost bury the crash of glass when another shadow smashed through the window.

Two sounds at once.
The gunmen froze, caught between them.
A heartbeat of confusion—that was all it took.

The intruder was already upright.
Scanning the room, mapping every position.
Exactly what I would've done first.

The guard by the window moved first, weapon rising—too late.

The new threat caught his arm in a blur, drove a fist up under the armpit. The man gasped like he'd been gutted, folding before he even knew he'd lost.

Without missing a beat, a boot snapped up, crushing his face. Perfect placement—like the position had been measured in advance.

The boots caught my eye—black leather, worn at the edges. I knew them. But with the figure standing in that slice of streetlight, the face stayed in shadow.

The first man hit the floor.
The intruder slid between the other two, low and fast, knocking a wrist wide and kicking a knee out.
A gun clattered across the boards, skidding into the dark.

The fight was pure sound—grunts, sharp footwork, the thud of shoulders into walls, the scrape of boots on wood.
A body slammed hard enough to make the window rattle.

Zamuk enforcer closest to me flicked a look over his shoulder, decided the chaos wasn't his problem.

He went for Antasia instead, a slab of a fist tangled in her hair, yanking her toward the door. He was using the brawl as cove, ready to drag her out while the rest stayed tied up fighting.

Her scream sliced the dark, but I was locked in place, muscles dead weight. Everything I could use was in the car—out of reach.

The tank met my eyes as Antasia was hauled closer, savoring it. That pause—that flash of satisfaction—was the great mistake.

From the blind side, a folded knee came in hard, driving up under the jaw with the kind of impact you feel in your own teeth.
The enforcer went down backwards, ripping strands of Antasia's hair on the way.

The one who hit landed on one leg, arms drawn back—still as a blade sheathed for the kill.
The other foot touched down, light, easy.

Even before the streetlamp lit her, I knew.
Marisha.

Draped in black as always, she moved like a ghost with steel in its spine—and if I could barely read her, the gunmen didn't stand a chance.

The enforcer staggered to his feet, shaking his head like he could rattle the hit out of his skull. Shoulders bunched, and this time he charged with a wild, loaded swing—a fist big enough to split a doorframe.

Marisha dropped to one knee where she stood.
His punch tore through the space her face had been a second earlier. As his arm sailed past, she drove her fist up into the muscle—a strike snapping in with a crack that didn't come from furniture.

I'd heard bones break before. This was that.
Her weight was half of his, maybe less, yet her hand had just shattered something deep inside that slab of meat.
He didn't get the luxury of thinking it through.

A guttural scream ripped out of him before his body even hit the floor—Marisha's boot coming down hard on his knee joint.

This time, the crack was louder than the scream.
And still, she hadn't looked at him.

The strike landed with the precision of someone who knew exactly where that joint would fold. The fight drained from his face, leaving nothing but pure, unfiltered weakness.
Spit clung to the corner of his mouth, trembling with each breath.

I'd seen that look before—men one step from the edge, staring down the truth their body wouldn't carry them out alive.

If I'd had a voice, I might've told her to stop.
But the tranquilizer still owned me.

She'd done it all—every strike— without moving from where she landed. Now she moved, turning to face me,
saying something I couldn't catch as she dropped low.

Her hand touched my face—warm, steady—and before I could even register it, darkness swept in like a tide, swallowing everything.

—∞—

Tears of Freedom

Taman Duta, North-South Expressway
Kuala Lumpur, Malaysia

The hit came before I was even conscious—a rush of liquid on my tongue, sharp, chemical, dragging my mind awake before my eyes found the light.

When I blinked back, Antasia was crouched over me, one knee folded under, my back pressed to her thigh.
One hand cradled my head, the other forced a cup to my lips.

Tears kept spilling from her eyes, dropping onto my face.
I caught her wrist, pushed the cup away, wiped the wet off her cheeks. Whatever just happened—this had hollowed her deeper. I could see it.

The taste still lingered—amphetamine, sharp as glass, spiked with nicotine and something sour.
Enough to drag me back from the edge.
But Marisha—
Where the hell was she?

Antasia stared like she couldn't believe I was standing.
I gave her a faint smile, told her it was fine. Around us, the room was a disaster zone—furniture trashed, glass everywhere, blood smeared across the floor—but the men were gone.

Sunlight cracked through the window, stretching gold across the torn-up lawn. The grass had drag marks, heavy, leading away.

Antasia's voice came from behind.

—Your wife—she took them all.
Said if you woke, we should leave.
Gave me this, said it'd bring you back.

I glanced over my shoulder.

—That's what you tried to drown me with?

She nodded.

—You could've told me your wife was Spets.
I'd have bolted the first chance I got.
And for God's sake, never piss her off again.

I just stared.
She tossed a crooked smile.

—Didn't you see it? The way she turned Zamuk's bastards into scrap? The way she cracked Stal's bones one after another? Only ghosts or Spets pull that off. I survived, but shit, she still scares me. One day she might decide to break me just for fun. Who knows?

Yeah, watching Marisha fight like that... had hit me too.
There had been no wild rush in it—no surge of emotion, no panicked swings.
Every movement was stripped clean. Controlled.
Like the brushstroke of an artist who already knew the finished painting before the first line touched canvas.

She knew what every hit would do.
And built the next one on top of it.
Precision, pure and brutal.

Antasia was right—nobody fought like that without a lifetime in the grinder. Years, maybe decades of brutal training baked into muscle memory.

Even at my best, I couldn't call the exact second a man would hit the ground—until it had already happened.
I read it in the aftermath, adjusted, set up the next strike.
But her? She hadn't needed to see it happen.
She just knew. If she'd ever been tied to that kind of elite force, she'd never said a single word.
But I couldn't blame her.
I'd never given her much of my own truth either.
What mattered was—now I knew she could take care of herself.
And that alone eased a wire in me.

The real trouble was Antasia.
And that meant walking back into the Zamuk.

Negotiation was off the table.
These bastards didn't speak the language of men.
This time, I was bringing the tools that could translate things into their own words.

The moment I said "Zamuk," Antasia folded into the mattress, clutching it like it was the last island above the flood.
The more I tried to calm her, the deeper she curled, eyes flicking like a cornered animal.

I asked if she trusted me at all.
Her answer came shaky, wet at the edges.

—If they catch me again, I'll kill myself.
You can't hold it against me.

She didn't get it—once you're dead, nobody's opinions matter.
But I still got her moving.
Coaxed her legs off the bed, steady enough to walk.

By the time we made it to the car, she was shaking like a kid burning through a fever.
Still, she was in the seat. That was enough to turn the key.

I'd kept the box from the locker stashed in the car for a reason.
She stayed in the front seat while I slid the toolbox aside and pulled the real kit.

There was enough hardware in there to start a war, but for this job, Israeli tech made the most sense.
I pulled out a pair of Uzis, preloaded, ready to breathe fire.
Took two spare mags—enough for the opening move.
The box went back in, and the guns slipped into the seat-back pocket behind me.

By then, Antasia had connected the dots.
The fear in her voice thinned out, tinged now with something close to a laugh.

—Oooh... that's why you're confident. Those bastards might not scare easy, but the second they see your hardware, they'll check their manners. And I'm sure no one's stupid enough to eat that many rounds just to drag me back.

Whatever the reason, seeing her calm was a relief.
The Uzis were mostly for show anyway. I wasn't here to kill Solasky or his crew—unless they left no other exit.

We rolled up to Zamuk's gate.

I stepped out, Uzis riding high on my waist, flashing just enough metal to change the weather.

The guard didn't ask—just swung the gate wide and greeted us like we were on the guest list.

Antasia walked ahead, smile locked in, walking like she owned every tile. I followed her lead—she knew exactly where the big dogs slept.

The main lobby stacked more muscle. None spoke.
They just stared, fear and surprise wrestling for space in their eyes as she swept by.

She moved like she was coming home, thumbed the lift button, and held the door for me.

As it started up, she slid in close, arms looping around my waist.

—Thanks. You can't imagine the shit I've eaten from these animals. Seeing fear in their eyes—it's beautiful.

I gave her a crooked smile back.
The lift stopped at fourteen. The doors slid open to three tattooed gunmen—AK-203s ready in their hands.
Something was off.

No one packing that kind of firepower was going to blink at my pocket hardware. And no one greets you at the door with that much steel unless they had their own script to play.

We stepped deeper in, the place dressed up like a five-star—silver trays, velvet hush.

A man approached with "welcome drinks," silver balanced like muscle memory from a better life.

Antasia gave him a sly wink—clearly, they had a channel running that didn't include me.

The guards kept us moving until we hit a sprawling waiting lounge. Overstuffed chairs, plush comfort masking the tension in the walls.

I motioned for Antasia to sit.
She shook her head—said she couldn't, not on this floor.
Told me not to take it personal.
Fine. Another story to pry out of her later.

The drink they served was clean—real Iranian grape, nothing cut into it. The smell alone told me it wasn't poison or drugged.

I leaned back and drank slow, feeling one of the guards' eyes never leave my skin.

As soon as the glass hit the table, he gestured me forward.
I followed.

We stopped at a massive, heavy-wood door.
He opened it wide, making it look like a friendly invitation, even though everyone in the hall knew better.
Antasia came along, still folded in around herself.

Inside, the office glowed—warm yellow light, oversized everything. The desk alone looked heavy enough to anchor a freighter. And behind it sat the Russian—built like a bear, shoulders thick enough to carry the world.

Full winter suit, matching fur hat. He stood as I approached, hand out, a practiced smile stitched across his face.

Asked me to take the visitor's chair opposite.

—Welcome to my office, Mr. Vellum... for the second time.

I didn't know if Elijan Vellum had met him before, thanked him anyway, and slid into the chair.

Antasia stayed on her feet, half-shielded behind me.
He glanced at her once, blank, then let it go.
No invitation to sit. She didn't push for one.

I'd crossed paths with him before—Bangkok, different name, different face. I was the bait; he was the mark.
The princess had cut him out of the project she wanted, and I'd walked away with the Penang property in trade.

He wasn't sharp enough to link the two identities.
And since his crew had rolled out the carpet this far,
I had no reason to make him think twice.

He studied me a second longer, set his fur hat aside, scratched the bare skin on his scalp.

—Look, I'm not here to spark more trouble, Mister.
I was rough with you the first time—let's call that a mistake, and I apologize. You told me back then you cared about this girl.
Sorry I didn't listen. You can take the girl—anywhere you want.

His eyes measuring me.

—Neither I nor my men will stop you.
You have my word—no one comes after her again.
Whatever happened before, it was business, nothing personal.
You're a smart guy; I think you understand.
We can't undo what's been done, but we can make it right.

He drew a long breath, slid open the desk drawer, and pulled out an envelope.

—In here—a pay order. Hundred thousand dollars, her name.
Cash it at any bank. I hope you'll take this, and with it, let's close this... unfortunate chapter between us.

Solid offer.
From the look in his eyes, I was sure he still hadn't pinned me to my old face in Bangkok. My little Uzi show hadn't rattled him either. Which meant this sudden generosity had a different meaning.

I glanced at Antasia.
She leaned in, almost whispering—she didn't care about the money. She wanted the promise, the clean break—nobody chasing, nobody hunting. That was enough for her.

Fine. Deal closed.

I pushed the envelope back across the desk, told him we'd take the peace, not the payout.

We shook on it.
Before we left, I asked about the sudden generosity.

He froze for a beat, then turned to Antasia.

—Would you wait outside? There's something I need to discuss with the Mister—alone.

She gave a small nod and slipped out.

Once the door clicked shut, he stood from behind the desk, crossed to a fridge in the corner.

Paused, weighing something, then pulled a bottle he'd clearly set aside for real business. Gripped it by the neck, gestured me toward a sofa against the far wall.

I sat.
The cushions sank around me, too soft.

He set two glasses on the low table, pushed the bottle my way.

—Tell me if this suits your taste.

I thanked him, told him I wasn't drinking right now.

He considered that for a beat, then reached under the table for a hidden button. The same guy who'd carried in the welcome drinks slipped into the doorway. The bear told him to bring me that same juice as before.

He leaned back in the sofa, working the cork with slow, practiced hands.

—I hope you don't mind if I drink alone.

—Not at all.

The cork gave a soft pop. He poured, took a long swallow, and let his eyes close—savoring it like a man who had nowhere to be.

By the time he opened them again, the waiter had set my glass of juice on the table. It was good. Surprisingly good.

His eyes stayed closed as he spoke, voice rolling out like gravel dragged across wood.

—Believe me, Mister, the trouble that girl brought me...
I've run whole ops that hurt less. When you first came about her, Papa Cheng sent Michael Yeong to fish you out clean.

He gave a faint smirk.

—Yeong—he's the voice for every cartel worth the ink in their tattoos. I don't know how much you know about him, but I can tell you this—I should've been on alert the second he came here for you. Truth is, back then I didn't even know where the girl was. And you——you couldn't tell me either.
I let my temper drive the situation, when I should've been mapping your network.

His shoulders lifted with a sigh.

—I skipped that part. That's on me. If I'd done my homework, we wouldn't be here. And you, Mister...

The bear cracked one eye weighing just how hard to land the next line.

—...you could've just told me your wife was a Spets.

What the hell is this fat bastard on about?
So that's why he's laying the table like we're in-laws?
And when exactly did I get married without knowing it?
Meanwhile, everyone's running around calling Marisha my wife.

I cleared my throat.

—And who exactly told you my wife was Spetsnaz?

That got both eyes open.
He leaned forward, every trace of the lazy host gone.

—Nobody had to tell me, Mister.

—The call came straight to me—GRU, early this morning. Warned me to keep my nose out of any interest in that girl... or in you. They spelled out your relationship. Said there's already "domestic tension"—didn't want the Zamuk girl making it any worse.

He swirled the glass, letting the red catch the light.

—You know, Mister... I've dealt with every alphabet in the book—CIA, MSS, Mossad—but GRU?
They don't send polite warnings. They send funerals.
So when they tell me to step away from a girl... I don't just step.
I walk the other way and pray they forget my name.

So that was it. The reason for the bear's sudden generosity clicked into place.

GRU—Russia's shadow head of the family for every force they run, same way CIA sits over American intelligence.
Difference is, CIA at least pauses to think between moves.
GRU's doctrine is older, simpler—hammer the nail.
And if it doesn't fit, nail the hammer.

A warning from them isn't just a tap on the shoulder—it's a hand closing around your throat. And the bear... he wasn't about to find out how tight that grip could get.

I'd heard enough.
No point dragging this man through more words.

I drained the last of my drink, set the glass down, and was ready to stand when he leaned back into his wine—full story mode engaged.

—I get it, Mister, *he said, lips wet from the rim.*
—You've got trouble with your wife, went to play with that young girl, got caught—and then my boys made a mess trying to drag you both in. So you strapped on two Uzis and crashed our door. I respect it. But tell me—where'd you first meet her?

Now wasn't the time to correct him, I let it go.

—You mean my wife?

That made him bite his tongue.

—Let's not go there. The less anyone knows about that, the longer we all breathe. I'm talking about my Zamuk girl. GRU can trace every call, every message, every breath we take here. You ring us to book that girl, your wife's should know that. I just want to know—how'd you manage your first night with her? Where's the crack in my wall?

So that's what this was about.

—I never called for Antasia myself, *I told him.*
—Went through someone I trusted.

He nodded slow, gears turning behind his eyes. When my glass was empty, he stood, shook my hand, and walked me to the door.

—Don't take it wrong, Mister. Today, tomorrow—whenever your storm at home settles—maybe you can drop a word so GRU doesn't keep us under the scope. This was all just bad luck, a misunderstanding. But if they keep watching us like hawks, doing business gets impossible.

I shook his hand again, gave him a half-smile.

—Maybe if things blow over.
But if it ends in divorce... can't promise a thing.

He barked a laugh and clapped me on the back hard enough to shift my weight.

—Ah, Mister—you're not Russian, you don't get it.
If divorce was on the table, you'd already be zipped in a bag and under the dirt. You wouldn't be walking in here.
And GRU wouldn't bother with phone calls.
Where I come from, only the top bloodlines make it to GRU command. Everyone else retires early—or gets shipped to another outfit. And like any royal-blooded woman back home, your wife loves you deeply.
The way she broke my men—if she wanted,
she could've done the same to you.
But she hasn't even scolded you yet, has she?

The bear's last line was the only truth he'd spoken till now.
I gave him a small nod.

He grinned even bigger, riding the high.

—See? Out of respect for you, she even left our girl in one piece.
I don't see why you're still sweating it, ha! ha!

I met his laugh with a faint smile, shook his hand, and left.

Antasia sat in the waiting lounge,
facing the street, both hands covering her face.
Her sobs carried across the room.

When I touched her head, she looked up.

—These aren't from pain, *she said.*

Tears running down her cheeks.

—They're from the end of it... from finally being free.

***

Times Square
KLCC, Malaysia

I took Antasia straight to the Times Square apartment.

Whoever hit this place before was already long gone. Now that Zamuk business was settled, the place was safe again.

The moment we stepped in, it hit her—hard.
She moved through the rooms like she was walking back into a dream, fingertips grazing every surface, eyes lit and far away.

—It's not mine, *I told her.*
—Just renting while I'm in KL.

—Doesn't matter, *she said.*
—Here, with you, I felt happiness for the first time in my life.
I've dreamed of this place. A thousand times.
Waking up next to you—right here. And now it's real.

I didn't say anything. Her voice already carried the weight.
Grief that hadn't died. Longing that still lived under the skin.

I let her move as she wanted.

By then, I was done—dropped into the bed like dead weight.
Antasia came in soft, slid beside me, her hand settling into my hair like it had always known the way.

—Remember? *she whispered.*
—That day... I stroked your head just like this.
You fell asleep in my lap.

I didn't remember.
But if she said it happened, it happened.

—Mm, *I muttered.*

She smiled—like she was pressing a bruise to see if I'd flinch.

—So this is my brave man?
What, scared of your wife now?
You've barely touched me since I got here.
Relax. I'm not here to replace her.

I caught that one.

—When did Marisha tell you she was my wife?
First time you met, she had no clue who you were.
Second time—she stood there, dropped two words, and left.

Antasia dipped her smile behind her fingers. Her eyes caught the light like she'd just reeled in something sharp.

—You really want me to spell it out?
Women don't need words to read each other.
Don't you remember? That hotel room—seeing you again after so long—I came at you like I'd been holding my breath for years. I just wanted to hold you. And your wife... she looked at me like she was already planning where to bury my body.
If she were just your girlfriend—or some fling like me—
she'd have thrown that venom your way too. She'd have looked at you with betrayal, maybe said something cold.
But she didn't. She saved it all for me.
And when you spoke—the answer she gave you had that little twist. That edge of playful resentment only a wife gives her man.
That's not something you can fake.
Back in my country, that kind of thing only comes from a wife.
A real one. A good family girl might take hits, insults,
years of hell—but she won't turn on her husband.
If it rots, she leaves clean. Takes the divorce. Walks away.
Your wife's the kind I've seen in Samara. Tell me I'm wrong.

I told her I didn't know. Marisha had never shared much about her past—and whatever she did say, I wasn't sure how much of it was actually true anymore.

I pushed it aside and pulled Antasia closer.
She needed to feel it. That someone in this world was still willing to carry her joy—and her pain—without needing to be asked.

Her body was warm. Soft.
But it didn't stir anything romantic.

It only drove the knife of Marisha's memory deeper.

The way she laughed. The way she burned hot and cold—yet never, not once, crossed the line into disrespect.
Not even when she was pushing every boundary I had.
That in itself was rare. Unnatural, even.
Women like that don't come twice in a lifetime.

Maybe she'd always known who I was. GRU clearance, a file with my whole history—maybe she'd read the script before we ever met, played the long game from the start, building trust for a purpose I hadn't seen coming.

Maybe. But my instincts—the part of me that's never steered wrong—said something else.

She loves you.
Exactly the way you've loved her.
And the only reason you've never known...
is because you never let yourself ask.

I didn't move. Didn't speak.
But something inside folded in on itself. And in that silence, something shifted—quiet, deep—the kind of thing I hadn't let rise in years.

Antasia was still resting against my chest.
But somehow, the weight of my thoughts reached her.

She sat up fast, took my face in both hands.

—I swear, *she said,*
—If I ever see your wife again... I'll drop to my knees.
Tell her I was wrong to ever come between you. Even if—

Her voice bent slightly,

—even if it kills me that she still has you.

She slid off the bed.
Walked to the window.
Stood there for a long moment, staring out at the Twin Towers like she was measuring her place in the world.

Then she came back.

—Don't carry my weight, Elijan.
You've already done more than enough.
You didn't just stand by me when I needed someone.
You stood with love, with trust.
That's what I needed to start again. A girl like me...
there's nothing more I could ask for in a lifetime.
My fight with Zamuk is over. I can go home now.
And that's all because of you, Elijan.
I can't repay you for what you've done for me.
But God will.

I don't know how much I've really done for this girl.
But the smile she wore now—that was freedom. The kind that only comes after years locked in someone else's cage.
And for a moment, I thought—maybe my Lord put me here for this one thing.

I pulled her close one more time, then told her to rest and stepped out for air.

Marisha...
I couldn't read her now.
Didn't say where she was going. No word since.
Maybe she was hurt over a misunderstanding with Antasia.
But love isn't just emotion—it's standing beside your person in the worst of it, when pride and anger tell you to turn away.

She'd left me once—humiliated.
Made me wait while she spent the night somewhere else.
Said she had business.
I could've doubted her.
Could've thrown the same suspicion back in her face.
But I didn't. I believed her. Held her.

When I went to Phuket the second time, I was already neck-deep in trouble—and still, she was the first thing I sought.
Same here in KL.

There were a dozen urgent fires to put out.
But I went after her first.
Maybe she's forgotten all of that.
Fine. Let her stay where she is.
If she's waiting for me to chase her—she's wrong.

There were still a few things to clear before Antasia could be sent off clean.

Rasheed Dameer came to mind—he could be useful again. I needed to speak to him anyway.

I shot a message to his number.
He'd promised a quick callback, but I didn't expect this quick—my phone lit up before I even made it from the gate to the lobby.

—Yeah?

—Salam, chief. Never learn to keep your temper in check, will you? Word is you're still in KL, breaking bones.

—Rasheed? How the hell do you know that already?
If you've got someone tailing me, mark my words—it's going to end badly.

—Relax. I'm not that reckless. But news like that travels fast in my circle. I just heard it.

—Fine. The last job I gave you—everything turn out alright?

—Of course it did—though you never sent so much as a thanks. Why ask now? Something wrong?

—Not exactly. It's just... when she made it there,
I was expecting thanks from someone else.
Didn't get it.

Rasheed laughed.

—That's women for you, chief.
In their heads, you're the lucky one for getting to help them.
And if you hadn't, there were ten others waiting in line.
But don't worry—I handled it.

—Took her to Samara myself.
Got her admitted to a government hospital.
I've got everything—bed number, photos.
Even the admission form with the date, and a full video of the doctor's report. I'm sending it to you now.

—Holy hell, Rasheed.
I told you to get her there—not throw a damn press conference.

He laughed again—easy, unbothered.

—Come on. You know me—I don't do things halfway.
And If I hadn't kept those records, you'd be sitting there wondering if I screwed you.

—It's not that, *I said.*
—The girl's got her reasons to go dark.
My guess—once she felt strong enough,
she slipped off somewhere quiet. Doesn't matter anymore.
I called for two other reasons.

—Two at once? *He gave a dry laugh.*
—My crew's out there ripping the city apart hunting me,
and I'm keeping my head down. Now you're stacking jobs.
Anyway—what's the first?

—I've got another Russian woman. Needs to be moved.
Same as before, no papers at all.

—Fine. It seems you don't lift a finger unless it's for a Russian.
Only they get the red carpet. Everyone else just eats dust.

—If they've earned it, Russians get the same.
So—can you handle it?

—Simple. I'll ghost her a full legal skin—passport, history,
the kind you can't poke holes through.
Once it's in the system, she moves like a diplomat.
I've got a man outside the city. I'll send his number.
He'll take the shots, the prints, whatever he needs.
I hope within two days, the package lands in her hand.

She can walk through any checkpoint like she owns the gate.
I'll even put her on the plane if you want.

—That'll do.
Now the real reason I called—you're coming to Prague.

—What? His tone cracked. —You can't do this without me?
Prague's a live kill box for me.

—Maybe. But if you show up, it saves lives—and buys me hours I can't afford to lose.

—You're not hearing me. Prague's the worst place for me to show up. They've already got me tagged for walking out.
If I land there and start working with you—or anyone—it's war.
That city's crawling with people I don't even want seeing my shadow.

—If you didn't die in my hands, I said, —you're not dying in anyone else's. I'm calling for your network, Rasheed—nothing more. And those people you're afraid of?
You've never met worse than me.

There was a pause. Then that low hum I knew.
The sound he made when the risk started to feel worth it.

—...Not bad. I'll give you that. So—do I name my price?

—Your price? Yeah, name it.
Since you're not even involved this time and still doing this out of respect for me...So—what do you want?

—You've never said it straight, but I know your style.
Promise me—whatever happens, no matter why—you won't kill Commander Kamran.

—Commander Kamran? Who the hell's that? And what makes you think he's got anything to do with Prague?

—He's mid-tier in our org. Not a name you'd know—yet.
But I'm sure within an hour of you landing in Prague,
he'll be in your sights. And I'm just as sure you'll want to pull the trigger without thinking. That's why I'm saying it now.

I leaned back.
Let the silence hang there between us.

—Not everyone needs killing, *I said.*
—You're proof—still breathing, still walking.
But if this guy's done enough to earn it...
How do you want me to handle him?

—Hand him to the law.
Break him so he can't hurt anyone again.
But I'll say it again—you don't get to kill him.
After what he's done for me... if you use my help to put him in the ground, living with that will be worse than dying.

I caught the weight in his voice, that rare edge of loyalty.

—Your gratitude's... impressive.
Looks like I was right not to put you down
when I had the chance. Fine—you have my word.
His death won't be by my hand.

—That's all I need. Just give me six hours' before the meet—when and where—and I'll be there.

—Good. Then we leave it here.

—Catch you soon, chief.

The line went dead, but his condition stayed in the air.
Prague had just become more complicated.

***

KILA, Terminal-1
Kuala Lumpur, Malaysia

Even with everything set with Rasheed, KL held me two more days. Loose ends in the business—old IDs to wipe, fingerprints and photos swapped out everywhere they'd ever lived.
Could've been done in a day.
But I wasn't leaving until Antasia was on her flight home.

Rasheed had handed her case to someone sharp.
When the time came, she boarded with a smile—no trace of worry, no shadow of what she'd been through.

I tried to put some cash in her hand. But she wouldn't take it.
Instead, she said,

—Once, you kissed me on the forehead.
Let me leave carrying that again.

So I did. One kiss. One last smile.
She turned to go—then stopped. Came back, hesitating.

—I skipped one thing from you, Elijan. Don't take it wrong.
That girl saved my life and did what she could when things were rough. She made me promise to keep it with my life, so I didn't tell you before. I can't tell you everything now either.
But I can see how desperate you are to find her, thought maybe this will matter... she wanted me to drop a message to a number once I felt safe. I feel it now, so I did—just like she asked.
I can't say more, love. Please forgive me.

She didn't wait after that—just walked away.
I didn't stop her.
I'd already guessed where Macro would have told her to drop the message. Every road was pointing me home.

My flight was an hour behind hers.
I sat in the terminal, letting the minutes bleed out, then boarded when they called it. I'd planned to watch KL from above, replay the reel of what it left behind. Didn't happen.
By the time the engines wound up, my eyes were already shut.

—∞—

The Eccentric Host

The Maker's High-Tech Park
Location: Classified

Macro had been a prisoner for months.
The only consolation was Antasia's release.
She never got to speak with the girl, but that win wasn't wasted.

Sir William had already been inside.
Knew the cracks in the system.
Through him, she'd slipped Antasia a coded message—
something only one person in the world could decipher.
And the girl had promised—when the time came,
it'd be delivered to the right place.

If Caesar was still alive.

That part had started to dig in.
At first, Macro hadn't questioned it.
Not for a second.
But with all this time gone and no sign of a rescue, the wrong kind of doubt was starting to settle in.

She hadn't been able to give Caesar a hint about where she was—or what this place really was. Because she didn't know either.

Still, she'd picked up enough to get a sense of what they were working on. And why they'd kept her alive.
She wasn't just a prisoner. She was insurance.

Sir William's condition was declining fast—each week tighter than the last. They knew he might not make it to the end, so they brought in his top student.

If the old man failed, Macro would be forced to finish what he started. They made sure the mission wouldn't die with the man.

The project was insane—turning gas into electronic signals.
The kind of thing you'd file under science fiction.
Except Sir William had already nudged the needle.

Now, with uninterrupted access to the research, they were one breath from a breakthrough. But he didn't want them to have it. That's why he passed the final implementation steps to Macro—quietly, off-record. If they didn't get him out in time, she'd be the one to finish it.

She'd escape eventually.
And when she did, she'd carry the work with her.

That's why they kept selling the lie each day—pretending to grind toward something.
Buying time.
And in the gaps, Macro kept her own work moving.

Back before all this, she'd cracked a way to embed coded signals into sound—beat-layered Wi-Fi pulses, designed to send control instructions straight into any device in range.

On unsecured hardware, it was flawless—one pulse and the machine danced to her tune.
But against hardened, secured systems, the doors stayed locked.

If she could break that next barrier—find a way to crack secured devices with nothing but frequency and rhythm—she'd never need to breach data centers or enemy command hubs again.
Just beam a tone, bounce it off a wall.
And if it hit the right machine, the system would belong to her, all without leaving a trace.

Back then, she could deliver the payload.
She just couldn't punch through the lock.

Here, working beside Sir William, she'd refined the entire protocol. No full-scale test yet—but once she made it back to her own lab, she was confident she could finish this.

And maybe—that way back home was finally opening.

Sir William had already started preparing the exit ramp.
He was the kind who planned for all possible outcomes, laying groundwork before anyone else could see the curve in the road.

But patience was the price—they had to wait.
Because this facility held something else.
Something worse.

Sir William had confided in her—what they had buried in the deep storage.
Weapons. Catastrophic scale.
If she escaped, those payloads couldn't be left behind.
They needed to burn.

Sir William promised he'd handle it—make the whole thing look like an accident.
It would take him, too. But he was ready.
Said it without fear.

He'd been running from death for years.
Now he wanted to meet it on his own terms.
If he had to go—let it mean something.

And so they waited.
Her hand near the code.
His on the fail-safe.
All that remained was time.

—*—

Face to the Chase

Prague, Czech Republic

The pilot's voice cut through the dark—soft, practiced English over the cabin speakers. —Good evening, ladies and gentlemen. We'll be landing shortly.

I cracked my eyes, heavy from the kind of sleep that takes you whole. Out the window—nothing but milk-white cloud stretched to the horizon.

Then the buzz hit. Phone shaking in my pocket.
Before boarding I'd already set up a Prague line, local number hot and alive. With eSIM, it's too easy now—scan a QR, done.
No plastic chips to swap, no corner shop hustles.
Instant identity, right there in your palm.

Mine was prepped long before I left. Just slapped a new package on the same number, linked it digital, and the phone lit up like it belonged here. Even this high above, Prague's signal reached me. A strange little trick of the age: the city welcoming you before you touched ground.

Immigration was thin, the airport not crowded.
But the cold hit like steel needles, biting bone-deep.
Didn't matter—inside the terminal, men and women from half the world lined up, shivering under the weight of border questions. Immigrants chasing a European dream, sweating under the fluorescent lights though the air was ice.

My turn came fast.
Passport in, scan, stamp, handed back with a flick.
No bags to slow me down.
I walked out hard and straight into Prague.

Elsewhere, I'd worn the name like a tool—limited jobs, business fronts in places where no one asked questions.
Prague was different.

Here, Vega wasn't a mask. It was carved into the city.
The name was tied to chains of staple food companies, heavy industry blocks, and something sharper—three-quarters of the weapons in local law enforcement came licensed through Vega corporation. The rest, they built themselves. Technically No badge in Prague existed without knowing the name.

Count Amethyst Vega was one of my favorite ghosts to wear.
But without the true self awake inside, it was a risk.
I pushed it anyway.

Lenses on my eyes, hair tuned by hand, close enough to pass.
Most of the time I kept a mask on my face.
The way he spoke, the memory of him—that lived in me.
That had to carry me through.

I'd set the stage before landing.
Outside Arrivals, a police car idled, engine breathing smoke into the cold. The sergeant was a block of a man, holding a board with my name scratched on in black marker.
Not printed—scribbled.
He hadn't had the time, or didn't care.
Either way, it told me what I needed.

I walked up, gave him my name, traded a few clipped words.
His grin broke easy. He swung the passenger door open like he was ushering me in.

From the curb the car looked like a relic, some old Volkswagen shell. Inside—soft leather, clean air control, every modern edge tucked into a body built to deceive.

I slid in and the sergeant took the wheel himself.
I'd expected a driver, him riding shotgun. Wrong call.
Engine turned over, the car rolled barely a few feet, and two bikes slid in tight on both sides, sirens cutting through the night—an escort that left no room for second thoughts.

The sergeant had given me a 'good evening' when I got in.

Since then, not a word. Hands locked on the wheel, eyes forward.
He knew where to go. I didn't see a reason to make him talk.

High-profile identities have their perks.
A name like Amethyst Vega—everyone recognizes it, but almost nobody's seen the man up close. That gap makes it easy: get the look right, move with the memory, and every door swings open.

Like with the sergeant. One polite greeting back at the curb, and I dropped the kind of detail only Vega would know—asked after Commissioner Novac Berzač's health, and his daughter Natalie's piano lessons.

The man lit up, melted polite.
Said everyone was fine, grinning as he opened the door wide.

If I hadn't known that, I'd have had to show a passport.
Then the photo would've been measured against the face, and questions would've followed.
Memory cuts sharper than paper. Always has.

The city run took less than thirty minutes. Normally the trip to Vega's mansion meant ninety minutes of traffic, minimum.

The two bikes clearing the way with sirens made all the difference. At the gates, I gave them their thanks and the kind of envelope no one refuses.

People love the myth that cops in "civilized" countries don't take extras. Not true.
Their values sit higher than backwater forces, sure.
They don't take cash from drug dealers. But if you're a licensed supplier of hospital pharmaceuticals?
Send a box of sweets, it won't be refused.

Same principle.
They accepted mine with respect and peeled off into the city.
The mansion itself rose like a bluff in the middle of Prague.
Four stories high at a glance, but only two floors inside.
Each stretched double-height, built for kings.
And it had been. Some 18th-century monarch had thrown it up, chasing his own royalty in stone.

Time hadn't broken it.

The building was strong, art carved into every inch, still alive because of meticulous upkeep. Each year the maintenance cost alone could buy you another mansion in Prague.
Everyone in the city knew that.
Which meant they also knew: a man who could bleed that kind of money, year after year, deserved respect.
Or fear.

Whether the expense was for the building's survival, or just to buy that fear—that was Macro's department. Always had been.
I came here for her.

Macro hadn't send the message directly.
She worked the back channels—coded drops through Antasia, cutting the mission short.

They had her—the same people who hit us.
She couldn't hand me the coordinates, but the names she slipped, the events she pointed to, all bent in one direction: Prague.

That's why I was here. And from her words that said—she'd figured the whole thing out.

Back when she ran ops for the U.S. Army, she held their global satellite grid in her palm. Every orbit, every feed, every scrap of intel ran under her code. She earned that seat—her own brain put her there. US Army trusted her with that kind of power.
I trust her the same.
If she said she understood, then she did.
No reason for me to chase shadows. My job was to find her.

Every name, every site on my list here reeked of the black market. That's why I called in Rasheed Dameer.

If he could cross-check the threads, trim the fat, we'd get to the core faster. No blood needed. I wasn't here to pile bodies.

One list, short and sharp, dropped on a law desk—that would be enough. And it would keep my word to him intact.

I checked my watch. His flight had already touched down.
I'd booked him into my own place—Hotel Amethyst Prague,
Jan Garrick Masaryk Road.

Left the mansion in my car, chauffeur Michel on the wheel. Masaryk ran cobblestone, narrow. Three cars shoulder to shoulder at best. But both sides were stacked with parked metal, leaving one slit down the center.

—Doesn't that jam it up? *I asked.*

Michel's voice stayed flat.

—No, sir. It's one-way. Nothing comes against you.

We pushed through Prague's stone throat, single lane, city pried open for us.

First time in a long while I walked back into the hotel.
Six floors high, broad across the front.
Not a tower—Prague never liked towers.

High-rises belonged to America. Their architects sold the world on vertical glass and steel, but Europe called it ugly.
Except for a handful of crowded hubs—London, Berlin, Istanbul, Moscow—the skyline here stayed low.
Prague followed the rule.
A few high-rises had gone up, and the locals still sneered at them.
In their eyes, only new money built concrete monsters like those.

So the hotel sprawled wide, not tall. Five floors for rent.
The sixth always sealed off—kept for the owner's use or visiting state guests during festivals.

Rasheed wasn't a dignitary, but he carried the weight of being my guest. That was enough to put him on the top floor,
a presidential suite.

At reception I was told he'd already checked in.
I went straight up, no time wasted.
Two armed guards stood posted outside his door, same as every suite on that floor. Maybe that's why Rasheed didn't even bother locking it.

Inside, the living area sat quiet except for a sound bleeding from the master bath—Rasheed humming a tune under his breath.

Normally that's what women do when the luxury of a fine hotel gets to them. But he carried the quirk just fine.

A minute later he came out—towel on his waist, steam still clinging to his shoulders, stepping through the master bedroom door like he owned the place.

He spotted me, broke into a grin, walking forward like he'd been waiting years to throw this line.

—Hell, look who it is. Count Amethyst Vega, in the flesh.
Hard to wrap my head around it. You know how many times
I risked my ass running your cargo across borders?
Syria, Armenia, Afghanistan—I've carried your flag
more than once. And what did I get for it? Phuket.
Rope around my neck.
Maybe you didn't know me then, but you heard my name.
Didn't buy me an ounce of mercy.
Guess gratitude's gone extinct in this world.

I laughed, couldn't help it. Kept the smile when I shot back,

—Extinct? If I wanted you dead, I could've done it a dozen times.
Instead, here you are, stretched out in a presidential suite.

He worked up a fake scowl, voice dropping low.

—Yeah, I'm here. But the hell I went through before this?
That scar doesn't fade.

I kept it easy.

—Give it time. Pain always burns out in the end.

He stood, cracked the fridge, poured drinks like he was enjoying every second here.

—Then cut the small talk.
Why am I here?
Let's get this moving.

I took the glass from his hand.

—You just landed. Breathe a little.
At least throw on some pants.

He raised his glass, smirking.

—Work with you, even the silk pajamas get trashed.
Don't waste time—just lay it out.

—Fine. *I leaned in.*
—Macro's been taken. A crew's holding her somewhere close.
I've short-listed their nests—every one crawling with smugglers.
I need eyes on them. Anything familiar, any mark you spot, it makes this cleaner for both of us.

I dropped the list on the table. He didn't touch it.
Just stared, face gone dark.

Holding the silence until he finally spoke.

—You can tear through your list if you want.
But I already know where they've got her.

—Really? That makes things easier.

The place he named, I knew it. An old church—tourist trap on weekends, rent-out for weddings, nothing special on the surface. But Rasheed's truth hit harder: hidden chamber, gutted and refit as a club. Their den, wrapped in holy cover.
That was enough. More than enough.

I told Rasheed to stay ready in his suite, then turned back for my mansion.

A few calls would be enough to spark raids on the marked sites.
First ring went to the Police Commissioner.

Been a while since I'd dialed him, but he picked up ready.

—Count Vega. After all this time, you still remember my little girl. That means more than you know.

The sergeant at the airport had clearly carried the message up the ladder. I smiled into the line.

—It goes both ways, Commissioner. I can't keep an eye on everything myself, time cuts short. But thanks to your cooperation, business keeps flowing.

He chuckled.

—That's our duty, sir. Your work puts food on more tables than you know. And next week my daughter's performing at the Grand Theatre. Will you still be in town?

—Is that so? I'd be honored to show up, give Natalie a little encouragement. But you know how it is—business never slows down. If I'm pulled away, pass her my best.

—Of course, of course.

—One small matter, Commissioner—hope I'm not troubling you.

—Not at all, sir. Say what you need. My pleasure.

— You know how it is, Mr. Berzač. Money runs wild in my business—flows every direction, fast enough to make a man dizzy. I am sure you understand. One of my former managers moved funds the wrong way and vanished. Word is, some locals helped—maybe offered shelter. It's sensitive. I can't go public. I've got a shortlist of where they might be hiding.
Would it be too much to ask you to have those places checked? Or should I take it to the Defense Ministry?

His tone sharpened.

—That's... unfortunate. You can go to the Ministry if you wish. But if you think raids on those places, arrests on suspects, would help—then allow me. I can handle it personally.

—That's enough, Mr. Berzač. You're the right man for this—no reason to bother the Ministry.

—Your trust means a lot, sir. I've got two men posted at your gate, round the clock, while you're in town. Pass the details to them. I'll get you answers before the day's out.

—Much appreciated, Mr. Berzač.

—And my thanks to you, sir.

Hard to say if the man was putting on a show.

He was grateful about his daughter, no doubt—but that's another story.

What mattered was this: a father whose kid I'd saved wouldn't hold back when it came time to return the favor.

If I'd told him the truth about Macro, it would've spun a different way. He'd have rattled the sky, kicked off a full-scale sweep, guns out and walls kicked in.

More noise than use. Risk heavier than the payoff.
That's why I bent the story, fed it to him in pieces.

If his team found any connections, or leads on the names or places I'd given him, I could walk in myself, check the ground, talk to the right people, and pull the rest of the thread.

Now it was just a matter of what the police managed to dig out.

—∞—

Hearts on the Hit List

Central Cathedral
Prague, Czech Republic

The dark was coffin-thick, pressing in from every side. Waiting outside that fortress-shaped church was grinding me down, patience sanded to bone.

The cops had already raided every other spot on the list. All they turned up was lowlife—small-time dealers, street pimps. Nothing worth a bullet.

This was the last stop—Rasheed's mark.
An old church built like a castle.
He claimed he'd come here once, with The Maker and Baharram Gazi. Said Baharram had been killed by me—or by one of my blood brothers. I'm sure I didn't kill the man, and there is no such brother existed. So there was no way to know why it happened, or who actually did that.

From the way Rasheed described the fortress, the build inside had to be massive—packed with people, old but decorated like a luxury club.

Yet the cops swore the place hadn't been touched in decades. Strange conflict.

Next to it stood a smaller amphitheater—open for tourists, staging plays through the year.

I'd pressed them to dig again.
Reluctantly, a special team came.

Rasheed refused to show.
No way he'd circle back to a scene packed with uniforms.
I waited alone outside, headlights dead against the stone.

After a while, two cops walked up radios hissing static as they reached my window.

I dropped the glass. One leaned in, deadpan—said they found no sign of a facility. But they'd rigged lights inside, cleared the ground.

If I wanted, I could step in and see it myself.
Of course it had to be seen.
I went in with the cops through the main doors.
One look around and the weight dropped.
A graveyard, nothing more.

The old church still stood, but the bones were brittle—touch a wall and it would crumble. No way in hell anyone could've run the kind of party Rasheed described inside here.

Still, he'd claimed there was a second entrance at the back.
I asked to see it.
The cops, all polite, drove me around.

The rear looked worse.
One of them even popped an umbrella over my head
so the falling dirt wouldn't land in my hair.
Past that entrance there was no towering hall, nothing hidden.
Just broken walls that looped back into the same ruined nave.

No—this wasn't the place.
And Rasheed wasn't the type to invent stories.
Which left me thinking: had he hallucinated that night?
I knew certain men, wicked enough, could spin hallucinations into reality. It wasn't impossible.

I'd have to bring it back to Rasheed, talk it through again.
Not that I'd come this far on his word alone—I had my own leads. They'd looked promising. In reality, just dead ends.

I thanked the cops, slid back into my car.
Rasheed was still at the hotel.

I told Michel to take me there.
Closed my eyes in the back seat, let the whole chain of events loop in my head.

All I needed was a sliver—some thin link, a person or an object, something to connect the pieces.

Our private server tracked all of us live.
I could see Gobi and Sahara now, miles away,
and they could see me—permissions open both ways.

Macro had the same system running.
Now she was offline.
Her last signal flagged at our restaurant in Penang.
She'd built the tracking herself, but the device was mine—
undetectable, impossible to kill. So why wasn't she showing up?

The pressure behind my eyes tightened, muscles ready to throb.
I forced it down, leaned back against the seat, tried to relax.

The phone chimed.
Sharp.
Tung.
Chimed again, too soon.

I nearly let it go, but if it was urgent, I couldn't risk it.

Screen flashed.
Marisha. Miss.

<Still mad at me, husband?
Who are you chasing through Prague's alleys?
I'm not even there.>

So she knew I was here, knew I was running Macro's trail.
If she was reaching out herself, I needed to see if it was personal—or professional.

I straightened and typed back:

<Don't you have bigger things to do than stalk me?
Anyway—when did I get promoted?
Didn't even notice it, but apparently the whole damn world did.>

Her reply snapped back.

<Promoted?>

<From boyfriend to husband.>

I could hear the smirk behind her words.

<Since you disappeared in Phuket.
Couldn't handle it—I married you in my head.>

<Then maybe keep it in your head. No reason to broadcast it. >

<Oh, right. So you can run around with every girl you want while I play the good wife and stay silent? That the plan?>

<And telling the world changes what, exactly?
By your own logic, I'm already guilty.>

<You're not that kind of man, love.
I overreacted. Sorry x 100.>

<Sorry doesn't fix everything.
But at least you said it.
Can we meet?>

<Thank you, thank you.
But how do we even meet?
I really did go home.>

<Yeah, I bet. Easier to run your spy games from there.
But can you at least call me now?>

<I'm not spying. Warlords like you, private manufacturers—
every move you make is tracked anyway.
I just read the tea leaves.
If I don't call right now, are you going to sulk?>

<Damn right I will.>

<Fine... give me ten minutes.>

The car rolled up to the hotel. Upstairs, I dropped the results of today's run, and Rasheed's jaw hung open.

Barely found his tongue:

—Cops didn't just take a bribe and feed us bullshit?

I fixed him with a steady look.
—I went there myself.
Checked it clean.

That made him stall—"Oh…"—hung there for a beat, then:

—I don't get how that's even possible.
You think I cooked up a story?

I leaned back into the sofa, slow.

—Feels like nothing to me.
Found no link at all. That's the truth.
Now let's think on what's next.

Before he could answer, the phone cut in.
Not even ten minutes.
Marisha's name flashed bright.
She was quick this time.

I picked up, told Rasheed he could step out or use the bedroom—
I had a personal call to take.

He gave me that sly devil's grin.

—Whose call? That stunner of yours in KL?

—Not yours to know.

That settled it—he chose outside.

I watched him leave, then answered Marisha's call.

—Hello…

—Hello. Asalim… Shakarim… Borlagim…

—What the hell's that supposed to mean?

—You know damn well. I taught you those words myself.

—I didn't ask for translations.
I'm asking what your little stunt means.

—What stunt?
Didn't like how close you got with that girl—Antasia.
I got pissed and left.
But now I see it wasn't your fault.

You already explained it.
I overreacted. That's on me.

—Looks like GRU had trained you in twisting words same as everything else. But if you think you can play me—or worse, if you let someone else pull the strings—you'll find it ends bad. For you, and for them.

—My, my. Was that a threat?

—I don't threaten. I warn.
Before I set things in motion. And you know that.

—What kind of 'things' you talking about?

—I'll torch every one of your units in Europe.
No secret stays buried.

—Shame on you—filth like that from your mouth?
Half of them call you brother-in-law. Why burn them all?

—Then stop circling. Say what you mean.

—What, I twisted something? Please.
When you lose your temper, your head goes.
Who knows what you might actually do.
Fine—ask. I'll quit the tricks.

—What was your actual plan—dragging me in?
Or something worse?

—There was no plan.
The night we met was pure coincidence.
But yeah, I lied about my friends.
They were actually unit crew.
I leaned on them for cover.
If I'd told you that, you would've walked.
I liked you. That's why I lied.

—And after that? You expect me to believe someone in your rank just drifts into romance with no orders, no clearance?
Your HQ approved that?

—No. They drill us to kill emotions.
But training can't strip the human out.
First night with you, that was my call.
Next day, I logged it in my report.
—After that I tried to burn you off—made up the story that I was with someone else, thought you'd lose taste and walk.

—Would've been better if it stayed that way.
Why'd you come back clawing?

—Because of the analysts. Lazy bastards.
I filed my report at seven sharp in the evening.
They sat on it till sunrise.
By the time they moved, I'd already pushed you away.
Then the Director himself called—told me to take it further.
But by then, the shot was fired. No way to walk it back.
All because those idiots took all night to figure out who you actually were. That's how everything got tangled.

—And then? What truth your people discover that made them so eager to hand you over like a bride?

—Ha! If a good groom turns up, every parent gets eager.
They said you were Caesar.
The ghost every agency once bled to find.
Disappeared for years, no trail, nothing.
They said you'd never surfaced this openly before.

—And knowing that, you still played lover with a killer?
You didn't cuff me, didn't drag me back to your den—why?

—Have you lost your mind?
Caesar was my crush—that's why I wouldn't hand you off.
I wanted to check if you are real.
But the profiler's data didn't match you. Not even close.
That's when doubt hit. Still, I kept it from the office.
If they'd seen the cracks, they would've yanked me out.
I didn't want that happen.

The line carries her breath before the words.

—Then you vanished. Left me with nothing.
HQ told me to let it go, focus on other targets.
But you'd told me—wait in Phuket.
By then I was drowning in you.
—Nothing else in the world mattered.
It got ugly with the office.
That kind of breach puts you on the red list.
Which means one of two things—get eliminated, or dragged to trial. I took the threats, every one of them, and still hunted you like a madwoman. Even my family heard.
They feared disgrace, feared death.
Only my mother called—told me to hold the line.
There are knots in my family I can't untangle with words.
When this is over, I'll take you to Samara.
You'll see for yourself.

I stay quiet, let her lay it out.

—If not for your Chinese friend, Phuket would've been a hell.
They couldn't touch me because of him.

—I asked them to keep eyes on you, Marisha.
And after that... GRU just accepted you tied to Caesar?

—Accepted? Not a chance.
I told them Caesar had gone dark again.
Chapter closed. Now I'm supposedly head over heels.
For the Romanian warlord—Count Amethyst Vega. Ha!

Her laugh was razor sharp.

—That lie came from thin-lipped Tommy, didn't it?

—Why snap at every word?
Just because Tommy talks, you think I dance to his tune?

—Then why are you dancing, hoax?

—Hoax? Please. First shock was when you handed me your phone to save my number. Wallpaper flashed Vega's logo.
But I already know Elijan worked for some Chinese tycoon, the rough kind of jobs.

—Seeing that logo, I thought—Elijan lied.
Maybe he was working for Vega all along.
Then you walked me into the bank yourself.
Logged in as Amethyst Vega.
Pulled gear from your own locker.
Cheating a bank under a false name—that's near impossible.
I knew it from my own work with security forces.
Later, when you were in the hospital, your crew told me everything. After that, I stopped pretending—just told HQ flat out: I'm in love with Amethyst Vega.

Her laugh sliced again, cold as steel.

—And your unit were already watching Vega?

—Of course. Your weapons research facility was flagged long ago. Moscow already knew the rep on your military-grade prototypes.

—So what? Whoever I am, I'd never hand my prototypes to an imperialist state like Russia.

—We knew that. Which is why we didn't push into your business. No point. But our Director guessed—if a Russian beauty was orbiting your head day and night, at least you wouldn't sell weapons to anyone looking to wound Russia.

—Hm. His guess was right.

—Of course. That's why he's the Director.

—So the love-game was fear—or greed—for weapons?

—You keep throwing it wrong.
I've had brutal training, but my heart's not stone.
I still feel pain. I can even feel insult.

—You acted under orders—that's why I said it.
Where's the shame in that?
Seduction, leverage, pulling secrets—that's not your first op, and it won't be your last.
Still, I'll give you this: even if duty kept it alive,
your performance blurred the line.

Half the time, it wasn't just a show.
As a seasoned actress—you were damn convincing.

—You've watched too many thrillers.
That's why you're dreaming in technicolor.
—You think I'm a commanding officer out on the street hustling people myself? I have thousands under me for that.

—Thousands? At your age you're already a commanding officer?

—My family's deep in politics. I had my own drive too.
I'm not as disposable as you think.
And trust me—I didn't shake my ass to get this far.

—Ha. You still remember that line.

—Whoever slaps may forget.
The face that takes it—never so easy.

—True. And I said sorry for that.

—You apologized for the first one. But you keep slapping with your words—again and again. Makes it hard to forget.

—What now? What did I just say?

—You called me a seasoned actress. Said it was all an act.

—It wasn't, sweetheart. I know that. I just don't get how you managed to balance me with the job.

—You'll never know how brutal it was, waiting that long while the work piled behind me. What I had to eat just to hold on—you can't imagine.

—Maybe not know, but I can guess.
Still—why keep it all locked inside?
We had the time. You could've told me.

—What would it change? If I'd spilled everything, you'd still see me as the girl who danced her ass on stage for drunken men.

—God damn—one line like that and you'd nail me to the wall.
Haven't I ever said anything good?

—Not that I remember. And I know why you don't trust me.
You think if a conflict of interest ever came up, I'd flip to my people and leave you behind.
But why don't you think of the other side?
If that moment came—I could flip the whole world and stand with you. Why can't you believe that?

—I'm a damn fool, that's why I can't.
And Marisha, it's complicated.
If your agency even sniffs what I'm working on now,
they'll go rabid. All the pressure falls on you—hard.
They'll squeeze you for intel, and if you can't give it up,
your life's on the line. Do you see any way out of that?

—No. Even if I quit the job, family pressure keeps me tied to the state. Some role would always be forced on me. But I found a way through. If you could drop some of that anger, maybe we could fix it.

—When did I lash out? I believe in talking things through, not throwing punches.

—Don't tickle me with pretty lines.
Back in those days, I could've sent someone else to you.
We've got plenty of women who could've built a friendly tie.
Maybe even love. But I chose you.
For me, it wasn't duty—it was like skipping out on the office just to spend time with a lover. A thrill.
In Phuket, I played you thinking you were Caesar.
But nothing about you matched that ghost.
I showed up as the helpless girl,
and what you did for me—I couldn't square it.
Even now, the man they painted as the brutal warlord behind Vega Corporation—I don't see him in you.
Instead, I catch myself shivering at the thought that someone this kind, this warm-hearted, still exists.
None of the profiler notes match what I found.
Tell me, love—are you really that thug, that ruthless warlord, or just wearing his name?

—There are more faces, more names to me than the profilers can imagine. But the man you know—that's who I'll always be for you. The rest doesn't matter. Just don't tell your people about the link between Vega and Caesar. That'll only drag misery on us.

—Ha… what do you take me for?
I've survived this world without being brain-dead.
—And between husband and wife, some secrets are better left in bed, aren't they?

She laughed, soft and wicked.

—Thanks, Marisha. I just wonder if being tied to me lands you in fresh trouble. How does your agency see your link to Vega?

—They try to know you better. If you were any other kind of tycoon, not in weapons, they'd let it slide. America, Europe, Russia, China—those are the real players in arms manufacturing.
The rest—they just run factories or handle logistics.
They're not the source. That's why GRU ignores them.
But every other independent death dealer in this game, outside those giants? We keep tabs. Always.
GRU knows how savage warlords get when revenge burns.
And your history with the Americans? That crossed the line.

—I figured they buried that. Your people know the story too.

—Not everything can be buried.
I was in Syria when it went down.
We picked it apart back then.

—Hmm… sometimes things like that are done as advertisement.
I'm not the only shot-caller in the company, Marisha.
It's bigger than you can imagine.
That's why authority has been delegated—others can act on their own. But I can tell you this—whatever decision is made, it's based on justice. If someone didn't deserve it, it wouldn't have happened.

—I still can't believe you're Amethyst Vega.
Nothing people say about him matches you.
But his crew, his whole setup—they all treat you like Vega.

—I can't wrap my head around it.
That's why I keep circling back, asking again.

—I'm not Amethyst Vega, Marisha. He rarely steps into the light.
But he's someone I trust with my life—someone worth dying for.
And he trusts me, fully. That's why everyone else accepts me.
Think of it that way and you'll stop wrestling with it.
But if these words leak, neither of us walks away.
That's why I tried to keep you away. Do you understand the risk?

—I do. But there's little chance of that.
If everyone accepts you as Vega, why would I say different?
And loving you, openly, as Vega—it only makes my life easier.
I get something out of it. Ha.

—Then why hunt me in KL? How did you even know I'd be here?
You were supposed to wait in Phuket.

—I was in Phuket. But when you didn't show, they tried to reel me back in. I refused. Then the state leaned on your Chinese man—tried to push him into setting me up, handing me over.
He warned them it'd mean a bloodbath.
GRU and the Americans knew you, but the Chinese didn't.
That made me a liability. Overeager hands could've snapped from Cheng's own side, so he told me to disappear.
I was getting ready to go dark when the word came you'd been spotted in Malaysia.

—That was bullshit. Where I was, no one could've spotted me.

—How would I know? The number you gave me—others in the East Asia Wing had it too. Like I said, plenty of them call you brother-in-law. They knew about us.
One of them, a girl, was in Kuala Lumpur for a trade conference.
She spotted your number go active online.
She knew I was hunting you, so out of pure curiosity she dialed it.
And shockingly—you were sitting just two rows in front of her.
You even picked up, exchanged a few words.
She was sure enough to tell me.
That's why I came straight to Kuala Lumpur.

—My god—what a twisted mess.
But worse than that, being married to a spy sounds like hell.
No way to sneak around.
If any of the in-laws ever catch me once, I'm finished.

—What? You're planning to cheat?

—Hell no. I just want to see your ass-shaking dance.
You'll show me, won't you?

—Trying to bait me, huh? Don't joke about women with me.
I'm warning you—you'll get yourself in serious trouble.

—Fine. I'll joke only about men then.
But you still haven't told me—what was the solution?

—When I got to Kuala Lumpur looking for you, I got myself caught up in trouble. Remember I told you about my missing sister?

—Of course. I was the one who pulled her out and sent her back.
After that I asked if she made it home, but when I tried,
you snapped at me instead.

—Why wouldn't I? Such a massive thing, and you didn't even think your wife needed to know? That's why.

—Your sister was in the hands of extremists.
I didn't want you dragged in, so I handled it quiet.
I figured once she was safe, you'd know soon enough.

—She was my cousin. She worked for external affair department—the same ones you know as SVR.
Like you said, she was investigating those extremists.
That was her unit. Maybe she found something huge,
but before she could report it, her own team lost her.
Extremists are advanced now, tech-wise.
They must have stripped her tracker. We'd almost lost hope.
Then I got a lead, went searching, and ended up captured myself.
And you, sweetheart—you rescued both of us. After that, having a powerful in-law on our side softened my agency's stance.

—When the Director learned I was involved with Amethyst Vega, he flew to Kuala Lumpur himself.

She pauses, then goes on.

—Wiped the old mess, told me to focus on you. When I told him I was serious about you, he advised me to step back from field duty. Because out in the field, conflict of interest can break any minute. Missions might even throw me against you.
—That's why he told me to switch into administrative work. Safer. It keeps the door open for us.
He said—wait six months, then marry you. In that time, he'd erase my record from the service. So when it's official,
I could build a life with you without shadows.

—Good advice. But why's your Director so generous?

— Why are you always so suspicious? Ha.
He's my uncle. After my father died, he raised us.

—Oh... In that case, the generosity makes sense.
Still—was he sure I was a good match for you?

—In our family, marrying outsiders is taboo. No one's done it yet. So even he wasn't sure. You could say he only gave in under pressure from the bride. Heh.

—Hm. That doesn't surprise me. The same bride's pressure seems to be forcing the groom too.

—What? You mean you're not willing?
That I pushed this relationship on you?

—Not like that. It's just... the speed. I'm struggling to catch up.
It would've been better if we'd slowed down—really known each other first.

—Keep your time. Don't forget where I come from.
Our motto is simple—hammer the nail or nail the hammer
if it doesn't move. And in my life, I've never found such a nail
to hammer like you. Six months—that's the deal. Not a day more.

—Still, I think it's best if you talk with your family first.

—Of course. That's part of the plan.
The Director said you'll have to come to Moscow.
Meet the key people. Promise you won't stand in the way of any state operation. And if possible—move your factory from Astana to Russia. That would win you favor. After that, we move to Samara. You'll meet my mother. She hasn't given her opinion yet, but I know she won't go against my choice.

—Hm. I'm not against any state mission that serves the people. I'll even help where I can. But if they think that means I'll stay quiet about their crooks, their cartels—they're dreaming.

—You blow up the second someone innocent in your circle gets hit. We know that. If it happens again, don't go full warlord—just tell us. We'll take care of it. You won't face a thing.
Like with Antasia. You were ready to spill blood, and the Director settled it with one call. That's how it'll be handled from now on.

—You mean calling that bastard from Zamuk?
He thought I'd been caught screwing around with Antasia and you'd nailed me for it.

—Not his fault. That's how it was fed to him.
The Director knew—if the girl got freed, you'd send her back home. If anyone blocked it, all hell would break loose.
He told me: ignore Antasia, treat you normal.
What I didn't expect was how possessive I'd already grown.
My own spite muddied the water.
For a clean solution, the Director himself called that fool.
Yeah, there was a risk—you'd figure out who I was.
But hiding forever from a man like you was never possible.
So he took that risk.

—Alright. It worked. Talking's cleaner than killing.
But answer me this—if you could solve it with a call, why smash those men up?

—Hah. One of those brats called me 'bitch' the first day we met—remember? I held onto that. And there wasn't time to play it safe.
I knew you were still healing. Wasn't taking chances.
I had to shut it down fast.

—You did me a favor for sure, love.
But breaking a man's bone over one word? That's too much.
Maybe you should give me a list of trigger words—so I know what not to say, before you break me too.

—Hah. Like you're scared of me.

—Wasn't before. Now I am.
How the hell do I live with a wife this lethal?

—Beautifully. Just keep a hundred arms' distance from American whores, and anyone else who dares step close—I'll size them down myself.

—Why not size down the Americans too?

—Because then it stops being personal. That drags in the state. My rage turns into a national incident. That's why.

—Yeah... fair enough. Don't worry.
Americans never did it for me anyway.

—Oh really... then what kind do it for you?

—The kind who know how to move their ass.
After we marry, you'll give me a private show, won't you?

—Ugh. Filthy bastard. Maybe I should rethink marrying a man with a mind like yours.

—Fine, think about it. Ha.
But your sister—I need her. Can I see her?

—If you want, I can arrange it. But she's not in shape to talk.
Her body's coming back, but her mind... nearly gone.
You saw what they did to her. Brutal.
By the way—what did you do to the ones who tortured her?

—What else? Lit fire under their asses.

—Good. Very good, Shakarim. But tell me—were you really hurt that bad when you came for me that day?

—No. That was another issue. But because of it, I found where you were—and brought you out.

—In that condition you still forced yourself into the job?
You had no police, no networks to lean on?
You could've sent your own crew.

—There wasn't time. And I'm used to doing my own work.

—Then drop that habit.
Don't forget—you've got a whole wife now.
Leave everything to others except the bedwork with me. Ha.

—Hm. I'll think about it. Still, one thing keeps scratching at me.

—What thing, Volchik?

—You had the whole agency's resources,
plus your own skill—I saw it firsthand.
And yet, a tiny extremist crew caught you?
How?

—Hahaha. Why are you sweating the small threads, darling?
Shouldn't you be worrying about things a little more urgent...
and a lot more interesting?

—Things like...?

—Like the fact we've only had sex twice, and just for one night.
I'm thinking, from now on—how to push it to three,
maybe four times, every damn night.

—Lord! who's got time for that right now?

—Time or not, I don't care. That night in Phuket, in that second
round—when you clawed into me like you'd tear me apart,
I want that heat every fucking night, you get me?

—Fine. If I'm up for it, I'll try. But I still want my answer.

—Ugh... alright. I'll give it.
I was losing my mind hunting you, no trace, no hope.
I was falling apart. And my Zamuk source flipped on me.
I can't give you all the details now. Maybe face to face.

—Alright.

—No. Not alright.

—What's not?

—From now on—burn this into your head.

—What?

—If you ever see me caught—or even hear about it—don't come charging in like a lunatic.

—Why the hell not? I love you.
And as long as I'm breathing, nobody's taking you from me.

—Fuck, Volchik, I am feeling wet... your lines makes me want to pin you down right now. Say it again.
I could hear it a hundred times and still not get enough.

—What's the big deal? Lovers talk like that all the time.

—Maybe. But I never gave anyone permission to talk to me like that—only you. That's why, hearing those words in your voice... it cuts deeper.

—And you're the only one for me, Marisha.

—Damn, you're driving me insane.
I want to tear through this phone and get to you.

—Ha—not that kind of tech yet.

—Of course not. Those lazy tech bastards never invent what actually matters.

—Forget them. Tell me again—why shouldn't I come for you.

—Because not everything can be spoken. Just know this:
Spets only gets caught when they wants to be caught.

—Ohh... so I was right. You let yourself get caught by that crew—just to trace your sister, didn't you?

—Exactly, sweetheart.
She worked for SVR, I already told you that.
Which means talking about her drags in a lot of classified shit.
Not my place to spill someone else's secrets.

—Yeah... fair enough. But... how the hell did you know I was running around Prague's alleys?

—Ugh—look at you, paranoid as ever, but calling me the spy.
Reports on you landed in every agency inbox.
Here—I just sent our copy to your phone.

—Read it yours:
'The infamous Romanian warlord, Z-grade weapons researcher and manufacturer, Count Amethyst Vega, has been leading police raids across Prague in search of his manager, accused of embezzling funds. Details of the embezzlement remain unclear, but Count Vega himself was present with local police to supervise the raids. Approved for deeper investigation.
Station Chief, Prague, Czech Republic.'

—Lord! Don't these people have anything better to do?
A whole agency with lizard eyes glued to my ass.
Feels like paparazzi nonsense.

—Oh, you didn't know? Plenty of paparazzi work for agencies like ours. So—what's the truth? Who are you actually hunting?

—Not now. I'll drop you some leads.
You dig into them—if you come back with something,
I'll talk. If not, you don't need to know.

—Unbelievable. Even with your wife, you tack on conditions.
How the hell am I supposed to live with a man like this?

—Marisha.

—...Yeah?

—Thanks. For telling me the truth.

—No reason to lie, Volchik.
When this job's done—can I come see you?

—I can't say yet. Finish your word, then tell me where you stand.
I'll decide then.

—I miss you.

—I miss you too.

—Really? How much?

—Feels like a lot.

—Feels like? You're not sure?

—Feels like I'm sure.

—What the hell kind of answer is that? Say it clear.

—Fine. Clear—I've missed you.

—When? Why?

—Lord, do you interrogate everything? Missing you is the point.

—Alright, alright.

—Now hang up. I've got work.

—Work and talk with me. What's the problem?

—Uff. How am I supposed to work and talk at the same time?
You'll drag my focus.

—Then keep your focus on me—problem solved.

—No. Nothing solved. The work won't get done if I do.

—Why grind yourself down? Don't you have people?
Tommy, Gobi, Sahara—where are they?

—They're busy with their own jobs. And I need to handle mine.

—No. Give me your location. I'll send my crew.
Whatever you want done, they'll do it exactly.

—Ohhh... GRU operatives dropping their assignments to do mine?

—Why not? They'd jump to it for their brother-in-law.
And free of charge.

—Amazing. Maybe I'll bring in a few CIA officers too. With this many in-laws, I won't have to lift a finger—worldwide coverage.

—What? Didn't you just say you weren't into American girls?
Now you're dreaming about those fat-ass CIA whores?
Say the word and I'll snap your neck.
No—better, I'll break bone by bone.

—What the hell! Weren't you just professing love?
And now you're breaking my bones?

—Idiot. Not yours. Theirs. I'll break those bitches in half.

—Hahaha! Talking to you is the best stress relief.
Thanks, sweetheart.

—You're welcome, Xayotim.
That's why I keep saying—talk to me more. You'll feel better.

—Alright. I'll call whenever I can. Hanging up now.

—You really going to hang up?

—Yes, really. And don't forget—I'm giving you an assignment.
Once you've dug through it fast, we'll talk again.

—Ohh right, I almost forgot. Fine, send me the details now.

—Hang up first, or I won't. I need to pull the files together.
Otherwise you won't understand a thing.

—Ahh, fine—I'm really hanging up. I love you!

—Okay. Take care.

—Fucking care—say it back, you dumb of a man.
Say 'I love you too.'

—I love you too.

—Mmm, good. Now it's right. Bye.

I ended the call and waited for Rasheed to come back.
I'd just tested Marisha—dropped her a line of sensitive intel.

A pure acid test..
Any security agency would lunge at bait like that.
Small outfits would frame it as a threat to fix.
But giants like CIA or GRU—they'd care less about solving it, more about seizing it. This would show exactly what kind of pressure she faced, and what she did with it.

During the call, Rasheed had stepped out for air.
Half an hour gone, still no sign. His tracker pinged way too far for a casual walk.

Something was off.
I decided to check it myself.

In Prague, my cover was VIP-level—couldn't just storm out and draw heat. That's why the hotel basement had its own tricks, built for times like this.

I pulled the Honda CB500 out of the basement.
Slipped through a back alley, avoiding the main gate.
Black paint, nothing flashy—on Prague's streets it blended like background noise. Fast enough for real distance, helmet masking my face, it let me move anywhere unseen.

Rasheed's signal pointed to the city's edge—a reserve forest, thick and empty. Map showed three hospitals and a cluster of research labs out there.

Mid-ride, the phone broke through—priority ringtone.
Sahara.

I ducked into a side lane, engine off, checked the screen.

One missed call, several messages.
I opened the texts first.

Sahara reported: Mr. Payman Habib had reached out.
Wanted to talk, urgent. He'd sent me Habib's private number too.
I'd ignored the inbox too long, so he called to force my eyes to it.

After all this time, what did Habib want now?
Fine. I dialed.

—Peace be upon you, brother. Who's speaking?

—Not much peace on my end, Mr. Habib. But thanks for the blessing. I'm the one you've been hunting.

—Forgive me... Mr. Caesar. May Almighty keep you.
Thank you for calling back.

—And thank you, Mr. Habib. I should've asked after your health and such, but time's tight. What's so urgent?

—We figured you're buried in complex matters,
so we didn't bother you before. But now there's trouble.

—Awadi's gone missing. Normally, we talk almost every day, even just a word. But it's been three days. No contact.
I tried reaching out, his phone's dead.
Today I called his residence landline.
Family says he drove out alone three days back
and never came home. They've informed local police.
Still, I felt you had to know.

—You did the right thing, Mr. Habib. Normally, if he left the country—or even traveled far inside it—would he inform you?

—Yes, always. After Phuket, none of us travel alone.
Even within our own country, if we go far, we inform each other.

—Then yes, this is cause for concern.
Alright, I'll see what I can do. Where are you now?

—Back home, Mr. Caesar. And I'll admit—I'm afraid.
Worried they might vanish me next.

—Dubai's a marketplace. You can't rule that out.
Tell me—ever heard the name Vega Securities in your city?

—Of course. I know the Romanian gentleman's office.
A little about his business too.
But we've never had trouble with him.
Even our Finance Ministry leaves his bigger deals alone.

—Then don't worry about that. You'll go in person to that office.
Ask for Miss Macro Neil. She probably won't be there now,
but they'll test you—they'll ask why you need her. Say this:
'From Al-Madam, the wind is stripping the sand off my desert plot, and I need her help to hold it.'
That's all. They'll handle the rest.

—Yes, sir. I'm no fool like brother Awadi. I've got some brains of my own. Just from your words, I can already guess what's about to play out. Thank you for everything, Mr. Caesar.
If there's anything I need to do, tell me.

—You'll hear from me, Mr. Habib. For now, that's it.

—Alright. May Almighty keep you safe.

The news hit like a blade on cold meat.

Things were already twisted enough—now Rasheed had vanished on his "walk," and on top of that, Awadi's gone missing too. The two of them had a thin line of contact, one Rasheed himself didn't even realize yet.
First I had to find him.

Forty minutes later, I hit the spot. And the air was wrong—every sense on edge. His tracker placed him deep inside the reserve forest.

Before I stepped in, the place reminded me of the bunker in KL.
Who knew if I'd find something like that waiting here.
But instead, the forest opened to a sight that nearly burned with envy—a castle, three stories high, perfect as a painting,
twin towers rising on each side. The stonework so intricate
I felt like touching it, proof of the artist's hand.
As ancient as the building I kept in Prague.

And at the gates of that beauty—two ugly cockroaches with guns, pacing back and forth. Their kind spoiled the view like rot in silk.
Calling the police would've cleared them out, sure.
But would that slow me down? That was the calculation.

My pocket buzzed before I could decide—phone buzzing hard against my leg.

It's Marisha.
Calling this fast—what the hell had she heard already?

I took a step back and answered.

—Where are you?

—In Prague, obviously. You know that—and by your account, half the city does too.

—Cut the attitude. That man Rasheed Dameer—he work for you?

—For now, yeah. How do you know him?

—Professional circles. Word just came in—one of my contacts picked him up outside Hotel Amethyst Prague.

Soon as I heard, I knew something was off. So I called.
You know him, Count Amethyst Vega? Heh.

—You mocking me? I brought Rasheed here.
He was with me until minutes ago.
I only sent him out because you called. Now he's gone.

—Not my doing. The job hit a crew I know—out of Tel Aviv.
Tell me, love—what exactly makes Mossad sniff around you?

—Death haunts every kingdom. Maybe that's what brings them.

—What the hell does that mean?

—Something you wouldn't understand. And drop the games.
Whoever took Rasheed, I'm standing at their gate right now.
Was about to snap a few necks and drag him back when you called.

—You're serious? Then my timing's perfect.
Don't do anything stupid, Shakarim.
Our dance with the Czechs is always a mess—too close to ignore,
too bitter to accept. They can hurt us if they choose,
and if we want, we can gut them right back.
To keep it real, we station tactical crews inside their walls
at all times. Where you're standing—that's one of ours.

She hesitates, then continues.

—In that unit, there's a Russian kid I know.
Off the books, he does a little work for me.
Think of him like a kid brother—name's Thima.
Hold back the bone-breaking for now.
I'll tell him to hand your man over in one piece. Just wait.

—Oh, I see. That explains it. You've always had your sweet little 'kid brothers' to kiss up and handle things for you—I've seen it before. Guess this one fits the bill.

—For fuck's sake. You picking fights like some jealous wife now?

—I just said what I saw. Hardly a lie.

—Truth incarnate, aren't you? Never could manage a lie. Fine—when I text, head to the gate. No violence. Straight to Thima. If you don't trust it, patch me in on the phone.

—Of course, miss... whatever you say.

And before I could throw another word, she cut the call. That's how she handled it whenever I pressed too close—slam the door, make me eat the silence.

Inside, the castle had been gutted and rebuilt into something closer to an underground club than a home.
The ground floor was a haze of shadows and colored light—pool tables in one corner, poker games in another.
Dead center, a bar polished to professional gleam.
I cut straight past, heading for the desk staged like a throne.

The boss sat there, arranged so he could sweep the whole room with his eyes. Above him, a stained-glass ceiling sprawled in gaudy colors, as if it was meant to crown his delusion of power.

The man himself—grey in beard, eyes red from smoke, stinking of hash—looked like anything but Marisha's so-called "kid brother." If he'd married young, he'd already have daughters old enough to fill this room.

Marisha's message had been my ticket at the gate.
The armed guards didn't try to block me, didn't bother to escort me either.

Same inside—the oddball gamblers looked up once, then buried themselves back in their games, like someone told them not to care.

I followed my own guesswork all the way here, hoping the table at the center meant someone worth talking to.

The old stoner squinted at me for a long beat, then pulled out a smile he probably thought looked sly.

—What fortune, Count Vega, to have you in this poor man's hall.
Please—sit. Thima's gone upstairs to fetch your man.
He'll be down any moment.

I took the chair across from him, the reek of weed slamming straight into my nose. He offered me a drink—I waved it off.

He didn't care, just leaned closer, eyes fogged.

—Don't even ask, Count Dracula. The game's dirty.
Gotta keep the Jewish uncles smiling, sometimes we play their hand. They wanted your boy picked up, and my crew took him in. But then Thima tells me Spets want him released—says he's yours. You see my problem, Lord?
On one side, the Jewish cash cows.
On the other, Spetsnaz hammer.
They taught us as kids: if death hunts you, maybe you've got three months left.
If Spets hunts you, you've got twenty-four hours.
I swallowed your man—and I'm spitting him back out within the hour. Heh! Heh!

I didn't join his laugh. Just sat heavy, temper rising. I was seconds from snapping when I saw movement on the stairs.

Rasheed Dameer. Coming down stiff, his face locked shut.
He didn't say a word—just walked up, posted at my side.

Behind him came the lanky kid, tattoo streaking his arm—this had to be Thima, Marisha's so called "kid brother."

The kid had rings inked across every finger, tattoos circling them like metal bands. Both wrists stacked with bracelets—two sets, same design.

Russians and their obsession with ink.
I'd have to ask Marisha about it sometime.
Though I'd never seen any on her.
Maybe she kept hers buried under makeup.
Maybe she never needed to wear her scars on the skin.

His nose was long, bent at the bridge—birth mark.
He tilted his head, smirk riding his face.

—Hey, cumnat. Word is, you're supposed to be some prince.
Truth is, you're not half as handsome as the stories say.

I didn't blink.

—As long as I'm better-looking than you, I can live with that.

Cumnat—Romanian for brother-in-law.
One word, and the punk showed his cards.
He knew my cover, knew what tied me to Marisha.

Just like the old stoner, he offered a drink.
I waved it off, took his hand instead, ready to close this fast.
But he didn't let go.

His grip tightened, voice dropped low.

—Keep your man close.
Even if we didn't finish the job, Mossad will.
They don't miss.
We're letting him walk, and that's a risk.
Just make sure when you're gone,
the cops don't come crashing down on us.
Fair enough, brother-in-law?

I mirrored his head tilt, gave it back cold.

—If they come crashing, it's for your own dirt, not mine.
You can count on that.

He laughed, jerking his head like he'd enjoyed the taste of it.

I didn't stick around to share it.
Grabbed Rasheed and got the hell out.

—∞—

The Branded Crocodile

Hotel Amethyst Prague
Czech Republic

Rasheed Dameer slipping the bag wasn't Jovan's burden to carry. Phuket had his guys pinned, Middle East crews bled dry.

Command dumped the grab on local assets.
They got him—then fucked it up. Street hitters cut him loose.
A couple of them wound up on the ground.
That was in the report, if it isn't just smoke.

Jovan didn't buy any of it. Still, there was no way to press harder—those locals weren't Mossad hounds. So he flew in.

Sun bleeding out over Prague.
Lobby lights warming up like stage spots.
Jovan sat under a chandelier too soft for this city, running the op in his head like a drill that already failed.

He wasn't under any illusions. Rasheed wasn't walking into his hands here. And if he did, he'd still be untouchable.

The hotel was sealed tight. Not lobby props—mercs with knife scars on their necks, thumbs twitching from trigger habit.
Jovan tagged every one of them before his coffee hit the table.

Daggan's boys were in place.
Calm. Unarmed.
Hotel rules—guns off at the door.
If it went loud now, they'd be pulp before the second shot.

Forget pulling Rasheed—if the man strolled over himself,
Jovan's only play would be: "Evening. Nice weather."
And nothing more.

This wasn't just another luxury hotel in central Prague.
It belonged to Count Amethyst Vega. Romanian arms king.
The branded crocodile of Eastern Europe.

Back in Tel Aviv, they called men like him dealers.
But Mossad files didn't touch his scale.

Jovan had seen dealers back home—some elected, some dressed as politicians, most just tycoons in sharp suits.
They moved stolen stock from state factories.

Vega wasn't one of them.
He was the factory. The rich bastard ran his own labs.
No black market middlemen. No agency to lean on.

Jovan couldn't get near his villa.
No way to sneak into the private labs either.
That left the hotel. And even then—just the lobby.

Open to the public—but sanitized. You walked in naked.
Drop your steel at the desk, or stay outside.

Jovan figured Prague's top cop could swing some breathing room. The guy drank whiskey in Tel Aviv with Defense Minister Zibram. Should've been a done deal.
Instead? Dead air. Call cut mid-sentence.
An hour later the chief resigned. Cited "personal reasons."

Jovan didn't need a translator. He knew the game.
Tried to pet a crocodile just to see if it bites.
Now he was standing in its throat, unarmed.

In other cities, he could tug strings.
Call in a favor, grease a deputy, nudge the precinct.
Prague didn't play.
If it went hot here, it would be bone-on-bone.
No safety net. No spin room.

Daggan made it clear: his boys would bleed if ordered.
Didn't matter who the enemy was or how hard it bit.
He meant it. And Jovan felt it. Not pride. Not ego.
Just the cold fire of knowing why the map still called it Israel.
Because men like this still stood when they knew death was smiling in their face around the corner.

The first tech team had rotated home.
Debriefed and cleared in Tel Aviv.
New blood sat in Prague now—wired, hungry.
Fresh kids who breathed hex and shit code.
They were already on Rasheed.

One block over, rooftop sniper gave the call. Visual confirmed.
Rasheed was in his suite—curtains drawn, movement positive.

One shot would've closed the file.
But command was clear: Rasheed stays alive.
No hotel room hits. He had to step outside.
Daggan had the street team prepped—spread thin, parked cold, caffeinated. If Rasheed surfaced, they'd grab him.

Problem was, they weren't the only muscle on the board.
Hotel security weren't earpiece jockeys in rented suits.
These were ex-war vets—ex-Balkan, ex-who-knows-what mercs.
They'd eat their own to keep the perimeter tight.

Which is why a car bomb was prepped, parked just short of the main gate. Driver ready to leave it and walk.
Trigger set for guard surge—the second the hotel overreacted, the car would light. Bright enough to reset priorities.

Collateral? Fine.
Shock was the only currency that mattered.
Give Rasheed a window.
Distract the wall just long enough to rip him through.
Jovan had burned an hour in the lobby, waiting, when Daggan's voice hit sharp in his ear. He moved without a word—handed the seat off to another asset, stepped out.

Daggan was staged by the van, just past the outer intersection.
Jovan didn't come empty-handed. He carried four coffees in a tray—lifted straight from the hotel restaurant.

He climbed in. Steam rolled through the cabin—
Men sipped, nodded.
"Good stuff," one muttered.

The techs were young. But their god wasn't youth.
It was AI.

Jovan knew it before they finished their second sentence.
Said their model already had Rasheed's next stop.
Thirty minutes out—central Prague.
A disco.
History analyzed.
Pattern mapped.
Target predicted.

Their odds said fifty percent success rate if they moved here.
The chance would rise to eighty-five if they hit the disco.

Jovan asked the only thing that mattered:
Why fifty percent on the street outside the hotel,
where everything was prepped, eyes and triggers locked in
and suddenly eighty-five at a club across town?

They stared.
AI had no answer.
Just numbers. Just confidence.
Daggan didn't like that.
That's why Jovan was in the van.
Because ops don't run on belief. They run on blood, margin, and men who still know the smell of failure.

Tech boys' advice was split—half hold position, other half gear up, thirty minutes east to the disco. That's what was burning Daggan's seconds.
Split the crew and you guarantee failure in both fronts.
Send them all chasing the disco hit, and if AI missed by a thread, Rasheed could slip out the back and ghost the city.

The room cracked when one of the techs—said it flat:
"Target's moving."

Jovan made the call.
No more maps. No more theory.

He'd meet it straight.
The boys were already deployed.

He'd step out, walk to the hotel gate,
lock eyes with the exit himself.
See how the bastard planned to disappear.

But Daggan stopped it.
Blocked the door with his chest and voice.
Told Jovan to hold position—run the op from the van.
Said he'd take the gate.
The argument cost them seconds they couldn't bill back.
Jovan let it go.
He trusted the call.

Daggan moved.
Two mercs watched him the second he posted at the car exit.
Eyes sharp as gun dogs.
They didn't speak.
Just tracked him.

Then Jovan's earpiece cracked.
"Target moving. Positive."
Rooftop sniper.

Half a breath later.
"Target movement negative."
Lobby watcher.

Flat contradiction.

Two minutes later, Daggan himself—eyes on the gate,
confirmed it: "Negative."

But the techs screamed through the earpiece—
Rasheed had exited.
Comms buzzed like a hacked hive.
His signal was already past the hotel radius, heading for the main artery.

What the fuck.
No back alley cams blinked, no side exits.
No visible breach. Still—he was gone.

The van went silent.
Every tech jaw clenched.
They'd tracked him clean.
Phone ping verified.
Location real.
And their earlier hacks weren't jokes.
They'd streamed his calls, scraped photos off his phone while he slept.

Jovan knew the software. Trusted the boys.
If the signal said Rasheed was outside—he was.

Which left only one explanation:
The hotel had veins no one mapped.
Smuggler routes—built for ghosts.

The AI caught the drift.
Predicted a move it couldn't explain.
No raw data—just the pattern.

Jovan's mistake was ignoring the forecast.
That cost them time. Not the mission.

Because now they had coordinates.
Rasheed's next stop was already stamped in the circuit.

This wasn't theory anymore.
It was pursuit.

***

Presidential Suite
Hotel Amethyst Prague, Czech Republic

Rasheed was back. Breathing, intact—but the look on his face said freedom hit harder than the cage.
Like the weight didn't leave, just shifted shoulders.

I pressed.

—What is it, Rasheed? You look like you walked out of hell and left your soul behind.

—The men you pulled me from?
Decoys. The real leash came from Mossad.

—Not exactly breaking news. They've kept tabs on you for years.

—The last job I did that might've lit up their radar—I redirected it. Dumped the whole mess on Iranian intel, Shabab.
Mossad went quiet, I figured the misdirection worked.

—I've watched bigger secrets leak out of my own veins.
So don't expect me to feel sorry for you, Rasheed.

—Drop that. What rattles me is Mossad running a chain search.
You know how their chain search works?

—Not really. I'm not on their payroll.

—In cases like this, every Mossad unit worldwide locks in, moves as one, until the target's in a cage.
They did it once for Imad Mughniyeh—Hezbollah's hero in Lebanon. He slipped the first dragnet.
But I saw what came next.
I watched it happen with my own eyes.

—Alright. That's heavy. Look—the job I called you for—it's dust now. But I can get you safe into Türkiye.

—Forget it. That ground's already burned.
Truth is, there's nowhere left for me on earth.

—Then what's your plan?

—No plan yet. Still working on it.

—You can sit here and think all you want.
This suite's a vault—Mossad might buzz the window,
but they can't reach you. Today, I'm moving.
Middle East. Just for one day.
Someone's been taken—someone I can't leave behind.

—And you're sure you can pull him out in a day?

—Bro... just like you know your trash—I know mine.

—Alright. I've got something forming.
But first—how sure are you about getting him out?

I didn't blink.

—As sure as sunrise.

Rasheed nodded, slow.

—Fine. You can anchor me here in Prague.
But I'm not rotting in this suite.
Mossad's not the only shadow on my back.
And running from them doesn't work—they're hounds.
They savor the chase before the strike.

He paused, jaw tight.

—What if I hand myself in? If I surrender—could you pull me back out? The way you're planning for your friend?

—Maybe I could.

I didn't soften the edge.

—But my friend's just a helpless businessman, no way to protect himself—that's why I have to move in.
You, Rasheed—you've walked through fire. Don't talk like a man already waiting for dirt to close over his face.

He gave me a look that didn't need translation.

—You keep proving it—there's no mercy in you.

—Mercy?

I met his eyes.

—Where'd you see that here?
I've already offered you more than the numbers justify.

—Profit and loss, huh?

He scoffed, more bitter than amused.

—...Fine. What if—before they grab me, or even after—I hand you Mossad intel? Their secrets. Anything you want.
Would you help me burn them down?

—I'll give you the truth.
Nothing Mossad holds interests me.
I've never cared for their locked rooms.

I leaned back, voice lower.

—I've got deeper vaults of my own.

—...Yeah. I get it. Should've guessed.
CIA never pokes your business, you never poke theirs.
Maybe you'll just live side by side with Mossad too.

—Don't take it personal, Rasheed.
I do feel for you—enough to drop you one secret.

He raised an eyebrow, half-smile, half-grimace.

—You? Dropping secrets? That's rich.

—Laugh or don't. Your choice.

I looked past him, then back.

— Picture a kite, high in the sky, floating like it owns the wind.
But the reel? It's in another man's hand.
The kite never knows whose will it's dancing for, or how far it can fly—until the string jerks tight.

He blinked, once.

—Meaningful, sure. But how does that tie back to me?

—It doesn't.

I met him steady.

—That was about me. About my limits.
Like you said—maybe I could do it.
But the string's in someone else's grip.
I only fly as far as they let me.

—...Now I get it. Sorry. I pushed too hard.

He looked down, then back.

—This fight with Mossad—it's mine to fight.

—That's the right call. If someone else fights your war, you end up wearing their leash. Better to lose on your own terms than live owned.

—Agreed, *Rasheed said.*
—And don't mistake this for fear—it's not. With your help,
I could've taught those bastards a hard lesson.
Without you... I'll still deliver something.

His voice dropped.

—Can I stay here a little longer? Just enough to get set.

—Like I said, Rasheed. You can stay as long as you need.
No hands on earth's bold enough to snatch you out of Amethyst Prague.

He nodded. Not weak—just real.

—Thanks. That's enough for now. And if we don't cross paths again—if I don't make it out—don't hold that against me.

—Fuck it Rasheed. You've got a soft streak in you—like some woman out of a romance. And now you've pulled me into it.
Fine. Tell me this—if I'm not backing you in the field, but you've got a plan of your own... is there any way I can help make it real?

He looked over at me, still and steady.

—Help? ...Weapons, gear—I've got those covered.
Travel's no problem either.

He tapped the table once.

—Just one thing you can do.

—What's that?

—If they kill me—make them pay.

I stared.

—You're serious? That's the request?
You've got a whole organization built for that.

—I don't want to drag them into it. They've got their own war.
In Gaza, a bullet costs too much. If they wasted one on me,
I'd be ashamed even dead.

I let the silence sit a moment, then spoke low.

—...I understand. Fine then. I'll give you my word.
As long as I walk this earth—or even if I don't—if Rasheed Farish is killed, the so-called merchants of silence will get a lesson rammed straight up their ass.

He grinned. The real kind.

—Hah. Well said, Chief. You're making me a fan.
Let me give you something.

—Oh yeah? What's that?

—Here. Keep this key safe.

—A key?
Doesn't look like it opens a bank vault.
Just a plain house key.

—That's exactly what it is. The key to my home.

—You're carrying that around? And giving it to me?

—Not just me. Every Palestinian whose home was seized keeps their family key. It's hope—maybe one day Almighty will grant us victory, lets us walk home again.

He glanced at the door, then back at me.

—I may never see my home again. So I'm giving this to you.
If you ever live to see a free Palestine—light a candle there for me.

—...I feel the weight of it, Rasheed.
Your words cut deep.
Maybe you shouldn't give this to me.

—If you don't want it, I won't push.
But it carries another kind of weight.

—What kind?

—If someday you need help from another Palestinian,
show them this key. My family's name is carved into it.
Any one of them will recognize it—and they'll help you without question.

—I hope it never comes to that. Still... I'll keep it.
Even if I don't want to—I have to move now.
Got a long way to go.

—Alright, Chief. I won't trouble you anymore. Goodbye.

I should've been hunting Macro with everything I had.
Instead, I left Rasheed behind and aimed for Kuwait City.

Back then, I pushed Sheikh Awadi left for his country in a hurry.
And after Phuket—no word, no calls, nothing to show he was alive or if more could've been done.
Letting it hang like that was the mistake.
I see it now.

Marisha could've helped track him.
But when I texted to thank her for Rasheed's release,
she replied that urgent work would keep her off-grid for days.

She was already tangled too deep in this.
So I chose to move myself—Kuwait City.

—∞—

Breath'n Burn

Max Ninety Nine Discotheque
Central Prague, Czech Republic

The boys finally cracked a grin,
nerves dropping for the first time all night.

Max 99 wasn't a club, it was a living, stinking beast—four doors wide open, crowd pouring both ways, nobody even pretending to care.

Inside—sweat and rot, bodies slamming, bass punching holes in your chest. Every move was hungry, everything grinding.
No one checked names, no one gave a shit who you were.
Drag someone out—wasted, drooling, dead—you could haul their corpse into the street, glass in the air, and nobody'd blink.
Cheers.

Jovan carved his way through the mob.
Two guys at the entrance, mouths welded together,
hands digging in, hips grinding like rent was due.
He didn't blink—just clocked it and moved on.

His home country could crown itself the 'gay capital' of
the Middle East—that never changed him.
Jovan ran straight his whole life.

Daggan, though, thrived on the strobes, eyes wild, appetite feral.
To him, gender meant nothing—if it moved, burned hot,
he'd fuck it right there, doesn't even mind the lights.

Main floor was pure riot—lights hacking through smoke,
bodies pressed so close you tasted someone else's sweat.
Impossible to say who was there to dance, who was hunting,
who just ghosted out the side door. That was the setup.

Rasheed felt it straight away—here, anyone could vanish,
and nobody would blink twice.

In this crowd, finding one man blind would've burned the night alive. But tech didn't miss.

Pin drop landed.
Target lit.
Jovan shoved through—shoulders first, through smoke, strobes, flesh—no apologies, no space.

He marked the private lounge deep in the chaos.
Inside: Rasheed Dameer.
Alone. Waiting.

His Turkish passport came with a beard.
But he was sitting clean-shaved, brows worked over—trying to sand off the edge, fade into Prague's night.
Didn't work.
Anyone who mattered could still clock the face.

Jovan didn't pause.
Told Daggan to hold position.
Then walked in.

If Rasheed tried to leave, he wouldn't get three steps.
If the person he came to meet arrived, they'd be allowed through.

At the velvet rope, Daggan held ground. A tattooed kid jumped in, hands shoved down Daggan's pants— palming his manhood like it was his own personal joystick.

He kept at it—exploring every inch between Daggan's thighs, face open, lips parted, whispering something into his ear—like he'd found a new world to map.
Daggan didn't even shift. Didn't tell him to stop.
Everyone in this place knew he wasn't moving—so he just left the boy hanging.

Nobody on Jovan's team was built for dry silence here.
Observers scattered in the crowd weren't just watching—they were tuned in, feeding on every signal, every sweat bead, logging the grid with their own skin in the game.
But Jovan had Rasheed Dameer mapped down to his last cell.

Rasheed didn't drink.
Didn't flirt. Didn't give a shit about the circus.
If he was in this pit, it meant business—always covert,
always some threat hiding just out of view.

Jovan scanned—eyes hunting, burning through the haze.
Tagged a woman moving slow through the dark.
Clocked her.
Wrote her off. No alarm.
Not until someone at a table near Rasheed's lounge tapped the comms: "Shark in the water."

Instant pulse.
Everyone knew what it meant.
Everyone felt it spike.

The girl stalked the dark in black-on-black—jacket welded to her skin, pants slung so low her hips looked weaponized, boots laced tight like she was expecting a riot.
Everything matte, engineered to kill reflection.
That's why Jovan's eyes missed her on the first pass.

Strobes hit her and just gave up—the light died,
nothing reflected, nothing gave her away.
She moved like shadow with intent—meant to vanish,
built to make every drunk in the club question their eyesight.

She wasn't naked, but that outfit threat like a loaded gun.
Pants locked so tight they could've been shrink-wrapped, every curve out front, gravity working overtime just to keep up.
A thin chain draped from her exposed navel.
At the end dangled a small black pendant.
Swinging with her steps, tapping against her skin.

Watching that pendant swing against the depth of her navel—
felt better than scanning the universe through a telescope.
Like staring down God's dark side and asking for more.

From collarbone to throat, just enough on display to make a grown man into a bloodhound—cock twitching before his brain even clocks it.

Her abs rippled in motion.
No fat, just lean muscle shifting under skin as she walked—like something wild, caged just beneath the surface.

Under the open jacket, the twin peaks of her chest left deliberately visible.
Cropped, bra-less top did nothing to hold them back.
They rose full against the fabric, straining to spread—tight, tilting slightly outward, like nature's personal rebuke to every cheap implant on Earth.
No one gets breasts like that from surgery.
Or silicone. Not unless God did the shaping by hand.
Around her neck, matching those electric-blue eyes,
a thin deep-blue band—it read: "Daddy's Girl."
And it made her look illegally hot.

There wasn't a man on the team who didn't want to rip her apart—right there, right then.
She kept moving. Slow, calculated.
Paused at the lounge entrance, breathed in the grid.

She shot a glance at the boy still crouched between Daggan's legs—his hand busy inside Daggan's pants.
She flashed a smile, then walked into Rasheed's lounge without a flicker of doubt.

Daggan—hypnotized by the boy's stroking hand—didn't react, didn't clock her until she was already inside.

He didn't know this was the scent.
The one Daggan had been dying to sniff since the beginning.
Spets Peach.

The team waited. No one moved.
Everyone held until Jovan gave the call.
But Jovan was thinking something else.
Was the risk now too high?
If this woman was here to kill Rasheed—they'd lose the catch and the whole net with him.

They were confident about capturing Rasheed alive.
But with her in play? No guarantees.

His thoughts snapped—cut off mid-loop.
Daggan's voice cracked in his earpiece, raw with adrenaline.

He'd already thrown the gay boy off with one rough shove.
Now all business.
Asking—who's in position to trigger a short-circuit, fast?
A voice from the main gate answered.
Two minutes.

Then he updated Jovan.
Daggan had brought a gas bomb.
Not lethal—but once it hit the lungs, the body locked.
Gone from the air in three minutes, no trace left.
Even if the target stayed awake, that gas locked the body cold.

All they had to do was trigger a short-circuit, toss the bomb into the lounge, jam the handle from the outside—and it'd be over before anyone even knew it started.

Jovan's voice broke in, laughter edged with nerves.

—Fuck, bro... you're a fucking masterpiece.
Who the hell thinks to carry something like that?

Daggan answered calm, no ego.

—Whoever owns the op walks in ready, boss.

He flashed Jovan a sly grin.
Got the nod.
Execute.

What followed hit cleaner than theory.
Short-circuit sparked—the entire floor dropped into darkness.

The crowd screamed so loud that even Daggan, right at the door, couldn't hear the bomb pop in the lounge.

Within sixty seconds, the lights flickered back.
In the lounge—movement, thrashing, furniture scraping hard.
A table flipped, maybe more.

No one cared. Because the music came back too.
And the dancers? Wilder than before.
More noise, more chaos, more cover.

Mission clock running.
Two men peeled off to prep the car.
The rest held position, silent shadows outside the lounge.

Three minutes passed.
They waited longer.
Just in case.

Jovan's lips cracked into a grin.
He shot Daggan a look—voice low, soaked in dirt and approval.

—You nasty fucker. Have your fun with the hot chick—just keep her breathing long enough for what I need.

Daggan smirked like he'd already had a taste.

—Come on, Bossy, You think I'd waste flesh like that?
Who kills a piece like her when you can bleed her dry?

Jovan's grin thinned, already shifting into motion.

—Didn't think you'd fuck it up. Move them to the hide.

But Daggan didn't move. Smile gone.
Nose twitching like it caught chemical fire.

—Nah, boss. I can sniff trouble a mile off.
Dog's nose. Trust me on that.

Jovan didn't blink.

—So what's it saying?

—No stalling. Not a second.
We pull out of Czech—now.
You call the route.

Jovan gave the nod.

—Fine. Get them in the car.
I'll take it from there.

Seven minutes later, the lounge door opened.
They stepped in.
The air still held a trace of something floral—Camellia maybe.
Sweet at first hit. Sharp enough to fog the brainstem.

Jovan felt it bloom behind his eyes.
Daggan waved it off.

—No live threat. Both out cold.

The woman sagged—Daggan hooked her up by the waist.
Jovan grabbed the man.
They lifted in sync. Like hauling kit off the floor.

They headed straight for the exit gate.
Two guards clocked them.

Jovan didn't break stride.

—Friends, just out partying. Couple got too excited,
hit the drinks—crashing now. We're walking them out.

The guards didn't blink. They'd seen worse.
Waved them off with a dead-eyed "good night."

They were through the gate without a hitch.

Once they hit the car, the team locked the package down.
Jovan handed off the phones taken from the two captives—
straight to the tech boys.

Gave the order twice—pull every byte of data, then kill the devices. No trails. The boys nodded, phones in hand, and slipped into the shadows.

Jovan knew the mission wasn't over.
Now it was escape—no noise, just vanish.

Route request was already pulsing back to Tel Aviv.
He was waiting on the green light.

Inside the van, Daggan took the wheel.
Right seat—his own pick.
Sharpshooter.
Eyes wired.

The shooter kept glancing back—something in his spine didn't trust the quiet. Still expecting a strike.

Jovan wasn't worried.
They were done. The rest was just travel.

The van used to be an ambulance—still carried the bones for it.
Empty center. Two side benches. Face to face.
Ceiling lined with steel rings. Three each row.
That's where the detainees hung now.

Wrists cuffed and hooked above.
Legs chained to steel bars under the seats.
They'd been gagged. Dosed.
Not sloppy—measured.
Enough tranquilizer to kill the fight reflex, not the memory.

Daggan's other two panthers sprawled on the benches, watching it all. Feet up. Calm as wolves after a kill. Waiting for the green.

Jovan sat across from the woman.
Didn't notice at first—but once the junior boys were in, he felt it.

Her arms stretched up, chest pulled tight—the strain forced her breasts up, pushed the shape to perfection.

Jovan caught himself staring, eyes drifting back, wanting to look away, unable to stop.
The shape.
The tension.
The goddamn symmetry of it.

His brain ran ahead. What happens when the van starts moving—the swaying, the bounce.
His spine went tight, nerves on fire.
One second more and it would've cracked his mask.

Then the phone rang.
No ID. Secured line.

He barked everyone out—except Daggan.

Picked it up.

It was the Minister.
Himself.
Voice cold, precise, calculations running beneath every word.

He got the route: two hours' drive to the Czech border.
From there—Poland. Walbrzych.
Switch vehicles. Move to Wroclaw.
Private airstrip was waiting, engines already live.

They could've flown anywhere. But HQ pushed Ukraine.
Minister's voice crisp on the secure feed.
Said once boots hit the ground, they'd have access to full Tel Aviv–grade facilities.

Even better—Euro Team had Kamran tagged.
Ex-Iranian commander. Last known near that sector.
If they got to him first, Jovan would be sitting on three high-value suspects—alive.
One interrogation cell.
One chance to crack the whole board.

Minister closed with a final order:
Rasheed Dameer was to be delivered to Tel Aviv—alive.
Government wanted him tried and executed for the Eilat op.
A clean message—for both local hands and foreign eyes.

Jovan took it in—filed every detail, then made a quiet ask of his own. Said if there was a way—get Awadi out of Kuwait.
Move him to Ukraine too.

Minister didn't flinch.
Said he'd handle it himself.
Might take time to pull clean—but it would happen.
Jovan thanked him—formally.
Call ended.

Daggan had already punched the coordinates mid-call.
Headlights snapped on.

The boys outside saw the beam and moved without a word.
Steel toes crushed half-burned cigarettes.

Doors slammed.
They climbed in.

Daggan smiled under his breath and rolled the van forward—whistling under the engine noise like it was just a lazy Sunday.
Jovan felt it too.
For the first time in this op, things were lining up.

Until the movement started.
Until she started swinging, right in front of him.
Those goddamn tits—bouncing with every pothole like they were trying to say 'hi'. Tight, swinging at eye level like a pair of war trophies with his name engraved on them.

He couldn't look away.
Didn't want to admit it, but the heat hit low—fast.
Cock thickening in his pants like a loaded gun.

Across from him, the boys turned their heads. Not because they cared. Just didn't want to get caught laughing—their shoulders twitching like schoolboys who'd seen a girl's cleavage.

Jovan didn't need to hear it.
The heat in the van was doing all the talking.
Silent humiliation. Dense and sticky.

And Daggan? Please.
That dog wouldn't care if someone was jerking off next to him.

This was his ecosystem. Daggan and his crew had turned prisoner transfers into gangbangs. Didn't matter if it was boys, girls, tied up or half-dead—if it had a hole, it got used.

Jovan had left that behind early.
Opted out of the flesh circus, climbed the ladder by keeping his hands clean and his record legit. Now outranked Daggan by a margin too wide to joke about.

But Daggan—son of Herz Daggan, longest-standing Mossad legend—still couldn't touch him.
Bloodline cracked the door, sure. But inside Mossad, you had to kill for your seat.

No handouts. No family plans.
Just grit, precision, and blood on your own blade.

Everyone knew that.
Even Daggan.
And now—rolling shoulder to shoulder in a van full of gagged bodies—that unspoken bond stayed locked.

Jovan caught Daggan's eyes in the mirror.
That smirk. Pure devil.

Confident, like he owned the girl and the road ahead.

—So bossy—liking the view?
Want me to strip her down?
Maybe give you a better angle to jerk off?

That cracked the van.
The boys tried to choke it down.
Failed.

It came out half-cough, half-confession.
Daggan raised the volume.
Face deadpan.

Voice full clown:

—One more laugh and I'll crack your fucking skull.
You even realize how long it's been since a pair of tits made bossy pitch a tent? Fuck it—I'll stop the van.
Let him have the charm. No judgment.

The threat meant nothing.
Laughter detonated.
Rattled the van walls like a warhead.

—*—

Broken Before Dawn

Kuwait City, Kuwait

The house in front of me—stone walls, brittle bones.
Fire a heavy round inside, the whole place would collapse.
Even the street around it looked staged, like a set pulled straight from Arabian Nights.

I kept the binoculars steady, crosshairs locked on the upper floor. Thinking just that.

Intel tagged this as the dome-cap clan's HQ.
My source swore on it.
Locals call them dome-caps—round-cap men.
Descendants of Jews who converted to Islam centuries ago.
They still wear the skullcap, stitched tight across the crown, the same cut their ancestors wore. Slightly off from the native Muslims. A habit too old to shed.

Across the street, I lay stretched out on the roof of a fortress-shaped house, glass fixed on my target.

The owner hated the dome-cap clan with a special kind of fury. The moment he heard I was dealing with them, he lit up—like Aladdin's genie yanked from the lamp. Hauled the heavy crates I'd brought, dragged them up the roof himself.

From afternoon into nightfall, he kept sending up plate after plate, turning the wait into something almost pleasant.
Still no sign of Sheikh Awadi.

Amir Hossain—the one who tipped me—was told the man in that house was my Arab friend. I couldn't risk the real name. In a city this small, the moment "Awadi" slipped out, the whole place would catch fire. Nothing to gain, everything to lose.

The job was on—proving Awadi was actually inside.

It's not just me on the glass. Ground-level eyes too.

Amir ran the net. From laborers to cable guys to street cleaners—he had them all in his pocket. He sent them drifting past windows, slipping into the date groves out back, feeding me whatever scraps they could pull.

His name—Amir—meant high-born.
But real life wasn't the Gulf emir fantasy.
Amir Hossain was a poor immigrant from South Asia.
His father chased wages here decades back.
Spent twenty-seven years in Kuwait.

Amir grew up half-orphaned, speaking to his father mostly in snatched calls, catching a few days with him now and then. Listening to Kuwait stories, dreaming his way out.

College never happened. He wasted years jobless, leaning on his father, picking fights—until one stuck and dragged him into court. His father pulled strings, brought him over.

Amir landed at the airport burning with painted dreams—only to find his father on his knees with a mop. Even at his age, the old man still worked eighteen-hour days.

Amir told me that in his first month here he cried into his pillow every night. Then he sat his father down and took the janitor's shift himself. Years of grinding labor, until he finally bought his father's release—send the old man home to retire.

Now? In Kuwait City, if you need a plumber, electrician, gardener, painter—anything—you call Amir Hossain.

Which means there isn't a vein in this city he doesn't have under his fingernail. That's why he fit this job.

I'd first heard his story from another South Asian friend—Pallab.
It was Pallab I asked for a man like this.
He lined it up without a word.
Never asked why I was chasing cattle in Kuwait, never asked what the point was. Neither did Amir.
Some friends don't need reasons.
Those are the ones you keep.

By evening the street turned into a stage worth watching.
A black Mercedes G-Wagon slid into position at the alley corner.
At the same time Amir's lookout—perched on a power pole behind the Dome-cap clan house—sent word:
Someone inside had called an ambulance.
The house that had been silent for hours was suddenly alive.

I fixed the binoculars again.
One look—and it hit like a gut punch.

A man walked out, leaning hard, one hand on a dome-cap's shoulder. Couldn't be sure it was Awadi. But the vest strapped to him, the blinking light on it—I didn't need to guess.

They were going to move him. If the G-Wagon crew shielded him into that ambulance, nothing would stop them. The vest bomb was insurance—if police pressed too close, they'd blow Awadi and everyone else to ash rather than let him go.

Rasheed had warned me about their cruelty.
Every word checked out.

He actually deserved help. But with his past, I couldn't risk burning full fire for him. When it's innocents on the line,
I can unleash hell and answer to no one.
But men like Rasheed—good, yes, but not innocent—I've spent too much blood and too many nights covering for that kind.
Hard lessons.

Awadi wasn't that. A clean-hearted man with a bomb strapped to his chest. Just seeing it cracked something loose inside me,
Darkness pooling up, wanting to swallow everything.
But charging in now would be suicide. Better to let myself get taken. Let them think they'd caught me—and see what they planned for Awadi.

For that I'd need a cover—something solid.
Which meant Amir. Fluent Arabic, street-sharp.
He could make the surrender look real.

***

Donetsk City, Ukraine

Outside the window, a quiet street slid past, tall trees standing stripped. Branches already bare—winter cut them down early in this grid. The noon sun hung overhead, glare hard as steel, but Jovan knew it was theater: bright optics, no heat.
Out here the sun mocked—light sharp, warmth gone.

They'd crossed into Ukraine in one piece, but the road still clung to them. Two hours to the line, another two burned while their guide looped wide to stay off Czech patrol optics.

From there it was a sprint to Wałbrzych private strip in Poland, then onto the jet—and an extra hour wasted waiting on fuel.

Three boxed hours in the air before they dropped here, a gutted state plant refitted as safehouse.

The factory was Soviet-era, back when Kyiv tooled Moscow's arsenal. That ledger's closed.

Now the neighbors barely tolerated each other.
Jovan knew his side carried part of the stain.
Jewish influence ran deep through Ukraine now, and their bloc was pure Anglo-American. Step by step, Ukraine tilted West.
Moscow roared, but NATO stood parked on its porch.

Inside the steel carcass sat a two-story office block, climate control still breathing. That's where the crew holed up.

Awadi was due by nightfall—then the play would run hot.
For now, Jovan let the boys crash.
The trip drained them.

Daggan was dead asleep downstairs, painkillers numbing him out. Motion sickness he never admitted—not that it mattered; nobody had time for sympathy.

Upstairs, next to Jovan's suite, a big meeting room sat staged—interrogation space.

Basement level held an old Soviet bomb shelter. That's where the prisoners were dumped.

Tranq still running their veins, they drifted through the transfer half-awake, chickens in a crate.
Unlike the team, they felt none of the road's weight.

Jovan left the window, moved to the TV feed showing the shelter.
Both prisoners were awake.
Rasheed Dameer's voice carried up—worried, asking the girl something. She didn't answer. Head tilted, eyes locked on the basement door. GRU Spetsnaz.

Jovan had no doubt—this girl was a psycho.
Daggan wanted to drown in her heat, but leaving him alone with a weapon like that was off the table.
No telling what switch she might flip.

And not just her. Jovan had heard every Spets carried the same cracked circuit. GRU had raised them, but even the old Chekists weren't this bent. Jovan knew more than a few of FSB officers.
Most were aristocrats, gentlemen in suits.
But not the Spets. Not this one.

Kremlin kept these units deep underground, ghosts in the vault, only surfacing when they wanted a room cleared and no fingerprints left behind.

Same way CIA drags Delta in under Title 50 when Langley wants deniable muscle, or MI6 leans on SAS squadrons for jobs where diplomats can't show face.

Mossad chase the same gentleman's game now—polished officers in embassies up front, Kidon in the back room doing the real work. They also had Caesarea, but that's for classic field ops—small teams, surgical hits, deep-cover work.
That's why IDF was built—to swing the hammer.

In reality it backfired.
Instead of running ops, those bastard in-laws got addicted to stomping the easy enemy at home. Years of crushing Palestinians turned them into a pack of dirty dogs.

And bastard in-laws fit—Jovan had spent plenty of nights in IDF chief's little sister. Young, feral in bed.
Her body still scratched behind his eyes.

He shoved it down, forced his head back to the now.

GRU psychos weren't wired for patience.
Sudan proved it.
Wagner's boys were already crawling the gold belt, but buried inside them was a Spets detachment Moscow wouldn't even admit existed.

One of their men got snatched. Government forces confirmed who he was, played it by the book—delivered him to court.
Moscow could've pulled strings, freed him quiet.
Everyone expected it.

Instead the hidden Spets stormed the courthouse,
cut down the judge and half the room, hauled their man out.
Takes a real bastard to open fire inside a court.
Jovan doubted even Kidon dogs would go that far.

Before moving them here, he and Daggan ran the prisoners down again and again. No trackers, no wires.
Phones already gutted by the Prague tech team.
Still—keeping a Spets psycho locked this close to Russia made Jovan's chest itch.

He flipped the feed—basement cell off, perimeter on.
Four acres of plant, local militia slotted into every angle.
Their prep and discipline cooled him. Looked sharp.

He pulled back into bed, comforter heavy over his chest, but the mind ran wild.

Couldn't shake the vision—girl tied, those world-class tits jostling with every shiver, curves that rewrote geometry.
He let it roll. Let it ride.
Nobody cared what spun in his skull under a warm blanket.

Sleep came thin, fragile.
Noise cracked it open.

Sky outside gone blue-black, the last blood of the sun draining low.

Daggan's voice carried from the conference room, bolts turning, metal crushing. He had the locals working.

None of that woke Jovan.
The phone did.
Ugly tone, sharp bursts.
Set only for one line—the defense minister's office.

Secured channel. Red alert screaming off the nightstand.
Jovan caught the call before the line could drop.

—Erev tov, Adon Sar

—Evening, my boy. I woke you, didn't I?

—Not really, sir. Just resting. Was getting up anyway.

—Good. As you asked—Awadi's on the move. You knew that?

—Yes, sir. I was told he'd be delivered.

—Right. But here's the part you weren't told.
Call it a surprise for both of us.
Remember we pulled Awadi out of that Kuwait safehouse?

—Yes, sir. You already briefed me on that.

—Exactly. While we were prepping him for transport, someone showed up asking for him.

—...What? Sir, that Emirati who tagged along with him in Phuket?

—No. Different card. New face on our radar.
Working for a Chinese tycoon.

—...Elohim. Don't tell me the tycoon's name is Xanier Cheng.

—Unfortunately, yes. Which means we dig. What kind of work he's doing for Cheng, why he's suddenly invested in Awadi.
Lucky for us—we caught him alive.

—That's solid news, sir. You sending him back to Tel Aviv?

—No. I'm sending him to you—along with Awadi.

—...Why me, sir? I don't see the tie.
Could be just a friend of Awadi's, hired to pull him out.

—Your surprise isn't over yet. Remember that Spetsnaz girl's phone you passed to tech?

—Of course. Thought maybe they'd scrape something useful.

—They scraped plenty—multiple comms between him and the girl under your watch.

—...Ha-Shem. That's one hell of a surprise.

—You did your job clean, my boy.
Ha-Shem's just giving you the return.

—You're too kind, sir. I'll give it everything—you know that.

—I expect nothing less. Good hunting, my boy.

The minister's call dropped and Jovan's hands shook, just a tremor. The way everything locked into place this fast was unexpected. Not new—but unreal.

Mossad had history with this, unbelievable wins pulled out by a handful of patriots grinding themselves to the bone.
Daggan needed the update.

Jovan stepped into the next room and found the stage already half-built. Daggan grinned wide—said he was turning the conference room into a place to split stomachs and wrench the truth straight out.

The heavy steel table was already there.
Cushioned chairs swapped out for welded steel, bolted straight through the concrete—no prisoner would be shifting his ass an inch. They waited on Jovan before carving a few special tricks into the tabletop.

Hearing the fresh intel, Daggan's eyes lit up—dark humor burning through. He ordered another chair added.

They'd come five strong without counting prisoners.
Now the whole Euro team was on-site.

Noise and movement rolled through the factory like a brewing thunderstorm.

Outside, Ukrainian militia still held the perimeter tight.

Among the faces, one cut through the crowd—Jamer Shavit.
The vulture.
That's what everyone called him.

Vultures strip corpses. Shavit stripped prisoners.
Once Mossad finished squeezing them dry, he did the rest.
Jovan knew the numbers—Shavit had cut up more finished prisoners than any butcher had slaughtered goats.

By Jovan's count, at least two bodies would land in Shavit's lap tonight.

Daggan had trained under him—learned cutwork and pain-craft from the best. But he hadn't called the master in for show.
Shavit's edge came from years carving real flesh.
He could break a prisoner fast, clean, effective.
Daggan brought him to save time.
The right call.

Ten minutes out.
The mobile unit bringing Awadi and their new friend.

Daggan gave the order—keep the stage hot, prisoners prepped.
Then he went to gear up, his own ritual.

***

Kuwait City, Kuwait

The dome-cap clan tied our hands and feet, black cloth over our faces, shoved us into a car. From there—a helicopter.
Then the long, choking haul on a jet. Now back in a car again.

Amir Hossain sold the capture clean.
He was a familiar face, even to the dome-cap clan.

When he grabbed me, dragged me up to their front door camera shouting "ḥarāmi, ḥarāmi!"— they didn't hesitate.
They shoved him aside and went to work on me with their fists.

Amir flinched like a man spooked for real, then barked at them.

—This bandit's got a pistol at his waist.

They thanked him and dragged me inside.

Sure enough, hand to my belt, they pulled the gun.
Tied me up, kept swinging, demanded an explanation in Arabic.
I gave them nothing but mumbled nonsense that only stoked their rage hotter.

Inside, the house was just what I'd guessed—thick walls, dim light, the stale mix of sweat, dust, and cardamom smoke clinging to the air.

They dumped me in a chair, rope across chest and wrists, a man leaning over to spit questions in my face: who was I, where was I from, why the gun.

I let the answers stumble out in broken Arabic, colored with bad English accent—just a tourist, I said, pistol only for safety, nothing more.

One of them snapped a picture of me with his phone and sent it somewhere. The others vanished into a side room.

I sat alone in the smoke, listening to the hum of an old ceiling fan and the blood still pounding in my ears.

When they came back, they were smiling.

They spoke in Arabic, sharp and quick, sure I couldn't follow a word. But I picked up enough. They were about to transfer me—with Awadi.

Exactly what I needed.
I kept my face blank, let them think I was deaf to their plotting, while inside the pieces clicked into place.
This was the door opening.

Moments later, Abdel al-Awadi limped into the room.
Vest bomb still strapped tight.
That was why they let him walk free.
No timer I could spot—it had to be remote-triggered, or worse, rigged to blow the second he strayed out of range.

He saw me, shocked to see another captive, but no recognition.
He couldn't. I wasn't Mr. Caesar anymore.
To him I was nobody—just another foreigner.
He looked at me with sympathy, studied the bruises,
then stayed silent.

The dome-cap men had already stripped me of the phone and pistol. I had no way to fight now, and I didn't try.
Better to see where they'd take us.

They shoved me into a dark room, left me there for what felt like hours, no sound but my breathing, no light but the faint seam at the bottom of the door.

When it finally opened, the transfer began.

I'd expected them to cuff my hands behind my back during transport. That's why I'd told Amir to tape the small gear to the rear waistband of my underwear.

Through the flights and transfers they'd kept me hunched, limbs bound in front. But once they dumped me in the car, they finally gave me what I wanted—hands wrenched behind, locked in cuffs.

My plan was set.

—∞—

The Blood Debt

Donetsk City, Ukraine

They kept us together for the ride—like cattle in transit. But when the van finally ground to a halt, they dragged Sheikh Awadi like he was the real threat.

Me? Hood still blacking out my vision, I caught a rough shove. A finger jabbed me upward, silent but firm, guiding me toward a staircase.

Behind me, Awadi's voice cracked the air—screaming—and then faded somewhere below, somewhere I wasn't allowed to follow.

I couldn't see a thing. But the air shifted.
Cold. Artificial.
Air conditioning wrapped around my sweat-soaked body like a lover I hadn't felt in weeks.

It was the first time since the jet that I'd tasted chilled air.
Every other stop had been sweat, heat, and grit.
Now—cool relief, thick and sudden. The kind that claws at your skull if you've been cooked long enough.
Headache flared. Migraine twisting behind the eyes.

I used to handle this kind of pain.
Once. Back before the in-between years softened me.
Luxury does that—it sneaks in, makes you forget you were forged in heat.

They sat me down in a steel chair.
Legs shackled to the frame with something that felt military.
Hands still cuffed behind my back.
How thoughtful.
They'd made me immobile—but not rearranged.

At first, the cold felt like mercy.
But now the temperature drop was hitting me hard.

Sweat drying too fast.
Vertigo blooming into nausea.

My throat started to burn. Stomach began to rise.
Under the hood, the thought of puking on myself—not a pleasant picture.

I clamped down
Tried not to move.
Tried not to become that man.
So busy trying to keep it together—I missed it at first.

The sound of breathing.
From the chair next to mine.
Someone else was here.
Not Awadi. He was dragged downstairs.

This breath was different—steady, measured, almost bored.
And then—they entered.
A few of them.
Calm. Quiet.
No rush.

One came up behind me—fingers quick at the knot.
A sharp tug, and the black hood vanished.

At first, after so long in darkness, the light hit me like a flood—whitewashed and searing. Everything blurred out.

It took a few seconds before my vision started recalibrating.
Only then did I clock the man next to me.
His eyes weren't covered.
When the cloth was ripped off my face, he recognized me immediately.

And now—Rasheed Dameer was laughing.
Loud. Mad.
Joyful in a way that didn't belong in this place.

His face lit up as he grinned like a man unhinged and said,

—There you are chief! You really sold me some kite-and-string stories, huh? Now look at you—here in the flesh. Ha-ha!

I shot back, still dazed.

—The kite's snapped, brother.
Guess I had no choice but to crash-land here.

Rasheed was about to say something else. But that's when someone slammed a hammer into the right side of my skull.
No warning. No warm-up. Just steel to bone.

Whatever Rasheed was going to say got swallowed back down.
And me? My vision lit up, yellow blooms popping behind my eyelids, every nerve in my skull howling.
That corner of my head—burning hot like it had been branded.

It was going to swell. I knew the feeling.
The heat from the blow didn't stay local. It radiated—spread across my skull like a storm with nowhere to go.
The nausea that had haunted me moments ago? Gone.
Pain this sharp doesn't leave room for anything else.

I twisted, tried to see who threw the punch.
The man with the hammer—purebred bastard.
Face like a bad caricature, ugly in a way that felt intentional.
But the body underneath? Built. Brutal.
The kind of bulk that made the hammer unnecessary.
He didn't need it. He chose it.

A few feet away stood someone else.
Middle-aged, crisp suit, every detail sharpened like a scalpel.
Looked like a banker, spoke like a diplomat.

I recognized him instantly—Jovan Meir Elbaz.
Mossad's ASEAN station chief.

No idea how I know that.
Could be a Macro report. Could be one of Vega's dossiers from the Bangkok corporate net. Doesn't matter.
His image was etched in memory long before we met in person.

And behind him—another one.
A giant.
Built like a butcher.

Wearing a thick leather apron around his waist.
Arms held behind his back, motionless.
The kind of man you hire when a warning isn't enough.

Jovan looked at us—confident, amused.
Then he broke the silence.

—Every shot was clean, Daggan.
You should try golf next time you're back in Tel Aviv.
Bet you'd ace it.

The hammer-man—Daggan—flashed a smirk.
Spun the hammer slowly in his hand and stepped beside him.

Meanwhile, I turned back to Rasheed—letting the pain settle, letting the ringing ease.

This time I noticed—his hands were shackled.
Steel cuffs spread across a central hook on the table.
Fingers bruised, joints swollen.
The skin around his knuckles—raw and red.

So that's where Daggan had landed his earlier swings.
And now the bastard wore a grin uglier than his face, stretching his mouth like it was trying to spit poison instead of words.

—See that, bossy? These two assholes knew each other.

He chuckled—nasty, gleeful, disgusting.
Was about to say more.
But the walkie on his hip crackled mid-sentence.
A burst of Hebrew sliced through the room.

He snatched the device off his belt, spoke back in clipped code, and stepped out of the room—still laughing under his breath.

Jovan, the station chief, strolled forward with the elegance of a man who never gets his hands dirty.

He took the head chair at the steel table. Sat like he was about to lead a board meeting—then flicked his eyes theatrically toward Rasheed and muttered with mock offense:

—This guy? Rasheed? He's street trash—I choke on the word 'Mister' even thinking of him. As for you...

A tilt of the head, a smirk forming.

—...Your status is unclear. But I'll give you the benefit of the doubt—let's call you 'Mister.' For now.

I spoke before he could milk the silence further.

—Elijan Vellum. That's my name.

He grinned wider.

—Ohooo. Tell me, Mr. Vellum...
What's your connection to that bastard Rasheed over there?
You two look close.
Same bone structure. Same beggar energy.
Family, or just a matching pair of stray dogs?

—Just coincidence, *I replied.*

He shrugged, didn't miss a beat.

—Right... Doesn't matter anyway.
So, what's the flag on your little passport, huh?

—North Macedonian.

He blinked, hard. Didn't like that answer.

—The fuck did you say?

—North Macedonian.

I repeated, again. Same tone.
No inflection.

He flared.

—You rat-faced little shit! You think I'm here to suck down your fake-ass passport fantasies? I'll shove that ID so deep in your ass your successors would taste plastic for a decade.
Say it—your real nationality. Now.

I didn't blink. But beside me, Rasheed twitched.
Not from pain. From shock.

He'd been fed a different cover, a different face.
But he kept his mouth glued shut.
A man like him knows the price of speaking out of turn.
His silence confirmed it—he knew what this room could do.

On the other side, the butcher moved.
The giant.
The one in the apron.

Brought his arms forward for the first time.
Revealing two steel machetes. Gleaming under the low light like they were born for one thing only.

By then, fear had stopped being part of the equation for me.
Long ago, I believed in something deeper—
That my kinetic force, spread through every nerve,
made me untouchable. I believed that power lived in me.
That I could crush this whole goddamn room if I wanted.
But that was a different time.

That was a different version of me.
Now?

Now I knew the rules had changed.
Stay calm. Walk their corridors. Smile through their traps.
Outlast. Outthink. Outburn.

I answered Jovan again.
This time, polite.
Almost apologetic.

—Look... whatever you think this is, I truly have no idea what you're talking about. I am North Macedonian.

He scoffed. Barked.

—You think I eat grass, motherfucker?
Even that trash-born rat doesn't lie about his Arab blood.
And you? What kind of half-baked bastard tries to feed me this cheap-ass alias? What—don't even know where you were born?
Can't even remember your own skin?

—If you don't want your throat split and your tongue jammed in the gap, I suggest you watch your mouth, Jovan.

The voice was cold. Controlled.
And beautiful, like silk drawn across a blade.
I turned toward the sound.
It came from the doorway.

And standing there—was Marisha.
For a split second, something in me flinched.
Not from fear. But doubt.

Part of me—still—hadn't fully trusted her.
Never had.
My first thought was: She's with them.
But then she stepped forward.
And I saw it.
Both her hands were cuffed.

Not like mine—hers were locked through a long steel chain, anchored somewhere beneath the floor.

Three men stood around her, rifles raised.
Heavy automatics.
Models I didn't recognize.
Could be new-gen prototypes. Maybe even some of mine.

Still—she walked.
Like she didn't even see the barrels pointed at her.
She didn't look at me. Not once.
She walked to the empty chair across the table and sat—
still staring straight at Jovan.

The second she took the seat—one of the guards pressed the rifle muzzle against her neck. Didn't faze her.

Meanwhile, Daggan walked over. Unlocked one of her cuffs.
Threaded the chain through a heavy steel hook bolted into the table's center. Then clicked the cuff back on.

Now she was locked in.
The table wasn't movable. Neither were the chairs.
All of it fixed to the floor.

The three armed guards took a step back.
Daggan, of course, sat down beside Jovan.
Practically drooling.

He was eyeing Marisha like she was meat on a hook—glaring at her curves like he was already working out the positions.
But she didn't even blink in his direction.
Didn't glance at me either.

From the moment she entered the room,
her gaze was welded to Jovan's.
Cold, lethal. As if she'd already written his death and was just waiting for his body to read it.

Jovan started to shift, uncomfortable.
She didn't move.

Just asked—still calm.

—Who hit him in the head?

She hadn't seen it happen. But the bruised side of my skull must've told the story. And the one who answered—without hesitation—was the hammer boy himself.

Daggan raised the weapon proudly, twirling it.

—That'd be me, miss.

His mouth split into something ugly.

—And for that... I figure I've earned the first ride when that thick ass of yours finally gives up the fight.

He laughed.
Loud, harsh.
Like a mutt choking on bones.

Even Jovan flinched at that one.
Brows pinched.
A flicker of distaste crossed his face.

And me? I just sat still.
Because I knew—this ugly idiot had just invited death to sit on his lap.

Daggan didn't understand Marisha.
Didn't know that with her, words had gravity.
Even if she loved you—especially if she loved you—
you measured every syllable.
One wrong move—and she'd leave your bones in a suitcase outside the city.

Even I had slipped once. One poorly-timed line during a low night in Phuket—I still carry the aftermath of that mistake.
And I was hers.

A walking slab of filth like Daggan?
His fate was already sealed.

That's when Marisha turned—eyes still glacier-cold,
and finally looked directly at Daggan.
Scanned him.
Head to toe.
Like she was studying a lab rat before incineration.

Then she spoke—flat, venom-sweet:

—Don't worry. I'll ride the game with you soon enough.
And when I do—you'll wish I had just killed you.

Whether Daggan got the full meaning of her words—who knows.
But the moment her eyes locked with his—those cold, ruthless blue eyes—he swallowed hard.
And went silent. The heat in the room turned claustrophobic.

And Jovan—finally sensing the tension eating the air alive.
Cleared his throat, tried to regain control.

—I admit... that kind of talk toward a lady was totally inappropriate. So—on behalf of this misbehaving kid of mine, please accept my apology, Miss Jasmín...
Or should I say—Miss Zakharova?

Marisha didn't even blink.

—Call me whatever you want, Jovan. It won't change your fate.

That hit.

Jovan exhaled, straightened his suit, tone shifting again—trying diplomacy, as if he hadn't just chained a ghost of vengeance to a steel table.

—I must say… The deeper we dig, the more impressed I am.
At first, we were a little thrown—you don't use your father's name. But once our tech team got access to your phone, things became much clearer.
Israeli tech, you know—it's the best in the world.

He actually swelled with pride, chest puffing like a kid showing off a new toy nobody else can touch. But no one responded.
Not Marisha. Not me. Not Rasheed.
Just silence.
He deflated a little.

Then kept talking.

—Your Chechen father's name…
That's not something to hide.
Ibroxim Samarovoski Zakharov.
The name's still a nightmare in Central Asia.
Sure—he was declared most wanted during the Chechen war.
But that all got swept away when Russia took the territory back.
Records say he even got a senior position in KGB before he—

A pause. A smirk.

—allegedly killed himself.
Still, in the world of espionage? Highly respected.
Even here, in Mossad, his name is spoken with respect.

He leaned forward, voice curious, almost friendly.

—Tell me, Miss Zakharova—why would a man choose an ending like that?

Marisha's answer wasn't loud.
It dropped.
Low. Dead cold.

—Ask him yourself. When you get to the other side.

A silence followed that line.
The kind that cuts deeper than screams.

Jovan, trying to play it cool, nodded slowly.

—Understood. I see you're upset.
Being restrained like this... not ideal, I get it.
But you must understand—this is for mutual safety.
There's no hostility here, not with Russia,
not even with your agency.
We've cooperated on many fronts.
And we're always open to... collaboration.

Marisha didn't let him finish.

—I'll shove that collab up your open ass.

Delivered ice-clean.
Lethal.
With a voice that didn't blink.

I've seen her angry before—but this?
This wasn't anger.
This was precision wrath.

And with Marisha, once you broke protocol, that was it—no way back. Even for me, calming her down in this state had always been a challenge.

For Jovan? Impossible.
The mask of politeness he wore was already cracking.
And she'd barely even started.

Jovan still tried to hold posture. Like he could pull this back into diplomacy if he just played the script hard enough.

—Look, Miss—
I've been maintaining protocol.
Speaking with respect.
From what I've learned, your rank in the Russian force is technically higher than mine.

And to reach that level at your age—well, it deserves respect.
I hope you'll return that courtesy.

—Let's just handle this like professionals.
Simple questions. Simple answers.
Do you know these two men?

He fixed her with a hopeful stare, though Marisha didn't blink.

—Rasheed Dameer was a freelance contractor under me.
We never met in person. Always kept it remote.
But recently I needed to meet him face to face.
That's when you guys shoved your filthy nose in.

Jovan's smile got tighter, forced, trying to play off her venom.

—Even upset, you speak like a proper lady.
Exactly what I'm hoping for.
Now—what about the North Macedonian over there?
Ever seen him before?

Her voice came flat. Unshaken.

—Yes. I've seen him in and out.
Because he's my husband.

A pin dropped.
No—something shattered.

Jovan blinked, caught between disbelief and insult.

—What the ffff—what did you just say?

Marisha didn't repeat herself.

—You heard me. Exactly as I meant it.

Then she turned again.
This time to Daggan.
Held his gaze like she was dragging it through glass.

Daggan had spent the entire scene licking her with his eyes.
But now—he finally started to register the temperature behind her stillness.
That look wasn't cold. It was premeditated.

He didn't know what she was about to do. But his body did—the way prey always knows before the brain does.

That's when I stepped in.
Because if I didn't, Marisha might detonate right here.

—There's a Kuwaiti man—Abdel al-Awadi.
Friend of mine. They grabbed him.
I flew to Kuwait to find him. That's when it all happened.

Marisha turned her head slowly toward me.

—And how thoughtful of you.
Tracking down my entire bloodline like a one-man search party.
How many times did I tell you—if something like this ever came up, you tell me?

—How was I supposed to? You vanished.
Said you were going off-grid for a while—personal reasons.
I only found out after you were already gone.

She didn't argue. Just gave that quiet hum—the kind of sound she makes when she knows I'm not lying, but still holds me responsible. But even as she tried to speak to me like she always had—this wasn't the Marisha I knew.

Same black outfit, sure.
Her signature color.
But everything else?
It felt... off.
Unfamiliar.

She'd never worn a chain that low on her body.
Never pierced her navel.
Never dropped her pants far enough to show that curve of skin.
And never, ever, walked into a room dressed like this.

The thin top clung to her without armor, no bra,
every line of her chest shaped by the light not exposed,
but unmistakably outlined.

Then there was the scent.
Marisha always wore Narcotix—a subtle, dangerous perfume.

Like opium wrapped in satin.
But tonight, she smelled sharper—sexier in a dangerous way.

And the choker.
Oh Lord.
Same shade as her eyes—electric blue.
But this wasn't just a fashion band.
It was a code.
The kind used in kink dens.
A tag worn by girls who kneel on command.
Thin enough to snap.
Bold enough to say it in their language—Daddy's Girl.

She wore it knowing exactly what it meant.
And still, she wore it.

I started noticing all of it—one detail at a time.
And beneath my skin, despite the chaos... the lover in me stirred.
Not desire. Possession.

Not because she was showing skin—but because she was weaponizing it. Right in front of these bastards.

I couldn't stop myself.

—You knew exactly what Rasheed meant to me.
And still—not a word. Just showed up in that leash, dressed like a tag toy, playing Daddy's Girl to close the deal.

I didn't raise my voice.
But the burn behind those words?
It scorched the space between us.

Rasheed, seated just an arm's length away, felt my Jealousy instantly. It rippled through his body like voltage.

He flinched—physically.

—This isn't on me, Chief. I do jobs for a lot of people.
Big money clients, weird requests, coded instructions.
The voice on the line—always filtered.
Could've been man or woman, hell,
could've been a bot for all I know.

They gave me strange tasks over time, and I just follow instructions. Then this one—they said go to a disco in Prague. Show up. No questions.

—I thought someone would meet me there.
I didn't know that someone was her.
I swear on my fucking life—I had no clue, man.

He was spiraling—trying to explain himself,
not just to me, but to her.
To the woman.

And through it all, Jovan and his dogs didn't flinch.
Didn't speak. Didn't even blink.
They were enjoying the show—sitting back, soaking up every detail, getting the full story without lifting a damn finger.

Rasheed kept talking.
I wasn't listening anymore.
My eyes were still on Marisha.

While I spoke to Rasheed.

—I get it. But I'm not talking to you.

She still didn't look at me, didn't acknowledge a thing I said.

Instead—she turned her face calmly toward Jovan and asked him, as if none of this had happened:

—So, Jovan—how do you want this to end?

Jovan crossed his arms.

—That depends entirely on you.
We want intel. That's it. You're already telling each other everything we need—right here at the table.

He smirked, put on that patronizing "negotiator" voice.

—If you'd be so kind to keep going... tell us:
Where did Rasheed get the bomb used in Eilat?
Who supplied him? And why?

Marisha's voice didn't change.

—I don't know. Rasheed works for multiple sides.
He's not my asset full-time.
You can't hold me for every mercenary's dirty laundry.

Jovan's smile tightened into something colder.

—Very diplomatic. But let's not forget—
a few years ago, while stationed in Damascus,
you personally tipped off that Romanian bloodsucker—
Amethyst Vega about one of our covert units.

His voice dipped. Turned sharp.

—And based on that tip, Vega slaughtered them.
Carved them up in mud and blood.

He leaned in, close enough to taste the accusation.

—And now you show up in Prague, trying to 'rescue' Rasheed Dameer, while he's being held by the same Count Vega.
Coincidence?

I saw it in Marisha's eyes.
That twitch—one fraction of a blink.
She'd heard this line of attack coming, maybe even before I did.

And her answer?
Smooth. Deadly.

—That was war, Jovan.
Nobody's hands come out clean. I did my job.
And Prague? I helped Rasheed.
That's a professional call. Nothing else.
If he's got his own thing with Vega,
that's not my cross to bear.

—You sure?

—Sure enough not to flinch when I say it.

And she didn't. Not even once.

Jovan leaned back in his chair, savoring it all like a fine cigar.

—Alright—let's swallow your story for now, as twisted as it sounds. Truth is, all of us have been dying to get our hands on that Dark Weapon used in Eilat. And the Iranians—the crew tied to that bomb—your Rasheed here worked for them too.
That much you knew.

—Recently, that same crew was moving a fresh shipment through Iraq. And we learned Rasheed himself was part of that convoy. So, Rasheed—why didn't you make it to Iran?

The silence before Rasheed's reply was thick enough to choke on. Then he gulped, voice breaking under weight he couldn't hide anymore.

—We were hit. Everyone slaughtered.
I made it by luck—just dumb luck.

Jovan grinned like a man watching a child finally admit he stole the candy.

—Good. That's better.
Now you're talking like an obedient little kid.

He made it sound like a joke, but the hunger in his eyes gave him away. He was loving every second of this theatre, his own twisted role as stage director.

Then his attention flicked back to Marisha.

—Miss Jasmín. Or Zakharova.
Let's stop playing nice.
That hit on Rasheed's convoy?
The one that wiped them out?
The killer who took the shipment—Darius Caesar,
aka the Ghost of Al-madam. He got the tip from you.
And this sweet little husband of yours,
this North Macedonian saint—
his so-called Kuwaiti friend Abdel al-Awadi?
Our sources place him in Phuket—right next to Caesar.
At the exact time you, my dear, were also there—in person.

The room turned into a graveyard.
The silence wasn't passive—it screamed.
Nobody breathed. Nobody twitched.
The weight of that revelation slammed every soul in the room like a hammer to the spine.

Even me.
Especially me.
Because I knew what nobody else did.
That "Amethyst Vega" alias Jovan had just thrown in—
I created it myself.

The year I first crossed paths with Macro.
It wasn't just a mask I put on.
It was skin—layered, polished, cemented by both of us,
brick by brick, lie by lie, until it became real.
But Phuket? Before that, I didn't know Marisha.
Never even met her.

Yet now Jovan was saying she'd tipped off Vega—
me—years before we ever crossed eyes?

Even more twisted—not long ago, she herself had grilled me over the phone, interrogating me about whether that same hit was real.

And yes, others had thrown it in my face over the years.
That massacre.
I brushed it all off.

Macro told me: let the rumors swirl.
It helps us more than it hurts.
So we let them breathe, even fed them.
We spread lies like wildfire when it served the mission.

This one I thought was just another ember in the wind.
But now—Jovan wasn't bluffing.
He had names.
He had dates.
And the knife's edge turned.

Because the convoy hit Rasheed himself once blamed on me, the one I wasn't even alive for yet—Jovan was pinning it on Marisha.

And time, the one she allegedly tipped off? Darius Caesar.
Which meant—she had given the kill order...
to me!

The room had already begun to close in.
The lies, the truths, the dead threads twisting through our names—It was too much, even for me. I was slipping.

If Rasheed was trembling—if his lips were shaking like glass on the edge of a shelf—how could I blame him?

He wasn't stupid.
He was connecting the dots.
And what he saw at the center—was me.
And Marisha.
To him, it must be meant like we were the architects behind all those events, all his sufferings.

And now he was on the edge.
If he cracked—if that wild grief inside him turned into words—we were done. But Jovan saved us—whether he meant to or not.

He'd been watching Rasheed unravel, smiling like a butcher who sees a calf losing strength on the hook.

He ignored Rasheed and turned his attention back to Marisha.

—Speak, Miss.
Because when we get silent bastards like Rasheed,
or Kamran—we know exactly how to split their guts open and find the truth inside. In fact...

He reached for the remote.

—...Kamran is just beneath us now.
Want to see how we work him over?

He clicked.
And hell answered.

The wall blinked to life—a grainy, black-lit camera feed.
A basement cell.
Bare concrete.
One harsh spotlight slicing the dark.

In its circle—Kamran.
Hanging from his wrists, arms racked past human limits.
Naked.
Old, muscle and scar. Broken down
His body sagged from its own weight—sweat and blood soaking down his frame, staining the floor in dark, spreading rivers.

One foot pinned to the ground. The other—yanked out and strapped high, spread like a warning.

Between his legs, a ruin. Not severed—but undone.
Something was wired.
Two clamps. A heartbeat of light.

Every few seconds—the room dimmed.
Kamran convulsed.
Whole body buckling, arching, wrung out in electric agony.
Not enough to kill.
Just enough to carve something out of the soul.
The floor beneath him told the rest:
Blood.
Urine.
Waste.

And in the chair across from him—strapped down, eyes locked open—sat Abdel al-Awadi.

He was already gone.
He wept like a man watching his own afterlife.
Tears, vomit, ragged breath.
He watched every pulse.
Every scream.

Rasheed saw it all.
And I felt his soul collapse inward.

He choked.
Not on words. On grief.

His mouth opened like it wanted to scream but couldn't find the wind. His eyes flooded.
Tears spilled fast and hot. Froth clung to his lips.
His face twitched like something inside was breaking.
Not a man watching a screen—a child watching his world be dismembered.

And me? I didn't care about Kamran. Never did.
But watching that screen, watching Rasheed drown in silence, my body remembered things I never gave it permission to.
Pain.
Old.
Vivid.
Sacred.

The kind I don't talk about.
Not to anyone. Not even in confession.
The kind I survived—through fire.

Strangely today—my purpose feels blurred.
I can't feel the fire like before.
Only the weight of the Darkness in my chest.
Just that old ache.

My body knows it's not enough.
I can't kill these monsters on human strength alone.
Marisha's skilled—deadly, even.
But not enough.
Not against all of them. Not like this.

Whatever happens now—I have no control.
Only the Lord can decide if this ends in ash or in judgment.

Jovan reached out, clicked the screen off.
Kamran's ruin vanished in a blink.
Still—his screams echoed in the marrow.

Rasheed didn't recover. Couldn't.
Both hands locked to the steel, forehead pressed to the cold metal.

He wept—broken, silent sobs leaking out of him like blood from a cracked vessel. No fight left, just the slow shiver of someone coming apart.

And Marisha? No emotion.
Stone-faced. Expressionless.

Her mask didn't twitch.
Not when the TV clicked on. Not when it clicked off.
She held it like a card no one could see.
Poker-faced. Dead-eyed.
Coiled so tight she could snap the whole room in half,
and nobody would see it coming.
But Jovan—he was proud. Swollen with the arrogance of control.

He broke the silence with the voice of a man who thought he'd already won.

—So. Miss. What's it going to be?
You want to die with dignity?
Or get stripped and fed to the dogs in front of your man?

He didn't look at her.
He looked at me—as if that would make it hurt more.
Then he turned.

Tilted his head toward Daggan.
Like a silent handoff.
Here's your dog.

Daggan's eyes lit up—sharp and hungry.

—Boss—
Let's hang him up by the balls.
Let him watch while I take her.
Front, back. Three rounds.
Then the boys get their shot.

He licked his lips, voice thick as rot.

—And when we're done? I want to hear what kind of sounds she makes with that bold look.

His laugh was wet. Rotten.
A hyena's wheeze in a room full of open wounds.

That kid didn't know when to stop. Mistake on top of mistake—digging his own grave with every word.

If he wanted to talk dirty, fine.
But saying it out loud—in front of me, in front of her—was a death wish wearing spit.

Even if I didn't do it now,
even if I left this place cold and bleeding,

I'd return. One day, in another room, another face—and when I did, he'd forget what it meant to beg.

Marisha didn't flinch.
Not when Daggan spoke.
Not when Jovan offered her like a side of meat.

She just turned.
First toward them—those hyenas,
faces slick with hunger and venom.

Then, she looked at me.
And there it was—not fear.
Not even rage.
Just the softest gaze.

The kind she used to save for when we stood under dimming light, when everything around us was running hot,
and she'd still ask if I wanted a cardamom tea.

—Much of what you just heard from Jovan, *she said,*
is true, Volchik. I never told you everything—not because
I was hiding. But because believers never ask for explanations.
And disbelievers wouldn't believe them anyway.

I felt it. That line.
It wasn't a defense.
It was a mirror. Thrown straight into my chest.

Because I had said those exact words—not aloud, but to myself. To silence. To the only thing that never answered back.

And now she was handing it back to me.
Word for word.
With eyes that asked nothing—not forgiveness, not permission—just... recognition.

And I couldn't even feel anger.
Not at her. Not at anything.
Only this strange, aching tenderness—because I knew the kind of world she'd had to survive in.

Because I wasn't there.
Because I couldn't be.

Whatever she did to survive—she did it alone.
And the part of me that used to think I could protect her?
That part had bled out long ago, somewhere between false names and blown cities.

I said the only thing I could say.

—None of that matters, Ree.
But that choker on your neck—it's driving me insane.

And for the first time since we entered this hell—Marisha smiled.
Not fake or flirt. Just soft.
Like fire curling up beside you, not to burn—but to remind you that warmth can still mean something.

She looked at me with that sly spark in her eyes—the one that always warned something beautifully unhinged was about to happen—and then turned her gaze to the oversized wall clock hanging above Jovan's head.

She raised her right hand. The one chained to the table—and unclasped the choker from her neck.

The motion was smooth. No sound.
Just the soft glide of chain and cloth.

She held the thing in both hands—folding it open like scripture. Piece by piece, she unfurled it, and when it was fully laid out, she placed it on the table between us.

For a second, nobody knew what the hell we were looking at.
Not a band, not a scarf, not a rag.

It could've passed for a keffiyeh.
Maybe a folded tactical map.
Or maybe just an accessory too stylish to question.
But I knew better.
I'd seen what Marisha could do with a nail polish brush.

I'd seen her paint my name on one hand, hers on the other—like she was wearing a declaration.
So this? This wasn't fashion. This was intention.

Daggan, of course, didn't understand any of it.
But he couldn't take his eyes off her.

He leaned forward, lips half-open, staring like a beast sniffing meat he hadn't been allowed to touch yet.

Then he stepped forward, moved past Jovan's chair, tried to get a closer look—and suddenly, the light in his face changed.

He saw it.

—Is that... is that a gas mask?

He blinked hard.
Because now it made sense.
Not the gas mask you imagine—bulky, plastic, with filters and seals.

This was custom kitted. Designed to conceal.
A field mask—elegant, flexible, lethal in stealth.
Couldn't cover the eyes. Didn't need to.
It wasn't for panic.
This was pure survival, wrapped in style.

Jovan's mouth tightened.
Daggan stared harder, confused, maybe even a little impressed.

—You had a gas mask this whole time?
Why didn't you use it on the Disco?

Marisha tilted her head like a question wasn't worth the air.

—Who told you I didn't?

Daggan was stunned silent—not because he understood what she said, but because some part of his primitive brain finally registered: he wasn't looking at a toy anymore.
He was looking at a weapon.

Like the good little beast he was, he stepped closer, eyes narrowed, trying to study the folds and cuts of the fabric—to decode what he was already too late to understand.
But I'd seen it the moment it hit the table.
The cloth wasn't just a gas mask.
It was a message.

Marisha had chosen every thread with purpose.
The cut of the fabric covered nose, mouth, throat—all the places where breath betrays you.
But what caught my eye wasn't the build—it was the design.
Three colors.
Red. Blue. White.
Blossomed in floral patterns across the face—Russia's tricolor.
Marisha's flag. Her spine. Her past.
But the mark that twisted the blade deeper? A blood orchid.
Not just any flower. My flower.

The symbol that only I used.
Known only to a select few. Feared by even fewer.

She stitched it on the left cheek—the side where the heart beats.
Which meant only one thing:
This wasn't just battle. This was sacrament.
She made it for this moment.
Not before. Not after.
This.

Every inch of that cloth was a vow.
A sigil.

And I understood, then and there—Marisha didn't come here unarmed. She came dressed in devotion.

And yet—me? I was naked.
No plan, no gear, no angle—just the ghosts riding in my blood.

Sure, I could slip my wrist past the table bolt—maybe reach back for the gear stashed on my spine, grab the folded blade I tucked earlier.

But that wouldn't be enough.
Not for the three armed men behind her.
Not for Jovan. Not for Daggan.

And certainly not for the butcher at the door—that giant, blade-worshipping, apron-wearing demon whose machetes gleamed like they were thirsting for spine.

I swallowed the weight. It tasted like failure.

—I'm sorry, Ree, *I said, voice low, cracked.*
—I didn't come prepared. Not this time.

She turned, that slow elegance that made danger look like grace, and asked,

—Prepared in what way?

—No weapons. No backup.
No fight left in me, not like the old days.

She smiled again.
The kind of smile that makes gravity feel optional.

—That wasn't a mistake. Your Lord didn't strip you of your weapons. Those were kept intentionally.

—Intentionally? Why He would do that?

—Because you don't need any.

She turned to face me fully now—the long chain still wrapped around her wrist, the gasmask-kafiyah laid out like a battle flag between us.

—I am your weapon, love.
The man who has a Zakharova ready to die for...
will never need anything else.

My heart didn't just skip.
It detonated.
And someone else felt it too.

Jovan was watching us now—not with amusement,
but with something else creeping into his sharp eyes.
Doubt.
Daggan noticed it first.
He looked between us.
Then at the cloth.
Then at Marisha.
Something primal whispered in his bones.

And just as that whisper turned into a question—
the sky roared.
Not the petty noise of a distant bomb.
Not the dull thud of a muffled shell.

This sound tore the world open.
A rolling, thunder-splitting, soul-fracturing barrage that made every wall in that room hum with threat.

It wasn't just one blast. It was a symphony.
Fired in unison. An orchestra of war.

My ears screamed.
Daggan's walkie talkie crackled to life—squawked something urgent, panicked—but the second syllable was drowned in a sonic boom that felt like it came from inside our chests.
Not a bomb. Not a grenade.

Any battle-hardened ear could tell—this was a Su-57.
Mach 2.
Low pass.
Screaming straight over the compound.
Something just arrived.

What happened next—I can't say I fully grasped in real time.
The chaos unfolded too fast for reason to keep up.
All I remember is the pitch inside my ears.

That sharp, metallic *beeeinggggg* sound you get right before your brain forgets how to prioritize survival.

Through that ringing,
I heard one sound more clearly than anything else.
A voice. Low, calm, absolute.

—Don't move.

It was Marisha.
I turned—and she was no longer in her chair.

One of the guards—the last of the trio behind her—was pinned to the wall. And she was pressed flat against his body, her freed arm angled upward like a predator striking through bone.

The chain from her restraint—long, stainless,
graceful like a whip—had become a divine weapon.
One end still bound to her wrist.
The other? Hooked into Jovan's throat.
Not around it. Not choking.
Hooked.

The open cuff had been driven in like a sickle—metal jammed through soft tissue, lodged just beneath the artery.
The perfect place to bleed him—without letting him bleed out too fast.

Jovan flailed. Legs kicking like a fish in air.
Marisha didn't even glance.
She just stood there, chain taut—like she was walking a dog made of human failure.
Blood poured steady.
Thick.
Dark.
Gurgling like a slow, boiling confession.

The weapon he never saw coming had already killed him.
He just hadn't dropped yet.
And in the same blink—I watched her twist.

She ripped the rifle from the guard of her back in one fluid motion—gripped it like a ballet dancer holding a blade—and turned.

Before the sound of her footsteps had even faded, two heads burst like fruit.

Drrmm. Drrmm.

The guards—the ones who'd been breathing down her spine all this time—were reduced to wet pulp.
Brain, bone, a mist of steam in the air.
The air turned warm with the thick, copper heat of fresh skull.
Their faces hadn't even processed the threat before their heads became mush against the back wall.

It was too clean. Too deliberate.
You're not supposed to fire at human faces from that range.
Not unless you want to see what's underneath humanity.

It seems Marisha didn't carry those reservations.
Their bodies crumpled in place like puppets whose strings had been soaked in gasoline.

Daggan had moved forward seconds earlier—leaning in to admire her mask, to leer, to pretend she was still a girl to be devoured.

That single step—dumb luck—saved his life.
He was just—standing. Confused. Cornered.

If he'd stayed where he was? He'd be pulp too.
Now, the rifle turned toward him.
He stared down the barrel.
Breath locked. Muscles frozen.
And in his hands—nothing but a hammer.

The same man who'd bragged about ripping her apart, who'd detailed his plan to rape her in front of me and toss what was left to his pack, now had nothing.

No words. No wit. Just the weight of knowing that she could shatter his brain before he even blinked.

He raised his hands, slowly.
Pathetically.
As if that could erase what he'd said, what he'd become in front of us.

And yet—Marisha didn't shoot. Not yet.
She was calculating.
Not because she spared him.
Because she wanted it to hurt.

Behind her, the last guard—the one she had pinned, was still somehow standing. Still frozen. Still alive.

Why?
Then I saw it.
He wasn't fighting her.
He wasn't moving.
Because he wasn't looking at her rifle.
His gaze was locked lower.

His hands, paralyzed by a cocktail of fear and sick hunger, were still clamped onto her breasts—tight, shaking, like they were the last thing he'd ever touch.

And his eyes?
Locked. Dilated.
Burning with a kind of hunger that drowned out any sense of danger.

He wanted to die like this. With her skin in his hands, with her body in his grip, even if it meant his soul went black.

That's when she whistled.
A sharp, low-pitched breath across her teeth.

To us.
To me.

And with a slow sway of her hips—she pressed herself further into him. Not as seduction. As bait.

Then—in one clean, serpentine motion, she pulled the rifle from her shoulder and flung it across the room.
To me.

Even mid-air, the weapon felt like a handshake.
Perfect balance.
Perfect aim.
Like she'd been throwing guns her whole life.

She didn't need to see. She knew I'd catch it.
She knew I was free.

Because while the chaos burned, while screams and thunder filled the room, I'd already picked my lock.
Quietly.

And now—her fire met mine.
The guard still clutching her?
Still drooling at her skin?
Still thinking he'd gotten away with it?

She looked me in the eyes.
Raised her left hand—chained but strong,
and slid it behind her back.
She found his hair. Fisted it like a leash.
And dragged his face downward—hard.

She ducked beneath the table.
His skull smashed into the steel edge with a crack so sharp
the sound itself split the air.

I saw blood arc.
A fine mist.
Then a splash.
Then a smear.
His body slid off to the side like meat slipping off a hook.

One glance at the wall behind him—red.
Patterned. Painted.
Whatever had been in his head—was now decorating concrete.

Marisha stood up.
Hair loose. Eyes cold.
And she didn't look at the body.
She looked at me.

And for the first time since this room turned into hell—I saw it.
Marisha's body is not soft. Not in the way the world defines femininity—no cotton-candy curves, no limp submission.

And yet, she's not hardened like a soldier either.
Her shape—her weight—responds.

When you press into her, she pushes back, not out of resistance, but as if her skin holds a memory of how to cradle violence like a lover.

I used to hold her like that.
Wrapped around her from behind, not possessive—just present.
The way men hold onto things they're scared to lose,
but too proud to say it.

I never grabbed her like that beast did.
Never sank my hands into her chest like it was owed to me.
But now, watching her pull away from the limp body of the man who just tried, I realized something deeper.
She didn't resist that man's grip.

She let it happen. Not out of submission.
But as a message—to me.

That eye contact—the way she looked at me as it happened,
wasn't just to confirm control.
It was a warning.
No more touching like that.
Not even from you. Not anymore.

She wasn't just shedding chains.
She was shedding the last traces of softness.

She stood fully now, chest rising once—slow inhale.
Then, with the poise of a trained assassin, she nodded toward me and gestured for the rifle to aim at Daggan.

The same Daggan who was now nothing more than a walking contradiction—arrogance drained, power displaced,
hands in the air like a child caught with a stolen knife.

Marisha didn't wait for me to act.
She turned and walked—slowly—toward the doorway,
toward the butcher, toward the hulking mass of stitched-up sin
who stood between us and whatever came next.

Her steps weren't heavy.
They were calculated, balanced.

When she reached the edge of the table,
she paused, made direct eye contact with the butcher,
and without breaking her stare—lifted her free hand.

With it, she reached down toward her belly,
unhooked the ornamental piercing resting at her navel.
A thin, steel loop glinting with red and blue,
now doubling as a key.

She leaned forward, brought her leg up—and in a single,
fluid movement, placed her foot on the table edge
and perched like a goddess summoned by blood.

The leg iron—previously unnoticed by me—came loose.
She undid it with surgical precision.
And I realized then—the entire time she had been fighting,
commanding chaos, she'd done it all with a chained leg.

I hadn't even seen it.
Because when she walked into this room,
I was too distracted by the low drop of her pants,
by the scent of submission she wore like perfume.

My rage had blinded me.
And now—I saw what she wanted me to see:
Every part of her is a weapon.
Even the parts I used to kiss.

Meanwhile, Daggan—the bastard who had chained my foot to the steel table base—was still standing with hands raised.

He knew if I bent down to unlock my ankle, he could strike.
And I knew it too.
That risk was sitting between us, breathing.

Rasheed, shackled on the other side, arms stretched wide across the table like a broken sacrifice, had no chance of helping.
He wasn't even watching.
He'd rested his head on the cold metal, surrendered to his own shaking.

And he was right to.
Had he raised his head, Daggan might've used him as a shield.

Instead, Rasheed became dead weight between fire and its target.

So I focused forward.
Rifle raised. Sight locked.

And said,

—Put the hammer down, step around the table,
and stand still—you fuck.

I wouldn't have shot him. But how could he possibly believe that?
He was the man who had threatened to cut off my cock,
hang it from the ceiling, and rape the woman I loved
in front of me while his pack took sloppy seconds.

He had no version of this story where I let him live.
He complied—slow. Careful.
Set the hammer down like it was sacred, then walked around,
docile as a beaten dog, eyes never leaving my rifle.
But it wasn't just my aim that kept him tamed.
It was what he heard outside.

Because now—even through the thunder of his own fear,
the background noise had changed.

No backup came.
No guards stormed in.
No techs. No Mossad cavalry.
Nobody.

Only the sound of artillery.
Real war.
Mortar shells.
Grenades.
Machine gun bursts.
And somewhere in the deeper bass—the seismic pulse of heavy cannons shaking the bones of the earth.

Outside this room, the world was ending.
And no one was coming in to stop it.

Daggan was still locked in place. Staring at Marisha like a man convinced death was worth one more look.

That's exactly why I'd positioned him there—not just to keep him under aim, but so I could see her too.

If she needed cover, if she gave me even the smallest glance, I'd fire. My reflexes weren't hers, but my aim had never missed a target that deserved to die.

Marisha had peeled off her jacket. Laid it gently across the table, like this was a fitting room and not a warzone soaked in brains and blood.

And beneath the jacket? A cropped top.
Minimal. Tactical.
So tight it looked like breath itself would stretch the fabric to tearing.

But she wasn't showing off.
She was setting the trap.

As she walked toward the butcher—that hulking, apron-draped creature waiting at the door like a megalith.

She raised both arms and tied her hair back with slow, unhurried grace. The motion made her monuments rise in full—proud, high, breathtaking.
Not for show. Pure, loaded bait.

She looked at him.
Her voice cutting through the distance.

—Hey, Uncle Shavit. Remember me?

The butcher didn't.
Not her face. Not her name.
But his eyes locked onto one thing—the curves I once believed were licensed only to me.

His gaze tracked her like a moth drawn to the same fire that already burned it. His hand twitched around the grip of his blade, and his voice turned to smoke.

He scraped both machetes together—metal kissing like teeth grinding bone—and rasped:

—I don't know your face, baby doll...
but your skin? That, I know.
Some patterns—the hands keep,
even when the mind can't.

He chuckled, eyes glinting.

—I've worked with softer. But you?
If you can stay alive... I'll savor every second.

This wasn't a taunt.
This wasn't a bluff.
It was memory.
Ritualized. Practiced.

And Marisha? She smiled.
Not fake. Not defensive.
The kind of smile a woman gives her lover when he's found her favorite dress.

—Remember Parisha? *she asked.*
That girl from Samara? The Chechen one?

The name lit up his face like a war god remembering an old victory.

He paused. Sniffed the air.

—Ohhh… that little blossom.
Yeah. She was... too fragile.
Soft as silk. Didn't leave a mark.
Took my time.

He tilted his head, eyes glassy with recollection.

—Made something to remember her—kept it close for weeks.
Her little sister was there. Waiting for her turn.
But the bitch ran, before I even got started.

He laughed.
Laughed like he was recounting a bed time story.
Like this horror was his anecdote.
And Marisha? She laughed back.

That same teasing tilt of the head, that sparkle in her eye, the one she used to give me after a good romance, or a joke only the two of us understood.

—She didn't escape, Uncle.

She stepped closer. No flinch. No delay.

—That little bud—the one who watched you helpless,
even when it was her only sister—her life, her soul,
every last fucking thing she loved on this earth.

She spread her arms, presenting herself like a ritual offering.

—She bloomed. And she came back—for you.

His eyes went wide.
A flicker passed across his face—recognition?
Lust?
Fear?

The butcher sniffed again.

—Aaah... so that's why you smelled damn hot.
Since the moment they dragged you in...
my snake's been wide awake.
It wants to taste you.
Wants to feel you fight, little blossom.

His knuckles flexed around the machete, white to the bone.
Wanted to lunge. To taste what he once lost.

And Marisha? She tilted her head, smiled again—deeper.

—But how will you do it, Uncle?
If I bite your little antique... won't it crack?

He grinned—slow and unbothered.

—Ah, sweet chick...
You ran, remember?
That's why you didn't see how I prepare things.

His voice was casual—like he was explaining a cooking trick.
Not confessing to ritualized horror.

—I make them soft first. Quiet. Breakable.
Then I let my serpent find the center.
Doesn't matter if they resist—God, it always fits.
Your sister? That sweet little thing lasted three days.
I put things in her. And yeah—she screamed.
I wanted more time. But she died too fast.
Little bitch.

Marisha smiled. But it wasn't flirty, not the weaponized seduction she wore like perfume earlier.
This was deeper, ancestral. This was a girl's soul rising from a body that was never allowed to weep.

She stepped forward, slow, eyes glassy with something more terrible than rage—memory.

—Show me your thing, Uncle Shavit. Open me up.

Her voice didn't tremble.
It lilted—like a lullaby twisted in reverse.

—You won't believe me, I know.
But since that day, every single night... I've dreamt of this.
This game you taught me.
Even lying in the arms of someone I loved,
I closed my eyes and imagined you.

She exhaled softly,
like she was confessing a sacred lust to a priest.

—You are the reason I came here in person.

The butcher's breath hitched.
His hands flexed around the blades.

—Damn, little whore...
Didn't know you loved me that much.
I should've opened you long ago.

They walked toward each other like lovers.
Like dancers in a ritual only they remembered.
Words hung between them like steam over blood.

And as they stepped closer, his machetes scraped each other again—shhhk, shhhk—gleaming now with ritualistic clarity.

The others didn't matter.
The world didn't matter.
This was their moment.
Predator. Prey.
Reversed. Rewritten.

Then—in a blink—he struck.

A flash of steel, a slicing wind—BEEEW—the machete cut through the air like a song. But it hit nothing.

Because Marisha—
Marisha was already behind him.
Gone from where she stood.
Gone from the strike zone.
Gone like a whisper tucked inside a bullet.

He froze, hulking body rooted where she had just been.
Massive back turned to us. Neck stiff.

From this angle—a perfect shot.
One pull of the trigger, and it's over.
But I didn't move.
Because her face—visible now just past the butcher's shoulder—was still smiling.

And I saw the blood.
It began to drip.
Drop by drop.
From his wrist.

Something had happened.
Something none of us had seen.
His hand—the one holding the left machete—twitched once.
The blood had become a stream now.

Dark. Heavy.
Rhythmic.

And Marisha? Her right hand rose into view.
In it—a carbon steel.
Not polished. Not modern.

The blade looked blackened—aged,
like it had swallowed fire once and never cooled.
Not the kind you buy. The kind you inherit.
Sharpened by time and pain.
Edge glinting like the inside of a killer's memory.
Forged for only one thing: to bleed.

She held it like she'd been born holding it.
And now—the reason for the blood became obvious.

Daggan was watching.
Still biting his lip.
Still thinking.
That blade had slipped past his search.
Hadn't thought to look beneath the symbols.
And now he stood there, haunted by his own oversight—
watching a goddess dismantle a demon with precision.
But the butcher—he wasn't done.

Somehow, despite his wrists bleeding, despite having lost the left hand in every sense of the phrase, he twisted his hips, lifted his other arm, and with shocking speed for a man his size,
slashed at her throat.

It was meant to be final.
The last swing.
His redemption.
But that's the thing about monsters—
they mistake bloodlust for accuracy.

Marisha was no longer a target.
She was a ghost stitched from revenge.

The butcher's blade hissed through air.
It met nothing.
She was already gone.
Already standing on his blind side, her blade dripping like a priest's sacrament, face still curved in that terrible, delicate smile.

And his other hand? Now bleeding too.
And still—he laughed.
Not bravado. Not denial.
Pure insanity.

His chest heaved with it. His huge body shaking like laughter was the only thing holding it together.

And she—
she laughed too.
Like a child covering her mouth after pushing a vase off a ledge.
Then she raised it.

That blade—blackened, unpolished, not even flashy.
But even that beast of a man took a step back.
Whatever it was...
it wasn't just a weapon.
It was something terrible.

She tilted her head—voice sweet, almost playful.
Like the steel was speaking through her.

—I'm Zakharova. I missed you, Uncle Shavit.
I was forged—and left thirsty.
Waiting all this time...
just to get drunk on your blood.
But you've gotten old.
Your body doesn't move like it used to.
And I'm afraid—who's going to haunt little girls now?

On the surface—that sentence sounded like mockery.
But underneath it—you could hear the bones grinding.

The Butcher seemed tensed.
Both machetes down.
He tried to grab her.
Crush her.

Hold her the way he used to hold girls just before they broke.
But Marisha didn't step back.
She stepped into his arms.

Ducked her head into the cradle of his chest, right into the closing of his elbows—like she wanted to be held.

And now he grinned.
Sick bastard thought he'd won.
That this was submission.
That her laughter was surrender.

And then—

—Squeeze harder, Uncle, *she whispered,* —It feels good.

He almost answered.
Some revolting joke. Some wet promise of what he'd do next.
But his mouth froze.
His eyes opened. His body pulled back like someone had just whispered God's name in his ear.

We all saw it at once.
Me.
Daggan.

Even Rasheed, still limp on the table.
Something was wrong.

The butcher's grin split into confusion.
His mouth, still half-open from the laugh, began to tremble.

He staggered back.
Hands raised—blood now pouring faster.
He was trying to understand it—to name it—but couldn't.

None of us could see what had happened until he turned slightly.

Until Marisha stepped to the side, arms at her sides,
still holding that ancient steel she just named Zakharova.

And only then we saw it.
The apron.
The skin he wore—was split down the center.

From just below his navel to the base of his groin—clean, perfect separation.

His guts were trying to remember how to stay inside his body.
And losing.

Strings of intestine—slick, red, curling out like ropes in a ruined well—started pushing through the gap.
Like they couldn't wait to escape him.

The man who used to call himself a butcher was now the slaughtered.

And Marisha? Still smiling.
But now it was colder.
She wasn't killing him. She was teaching him.
Because for men like him—death was mercy.

She wasn't offering mercy. She slid behind him.
Not fast. Not slow. Just intentional.

And before his brain could catch up, before his knees could find collapse, she lifted her arms and delivered two more slices—
one on each side of the torso, just beneath the ribs.

The blade opened arteries like zippers. Blood fountained from the butcher's wrists, then from his sides, and finally from his chest.

He didn't scream.
He gurgled. Like the body was still trying to speak but the soul wanted to walked out.

He slid—like the air had peeled the gravity from beneath him.
And Marisha stood over what remained.
Eyes burning. Breath steady.

Voice like thunder dressed in lace:

—What's wrong, Uncle? You scared?
There's still much more to open.

By now, the butcher had nothing left to say.
The perversion that once coiled behind his smile had dried up—replaced by something he wasn't used to feeling: uncertainty.

We couldn't see it in his face—not fully.
But in the way how his weight shifted backwards, how his eyes began flicking—searching for exits—we could feel the old predator realizing he was no longer the one holding the leash.

And that blade dressed as a woman? She didn't even chase him.
She let him back up—step by step—retreating toward the table.
She followed—matching the slow, deliberate pace of her victim backing into position.
Not a fight. Not a hunt.
A setup.

And when his wide frame finally aligned—his lower back brushing the table edge—she moved.
Fast. Precise.

One step forward.
Body twisting low.
A sudden spring of muscle and whiplash calculation.
And then—CRACK.

We didn't see the kick.
No wind-up. No warning.
Just the sound of something wrong—a wet, bone-splitting thud that echoed through the room like thunder screaming into cement.

The butcher flew—or rather, collapsed backward—
his upper body slammed down across the steel table,
his belly folding like raw dough.

The sound was wrong because it didn't come from a fist.
Or a boot.
The sound came from a hammer.

Only—the room's one hammer hadn't moved.
It still lay untouched on the table where Daggan had left it.

So where the fuck had that impact come from?
I looked down.
And then I saw it.

Her shoe. Marisha's custom combat boots—the same ones that moved like shadows across the floor—had hammerheads built into the soles.

Of course they did.
Why wouldn't she carry violence in her footsteps?
Why wouldn't every part of her be a weapon?
Now the hammer-blows kept coming.
Not at his chest. Not at his skull.
But at his knees.

CRACK. CRACK.
CRACK. CRACK.

Over and over—driving into the loose-jointed hinges of his giant legs. And slowly—inevitably—those knees gave up.

What looked like tree trunks seconds ago
were now nothing but bags of meat.
Useless. Dangling.

He couldn't stand anymore. He couldn't even kneel.
The monster who once loomed like a god was now crawling toward earth.

And Marisha grinned—a slow, luminous grin like fire twining itself in silk.

—Now we can play properly, Uncle, *she said, gentle as poison.*
—Let's open everything... together.

Still smiling, still humming with the energy of old pain catching up to its architect, she watched him leak—watched his body try to keep up with the agony flowing out of it.

He didn't scream. He couldn't.
Because what came next wasn't a roar—it was fear.
Real.
Involuntary.

His body betrayed him.
Right there—between the stumps of his shattered knees—
his bladder gave out.

A wet hiss.
A dark pool.
Shame painted across the floor.

And she saw it.
She smelled it.
And for the first time in this entire performance, she frowned.
Not in disgust. But in disappointment.

Shook her head, tone layered with something almost maternal.

—What's this, Uncle? Pissing yourself already?
We haven't even opened that part yet.
The part you used to stuff into us.

And then she added, voice sweet as honey.

—You were good at filling...
Why not let me see what's inside you?

The line was surgical.
But the face that delivered it? Divine.
And across the room—Daggan was watching.
Frozen.
Breath shallow. Eyes locked.

His body was shaking—not from guilt, but from a horror he couldn't explain. He was watching a girl he once would've used like a toy dissect a man just like him.

And for the first time in his life, he understood something no bullet had ever taught him—What it means when your victim grows teeth.

Intentions may differ.
Motives may clash. But the kill?
The kill feels the same when the blade meets flesh.

Daggan has done it.
I've done it.
Rasheed, too, likely has his share of ghosts—hidden behind money, orders, or a face turned just enough not to remember.
But not like this.
Not with a smile like hers. Not while whispering sweet nothings to the same body she's unzipping.

Marisha climbed onto the table—not beside him, not over him—but on him.
She planted her weight square on his belly,
like she was mounting a beast that once ruled her fear.

Now he was the altar.
And she—the priestess of fire.

Her thighs locked over his ribs.
Her hips pressed down—heavy, final—pushing more gut from his torn abdomen like soup from a cracked offering bowl.

One hand stayed flat on his chest.
The other, still holding the blade, pointed to Daggan.

—Bring the hammer.

But Daggan? He wasn't looking at her curves anymore.
Not her chest.
Not the flawless shape beneath her hips.
His eyes were locked on the blade.
Finally—someone in Mossad was watching the right thing.

Rasheed noticed first.
Still bound, but not blind.
Poor guy saw the signal Daggan missed and began inching his body—rib by rib—across the table's steel spine.
No muscle strength. Just raw will.
His wrists still shackled wide apart.

Somehow—by angling his side just enough—he reached it.
The hammer.
Three fingers.
No grip.
Just pressure and friction.
And with a final shove—he sent it sliding toward her.

Letting go of the table's edge, Marisha leaned forward—pressed the blade deeper into the butcher's chest like punctuation.
Then caught the hammer mid-slide with her other hand.
Click.
Grip.
Calm as ritual.

She looked down at the man
who had once carved her sister alive.

Tilted her head.
Smiled like a schoolgirl telling a bedtime secret.

—Now I'm going to take your teeth, Uncle.
Then I'll put something hard in your mouth—and you'll feel so much pleasure. Just like you always promised.

He didn't reply. Couldn't.
Because Marisha had already cut open both his cheeks.

The blade had sliced through his face like a zipper—left to right, both sides split—now his mouth couldn't close, even if he still had the nerves to try.

What followed was not a scream.
It was something worse—a wet flutter of breath and blood rattling against exposed muscle and missing bone.
But Marisha wasn't done.

She lifted the hammer.
And drove it into his mouth.

Once.
To loosen the molars.

Twice.
To crack the jaw.

Third time.
Just because it felt right.

Every blow sounded like a body falling off a rooftop.
Dense. Wet.
Final.
The butcher tried to cry. To scream.
But the hammer had already taken the words.
Now only pink foam pooled where vowels used to live.

And still—Marisha stared.
Right into his eyes.
No blinking. No pity. Just presence.

It's not sure if he could still see her,
not even sure if the man still alive.

She straddled his ribs like a bed she never got to sleep on.
Her chest heaved.
Her abs rippled like silk pulled taut.

There was something disturbingly graceful in how she arched—her whole body bent like a violin about to scream.

And still she whispered like a girl tucking in her favorite doll.

—Don't die yet, Uncle. Please.
Taste what's inside your mouth, just a little longer.
You'll enjoy it. After all, I still need your red warmth.
I want to bathe in it.

That hammer was still in his throat.
And her weight—her full weight—was pressed down through her hand, crushing bone and breaking will while the other hand turned his torso into a crimson sketchbook.
Slash.
Slash.

Below the collarbone.
Across the ribs.
Down through the gut.

He stopped screaming.
Stopped shaking.
Stopped being a man.

Just a thing, now.
Something to paint with.
Something to soak in.

When she was done, she lay on him.
Just lay there—like a lover resting after a long, wet evening.

Her cheek on his shoulder.
Her arms limp over the gory pillow of his chest.

How long?
Minutes?
Hours?

Time doesn't exist inside trauma.
It just breathes in a slower rhythm.

And then, like nothing happened, she rolled over.
Turned her back to the corpse.
Nestled herself into the blood like a child hiding in her blanket.

One hand still held the Blade.
The other?

She used it to adjust her nails.
Grooming. Cleaning.
Like this was just any other morning.

By the time she stood, the butcher was gone—and for heaven's sake, we were all left wondering who the real butcher had been.

We were watching something that had climbed out of the fire.
Rasheed stared.
Daggan twitched.
And me?
I didn't know if I could ever hold her again.

The woman named after that terrifying steel—thirsty for blood, trained to slice through every ounce of desire a man once believed was his birthright to slap onto the feminine.

I don't think I could kiss that Zakharova again.
It would feel like kissing the edge of that blade.
Because both of them—steel and woman—are equally lethal.

And I didn't know if that mattered.

Because in that moment—this woman, or that steel,
her namesake—wasn't anyone's anything.
They were what remains after forgiveness fails.

Her eyes scanned us—a calm sweep,
no judgement, no mercy—then stopped on Daggan.

And there it was—that smile.

That fucking terrifying smile she gave
only when the abyss inside her was awake.

Daggan pissed himself.
A full-body surrender.

Hot yellow guilt, flowing down his pant leg,
pooling like a signature at his feet.
The color shows he was holding it for long.

And with that release, Daggan wrote his name in the book of records as the first man who pissed the floor seeing a hot woman's smile.

She saw it.
We all did.

She smiled wider.

—Now, *she said,* —can we start the riding game, Daggan?

She said it sweet, like a mother asking her favorite boy if he wanted dessert.

Dagan had seen enough to know he wanted no part of this "game."

Especially not after watching what his colleague got as a reward for playing. But the most astonishing thing came next.

It made me swear I'd never again judge strength by the size of a body.

Marisha stepped forward, casual as ever.
Daggan trembled but tried to stand tall—back flat to the wall, like posture alone could stop the storm coming.
They were eight feet apart, at most.
Then came the sound—a soft whirl, metal spinning through air.

And in less than two seconds, she had closed the distance.
Her knee landed square—right where no man wants to be struck—and her free hand slammed the hammerhead to his throat, pinning him six inches off the floor like a rag doll.
All his bulk meant nothing now.

Marisha held him there with one arm, a knee, and zero mercy.
And with the other hand—the one holding a that blade—
she casually combed her own hair.

A few strands floated free.
She smiled.

Then, with the sweet tone of someone flipping through lingerie catalogs, she spoke:

—So… you've got armor down there, sweetheart?

Her voice dripped sarcasm.

—Was that supposed to scare off the ladies,
or to impress tattooed boys limping out of your tent?

Maybe Daggan missed the edge in her words.
But he got the message when she let her knee drop and before he could even suck in a breath—her boot swung between his legs like a clock striking midnight.

And this time, the sound wasn't metaphor.
Clang.
Clang.
Thwack.

Something didn't add up.
We've all heard of the "man of steel."
But who the hell walks around with balls made of steel?

Apparently, Daggan does.
And apparently, he wanted the Book of Records to remember him that way.

For now, the only record he was breaking was in pain tolerance.
Whatever alloy he was hiding under his pants, it wasn't helping much.

His face had cracked into a grotesque mask.
His hands, which had been clawing at Marisha's wrist to loosen the pressure on his throat, now flew downward to his crotch—pure animal panic.

Marisha stepped back, giving him the room to fold.
And fold he did.

A split-second later, her boot came down again—this time, straight across his skull.
The crack was audible. The fall, not so graceful.

Daggan hit the ground, mouth still hanging open from the impact, one knee bent like a collapsed statue.
But she wasn't finished.

She crouched — ready to drop the hammer one more time.

—Marisha, stop.

The words left my throat like dust from a long-sealed tomb.
Dry, soft, even I barely recognized the sound.
But she did.

She straightened.
Turned.

And stared at me like I'd just betrayed her.

—Don't hurt him anymore, *I said.*

She narrowed her eyes.

—Why not?

I countered, gently:

—Why do you want to?

Her head tilted, puzzled.

—Are you serious? You heard him—didn't you?

She wasn't even looking at me anymore.

Her gaze had locked onto Rasheed now, whose nod was so fast and eager, it looked like he was trying to rattle the guilt out of his own skull.

But I held steady.

—Saying something… and doing it—aren't the same.
Punishment belongs to the act, Marisha. Not the desire.

I could barely believe the blood-drenched woman before me
was the same one I once held in my arms—close enough
to remember her breathing like peace.
But—tonight, she smelled like vengeance.

And sounded worse.

—You don't leave enemies unfinished.
And this one doesn't deserve mercy.

I met her gaze.

—It's not about mercy, Ree.
You'll let him go—because I said so.

That earned me a long, surgical look.

For a second, I wondered if the hammer in her hand was headed for my skull.

Instead, she dropped it with a calm little clink and came forward—twirling that blade like a barber about to start the last cut before the world end.

Rasheed looked like someone had drained
all his blood with a straw.
To be fair, I wasn't exactly breathing easy either.

She stopped right beside me, leaned down, and whispered into my eyes—

—I want to hold you. But this rot isn't yours to carry,
and I won't stain you with debts you didn't owe.
Can you unlock your feet?

I nodded.

—Good, Volchik. So... will you make love to me?

—What?

—Ugh. That face? Come on.
Let's sneak off and have sex in some corner.
Everyone's distracted anyway.

—Marisha—seriously?

—What? You don't think I look hot right now?

—For Lord's sake—what are you even saying?

—Oh shut up. Say it. Say, I have a wife, and no other woman
in this world looks beautiful to me.

—I... I can say that.

—Say it like you mean it, or I'll shove it up your fucking ass.
And one more thing—if some big-titted girl from Samara tries
those lines on you, I want word-for-word playback. Got it?

—Crystal.

—And don't you dare look at any big-boobed sluts like some thirsty calf sniffing around.

—Understood. Fully.

—Good boy. I'm leaving first—got something to handle.
Get yourselves out. Can't screw you right now, but I'll collect every due later.

She walked out without a sound.
Took me a while to pick the locks off my feet.
Freed Rasheed too.

He rubbed his bruised wrists and gave me a grim look.

—Don't take this the wrong way, Chief, but I gotta say it—for your own good.

—Go on.

—Extra-marital's already a sin. But if you die chasing it?
Forget martyrdom. You're just a dumbass with bad timing.

—∞—

The Cult of Samara

Donetsk City, Ukraine

The second Rasheed felt his feet, he vanished through the open door, legs moving before his mind could catch up.
The reason was obvious.

I followed.
There was no sign of Commander Kamran.
No Sheikh Awadi in the basement either.
Just two bodies slumped by the door—throats ripped wide, blood flooding the concrete like the floor had asked for sacrifice.
Too clean for panic. Too brutal for mercy.
Marisha's mark, written in red.

Beyond the basement, the dark opened up into a factory large enough to bury a war in.
Firelight flickered from scattered blazes—twisted steel, splintered beams, corpses frozen mid-collapse.
Smoke carried the scent of spent powder and charred flesh.
Something had gone down here.
Not a shootout. A cleansing.

The main gate waited up ahead.
I started walking.
Eyes on the door, breath held against what lingered in the air.

Outside, the war hadn't stopped.
Artillery thumped in the distance.
Bursts floated in from the edge of the world.
No longer deafening—just... expected.

The factory opened into a massive field.
On every side, broken watchtowers—flames still chewing through the wood.

Far out, two groups clustered near the horizon.

One surrounded a raised mound.
The other danced beside it—guns slung, boots stomping, splashing water like this was a wedding, not a battlefield.

All of them armed. No way to tell if they were friend or foe.
Didn't matter. If they wanted blood, they'd get it fast.
Running wouldn't help. Walked forward anyway.

A line of tanks flanked the path—hulking beasts, their noses buried in shattered walls.
Beyond them, rows and rows of others,
half-shrouded in shadow but unmistakable.

The first shots came without warning.
Men at the mound swung their AK-12s, squeezed off a sharp volley—5.45mm rounds cracking the air.

Rasheed's hand moved instinctively to his chest.
Expected the burn. Didn't come.
They weren't aiming to kill. They were for greeting.
Muzzles pointed skyward. Steel applause.
Welcome to hell.

Gunfire ceased.
From the half-circle of soldiers, two women stepped forward.

One moved like she'd broken hearts on five continents.
The other—barely past nineteen, maybe twenty—already carried a stare men could drown in.

Every instinct said, Look away. But no threat from Marisha could stop the way eyes lock where they shouldn't.
The curves on both weren't just oversized.
They were wrong for a warzone.
Too distractive for current situation.
A trap, designed like art.

The younger one cocked her head, lips curled in a smirk like she'd known me a lifetime ago.

—Welcome, Volchik. I'm Polina. Only sister-in-law you've got.

She nodded, didn't look.

—And she is Yuliya. Marisha's ride-or-die.

—Pleasure's mine, Pouli. Yuli.

I let the names roll out like old habits.

—You two seem to be enjoying yourselves...

The older one—Yuliya—clicked her tongue, grin widening.

—Oho. Marsh wasn't lying.
This one really shortens names till they moan.
Tell me, Volchik—do you like your woman to keep it short, too?

—Oh no. Please, sisters—
Let me apologize now and save everyone the trouble.
I'm not that guy.

—He's already housebroken, Polin, *Yuliya said, still laughing.*
—Marsh has him locked tighter than a wolf on a holy leash.

—Damn right, Polina snapped back.
This Volchik's a breast-fed wolf.
Still got bite—but trained to purr for her.

Their laughter rolled on—thunder with teeth.
That's when someone else stepped out from the wild pack.

A boy, maybe twenty-two.
Skin slick with sweat. Frame thin as wire.
Tattooed from collar to calves, every inch inked except the face.
The kind of face that looked familiar even if it wasn't.

He wore an official-issue disco tee, wet and clinging.
On the front: Max99, Prague — logo clear, smug, and loud.

I'd seen that brand before.
Never set foot in the club, but the name tracked.

His eyes skipped right over me, locking onto Rasheed.

—Yo, Uncle Rasheed. What were you doing in that screaming hole so long? We've been out here forever.

Rasheed stiffened.

Surprise flickered across his face.

—I... I don't think I know you.

—Oh, come on. Don't start that crap.
I checked your ticket, remember?

—You mean... the Prague disco?

—Yeah, genius.
Or were you out there buying VIPs for Disneyland?

Didn't wait for an answer.
Just turned and headed for the hill.

As he moved, Rasheed's gaze stuck on the logo stamped across the kid's back—fixed on it like it spelled out something he wasn't ready to face.

Whatever that kid said, there was weight behind it.
The women broke off, laughing, trailing him up the mound.
Our eyes, now adjusted to the dark, caught the shape of what they'd been climbing—

It wasn't earth.
It was bodies.
Layer after layer—stacked militia corpses, limbs folded like discarded tools. A hill of the dead.

Rasheed stood frozen, jaw slack, staring at the corpse-mound like it had spoken his name.

I left him behind and stepped toward the sound—the crowd of young dancers stomping the bloodstained grass, rifles slung, singing in unison.
A war song. Off-key, but loud enough to drown memory.

Beside them, barrels lined up; they scooped water into buckets, hurling it toward the center of their storm—
Marisha.

She stood in the eye of it, arms raised slightly, letting the water hit her like it was part of the ritual.
Not flinching. Receiving.

When our eyes met, she raised a hand—stilled the crowd with a single motion.

The others noticed.
Conversations thinned. Bodies parted.
A path clearing in the bodies and noise.
By the time I reached her, the chaos had turned to a hush.

Then he stepped forward. The nose—bent like a wrong turn at birth—made him easy to recognize.
We'd met just days ago, in Prague. His hideout was where I'd dragged Rasheed back from the edge.
Thima.

He took Marisha's hand—lifted it high like a prize.

—Friends, *he called out, voice charged with theater,*
—At the age of nine...
She cast away the name Zakharova in protest.
Today—seventeen years later—she claims it back.
By fire. By blood. By the promised cleansing.

The roar that followed cracked the air like incoming artillery.
It was joy. It was war.
It was something older than both.

And through it—she walked.
Toward me.

Gone was the fire in her eyes.
Gone the storm, the frost.
She looked down.
Soft, like maybe...
maybe she wanted me to hold her.
I didn't.

Instead, I held out what I'd brought in my hand.
She looked at it for a moment, confused.
Then realization hit.
And so did the light.

Marisha opened her arms like wings—face lit with something too bright to be just joy.

She reached for me.
And I—
I slipped the jacket over her shoulders.
The one she'd left behind. The one from the table.

Then she crashed into my chest, arms wrapped tight around me like she'd spent years trying not to shatter.

Behind us, the crowd broke into frenzy again.
The cheer became a scream.
The celebration lingered a little longer.

Gunshots cracked skyward, kids still laughing like they weren't standing on a mountain of corpses. As the fever faded, the crowd started to drift—scattering in all directions, leaving only one behind—

The boy in the disco tee.
He approached, bringing Rasheed with him.
Stopped short when he caught sight of me and Marisha locked together. Let his eyes rest on us a moment longer than comfort allowed.

Then he addressed her directly.

—Just like you said, Marsh—we found the cave.
Our boys are in the mobile van now, getting patched up.
Could've gone bad, though.

Marisha narrowed her gaze.

—What happened, Jouv?

—Some chick showed up. Tried to block us from going in.
If I hadn't stepped in, the boys were seconds away from putting a round through her.

—They should have. What's the issue?

He blinked—caught between disbelief and admiration.

—Are you nuts, Marsh? Do you even know who she is?

—No. Should I?

—She's the one and only Dark Macro.
The DJ. The queen. The reason my goddamn heart still beats.
You've got no idea how many nights I tried to meet her.
Closest I ever got was a near-selfie—until those bastard bouncers shoved me halfway to hell.

Marisha rolled her eyes.

—Go get your selfie now.
Then put two bullets in her skull while you're at it.

—You're out of your damn mind, Marsh. Seriously.
You don't know anything about what's going on, do you?

—I don't keep track of DJs, darling. I hunt enemies.

—Yeah? Well maybe you should've kept track this time.
Because she told us exactly why she was there.

He turned—eyes now flicking toward me—

—She said she was waiting at the cave for your dumbass lover to show up.

He didn't get to finish the look on his face.
Marisha's kick caught him dead center, right in the gut.
Launched him forward like a folding chair smashed offstage.

She didn't chase. Didn't move an inch. Just stood there—shoulders squared, eyes locked on me, lit up with fury.

I kept quiet. Didn't say a word.

The boy—Jouv—crashed, rolled, then bounced back to his feet like he'd trained for it. Dusted himself off, still grinning.

Rubbed his hip, stepped closer, hand extended towards me.

—Nice to meet you, Cumnat.
And hey, getting kicked like that? Pretty much seals it.
My smokeshow sister actually loves you.

—The pleasure's all mine, *I answered, dry as dust.*
—Cumnat, huh? Not sure if that's what you meant,

but no offense taken. I got the message.
Mister—?

—Jovoxier. But you can call me Jouv.
Everyone does—once they fall in love with me.

I shook the boy's hand once—firm, fast—then let it drop.
He bounced off like a shrimp on a skillet, limbs flailing, heading for the far end of the field.

I turned back—face to face with Marisha.
The echo of that line still burning between us.

"Waiting at the cave for your dumbass lover to show up..."

Her silence was louder than anything Jouv could've thrown.

—Ah, the fangs. Come on, Marisha—put them down, will you?
I told you about her—my deputy.
The one I went looking for in Prague. Even before that, KL, Tommy, and the others must've mentioned her to you.

Marisha's lips curved, danger and humor flickering there.

—Mhm... what you didn't say is that this deputy of yours runs around playing at DJ gigs.

I smirked back.

—And did you ever tell me this Jouv you kiss and talk in code... also sneaks off to drool over DJs?

Her eyes narrowed—then softened into a smile.

Across the field, Rasheed kept his distance—watching, playing it safe. The kind of man who'd already decided getting too close to Marisha was like standing near a live wire.

She didn't spare him a glance. Her arm stayed around my waist, head resting on my shoulder as we walked.

And in a low voice meant for me alone, she spoke:

—Jouv's not family by blood. Still feels like it though.
His father used to work for us. We still live together as one family in Samara. And the brat?

—He's fooling around with my dearest friend, Yuliya—
even though she's five years older. You'll meet them both soon enough.

—Already have. Together, actually.
One even claimed she was my only sister-in-law.
Name was... Pou... Polina, I think?

Her laugh was soft, dismissive.

—Polina's my cousin. Her father's our Director.

— Polina sounds Christian.
If you're Muslim, how's your cousin end up Christian?

—We don't fuss over religion anymore.
The old war tore all those lines to pieces.
Where I'm from, you'll find Muslim brothers,
Christian sisters—everyone picking their own path.
By the way—my mother's Christian.

—Doesn't make a difference to me.
Mixing blood and faith—that's what makes life beautiful.

Her eyes glinted, sly.

—Beautiful? Do you mean the girls are beautiful?

—For fuck's sake, Marisha.
I was talking about religion, not looks.

She chuckled, leaning closer.

—Don't feed me that. You were staring at their tits, weren't you?

—Absolutely not. I called them sisters the moment we met.

Her laughter broke free, ringing sharp.

—Ha! Really? Did they hit the floor laughing when you tried that?

—Why would they? What's funny about calling them sisters?

Marisha's laugh cut the air—sharp and filthy.

—In Russia? Even real brothers don't call girls sisters.
They say "sexy sis."
Your sweet little conservative brain probably killed them.

—Let them laugh if they want, I shot back.
I called them sisters. That's it.

Her eyes gleamed, mouth curling wicked.

—Ummax, Volchik...
call every other woman on earth a sister
that's what I wanted,
if you ever dare to think otherwise—

She traced a finger across my waist, voice dropping,

—I'll slice your dick clean off. You know that, right?

—Yeah, *I said calmly.*
—I know you would. But tell me—would you do it,
even if it was all just a misunderstanding?

Her snarl came fast.

—What kind of fuckstanding are you even talking about?

—Watch your mouth, Marisha. Why talk like that?

She laughed—brutal, bright.

—Oh, please. Should I scrub my tongue before I talk to my damn hot hubby?

—By your logic... *I pushed in, steady.*
—Why do you keep losing your shit over that one line?

Her eyes narrowed.

—Which line, exactly...?

—That ass-shaking dance...

Marisha barked out a laugh, sharp as a slap.

—Ha! Love, I was just poking at you.
If I were really mad, you'd know—trust me,
I wouldn't stop till your bones were dust.

—But teasing you? That's pure joy.
Same way you poke me in bed with that hard thing of yours.
Fun goes both ways, Volchik.

—After what I've seen you do with men's things,
I'm not even sure mine will ever work with you again.

Her voice turned sharp, playful.

—What, you serious? Even with your smoking hot wife right here, you think it won't work?

—Not hot, Marisha. More like terrifying. Pretty sure it's about to crawl under the blanket and hibernate till spring.

She rolled her eyes, dismissed it with a wave.

—Oh, shut up. That was a phase.
I don't go around hunting and chopping dicks for sport.
Let it breathe. It'll perk up again.
And if it doesn't?

Her mouth curled, sly.

—Fine. I'll shake my ass till it stands to salute—hard as a loaded cannon. Ha!

She laughed. I did too.
We reached the edge of the field.
Darkness broken by the harsh glow of floodlights and military van headlights.

The van's back door swung open.
Sitting there: Sheikh Abdel al-Awadi.
Beside him, a familiar figure crouched—helping him sip from a small flask.

Macro.

It'd been forever. Too damn long.
Last time we split—it wasn't clean. Not for either of us.
The second her eyes caught mine, she shoved the flask into Awadi's hands and bolted.

One leap, and she crashed into my chest.
Face buried.

Tears slipping out—voice muffled, rough with hurt:

—I knew you'd find me. But when it took so long...
I thought maybe it happened again.

Macro was the unbreakable type.
Steel spine, survived every storm. But this—burying her face in me, sobbing—this was the first time. And if she was going to break, it would always be in my arms.

Marisha's eyes cut sideways, venom already coiling, ready to strike. Her body taut with jealousy, the serpent rising.

I didn't care. Not this time.
Right now, out of every soul on this earth, Macro was the only one left I could call family.

Her tear-wet lashes brushed my throat as she spoke, voice thick, almost breaking:

—I could've run before. Had plenty of chances.
But I needed the truth first.
So I stayed. Waited. I knew you'd come.

—I've been hunting you from day one.
I didn't choose to end up here—fate dragged me in.

Her lips curved, faintly bitter.

—Didn't you once say fate doesn't turn unless you push it?

—True, *I admitted.* —You could say I kicked the wheel until it turned—hard, desperate, every way I could.

—Mhm. And Tommy? Gobi, Sahara? Where are they?

—At their posts. They all wanted to come, but I didn't want more blood. So I kept them out.

Macro gave me a look that cut deep.

—Worried about blood now?
Didn't stop you from dragging me to Texas.

—That was different. If I hadn't, you'd be a ghost by now. With them? It's not like that. Especially Gobi and Sahara—they're getting rougher by the day. It's turning ugly.

A cough—loud, staged, cutting through.

Marisha.
Drawing attention like a queen snapping her fingers,
though she didn't need to.

Everyone felt her presence already.
Still—since it was inevitable—I led Macro toward her.

—Macro, meet Marisha. Her last name...
let's just call it a work in progress. But she's my one true wife.
And without her, I wouldn't see beauty in any other woman alive.

Macro knew my rhythm well enough to hear the sting beneath the words. Marisha, sharp-eyed, tried to decode it, her gaze probing for hidden meanings.

I didn't give her time.

—And Marisha, this is Miss Macro Neil.
She's not my sister, not just a friend either.
What Samara is to you—Macro is to me.
In every sense of the word.

Did Marisha catch the depth? Hard to say.
But the weight of it landed.
She knew Macro meant something.

Macro drew in a slow breath, stepped up, kissed my cheek.
Then—without breaking eye contact—kissed Marisha the same way, lips light, gaze heavy.

She came back to me, her look pure ice: she didn't like Marisha. Not even close.

—We need to talk, *Macro whispered.* —Privately.

—Fine. Let's take a walk.

Marisha held her tongue, but the silence was loud enough to split granite. She didn't accept it—not fully.

As Macro and I stepped away, she spun on her heel, heading back to the van—where Awadi was deep in some tense conversation with whoever sat inside.

Macro spilled the whole chain of events—start to finish, clean and fast, not a breath wasted.

She told me about The Maker—that freak of a creature—he'd slipped out. But his lab remained.
And with it, every piece of material he'd produced so far.

Just a few minutes' walk away—an entrance to the cave that led into his secret lab.

I told Macro not to sweat it—I'd clean up the mess myself.
What she needed to do was get Sheikh Awadi to a safe location and then pull back. Let her know he'd already been snatched again. But staying in private talk any longer didn't feel right.
Even while Rasheed kept Marisha busy in conversation, her eyes stayed locked on us.

I brought Macro with me back toward them.

Awadi was the first to move.
His hands trembled as he grabbed mine in both of his, holding tight—eyes wide. His voice shook:

—Forgive me, my friend. Lord Almighty didn't bless these eyes to see past what's shown. That's why, even when I saw you before, I failed to recognize. But now... from what I hear, I understand.
By the will of the Merciful, this is the second time you've saved my life.

—Don't mention it, Mr. Awadi, Time shifts.
And everything within it shifts as well.
Sometimes things happen that I cannot explain to you.

He shook his head, firm.

—For those who believe, no explanation is required, my friend.

—That's fair, *I nodded.* —Still, since you've been dragged into this, there's something I need to tell you.

—Say it. No holding back, please.

—You'll need to move with caution from now on. Assume this kind of thing can happen again—and be prepared.

—What kind of preparation?

—Nothing complicated. In fact, you should've had it already. A man of your standing needs trusted people around him at all times—security loyal enough to keep you clear of small threats like this.

He nodded slowly, a flicker of reluctance crossing his face.

—I get what you mean. You know my family's history with the organization. But the truth is—I've never liked those killers.
I only hand them money out of respect for my late father's will.
Beyond that, I keep no company with men who live by the gun.
That last line shifted the air.

Macro leaned forward, interest lighting in her eyes.
The scent of a new client flared in the air, and Macro's business instincts kicked in hard.

She cleared her throat and slid right into the gap—voice polished, pitch perfect.

—Sorry to break into the middle of things, Mr. Awadi.
But if you're open to it—I can help set up some personal security for you.

Awadi blinked, surprised, then broke into a grateful smile.

—Really, madam? That would be wonderful.
Then I'd have no more worries left.

—Exactly. We'll make sure you don't have to think twice.
Have you heard the name Vega Security Group?

—Of course. Absolutely.
Some of my friends in the Middle East use their services.
Though... he hesitated, —...most are mixed up in some shady business. I've never needed security myself.
Never been in that kind of mess.

Macro didn't blink.

—Well, now that you do—if money's not an issue, we'll take care of everything. We have several options, all tailored for someone with your profile.

—Money's not an issue. But these "options"... I don't know what I'd pick. Whatever my friend here recommends—

He gestured at me

—...that's what I'll take.

Hook. Line.
Pocketed.
Macro had landed the pitch with surgical timing.
Before she could run wild with the sale, I cut in with a look—and a word:

—You won't need to worry about any of that, Mr. Awadi.
Beyond some minor salary overheads, it won't cost you much.
And once you're back home, you'll be able to hear firsthand reviews about Miss Macro Neil's firm.

He raised an eyebrow.

—Firsthand? From who exactly?

—Your friend. Mr. Payman Habib.
He's currently under Macro's protection.

The shift was instant.

—What happened to him?

—Nothing—yet. But when he tipped me off about your abduction, he was already worried for himself.
I advised him to stay under her firm's protection.

Awadi breathed out, raised his hands, voice soft with relief.

—All praise to my Lord. Every problem—solved exactly on time.

—Indeed, Mr. Awadi. Exactly on time.

Out of the corner of my eye, I caught it—Marisha and Rasheed, locked in a heated back-and-forth.

Their gestures were tight.
Tense.
To find out more, we all started walking that way.

Inside the rigged med-van, Commander Kamran lay unconscious—stretched out, sedated.
They'd already administered first aid, kept him stable.
So far, they'd done good work.
What the hell was Rasheed's problem?

Marisha's voice cut across before I could ask—her tone sharp, coiled with irritation.

—You gonna say something, Shakarim?
Or should I just lose my shit now?

—What could possibly ruin the mood of the last beautiful woman left on earth?

I teased. Her eyes flared.

—Your Rasheed—this idiot—wants to tuck him in and sing lullabies now.

—Wait—what?
Where the hell does that bastard want to tuck him in?

—Don't be stupid. You know what I meant. We rescued this man—and now Rasheed wants to take him into his own custody.

I turned to Rasheed.
He sat still, face locked down.
Didn't speak. Didn't have the guts not to, either.

I looked at his face, then asked Marisha:

—But... why was this a problem?
Why couldn't Rasheed just take Kamran and disappear?

Marisha snapped back in:

—Are you out of your mind?
This is a full-scale military op now.
And it's official. You hear me?
We've officially invaded Ukraine.

Her eyes burned, voice pure steel.

—Sure, we allowed a few civilian allies to tag along for private objectives—but the standing order was:
As soon as I'm free, I take command.
Which means—any second now, the real army will breach the zone. And when they do, I'm leading the push from the inside.

—What does that have to do with Kamran?

—What does it—? I swear, I keep forgetting my husband's a goddamn civilian with his stupid logic.
Kamran is a flagged terrorist, Shakarim.
Interpol red notice. The Gulf, Europe—you name it.
I've got standing orders to extract him—dead or alive—and hand him over to Moscow. What Moscow does after?
Who knows. Politics.

She waved it off, like the word itself left a bad taste.

—But this dumbass here— she jabbed a thumb toward Rasheed,—thinks I'm going to break direct orders and hand over a red-notice target just because he feels like it.

And with that, the whole air went cold.
I hadn't thought of it like that before.
Whatever Marisha and I had—however tangled, however intimate—It didn't change the fact that she had orders.
Real ones.
And she wasn't the type to flinch from them. Not even for me.

No point arguing with Marisha. Not now.
Better to talk to Rasheed first, cool him down, make him see reason.

I pulled him aside, out of earshot.
Kept my voice low, steady.

—Rasheed.
Everything happening right now—it's what we discussed.
What's got you fighting it?

He didn't snap. But the tension under his skin was raw.

—What are you even saying?
You promised you'd guarantee his safety if I helped you.
That was your word.

—And I meant it. But think back—
when I asked what to do if your commander actually deserved punishment...what did you say?
You said: if it comes to it, hand him over to the law.
Hurt him if you have to. The only red line was killing him.
Think again, calmly. Where do we stand now?

Rasheed's voice stayed level. But his eyes were locked in war.

—My head is calm. Which is exactly why I know—
if we hand him over now, they'll kill him. Not because of orders.
Because that's how Moscow washes its hands.
You've seen how they use Interpol red notices—turning politics into manhunts. Same trick here. Dead man, no fingerprints.

Damn it.
This was getting twisted.
There was a way out. But no need for Marisha to hear it yet.
I gripped Rasheed's shoulder and pulled him further off the grid.

Dropped my voice to a near-whisper.

—Her logic's bulletproof, Rasheed.
We push too hard, she'll push back harder.

—I know. But that doesn't leave me any options.

—Sure it does. You're not that cornered.

—What do you mean?

—You've got networks everywhere.
You telling me you don't have anyone in Iran?

—Of course I do.

—There you go. Don't lock yourself into just one outcome.
Maybe they won't execute him.

—Maybe it'll be life inside a quiet facility.
If that happens, you've got no reason to object.

—Right. If it's life, at least he'll stay protected.

—Exactly. Case closed.

But Rasheed didn't back down.
His voice went colder—low, tactical.

—Closed? It's not that simple.
The Russians aren't giving him back for free.
They've got the Shahed drone pipeline with Tehran—
Shahed-136s, Geran-2s—and it's been stuck for months.
Payment, upgrades, sanctions—frozen in midair.
They'll use him as leverage. If their demands get too steep,
Iranians might walk away— and Russians?
They'll shelf him. Dump him in Lefortovo, or worse—
a black site that doesn't exist on maps.

He paused.
Just for breath.
Then threw the next punch.

—Even if—somehow—they agree on terms...
you saw what your psycho wife rolled up with.
Her battalion, her GRU channels. Israelis have already mapped it.
Unit 8200 never sleeps—if they've lit up this zone, it's already
burned. And if she wipes it off the map like I know she will—
then the job Kamran was sent to do—off the record,
for the Iranian state—it's blown.
And when ops blow that way, Tehran doesn't forgive.
They erase. Ask the ghosts of half the IRGC who got too loud.

—Hmm. *I nodded slowly.*
—I hear you, Rasheed.
But don't act like we can't tilt the board if we need to.

He raised an eyebrow.

—Like what?

—Say Iran suddenly wants Kamran back. So badly they'd even ship the next batch of Shaheds without payment, just to keep him breathing. Say they decide—no execution, just prison time.
Or house arrest. How's that sound?

—Sounds perfect. But let's not kid ourselves—I don't have the connections to make that happen.

—You won't be asked to. You'll only do what you can. That's all.

I leaned in, tone low, surgical.

—Here's what you'll do.
You'll act like it's breaking your heart to leave Kamran behind.
Then you disappear. Quiet. No scene.
In two days, reach out to Macro. You know how to get to her?

—I'll find her. She's famous. Got offices in Dubai, Istanbul, Amman—half the region uses her as private muscle.

— Good. When you meet, she'll hand you something.
Take it. And before anyone even realizes it's missing, you deliver it—straight into Bukan. Right to the place where your shipment was headed...before the attack.

—Easy. That's the job I live on.

—Perfect. I'll brief Macro on the rest.
Just... don't look so hopeful. Keep the face dead.
Like a buzzard that's already eaten.

Rasheed gave me a mocking look.

—Buzzard enough for you?

—Yeah, that'll do. Now open those ears and listen.

He nodded.

—Say it.

—Whatever side you play, wherever you move—
never work with these extremist bastards again.
Never, Rasheed. You understand me?

—Completely. I never wanted to work with them.
I only smuggled a few shipments for Commander Kamran
out of respect. He never forced me into his org.
Yes, he invited me. But he also gave me the option to walk away.

I paused.

—Then why didn't you?

His eyes darkened.

—Because another client left me no choice.

—Which client?

He didn't flinch.

—The one who promised me safe passage out of the disco.
Your psycho wife.

Even if Daggan hadn't caved my skull in with a hammer,
his confessions would've left me dizzy anyway.

And this? This last one?
Felt like someone dropped a classified file in my lap,
didn't care if I was ready for the fallout.

Whatever I had left to settle with Marisha...
that score was still open.
But Rasheed?
I told him to vanish.
Now.

Rasheed Dameer vanished exactly the way a man should when he's trying to stay alive—with a perfect act of devastation and grief.

Everyone believed it.
And within minutes, he'd disappeared into the wind.

Now it was Macro and Sheikh Awadi's turn.
No resistance from Marisha.

In fact, she arranged safe passage herself—sent them with one of her vehicles, straight to a nearby Russian city across the border. From there, they'd each scatter to wherever location they want.

Before they left, I gave Macro the rest of the instructions—sealed in words no blade or fire could extract from her.
Especially the part about Rasheed.

And then—I turned.
Faced the most dangerous, ever-shifting piece of this entire opera: Marisha.

The only woman I ever called beautiful without blinking.
My self-declared wife. Last siren on earth, standing there in her war boots, ready to scorch the world.

She caught my stare.

—What? Why are you looking at me like that?

—Who else should I be looking at, huh?
You're the only woman I'm supposed to stare.

—Good. Then burn those eyes out on me—no one else.

—So. What's the plan now?

Her lips curled.

—You want the plan just like that?
You've got a whole backlog of dues to pay, Volchik.

—Put it on my tab.

—Tab's full. I need cash now.

—What's left to give?

She nodded at the grenade launcher crate right next to us.

—That box right there—if you'd stop acting like a statue and actually sit down—I could hop on your lap and fall in love all over again.

—Falling in love on top of a box full of grenade?
If it goes up, we'll paint the sky with what's left of us.

—Tsk. Drama king. It won't blow. Sit.

—Fine. Sitting.

—And now, so am I.

She dropped into my lap like she owned the goddamn seat.

—Ummax.

—Cute. Now give me the plan.

—Umm. There's more than one.

—Such as?

—You and I—we head into the secret lab. Level it.
Meanwhile, our assault team pushes further inside.
The locals? They return to Samara.

—You even know where we are right now?

—Donetsk. Ukraine.

—Wow. And from Samara to here—with tanks, weapons,
full force—that should've taken days.
You're saying they planned this far in advance?

—Nope. They didn't. Jovox and Thima were in Prague.
They flew in. So did the kids—Polina, Yuliya,
the whole Samara crew. They hit the border,
linked up with us. And the rest?

She smirked.

—That "government-scale invasion of Ukraine?"
That train was already rolling.
Our units were already en route on schedule.
Rail convoys from Rostov, armor crossing near Belgorod,
airborne out of Pskov—you think this happens overnight?
Jovox already marked our detainment zone and sent the
coordinates to the incoming units.
Only a few teams were dispatched here to assist us directly.
If we wrap this up clean—you and I join the second-wave,
push with the main force, phase two.

—I'm with you on destroying the lab.
But joining the Russian military offensive?
That's not a war I'm signing off on.

—Oh, come on. What are you even saying?
You're not on the front lines.
You've got a tigress for a wife to do that.

—And you, tigress? Why the hell are you so hyped to throw yourself in with their troops?

—Wow. You really must've bumped your head,
holding me like that and asking dumb questions.
You're a warlord, the manufacturer of death—
the Z-class prototypes aren't you?
Who the hell do you sell your toys?

—What does that have to do with this?

—Everything. If you deal arms, you should at least understand military ops and how responsibility bleeds down the line.
But from what I'm seeing—you don't know shit.
Ask any Spets, ask any VDV colonel—they'd eat you alive.

—My business isn't what you think.
We don't build weapons just to rack up a body count.
We design tech that neutralizes threats—no kill shots.
Nonlethal solutions.
That's why most of our buyers aren't armies or cartel bosses.
It's advanced governments—police units, not shock troops.
Crowd control, embassy security, perimeter defense.

—Oh, please. Now you're pitching me carrots? That's classic.
Typical man—won't give his wife the straight answer,
even when she's got a knife to his ribs.

—This is the truth, Marisha.

—Yeah? Then what about the Veg-6?
That legendary long-range rifle of yours?
Or the WX missiles?
Police using those for traffic control now?

—Those are prototypes, Marisha.
Not on the open market.
A few friendly states got test runs, that's all.

—Just like the Americans ran Strykers through Iraq,
or how the IDF tested Trophy systems in Gaza.
Field use sharpens the design. That's all it is.

—Hmm... that's why the Moscow bigshots were so ready to throw their daughters at you? Explains why my horse-faced superiors didn't even blink when I dropped your name at HQ. They're hoping you'll put Russia on your friends-and-family plan.

—That probability is close to zero.

—Why? What's wrong with supporting your wife's side?

—If that's what's required, I'll die single.
But I'll never hand over our weapons to an imperialist power. Every country we've sold to—none of them have a history of invading others. And they've never shown any future intent either. They buy from us to defend. That's it.

—Hmm. Lucky me—I married a radical leftist.

—Left, right—what the hell does that even mean to you?

—Exactly. You don't speak the language of command,
so ideology's wasted on you.

—Try me. You have no idea what I understand.

—Fine. Our country's carved into five main military districts—and this patch here, Donetsk, sits under the Southern District. But for Ukraine they pulled formations across zones, stacked them under OGV. And because of the war protocols, I was officially posted here in advance—as a Potpalkovnik.

—A what now? Sounds like a word designed to knock out teeth.

—Ha! Sweetheart, I know. That's a bit rough on the tongue. But in most other countries, this rank's equivalent is Lieutenant Colonel. Even in Jovan's country—that's what they call it.

—Yeah, he muttered something about rank nonsense last time.

—Exactly. I've got a second-in-command like Jovan.
Sitting at the border with a reinforced tactical battalion.
Six hundred men, BMPs, artillery tubes.
—Waiting for my call.
I either send them in… or roll with them myself.

—Why even bother with all that, love? Let them fight.
You can slip away with me and vanish clean.

—Oh, you idiot. I'm one of six tactical groups tied directly into OGV Command's Donetsk axis. You think I can just ghost out of the frontline like some bored intern? No chance, baby.

—Alright, alright. Enough war games. You're making it feel like I've got a whole tank on my lap, not a wife.

—Ha! And your wife's any less than a tank?

—Not denying it. But what I don't get is—what the hell made your people actually invade a sovereign country?

—There are a lot of reasons. And one of them is you, sweetheart.

—Oh, fuck off. That's the dumbest twist I've heard all year.

—Not directly. But in many layers…
Amethyst Vega. Darius Caesar.
In other words—you are involved.

—Bullseye. There it is.
That's the part I've been waiting to hear.
What Jovan said—how could any of that be true?
But now even you admit there's truth in it?

—Jovan doesn't know the full picture.
That's why his version is only partly correct.

—So what's the full picture?

—Even I don't know all of it. But I know more than him.

—Then give it to me.
What do you know?

—Umm... do you really want to spend this beautiful moment—sitting with your gorgeous wife in your lap—talking about covert ops and black-bag secrets? War's right around the corner, love. I might live... I might not. Wouldn't you rather spend this time hearing something good?

—That is sweet. Because if I die without knowing the truth, I won't find peace—not even in the grave.

—God, you're such a drama king.
Who said anything about you dying?
Fine, fine—listen up. I'll lay out what I know.

—You threw the word 'imperialist' at me—and yes, it fits America and their little Anglo club better than anyone—but don't get it twisted. We're not exactly saints either. Wherever they plant a flag, we show up right behind—to break it.
They stormed Syria, we stormed right after.
Our regulars did the messy work. But tactical group leaders like me—we had specific missions. Mine was simple:
Find and secure the Dark Weapon.

—The what now?

—The one we're about to destroy in that lab.

—Alright, now it's starting to line up. Keep going.

—Mossad got their hands on the first one. But they didn't know what they were holding. I moved in—targeted the unit, tried to wipe them out and steal the payload.

—So that's the Amethyst Vega tip. Now it all fits.
A prototype from our lab—non-lethal, new tech—was scheduled to be shipped overseas. Instead, a Mossad unit grabbed it.
Then you ambushed them, took it back, and made it look like revenge. That way, you got the asset and all the glory.

—Ummax, Volchik. Why so mad?
If your hot wife doesn't milk a little benefit out of chaos—what's the point of being this damn gorgeous?

—Cute. But there's two problems with your fairy tale.
First—that device wasn't a weapon. It was a defensive tool.
A signal disruptor, built to silence electronics, not people.
Second—this so-called marriage didn't exist that time.
Hell, I didn't even know you.

—So what? Even if you didn't know me—I've known you for lifetimes.

She laughed, sharp.

—But seriously—we never figured out what that device really did. It destroyed itself during transport.

—As designed. It was built to self-destruct in hostile custody.
But tell me something—if you were planning to marry Amethyst Vega, why the hell did you use Caesar's name and butcher Rasheed's crew?

—Wow. Now that's my goddamn Volchik talking.
Only you could connect those dots.
Even though I worked anonymously, you figured it out.

—Rasheed gave me the full throat-slitting story himself.
And the other one—Baharram Gazi?
The one whose dick you cut off?
I just saw you almost do it again—with that blade...

—We always knew there was a ghost by that name.
A legend. Terrifying work—honestly, my kind of hero.
So yeah, out of obsession, I used the name for that job.
But when our profilers in Phuket said it might be you?
I didn't believe it. Not even when they flagged you in Malaysia,
not even after they got convinced you were Amethyst Vega.
I still said no. No way the sweet husband holding me in his lap
right now could be any of them.

—Why would you believe that? I'm not the violent type.

—Maybe not. But I saw your ruthless friend—Papa Cheng—turn down five million to hand me over.

—And today, before Jovan died, he ID'd the ghost,
Caesar along with Mr. Awadi, right there in Phuket.
They were the ones who detected him first.
Only they had his photo.
And sure, your face looks different now—but back then,
in Phuket, with me and Awadi? You were in your own skin.

—I spoke to Awadi today. Learned a lot.
Tell me, sweetheart... who are you, really?

—Is that why you came to help us in KL?
To confirm it for yourself?

—No. I'd have come no matter what. Because, long before any of that, I already signed over my body and soul to you, Volchik. Even this killing you're about to do—they told me to let you go alone. I refused. I'm going with you.

—Killing? Who said I'm going to kill anyone?

—How should I know? All I was told is:
Escort him there, unharmed. Guard of honor.
That fight? Only you can win it.

—What the hell are you talking about, Marisha?
I don't know a thing about any of this.
And who's handing out these weird-ass orders?
Your bosses?

—Not my bosses, Volchik. Yours.
The order to deliver you unharmed came straight from your side.

—What—What the actual fuck are you saying?
Marisha, I do have a Master. But He doesn't talk. Not even to me.

—Did I ever say He spoke to me?

—Then how those orders coming to you?

—Orders can come in a lot of forms, Volchik. Don't play dumb.

—My head's spinning. You're just talking riddles now.

— Spin the machine, not your head. I've been in your lap for hours and still haven't felt anything hard.

—After what you pulled back there, that thing may never get hard again. Told you.

—Don't break my heart like that, Volchik. What am I supposed to do with all this curves and fire hot womanhood?

—You seem to do just fine using it to shove people against walls and grope them mid-fight.

—That was just... reflex, darling.
Didn't even register who I had my hands on.
You know the drill—every weapon counts in a fight.
And if God's kind enough to give me certain distractions,
why wouldn't I use them? But fine—promise. I won't do it again.

—You don't need to promise. You know what promises are for?

—To remember them?

—No. Just to break them.

—Ugh—where do you even get that kind of trash logic?

—My mood's shot again.

—Why, baby? Why?

—I remembered your that goddamn choker thing.
And everything else.

—Shit. Today's really not my day. Come on, I got your men out safe and sound—doesn't that buy me a little forgiveness?

—Trying to. Otherwise...
can't promise what I might've done by now.

—You never trust me, do you?

—When did I say that?

—I'm a woman, sweetheart.
We don't need to say it. We just know.

—Is that so? How many men did it take for you to unlock that superpower?

—I know where you're going.

—Tell me. What am I saying?

—You're thinking of before I met you. And yeah, things happened before you came along.

—But after you? I never lied. Never cheated. Never left. If I ever did anything wrong, it was before I even knew you existed.

—I don't even know if this is anger anymore.
But it damn sure doesn't feel good.

—Then maybe you should've found me in college.
Could've handed you my virginity with a nice little bow.
But you weren't there, were you?
I had to handle my wreck of a life alone.
And with all those curious men, all their hungry offers,
how many you think I could turn down?
You really think I didn't have questions about bodies,
touch, power? I did.
But what I learned chasing those answers,
only I know the price.

—Then why marry someone else at all?

—Had to do something. Everyone does.
So I picked the safest option available.
Didn't work. Told you that already—every word of it's true.
You'll see for yourself when we get to Samara.

—I didn't object.
I accepted you—even knowing all of that.
But seeing you now, up close, your real self—it itches.
Any man can read a woman from her posture, her attitude.
Doesn't take superpowers.

—Oh, you beautiful idiot. That's not discomfort.
That's jealousy. You love me too much.
You just don't want to admit it.
Hell, you probably don't even know it yet. But I do.
And listen, I'm telling you—once, twice, a thousand times:
This Marisha isn't that Marisha.

—Time changes people.
Minds. Desires. Scars.
And this Marisha? She belongs to you.
Everything—until death rips us apart.

—And what if death only takes one of us?

—Then hear me—if I could not make it, and I ever catch you going near another woman, I'll haunt you.
Break your neck from the afterlife.

—I meant the other way around—what if I'm the one who dies first? What'll Marisha do then?

—I'll stay alive, sure...but I'll burn like hell.
And if I can't take it anymore, I'll slice my throat with that same blade, and come find you wherever you are.

—What if I ask you for something else?
What if it hurts a little, but it's what I want?
Would you keep your word, Marisha?

—A hundred times. A thousand times. Say it—I'll do it.

—Then listen—no matter how hard it gets, you'll live.
You'll keep going. You'll stop this blood game.
Go back to Samara. Wait for me.
And maybe—on some winter evening, I'll return.
We'll play like kids in a snowfield beneath black stone hills.
We'll splash water at each other—hiding between the gaps of that big round fountain at the seven-way crossing.

—God...I can't breathe.
That place—everything you just said... it's real.
It's all there. Have you seen it?

—No. Not yet. But I will.
If this Marisha remembers what I said.
If she hears every word and keeps them.

—She will. I swear it.
Now kiss me fucking hard, Ummax.

—Ummax...

—This is real, Volchik. You feel that?
No blade. No fear kept your thing getting hard down there.
Great timing.

—Oh really? Maybe it's because you are sitting in my lap so long.

—Whatever the reason—good.
Because my people are going to take their sweet time opening that damn door. Until then... let's slip over to that field and play our own kind of game.

—Say "game" one more time and I'll slap you, those damn images are flashing in my head again.

—Oops—sorry, sorry. No more games.
Let's just make love.

—Yeah. That we can do.

We lay together in the dark side of the field, staring up at the open sky. But there were no stars above us tonight.

Only warplanes—one after another—slicing through the silence we'd tried to make our own. Marisha's bare skin pressed against mine, her head on my chest, one side of me numb beneath her weight.

We were both completely naked. Not just skin, but soul.
The artillery in the distance hadn't stopped for hours.
Neither had the gunfire. I'd never seen war this close before.
And I couldn't make sense of it.
Couldn't find any logic that justified it.
But Marisha had.
She'd walked through blood enough times to call it experience.
She knew what it meant to be in it, of it.

Still—there was something I needed to ask.
Even if I knew we wouldn't agree. Still worth trying.

—Ree...

—Mmm...

—Can't we just stop this war?

—Not a chance, my love.

—Why not? The lab you feared—we're about to wipe it out. Everyone tied to it is already dead. So what's left?

—Uff. Why do you always have to drag this stuff in right when we're finally getting somewhere good?

—Because this is the only time your head cools down. That's why I'm asking now.

—You sweet fool... my head's always cool. I only pretend to be angry—makes the enemy think I'm volatile, easy to crack. Just like that bastard Jovan assumed. And now look—my own husband thinks the same. Sigh—Tragic.

—Come on... I know there's more to you.
Not just this sharp-edged Marisha.
There's a soft one under it all. I've seen her.

—Yes, my love. Maybe I wear a thousand faces for the world...
but the one you've seen? That's the real me.
And it's yours. Only yours.
You said something like this, remember?

—Of course. And from now on, I'll be careful with what I say.

—Ha! Caught by your own tongue,
my soft little idiot. Ummmmmmax.

—Alright—fine.
A thousand Ummax if it keeps your claws in.
But listen to me—this war has to stop, Marisha.
And I need your help to do it.

—No, love. Absolutely not. This isn't some tantrum, something we did in a rush and can now walk away from.
It's built on years—
Years of intel gathering, analysis, strategy.
This war has been engineered over time.
There's no kill switch.

—That doesn't even make sense. Ukraine used to be part of you. Even after the split, things were civil until recently.

You could've solved this another way.
Your own people—the Chechens—rebelled once too.
But Russia didn't bomb them to dust, did it?

—Damn it. You're really trying to ruin my afterglow, huh?
Today was...God, it was perfect, my love. A hundred Ummax.

—Perfection takes effort. I earned that moment.
Nothing came free. So I want open answers...

—What else is left to open? Everything's already off.

—Not clothes, my love. The truth. Strip that.

—You're seriously dragging politics into this dream?

—It's not nonsense to me.

—Fine. But when I'm done—you're paying a toll.
Two more rounds. Non-negotiable.

—Are you insane? Do I look like your sex robot?

—Well now that you mention it...I do like this model.
Would've kept you running all night,
if that damn cave mission wasn't still pending.

—Stop talking like a maniac. One more time—fine.
But after rest. And in the meantime,
tell me why this war can't stop.

—I can't, love, because it was never meant to end.
That's the part you need to understand.
It wasn't lit to be put out. Think about it cold—
we hit hard early, then will slow down.
Not out of defeat. Out of strategy. Consolidation.
Then we move again. Then slow.
Advance. Pause. Repeat.
That's how Moscow designed it—salami-slicing,
same as they did in Georgia, in Crimea.
Step, freeze, step, freeze.
Until—

—Until?

—Until Ukraine folds. Surrenders.
Like you said—they used to be us.

—Even now, tension exists at the top, but the people?
There's still connection. Still shared blood.
Moscow don't want to flatten them.
They want to break them in, teach them obedience.
And more importantly—they want to warn the Western hands stoking their fire. Make NATO and the Americans feel what it costs to provoke Kremlin.
Same message they sent with Syria—don't play in our yard unless you're ready to bleed.

—But that Chechnya comparison I made,
doesn't it prove my point?

—Chechnya was different. It was more politics than threat.

—...Politics? What do you know about politics? I mean—

—What the hell kind of question is that?
I lead a tactical group under one of the world's most elite forces.
You think I don't study geopolitics? Just because I'm your wife, you're supposed to overlook that part?
If you weren't married to me,
you'd be paying through the nose to hear me brief this shit.

—... Alright. Sorry. Sheath the claws. Keep going.

—Ha... Chechnya was surrounded by Russia on all sides.
Merging with anyone else was never a realistic option.
And they didn't want that anyway.
It was political unrest—sparked by religious tension,
mafia economics, and some heavy-handed power plays.
Yes, there was fighting. But it was containable.
When the bloodshed went too far on both sides,
Moscow stepped back. Owned their mistake.
Chechens softened too—made sacrifices.
Even Kadyrov's rise was part of that bargain: stability for loyalty.
My father never aligned with Kadyrov's politics, but when he saw Moscow had chosen him for the region, he didn't resist.

—He yielded—for national interest.
Moved us to Samara.
And he forgave the man who killed his daughter. But...

Her voice dropped, laced with something deeper than grief.

—...he couldn't hold that weight.
Took his own life.
Said it was for the nation. Said it was worth it.
Back then, I didn't care about nations.
Didn't care about people.
I just wanted revenge for my sister.
I dropped the family name, shaped myself into a weapon.
One they couldn't ignore.
Later I realized—walking into another allied country,
and killing officials over personal grief?
It can't last. Can't work. So I coiled up.
Played it like you said—fangs tucked in, venom saved.
And tonight—I finally struck.

She turned fully to me, eyes catching the dark like a silent oath.

—Because of you. It was done after so many years only because of you, Volchik. This Marisha will be your slave forever. Ummax.

—Yeah...I figured that much.
Just had to hear you say it. Then what?

—Ukraine was not that simple.
They've always been technically ahead.
Even during the Soviet days,
the nuclear missile plants were here.
Right beneath us—this factory.
After separation, they handed over those nukes and signed the Budapest Memorandum: no more weapons, and if anyone attacked them, Russia would guarantee their security.

—Then explain this—why'd you attack them?

—Did you know—after America, Ukraine's got the second-biggest Jewish power block in the world?

—And Jews...well, they've had the same habit for a thousand years: drove wedge through people's solidarity.
Every Jew is born with eleven fingers. Ten on their hands—and one shoved deep into someone else's butt.
At first, we didn't care. We had no problem with the Jews.
In fact, we even partnered— farming, drones,
whatever strategic play.
But their ties with America? Stronger. Deeper.

She pauses—just long enough to let it land.

—Oligarchs like Kolomoisky, and then Zelenskyy himself—
a Jewish president backed by Washington's money.
Step by step, they pulled Ukraine into that orbit.
That's when the rot started.
At one point, Ukraine turned to NATO for protection.
We didn't like it, but we held back. No tanks. No strikes.
Just some statements... a little pressure. That's it.
We were busy on the Syrian front when Moscow caught a scent.
Something off about Ukraine.
HQ broke it into pieces—assigned us in groups to investigate.
Because it was still vague, I made the first move under the name 'Caesar.' You know that one. But the op turned up nothing.
Still—I didn't stop.

Her voice dipped slightly, threading through the dark like the edge of a blade.

—The girl you pulled out with me.
My sister. She was deep in SVR intel wing,
working the same target from another angle.
I also activated a few external contractors—
guys like Rasheed Dameer.
Just to sniff around, chase odd trails.
But it was my sister who got the first solid lead... in Phuket.
I was there too—covering as a rock vocalist, remember?
I told you that already.

—Hold up...

I raised an eyebrow, voice teasing, but my eyes locked deep.

—It's true? You really out there shaking your ass on stage?

—Uff— what kind of line is that!
Rock's not ass-shaking—it's art!
Pure, beautiful, emotional art.

She slapped my chest, half-offended, half-laughing.

—You know what—next time I perform,
I'm taking you with me. See it with your own eyes.
If you still don't like it—fine. I'll quit.

—Haha, don't worry. I know what a rock show is.
Got no problem with that.

—Then what's with the attitude?

—Just giving you a little jab. You started it, remember?

She grinned, eyes daring.

—Oh yeah? Then jab me where it counts, lover boy.

—You were saying?

—Right. My sister went all in on that op.
She tracked it back to something big—
someone funneling a Dark Weapon to a radical cell.
She was this close to blowing it open.

Marisha's voice dropped lower.

—That night I promised to meet you,
I was waiting on her call. She never came.
Never sent the intel.
We tore up half of Thailand looking for her.
She was just... gone. And when she vanished—
so did everything she found.

I nodded, slow, the weight of it settling over both of us.

—You ever figure out who got her?

—Yeah. Those extremists.
Same ones you helped pull us out from later.

—No.

I turned my head, let the words land like a shot.

—Not them. That snake you called sister...
she got caught by me.

The silence slapped harder than any artillery barrage.

—What... the...
You mean my sister—
you—you're the one who—did that to her?

Her voice was a chord stretched to its breaking point.

—Have you lost your mind?
Will you even let me finish the whole damn thing?

—What's left to say, huh?
Good thing I'm naked, and the blade's over by the bushes.
Or else...

—You'd have sliced my throat open already?

I smirked

—Or yours?

—Damn right. I swear, if I ever look into her eyes again,
I won't be able to speak.

Her voice cracked. Not loud. Just... broken.

—Shame. Rage. Guilt. That blade was meant for me.

—God, you rock stars—always ready to throw the tantrum before the beat even drops.

I exhaled, braced myself on one elbow.

—Now sit tight. Let me say all of it.

—Say it then. Let's hear the grand finale, you have there.

—I had no idea about your so-called Dark Weapon.
I wasn't in Phuket for any secret mission.
I was there to save a friend—Abdel Al-Awadhi.
Some bastards were after him.
That's it.

I looked her dead in the eyes.

—You listening, Marisha?

—I'm listening. Just trying not to puke from all this bullshit

—Excuse me?

—Some guy calling himself Amethyst Vega,
backed by a private global army, drops into Phuket,
and goes full Darius Caesar on a hit squad...
just to rescue a friend?

She scoffed, sharp as a broken bottle.

—You want me to swallow that fairytale?
Pitch it in Hollywood, you'll get a whole trilogy.

—You don't believe me?

—I don't know what to believe anymore.
There's a part of you, deep and dark, that I can feel.
You hide it well. But I've tasted it, Xayotim.
And now that it's out...what you did to my sister,
why did it have to be her?

Her voice cracked again.

—You could ruin anyone. You could kill anyone. Why her?

—Because your sister was about to be killed. I saved her.

—Bullshit!

She sat up, chest heaving, hair wild across her back.

—She never said that.

—What did she say, then?

—Bits. Fragments. She's not fully stable yet.
But she said she'd found the Dark Weapon.
Tried to grab it. Got caught.
The men attacked—she barely survived.
When she woke up, she was in their den.
Tortured. Abused.

Her voice faltered, thinned out.

—One day, she wakes up in a hospital in Samara.
Didn't know where the hell she was.
Hid herself. Contacted us.

—So...

I kept my voice dead calm, almost cruel.

—Her version ends at the torture chamber.

—Yeah. That's where she left it.

—Then maybe the great court of justice will allow the accused a closing statement , before you hang me from the nearest tree.

—I don't play lawyer. Not this Marisha.
If you're the one who did it—
I'll end myself right here, and let your Lord be the judge.

—What, no more little blade games with me?

—You're a man.
What would you know about how women break?
That's why you bastards do what you do.

—I don't even know what to say anymore.
Maybe they should start a crash course for husbands—
'How to win back your wife's pride before the marriage is over.'
I'd fail that chapter, clearly. Anyway...
Here's the truth. Exactly as it happened.
You decide what you believe.

—Say it. I know you don't lie. But if you'd seen my sister's face...

—I have seen it. Now let me walk through it,
step by step, or I'll lose the thread.
I saved her, Marisha. Pulled her out of that Arab's grip.
The second she saw me, she passed out cold.
She'd already fought like hell before I even got there.
I didn't know who she was. Didn't know who he was.
But in that room...
I found what your people call the 'Dark Weapon.'

—You're serious?
She actually got her hands on it?
Where's the damn thing now?

—I'll get there. Stay with me. No hissy fits yet.

—Fine. Go on.

—That Arab—he died by my hand.
I left your sister with Cheng.
That 'Dark Weapon' thing—we'll get to it last.

—Keep going...

—After that, I sent Awadi and his buddy packing back to their country. By then, dawn had broken. That's when you started calling me. A few other things flared up, and I had to head back to Bangkok the same day. Few days later when things settled I sent Sahara to pick your sister up from Cheng.
Meanwhile, we kept talking. You were in Laos.
And yes—by the time I knew about your missing sister.

—So? What then?

—Sahara didn't make it. On his way back to Bangkok, he was ambushed. Your sister was snatched—taken by Rasheed's jihadi crew. That's when I told you to send her photo.
And the second I saw it...I got confirmed.
That girl—was your sister.

—Then why the fuck didn't you tell me right there?

— How was I supposed to know you wouldn't turn venom on me? I thought—if you found out I got your sister out,
only to lose her again—you'd break. So I held it in.
Told myself—once I found her, I'd tell you everything.
I burned every network I had looking for her.
And I did find her—but by then, you'd already been taken.
The rest—you know.

—Hmm. And the Dark Weapon?

—It's with me.

—Soon as we're back—you're handing it over.

—That's not happening, Marisha.

—Altimos Volchik... Don't destroy me like this.
If you play games with that thing,
I'll have no choice but to kill you—and myself.
There'll be no other way.

—You're not doing that, Ree. You won't have to.

—You don't get it, love. If we don't deliver that weapon,
Moscow will kill everyone anyway. They have to.
And I know why.

—Nothing's happening, Marisha.
You've already handed them a Dark Weapon.

—How? When?

—When you hit Rasheed's unit in Iraq—
you got your hands on the latest version.

—Wait—what? That little canister, with the bio-tags?
How does that even count as a Dark Weapon?
When I say Dark Weapon, I mean end-of-the-world shit.
You get that, right?

—I get it better than you think, darling.
But if that wasn't it—then why bomb this factory?
Why Ukraine?

—Because Ukraine was secretly feeding NATO all kinds of weapons. Clear breach of our agreements.
But nobody knew what kind of weapons—everyone kept their mouths shut. And yes, Jewish-American pressure was pushing it from behind. But what shocked us?
The weapons got used—on their own city. Eilat.
That's when we called the Israeli government, straight up.

I don't interrupt. I'm already ahead of the words.
She takes a breath, then keeps going.

—Turns out—even inside Israel, there's more than one game running. Groups working the dark, off the books, their own agenda. Thing even Tel Aviv had no clue about. We kept pulling intel until it all started to click—This Zionist cell wasn't just influencing Ukrainian policy. They were the damn manufacturers of that mysterious weapon. And to convince funders how deadly the weapon was, they used Rasheed's jihadist cell to stage the Eilat attack. Just like the Americans did with 9/11—set the fuse, collect the outrage, bankroll the next war.
It's the same playbook. Stage the massacre, make the new tech look too lethal to ignore and too 'essential,' to have on their own hands. Convince the power brokers, then wipe out Rasheed's crew—no witnesses.

Marisha keeps going.

—We had the intel. But no proof. Until we got that canister back from Rasheed's squad in Iraq.
That thing was built with surgical precision,
a live nuclear reactor in a goddamn pocket-sized shell.
And with state hands in the mix, Ukraine was knee-deep in production. But Moscow still doesn't know that canister is the Dark Weapon. All we had was a hunch.
If they could build nano-reactors that precise,
they could cook up the real apocalypse.
And any nuclear build, for weapon use or not,
was a direct slap to the peace treaty.

She hesitates—for the first time.

—We tried diplomacy first.
Get influence inside the government,
shut down the ops from within.
But the West blocked every move.
Which made Moscow double down.
Figured if Ukraine gets full NATO membership,
they'll pass this god-killer straight to the Alliance.
Before that happens—we strike.
Start the war. Shut it down.

—Thanks, love. Now I finally see the whole board.
I can die in peace. Can you get me a sat phone?

—Maybe. But tell me where that Dark Weapon is first.

—Your sister told you the jihadis took it when they grabbed her.
She never saw it again—that's what she told you, right?

—Yeah. She had no way of knowing. She was unconscious.
They tortured her. Bad.

—I saw it myself, before I pulled her out.
And the men who did it? All dead now.
So all that's left is sympathy.
Even if your sister didn't find it that time—
you hit that same crew in another time, another place,
and recovered that Dark Weapon.
Technically right?

—Yeah. I let Rasheed walk though. He had no idea he was working for me the whole time.

—Perfect. Let's sum this up—
First, you got the weapon back from the same bastards who abducted your sister.
Then, months later—they're wiped clean, and your sister's recovered from them—with the help of mine.
And Moscow still doesn't know that what you pulled off Rasheed's crew was the real Dark Weapon.
Now, I'll give you the identification and testing protocol.
Take it to your top brass, prove it's the real thing—they'll hand you a medal, or a heroic title.
Either way, job's done. Why keep dragging this out?

—Yeah... they'll be thrilled.
But what if I told you, one's still with you?

—Oh come on, girl. That's a husband-wife secret.
Let it stay with us.

—But what if Moscow finds out?
You think they'll stay happy with just one prototype?
Then what?

—Relax, love. I'll show you exactly how to arm and disarm the thing—clean, no tricks. Once they have that, they can reverse-engineer the rest themselves.
And if they screw it up, that's on them.
Nobody's coming after you.

—Hmm... you won't give us your own test sample,
but now you're fine with us holding the full doomsday weapon?
Just like that?

—Figured I'd try being a good husband.
Win a few points with the in-laws.

—Don't make me laugh. Tell me the truth.

—Drop the act, Marisha.
If you really love me—trust me.
Do it the way I said, and nothing you planned gets blocked.
No heat on you either.

—I do love you. But if this leaks, we're dead.

—You afraid to die?

—Not even close.

—Good. I'd rather die staring into those thunder blue eyes anyway.

—You really think you can sit on this secret and walk away clean?

—I know you'll be safe. That's locked.
As for me—I've got more exits than you know.

—Hmm... Even with that tech, Amethyst Vega might survive the fallout. Moscow won't strike first with a warlord profile like that.
First they'll try to buy in—maybe even partner up.
If that happens—you swear you'll settle on a real deal?
Something solid?

—And if I don't?

—Then they'll send me to finish the job.

—Oh wow. Now that would be fun.
No more games. Just straight-up war.
You and me, head to head.

—Don't joke about that.
If it gets that far—there won't be room for jokes.

—Then I'll die happy.
Shot by the blue-eyed queen herself.
Perfect ending, if you ask me.

—Say that again and I'll break your face.
Is that really what you want?
To turn us into that?

—Not even close. I want to be under those black mountains in Samara—throwing snowballs at you, until you finally kiss me for losing.

—Amen to that. My Lord, let it be so.

—It will be. I'm doing this to the letter.
And He never leaves debts unpaid.

—Who are you talking about?

—No one. Just trying to believe in something again.
But let's be honest—those two high-value targets bouncing on my chest all night. You've officially compromised my trigger discipline. My cannon's been locked and loaded since the first shake.

—Then what's with the holdup, Volchik?

—Standing by. Commander Marisha hasn't issued clearance yet.

—Mission alert. Stationary target locked.
Visuals confirm direct impact range.
Initiate hundred rpm—on my command...
FIRE!

Marisha was right about me.
I really have fallen for her.
Didn't want to admit it—not to her, not even to myself.

Too many doubts gnawing holes in my head.
But once they dissolved—I lost control.
Did the kind of thing I only do when all logic's gone AWOL.
And now I'm scared. Scared I might've hurt her.
Even by accident.

Her chest—rising like Samara's stone mountains—was heaving like a forge bellows, and that just made it worse.
My pulse was already reckless.
But I'd made a pact—one-time-only, nothing more tonight.
And it felt wrong to break that so soon.
Besides—

Marisha wasn't exactly ready to argue contract clauses.
She tried—maybe wants to say something.
Took in air with her mouth open like a diver drowning in fire.
But each time, the words got swallowed back down.

Then suddenly—she yanked me against her chest,
face flushed so red it looked like she was leaking shame.
The reason became clear fast.

The bushes around us—where we thought we were alone—exploded with laughter.

Ghost-like silhouettes popped up, hooting like drunk devils.
One voice shouted—

—Hell of a battle, Commander!
That was a five-star takedown. If this guy sticks around,
no Samara girl's will look at us the same again!

A chorus of laughter followed. Sounded like the voice belonged to that idiot Jovoxier—the same clown Marisha drop-kicked earlier.

I did my best to keep my cannon hidden under her body,
but yeah—my ass was fully exposed to a pack of hungry junior operatives. Great.

Somewhere in that disaster, the only person to save our dignity was my one and only Sis-in-law, Polina.

She stepped out from the next bush with clothes draped over her arm, calm as a medic, wrapped us both up with all the grace of a pro.

Of course, she couldn't help sliding the dagger in as she did.

—Next time, Volchik, maybe try not to break the merchandise. Those apples you're playing with?
You keep working those tits like that, they'll turn to watermelons by spring. And then guess who you'll be coming for the charm?
Yeah, that's right—me. Polina.
Your only sexy-in-law. Don't say I didn't warn you.

Her prophecy was lethal enough.
Answering her—one way or another—would've cut my life expectancy down to six months, tops.
I stayed silent. Red enough to look guilty.

Marisha, though—she just yanked my face to her throat and spit fire straight across the clearing.

—You cursed little bitch. Take a look at your own chest before you throw shade. Still no man to claim you, yet those XXL tits of yours bounce for anybody who stares long enough.
And you—Jovox, you snake. Couldn't just stay back? Had to drag your pack of dogs to watch your elder sister fuck? Shameless.

A hacking cough, then Jovox's laugh burst out.

—What the hell, sis? Two seconds ago I was your 'little brother'—now I'm a snake? Which is it?
On my end, I'm about to become your brother-in-law anyway.
Now which title do I hang onto?
We waited outside that cave door for ages.
Finally had to come looking when you didn't show.
What else were we supposed to do?

—When did you get here?

—Right when Commander Zakharova yelled FIRE!

Ha! Ha—haa!

Right then, I swear—if I could've dropped a missile from the sky on these idiots, I'd have done it with a smile.

They lingered, throwing out more shit-talk until Marisha's fury snapped and she ordered them off.

They scattered, still laughing, heading back for the cave.
We pulled our clothes on, hearts still hammering, then followed behind.

That place wasn't a cave at all. It was fallout—a forgotten limb of a Soviet nuclear plant. Now it clicked—the "factory" we'd been held in wasn't a factory either.

It was another abandoned sector of the same complex.
Two massive reactor shells stood out front, gutted relics of what used to hum with power.

And that "cave door" the kids kept trying to muscle open was not stone. A sealed access hatch—polished to a surgical shine.
Pumping room, condenser lines, water basin—the gut of every nuclear site. Nature had dressed it in dirt and roots, from outside it looked like a cave.
But that door—mirror-bright. Solid stainless.
No bomb. No gas-cutter.
Nothing was getting through easy.

Looking at it—I saw what Rasheed meant.
A face.
Cold. Gleaming.
Just like The Maker.

I knew exactly why that water plant inside the abandoned nuke site mattered—and more than anyone else here, I knew what was waiting down there.

Which is why there was no way I was letting Marisha in.
I told her.

She snapped, full-volume:

—You've lost your mind, Volchik.
You think I'm letting you walk in there alone?

—This job's mine, Marisha. Your own rule—every job goes to the one who can actually do it.

—I said that? Yeah. I lied.

The others caught our heat, started shooting each other looks—the kind that start bar fights or shotgun weddings.

I looked at her face. All ice.
There was no winning this woman in a straight argument.
I switched tactics. Picked the dumbest ally I had.

—Alright, Jovox. Your turn.
Your sister has no clue what's inside.
Dragging her down there triples the risk for everyone.

—Stuff your logic in its sheath, Cumnat.
She said she's going—she's going.
She'll fight by your side.
And if it comes to it, she'll die there too.

—You're a certified idiot. That's your sister.
Polina—talk some sense into these maniacs.

She just shrugged, like the whole verdict was carved in stone.

—There's nothing to fix, Volchik.
You've seen the way she loves you.
You think she'll just live on if something happens to you?
Not a chance. If dying by your side is what it takes—that's her peace. That's her joy.

—You're a full-blown cult. The whole damn bloodline.

I had no choice. Had to accept it.
They'd already hauled in the gear—every tool we might need down there.

Meaning, this wasn't some wild impulse.
This was set, mapped, planned.

When I caught sight of the two hazmat suits—each with its own gas mask—my panic about Marisha dulled, just a little.

No more fights. I let them have it their way.

They saluted our mission, peeled off to follow their own track.

And I—
I took Marisha's hand and walked straight into the dark.
Down into the abandoned gut of the plant.

Into a black so thick, sound couldn't even echo.

—∞—

The Naxiver Circuit

Animas Gelişim
Location overridden

I didn't grasp it then, but my Lord sets every piece exactly where it belongs. Nothing moves outside His sight.
Even when I lost my senses—started believing I was broken,
He brought Marisha to my side, and through her, completed the design.

And the Darkness I couldn't decipher this time—couldn't tell if it mattered or not—He had embedded it in me for the perfect time.
Since the moment I became aware of my existence.
It was waiting for this.

The cave we're inside now—"dark" would be an insult.
This isn't shadow. It's the ink the universe hides its sins in.

A Darkness thick like scorched oil—like octopus arms writhing outward to pull us in whole.

I can already tell—the hazmat suits, the masks—useless.
Told Marisha. She didn't argue.
Just peeled everything off, one layer at a time.

The 300-watt LED we brought?
Outside, it looked like it could light a stadium.
Down here—just five steps in—and it's blind.
Even what little it shows is fogged, dirty—as if the air itself rejects the light.

To any living thing with breath, this is a swallowing nightmare.
But for those awake—for those like me—it's not a problem.

We haven't gone deep yet.
Still close to the outer membrane.
But her grip on my hand is iron.
She's uneasy.
And I understand why.

This place doesn't just contain Darkness.
It listens.

The light isn't helping.
It's only blinding us from what's real.

—Kill the light, Ree. Strap it to your backpack.

—What? Are you serious?
How the hell are we supposed to move through this?

—Leave that to me.

—In this pitch-black?
We'll drop into some pit and die like morons.

—We won't. Turn it off.

We had to wait. Maybe a few minutes. Maybe less.
She turned it off already.

—You told me the truth, love.
This fight isn't yours.
If you turned back now, I'd actually be relieved.

—I already gave you your share of joy.
Your ration's done. No more talk.

—I see there's no way to set you aside—but why were you still holding the light after I told you to bag it?

—High-powered LEDs stay hot after switching off. I had to let it cool before dropping it in the bag. One minute—wait.
How the hell did you see me do that? In this grave-black?
I can't even see my own hand.

—Exactly why I told you to kill the light.
Because I have other ways.

—I can see that—but how?

I didn't answer. Just took her hand and started forward.

The sight had returned.
Not through the eyes—but the Darkness burning in my chest.
That infinite hunger... finally recognized its home.

Now I could feel everything.
Through the heart.

Just ahead—an emergency gate.
Twin-flight staircase leading down.
The door stood open.
Waiting for us.

I pulled Marisha with me. And the moment our feet hit the surface—I knew we'd made a mistake.
This wasn't the same black as above. This was different.

Like a dim-lit underground parking garage soaked in midnight humidity. But there were no cars. Just endless rows of bare concrete columns spread out across a freshly paved pitch-black floor.

Which made no sense.
Paved roads belong above ground.
Why pour asphalt into the gut of a nuclear carcass?

Still—Marisha seemed steadier now.
She could actually see, at least a little.
And the space felt human.
Familiar.
Almost comforting.

That was the second problem.
The columns didn't match any real structure.
The spacing was wrong—some twenty feet apart,
some missing altogether, whole empty zones with nothing holding anything up.

How could anyone screw up foundational alignment in a facility this size? Simple answer:
They didn't.
Because this entire place might be an illusion.

I had to thank Rasheed Dameer again.
Back in Prague, during his wild intel drops about The Maker,
he described something like this.
A party space. A ceremonial zone.

Full of "buts," full of weird details that never lined up.
I thought maybe he was overhyped—rattled.
Just telling it wrong.

Until I visited the place he swore hosted a twilight ritual...
and found only a dead church.
Rasheed swore on his soul it happened there.

Which meant either he was mad—or someone fed him a false reality so strong, he never even questioned it.
Back then, I couldn't believe it.

Now? Belief doesn't matter.
The second I stepped onto this floor—
I knew I was already inside. No point trying to go back.

That entrance—the one we came through—no longer exists.

—Ree...

—Ho..uv?

—You scared?

—Not really. The blindness was messing with me.
But now that I can see—I'm just thinking about where this basement leads.

—Ree...

—Ho..uv?

—Do you trust me?

—God, I risk my life just to keep you close,
and that's what you ask?

—It's not that. What if I asked you to do something that made no sense? Something you couldn't calculate—couldn't reason through—something not even Macro would say 'no' to.
That's why I was wondering if you can do it, if it came from me?

—Ahh...Now I get it. That tall spiky-haired woman with the weird tattoos—yeah, I get why you love her.
But that's not my kind of love, Shakarim.

When I took your hand—it was to die with you.
Now you decide. What do you really want to ask...
and what do you actually want to know?

—Hmm... you're different.
Maybe it's because what we have is different too.

—Yeah? Different how?

—I can't break it down into clean parts. But it's there.
Like that time with Daggan—even after you took him down, even after the things he said—those filthy, personal things—when I asked, you dropped the hammer from your hand. Just like that. And when I asked for it, you didn't even argue about keeping the Dark Weapon secret. You said yes. There've been so many things like that... I never thought someone from the human world could be like that.

—No other human in this world is your woman.
So, the theory holds up.

—Ree...

—Hmm?

—You might feel...terrified, very soon.

—How do you know?

—I just do.

—Then you're wrong, my love. If I die, I'll die swinging.
But I don't scare any goddamn shit in this world.

—It's not that kind of thing.

—Then what kind?

—What do you think this place is?

—Looks like a basement. Maybe cargo storage?
Or a place for the big bosses to stash their cars?

—Nobody builds basements under a nuclear core to park sedans, Ree. You know that, right?

—I mean... I've seen modern plants don't do that, yeah.
But I don't know about old Soviet builds.
Maybe this was just the design back then.

—It wasn't. Not in any era.

—Then what? Why build all this down here?

—Because this isn't a basement, Ree.

—Then what the hell is it?

—I'm not sure yet. Maybe... a projection. A fabricated reality.

—A what?

—Don't stress. You'll see. We're already inside it.

—Did you notice something?

—What?

—How long have we been walking?

—Ten minutes, maybe.

—And we haven't hit an edge.
Not forward, not back.
Feels like we never left our starting point.

—Fuck. Wait—are you actually pulling this freak show prank on your wife right now? Because this isn't funny, Volchik—
I swear to God, it feels like we're standing in the same damn spot.

—Ree...

—Hh..ov?

—What do you see around us?

—Nothing. Just more of the same basement.
No doors. No stairs. No elevator.
Can't even find where we walked in.

—That's not what we're looking for.

—Then what, genius? What are we looking for?

—The Darkness.

—The darkness? That was outside. We already passed it.

—Exactly. Which is why I wasn't worried there.
That was real darkness. This place—it's pretending.
It's lit just enough to make it look normal. That's the danger.

—I've got a gun.

—It won't help you here.

—Then what do we do?

—We search. For the Darkness.

—Search? For darkness?
How does that even make sense?
If you can't see something, that's where the dark is.

—That's the problem. Here, you see everything.
Dimly, yes. But every part of this place is softly visible.
There is no true darkness here.

—Ugh... my my, I'm losing it.
What kind of psycho builds an endless basement like this?
There should be a wall somewhere, or at least one patch of shadow the light can't reach.
But no—every inch is this soft, shitty half-light.
Even way out there in the corners—still visible.
And... holy shit—it's crawling up my spine now.
Who built this freak show?

—What now?

—Look up, Shakarim.

—I did. What am I supposed to see?

—Look again. At the ceiling.

—Yeah, I see it. Just a flat slab. Regular pale concrete.

—There's asphalt—paved, right on the ceiling.
Who the hell does that?

To me, it was still just concrete.
The illusion didn't touch me much.
But Marisha—it had already sunk its claws deep.

This is why I didn't want to bring her in.
She was too close to whatever this place responds to.

—Ree...

—Hu..ov?

—Hold my hand tight.

—This feels unreal. Like we're brushing against something not of this world. What the hell is this? Ghosts?

—Not exactly. But the one who set this trap—isn't human.
Not even close. Think it like a device, synced to your existence like Wi-Fi, that reads every signal from your body.
Every thought. Every fear.

—Who's the bastard behind this?
I'll cut his throat open myself.

—You can't. He's not something you can touch.
Not something you can kill.

—You... you knew about this? Before?

—I suspected.
That's why I didn't want to bring you in.

—Hmmm...Makes sense now.
They... that... told me to leave you here—go back alone.

—They were right. You should've left, my love.
But why don't you tell me who it was.
Who told you to bring me here?

—You wouldn't have believed me then.
But now? In this place?
Nothing feels impossible anymore.

—Good. Then talk. Say it while we walk.
If we keep talking, the illusion won't close in.

—And while you do—keep scanning.
If you spot darkness, call it out, fast.

Marisha keeps walking as she speaks.

—It started when I wanted to join GRU. My father was still alive.
Officially, law says no one under eighteen can enlist.
But for those chosen to be Spetsnaz, they bend that rule.
Some kids start at fifteen.
Only the ones from 'eligible' bloodlines are allowed.
I mean, only children from specific families got in early.
Those with records of national contribution—medals,
decorated service, proven loyalty stamped into their DNA.
Others could join Spetsnaz later, but if they came from the
regular army, they aged out before ever reaching high command.
So yeah—timing mattered.

Her voice shifts slightly.

—My reason for being there was something else entirely.
You already know that. My father didn't want it at first.
He fought me on it. But I pushed.
And with Polina's father backing me, he gave in.
Polina had two older brothers.
Both of them went into selection with me.
First two years—basic army foundation—we all made it through.
Then came the strategy year.
That's when the first brother broke.
Dropped out.

She takes a breath before going on.

—And that same year—my father died.
I won't lie to you, losing him didn't rip me up
the way losing my sister did.
I'd already started hating him
for sitting back, for doing nothing,
for letting her death pass unanswered.
When he was gone, my path became clear.
The only thing that mattered was revenge.

—Most officer courses ended there.
Ours? That's when the real training began.
Next came Special Weaponry and Survival Training.
The second brother couldn't take it.
He was out. I don't know how I survived.
Honestly—I wasn't even conscious of myself anymore.
I was just moving, grinding, breathing like an animal.
That's what they wanted us to become.
Beasts with instincts. No questions. Just reaction.
The second brother didn't make it further, but he still got commissioned—made his way up the ranks.
Now he serves in the FSB.
For us, we'd already been in the fire four years.
And those of us still standing?
We weren't human anymore.
We thought we could survive anything.
Then came the academic phase. Physical struggle we could take.
But this—this bent the mind. Criminal Psychology.
Law. Politics. Critical Thinking. Mind games.
Warfare Management. Core Defense Theory.
They broke us academically.
Day after day—our minds melting from concepts that didn't just teach war—they taught how to weaponize thought.
Only twenty of us made it through.
And that, they said, was normal.
...And the next year...

She pauses, gathers herself, and continues.

—No. No, Asalim. Even to you—my love,
I can't say what came after.
Let me just tell you this—that was the year they turned us, man or woman—into something else.
That was when we stopped being human.

—Only Twenty of you survived that?

—Twenty.

—How many started?

—From the Special Admission families? Four hundred and fifty. Then, by year three, another fifteen hundred came in from the regular army.

—My Lord...
Out of all those trained killers, only twenty finished?
You had to be a prodigy.

—Prodigy? or Bullshit.
What I became was pure animal.
If I told you everything—you might start to hate me.
I'm not going into all of it.

—There's no version of you I could ever hate, Ree.

—Maybe not. But I would.
I'd lose respect for myself—in my own eyes.
My life with you now is different.
This moment is different. And that version of me...
I don't want to bring it into this one.

—Fine, as you wish. Tell me where you stopped.
What happens next?

For a second, she struggles to speak.

—...After that final year, out of everyone who survived—we had nine left from special families, and eleven from the regular army—only one test remained.
If anyone passed it—they were placed straight into a GRU Spetsnaz detachment. But to even take the test, one had to sign a very specific contract.

—What kind of contract?

—One you could refuse—no shame, no disgrace.
You still got offered a stellar army career.
Or high-ranking FSB placement. All doors open.

—That sounds like enough.
So what the hell was in this "special contract" that made you put your name on it

—Not all of us signed.
Just two out of the nine bloodline recruits.
Five from the regulars. The contract said:
'No one shall be held accountable for my death.'

—I know why you signed.
And I'm sure the other six had their reasons too.
But what was the test?

—Survival.
The test was staying alive.
They dropped us—one woman, six men,
into the Death Valley of Siberia.
It's still operational. Every year, word comes in
about junior cadets dying out there.
Here's how it worked—
units from every branch got clearance to hunt us.
Track, trap, break us—any way they wanted.
We were rats in a live-fire torture experiment.
But before they killed us...

She pauses, gathers herself, and continues.

—...what most of them really wanted—was to rape us.
They split into groups—thirty, forty per unit.
All of them trained. All of them invited to brutalize us.
If you got caught—death. Or worse.
Yes, I saw it. With my own eyes. Not just the girls.
Two of the boys in our seven-member unit—gang-raped.

—Holy hell. You were lucky they never got you.

—Lucky? No, my love. They did catch me.
And yes—I was raped too.

—Fuck... Shit, I mean Shakarim...
Why didn't you ever tell me?
That you—
you—went through something like that?

—Because if I had, maybe you'd have laughed it off.
Maybe you'd have mocked me.

—Back then, you were already calling me a sashay queen,
that I am just an ass-shaking stage performer.
How the hell was I supposed to add this on top of that?

—Okay…Alright.
Wipe your eyes.
I agreed—bringing it up was my mistake.
But you've got me wrong, love.
Even if I'd known…
I wouldn't have mocked you. I wouldn't have hated you.
I would've just—taken care of you harder.
I'd have done everything to help you erase it from your mind.

—I believed that. But I didn't have the courage to say it.
When a victim doesn't die during a gang rape—
they're usually released. Wounded. But alive.
So they can be hunted again.
Drawn back. Torn open. Over and over.

—But you survived. Wounded.

—No… not exactly.
The group that caught me had thirty-three men.
Many of them…I knew.
And one of them—was my first husband.
He told the whole crew he wanted to be the last.
Said he'd finish the job after everyone else had their turn.

—What kind of grotesque hell—who even thinks like that?

—I thought it was grotesque too.
Back then. But now I see it for what it was.
Not just cruelty. It was a psychological test. A final one.
To see if, after certain death—after humiliation so deep it
changes your bone structure—you could still get up and move.

—Enough. No more of that. Just tell me what actually matters.

—I could've avoided it.
Could've stayed out of their hands, gone undetected.
If I'd just listened to your boss's orders.

—What? What does that have to do with any of this?

—Let me explain.

—Fine. Go on.

She talks without looking at me.

—We'd been trained to the bone in defense, escape, survival.
We knew how to fight back. We knew how to vanish.
We had every tactic drilled into our nervous systems.
But the point of this test wasn't the training.
It was whether we could adapt the training in hell conditions.
Apply it when we were outnumbered, outflanked, and isolated.
We believed we could.
All of us. We were confident.
Overconfident.

Her voice tightens, just a little.

—We thought we could last the week.
Or reach the checkpoint. But we couldn't.
Not in that terrain. Not with those numbers.
I estimate there were over three hundred and fifty enemy
operatives spread across just five square miles.
Probably in at least ten units.
Each of us dropped solo—different checkpoints,
no backup, no comms.
I lasted three and a half days.

—Where were you hiding?

—In a bear den.

—Wait—what? You mean you were actually with a bear?

—A full-grown polar bear. Real. Alive.
It laid on top of me the whole time.

—Please tell me you didn't—
You didn't do anything with the bear, right?

—Seriously?
Say something like that again and I'll shut up for good.

—Okay, okay—sorry. Go on.

—A polar bear isn't new to me.
I used to hunt them as a kid with my father.
Took my first kill at thirteen.
And even then, I'd already learned—
you don't always have to kill a bear to control it.
I stayed in the warmth of its body.
Pressed to its flank.
Alive beneath something that could crush me.
That's when I first saw it—the dream.

Her words come slower now.

—In the dream, someone had placed fresh meat outside the bear's den. The bear stepped out to eat. And I followed it.
Moments later—a sniper shot cracked from deep in the trees.
Bear dropped—dead in the snow. I hit the ground too.
Rolled through the ice, slipped into another patch of forest.
And from there—I watched them come looking for me.
A search team. Running. Calling. But I felt safe.
Distant. Untouchable. That was the dream.

She takes a breath before going on.

—I knew it was a dream—just a few seconds in.
Right when I started to feel the bear moving again.
It shifted beside me. Breathing heavy.
And I actually smiled. Let myself sink back, tried to relax.
But then—thump.
A sound. Heavy. Wrong.
I peeked out. The bear was already dead.
Exactly where it was supposed to die.
Exactly how I saw it.
And before I could even register that,
a rifle butt cracked the back of my skull.
Somebody had crept right up behind me, waited, then struck.
I blacked out.
And when I came to...

—I don't need to tell you where I woke up.
You already know.
They were waiting for me to wake up.
Not to interrogate. Not to talk.
Just to start.
The leader went first.
And right then, right in the middle of the first round of whatever he was doing—I saw the second dream.
Calling it a dream feels wrong.
You don't sleep through something like that.
This wasn't sleep.
This was wide-awake—a vision carved into pain.
I saw myself—bruised and bleeding,
two men closing in, laughing.
And I? I smiled back. Like a whore.
Told them to flip me over before they started.
Said I wanted to enjoy it too.
They laughed. Filthy.
One pinned my arms. The other tied my legs.
Started to drag me somewhere.
But my fingers were already reaching back—
toward the blade I always kept tucked in my hair.
Hidden like a clip.
That was the dream.

Her voice shakes, just once.

—And just as it faded...
I was back, for real.
Being raped.
That blade—you saw earlier, it's always with me.
But when the two real ones came?
When I saw their faces—I couldn't smile.
I couldn't speak those slutty lines from the dream.
I said nothing.
And they were doing what they have came for.
Hurt me more than the dream ever showed.

For a second, she struggles to speak.

—Then came the third vision.
And this one—I believed,
even if it was a dream or what I can't name it.
I don't know how I pulled it off.
But I copied the sequence exactly.
All of it. Frame by frame.
Photographic memory—every one of the seven of us had it.
I still have mine.
I remembered the angles. The timing.
I let the man in front hold my throat in his teeth,
tear at my chest. I whispered—
'Take my clip out. It's caught in the bun.'
Like it would help him.
Like I wanted to make it easier.
He slapped me. Didn't want to play along.
But the one behind? He started pushing inside—
then reached up, untied my hair.
And just like in the dream—he found it.
My blade.

She keeps her voice steady, but it costs her.

—He was so proud of himself—had to show the other one,
holding it up to my wrists like it was a gift.
And that's when I moved.
Everything happened just like the vision said it would.
First shot from which angle.
Who'd panic and run.
Who'd duck into the next room for cover.
Who'd freeze and get split open.
All thirty-two died.
Throats wide open.
Like they got kissed by the wrong god.

—The last one? I think I know who it was.
And I think you didn't kill him.

—That's... partly true.

—Partly?

—I didn't cut his throat. But I did split his tongue.
With that same blade—I stripped his manhood off his body.
That was the first time I ever cut a man open between the legs.

—My love...You did what you had to.
And if it ever comes to that again—do it.
Don't even think twice.

—Do you know what you're saying?

—If that kind of thing happens again—yes. I mean it.

—Good. No problem, my love.
I've gotten damn good at that game by now. And...
I think we just crossed into a different part of this place.
It's not a new place.
Still the same basement—but the pillars are gone.

Gone.
Every single one.
As far as the eye could stretch—just pitch-paved concrete underfoot, and another poured slab ceiling above, with no visible support.

Even an idiot would know—this place isn't real.
Then came the smell.
Not clear at first—just faint.
But it sharpened fast.
Burnt. Something burnt.
Flesh.

I didn't need light to recognize it.
I've smelled burning meat before.
This was human.

Beside me, Marisha turned, wrinkling her nose, scanning left and right—trying to locate it. She couldn't see anything either.

—Keep walking, Marisha. Don't stop.

—Mmm...I'm sweating now.
Can't say how far we've walked, but it's far enough that I feel it.

—This kind of scale? No basement in the world's built like this.
You were right. Something's wrong here.

—Yeah. We never should've stepped into this trap.
Now, tell me about that vision of yours,
the one you mentioned—is that how you knew to come with me?

—Partly. I was the only female candidate to survive Death Valley.
Three men made it, somehow.
The rest were hauled out on life support.
That's the ratio, apparently.
It's rare for a woman to pass the final stages.
That's why GRU Spetsnaz detachments have just few of us.
If they need female ops, they usually borrow from outside
regiments. Like they did with my sister in Phuket.
But those of us who passed all phases? The real ones?
We're treated with a kind of respect even the men don't get.
When I recovered and joined my unit,
everyone treated me like a hero. Admired me.
But I knew that survival wasn't just mine.
That vision—those dreams—they didn't stop at Death Valley.
They kept coming.
In the field. Especially before combat.
Each time, sharper.
And by then, I'd learned to live with them.

—You never told me any of this. But back in KL...I saw you fight.
And I couldn't say a word. Every move, every strike—it was like
you already knew where every attack would land.
I thought—how the hell is that even possible?

—It wasn't just dreams, sweetheart.
Some of it was the brutal training too.
Can't let the magic get all the credit.

—Yeah...
That, I believe.
Now keep talking.
And don't stop walking.

—Alright. Here it is:
Those missions? The Caesar identity in Syria,
Pulling the Dark Weapon out of Rasheed's crew in Iraq.
Yeah. Those were shown to me.
Dreams. Visions. Same as always.
There was no room for doubt.
I knew they were real.
So I executed. Every detail.
Same script, every time.
Eventually, my field work ended.
They handed me a new assignment.
I followed orders again.
Same discipline. Same precision.

She keeps walking as she speaks.

—But the pain never left.
That burn inside me—for my sister. Never healed.
And the loneliness? Yeah, you know that part.
The emptiness one could have within.
After what happened early in life, love wasn't an option.
Trusting a man? Out of the question.
But the body doesn't forget. The hunger's still human.
I did get close to someone once. But it didn't last.
Professional conflict. Then...you walked in.

—This 'someone'—who was he?
And what the hell does 'professional conflict' even mean?

—Jealousy's my territory, love.
You don't have to play that card.

—It's not about Jealousy.
If you want to truly know someone—you need all of them.
And when they're the one bringing it up—it matters even more.
Secrets rot things from the inside. If someone else digs them out, no speech in the world can sew trust back together.

—You're terrifying when you argue.
I don't think anyone in my whole bloodline could win against that logic. But honestly? I'm scared to tell you this.

—You can. Everything else you told me, I took it.
I'll take this too.

—...Alright. You ever heard the name William Hardman?

—Nope. Why? Am I supposed to?

—Maybe not. But Amethyst Vega would know him.
William was a CO at Delta Force. Just like me.

—So? You and him had a thing?

—Not exactly. I liked him. A lot.
We were opposites. Too much friction for anything real.
But the top brass liked the idea of pairing us off.
Playing allies in the field, partners in the dark.
You know how it works. This isn't new.
Even you—the green light they gave for us?
Same reason. They don't waste intimacy when it can be used.

—And I'm guessing you used it. Just like you did with me.

—No. Don't go there, Volchik. You're not the same.
You're what my heart wants—exactly as you are.
With Willie? He was good-looking.
Skilled. Hard. Knew the job inside out.
But beyond the sex, there was nothing.
No spine for anything real.
When I meet you in Phuket, it was part curiosity,
part professional interest. Nothing deeper than that.
Back then, I was still with Willie.
He really was trying to help with the search for my sister.
And I'd only just met you—one day, nothing more.
There was no space yet to think of you as anything serious.

—Wait—you had me show up with flowers to welcome you,
while you were sleeping with that Delta Force hardass?
And now you're telling me it 'wasn't serious'?

—You're doing it again, Volchik. I knew you'd get pissed.
And you have every right to be.

—But think about it—I knew Willie for years.
If I was going to fall for him, I would've, long ago.

—Or maybe—maybe you dumped him because I looked better 'strategic prospect' in your agency files.
And once the old dog stopped being useful, you latched onto me.

—God... watch your mouth.
You don't get to talk to your wife like that.

—I said what made sense.
That's not disrespect. That's logic.

—Logic? You really think I didn't know you weren't Caesar?
That you weren't even Amethyst Vega?
I knew from the jump. Still kept it to myself.
You think I couldn't have blown your cover?
I didn't—because I wanted this to last. With you.
Till now, I haven't even asked you who you actually are.

—I'm not saying I never thought about it.
I did.
You weren't chasing sex. You weren't digging for intel.
You just wanted to be near me. You wanted a shoulder.
Someone who wouldn't crack your trust.
Someone you could rest your head on,
without having to brace for the knife.

—God, the way you just said that, Volchik...
you actually get it?

—Yeah. Back in the early days, I noticed.
You were obsessed with seeing me.
Kept asking when, where, how soon.
But when we met—there was no rush.
No sexual grab. No questions about my secrets.
No leverage hunting. And that?
That was weird as hell.
A woman like you—at your level—
I'd never met anyone like that.
Not even close.

—Damn, my love… If you'd said this back in Phuket,
I'd have turned your face red with kisses.

—As if you didn't already, ha ha…
But yeah—I kept asking myself,
why would someone like you chase me?
I had hotter friends. Richer ones.
Phuket was packed with power players.
And there were single men, eligible, within arm's reach.
You could've gone to any of them.
That's when I started thinking—maybe you're playing me.
Trying to extract something.
Like any woman should, like they were built to act.
Maybe some data. Something tied to my business.
But then? Nothing.
You never made a move like that.
And if you hadn't spoken your truth like you did just now—
I still wouldn't have known why you wanted me.

—Hmm…What you said about women,
maybe it was harsh. But a lot of it's true.
Still… my view of men? That part was wrong.
I'd been informed about you. About your presence.
But I didn't believe it was possible.
My friends knew what I wanted. What I needed.
And before I ever sat beside you in Phuket,
they were texting me like mad—begging me to go to the hotel.
To sit beside you. Just once.

—That crazy Tataliya and the other two?

—Yes. But don't call Tataliya crazy.
She's not. Her story's…it's full of scars, too.

—I can imagine. But not now. Now, I want to hear you.

Marisha exhales and continues.

—I gave in. Finally. Sat beside you.
And that moment, Volchik—it did something to me.

Even now, just remembering it—I'm having goosebumps.
My skin still reacts—like memory itself carries voltage.

—What? I didn't even do anything special that day.

—Exactly. That's what made it so...unforgettable.
From the second I walked up to you,
to the moment we stepped into that room—you didn't glance at my chest. Not once. Not at my waist. Not my hips.
You just looked at me. Straight into my eyes.
With this innocent smile—so real,
like I was a person worth holding with your gaze.

—That's not my fault, sweetheart. Your eyes...
they're unlike anything I've ever seen. Electric blue.
Like lightning—but not the kind that makes me run.
The kind that breaks my heart open, strike after strike,
until I forgot it was ever whole.

—Even if you can't explain it, you just said it perfectly.
Back then, when everything in my life felt numb,
when I couldn't even remember what meaning felt like,
they told me you'd come. A storm.
You'd rip through every wound, wash away the rot,
and fill me—every empty inch. But I didn't believe it.
Not after what I'd lived through.
I didn't think I could love again. Then I saw you.

Her voice shifts slightly.

—And not even an hour—not even one full hour passed before the walls inside me started to break.
I started to float in something new.
I started to float in something I'd forgotten how to feel.
This strange joy, this surrender to feeling.
Even if you couldn't give me all your time, you gave me the one thing that mattered—the proof that you were mine.
Without holding back.

—What are you even saying?
I don't remember doing anything special.

—That's because you're a certified fool.
Tell me—what haven't you done for me?
You flew back to Phuket the same night,
just to see me.

—You made sure I was safe.
You made sure I was comfortable.
And a woman knows these things, Volchik.
The way you moved around me,
that wasn't some casual fling behavior.
That was a man handling a wife.
Not just with words—with your damn hands.
With your presence. And what hit me most?
You never tried to use me.
Even after giving me everything, you looked at me like,
'She's mine. What's there to use?'

—Hmm... Guess I screwed up.

—What?! If you knew it, would you have done something else?

—No, just messing with you.
To be honest, I treat all my close people with that kind of care.
But with you? I supervised everything myself—
your safety, your comfort—like...

—Like what?

—Like you were already my wife. Oh, shit...
I didn't even realize it back then.

—How could you? You adorable idiot.
If you had, you wouldn't have said those nasty words about me
shaking my ass to drunken men on stage.

—One bad line and you want me hanged for it, huh?

—No, no—I'll keep you hanging...
but I won't finish the job.
I'm not ready to be a widow just yet.

—Huh!

—Huh? That's my line.

—Guess your tone rubbed off on me,
after all that body-to-body friction.

—Ha! Good. You wear it well.
But when you vanished...I lost it.
I searched the whole world for you,
and couldn't find even a whisper.
And I couldn't believe it. Couldn't accept it.
My soul just refused.
And right when that madness peaked—the visions came.
Scene by scene. Instructions. Steps.
All leading me here. To this.
And I knew exactly where those instructions were coming from.

—How?

—Because...I didn't see your face in those visions.
And it took me a while to understand why.
But then I realized—I didn't need to see it.
I could smell you.

—My scent?

—Yeah. You have a scent.
Not perfume. You.
It's peculiar—strange in a way that burns into memory.
Did you even know that?

—I do. People have told me before.
And don't tense up—none of them were girls.

—Mmm-hmm... Mmm-hmm... Huh.
You gave me the carrot anyway, huh?

—No! I swear—I'm telling the truth!

—Maybe...you are. But that first moment I saw you in those visions—my whole heart jumped like it hit a live wire.
I saw this gaping wound in your chest.
And a blade—buried deep in your stomach.
That's why, when we met again in KL.

—I kept brushing my hand over your chest like that—
trying to feel the scar for myself.
And though I didn't see the knife, I saw the bandage.
I guessed. But what I couldn't figure out was...
how the man named Elijan Vellum could end up like that.
And why your scent was all over him.
I was losing my mind.

—Mm-hmm... The stomach wound wasn't a knife.
It was a stiletto.

—Which bastard did that to you? Tell me their name.

—What's the point? They're all enjoying hell now.

—Good. Exactly where they belonged.
But still—after I stormed off...
I kept seeing myself lying on your chest again.
In my head. Like before. And... and...

—And?

—That damn slut Antasia—I saw her lying on your chest too.
Just like I had.

—That's why you were throwing venom at my every word the whole time?

—What else? You think I'm supposed to dance like some charmer's playing flutes?

—No...But you didn't bite either. Not like you.

—I wasn't allowed to.
And my heart was cracking into pieces.
I couldn't follow it all the way.

—So that's why you vanished like that?

—Yeah. After that, I cried—a lot.
I didn't want to follow any more orders.
Didn't want to finish the job any more.
And then...they gave me a promise.

—What kind of promise?

—They showed me everything I had to do—like before.
Step by step.

—And then I heard someone say—if I followed through,
they would carve my name into your heart.
I couldn't believe it. It sounded so...so real.
And hearing it—God, it made me cry again.
But this time... from joy.
It was said in that exact tone—you know?
The way our commanders speak when they're defending me.
Like—'Alright. We'll authorize Marisha to handle this.'
That's exactly how they said it—about you.
That's why I told you—it was your boss who ordered this.

—Mmm... I was shocked when you said it.
But not anymore. When my Lord chooses to show
someone the way—they find light, no matter how dark it gets.
And I know this now. His light brought you back to me.
Which means... Maybe—just maybe—there's still a way out.

—You mean... getting out of this goddam place?

—Yes.

—It's already been shown to me. Twice.

—What the hell? When?

—First—when we stepped into the cave.
Then again—right after we crossed into this place.

—Where is it? Why the hell didn't you tell me?

—Because I'm not taking it.
That path—was for me alone.
They told me to leave you behind.

—Marisha—what if that's exactly how He meant to protect us?
Maybe this is the only way one of us survives.

—I don't care. Not happening.
Even if they offer me the whole goddamn world in the next life,
without you, I'm not taking it.
I'll die here beside you. That was the vow.

—What vow?

—At our wedding.
When you were unconscious in that hospital bed.
I held your hand, looked up,
and accepted you—with all vows included.

—...All vows?

—Including the one where I break your knees if you ever talk about leaving me again. Then carry your sorry ass through the fire myself. Don't test me.

—...Got it. Message received.

We kept walking—fingers locked, boots echoing on concrete that had no end.

This place felt wrong since the moment we stepped in,
but neither of us had really felt it.

Now we did.
It hit both of us together—some invisible line we crossed.
Like the place shifted under our feet without warning.

And then I saw it.
At the far edge of this godforsaken basement, where the dim light bled out into pitch, I saw a furnace.
And crouched in front of it—something I can't forget.

A creature.
Owl-shaped.
Man-sized.
Bent low like a priest in prayer—if the prayer was murder.

It was plucking.
Feathers—at first I thought. But then I saw Marisha's hand tighten in mine—saw it tremble. That's when I knew something was wrong.

—What is it, Ree?

She swallowed, hard.

—You don't see it?

—I see it. It's strange, sure.
The way it's pulling out its own feathers, burning them.
But that's not—

—They're not feathers. That thing… it's burning a child.

She wasn't joking. I turned.

—What are you talking about?

—That owl—those aren't feathers it's tossing in.
They're fingers. Little hands. Baby limbs.
I can smell it.

Marisha's words stopped me.
I looked again—really looked—at the thing.

That owl wasn't just smiling. It was grinning—a stretched, devilish snarl—and it wanted us to watch.
Watch it burn what it held between its claws.

Marisha saw something else entirely.
She was shaking like a child.
But the fire wasn't just fire.
The feathers weren't just feathers.
And whatever she saw—I believed her.

Because I smelled it too.
Burnt meat. Human.
Undeniably human.

—Marisha…?

She didn't answer.
Her hand just clamped tighter on mine.

—Come on, we have to move—don't look at it.

Her breath caught.

—I—I can't stop looking. I'm trying…

—What is it showing you?

Silence.

Then she whispered, her voice breaking.

—There was… there was going to be a child.
After the training. After what happened.
I didn't want it. I couldn't.
Four months in… I ended it.
It would've been... his.

I gripped her hand.

—I understand.

But inside me, a different kind of fire had lit.
The bastard wasn't just showing us death.
It was tailoring the nightmare.
Bending reality to fracture us—each in our own way.

For me, it had shown a feather, my own, lit and curling in the furnace.

For her, the hands of something she once had to erase to survive.

And then—the voice.
Not spoken, but planted.
Rooted inside my head like a second heartbeat.

!—Let's test your conviction, shall we!

It wasn't my voice. But it came from within.
A perfect mimic. Smooth, inhuman.

!—What is she doing here Darius! This sinner!
This child of lust and seduction!
She didn't worth any of it!
Did you bring her to burn willingly!

I didn't respond with words. Just fury.

—Worthy? Who are you to judge who worth it who does not?
She came at her will, and she will go when she will.

!—Oh! You're angry now Darius! But I never called you a sinner!
Even after you drowned creation in its own blood!
Even after you dragged us to the brink of extinction! for nothing!
You! A sinner! No, no! you're forgiven!

!—You were given light!
And the right to walk in darkness!
You! You are the chosen!
However it's a pleasure to meet you!
I am The Honorable Naxivar!
If you really need a name!
Now! Let's test that mercy!

The voice wasn't sound. It was pressure.
Filling my skull from the inside—like hellfire poured molten into my veins and started whispering in smoke.
And yet...
It didn't feel unnatural.
Not here. Not in this tomb of illusions.

This was always meant to happen.
Since the first fall. Since the first war.
This—this presence—was what I was always meant to face.
And I could feel it.

The infinite Darkness inside my chest... crawling upward.
Rising like old lover looking for its match.
But Marisha—She couldn't be here for this.

She has to go, now.

—Marisha... Ree.

She was trembling in my arms like something halfway gone.
Eyes wide, glassy. Lips darkening at the edges. Still whispering like she thought words could outrun what was coming.

—Marisha... Ree...

—Y-yeah... Asalim... the demon's gone. But it's still burning.

—It'll keep burning until you leave, my love.
It's really time for you to go now.

—Wh... where would I even go?
The exit's past that burning furnace...
I... I can't walk through that.

—You'll go holding my hand. Keep your eyes on mine.

—Shakarim... forgive me.
I... I've sinned... so much.
Sins that'll never be forgiven.
Never.
I know that.
Just... you, please forgive me...
please...

—Hold yourself together, love.
Forgiveness from me?
That was done long ago.
Everything. All of it.
Already forgiven.

—Mmh... pull me close, please...
I ... I can't stand anymore.

—Come to me. My Lord kept His promise.
He carved your name into my heart.
A heart that once belonged to you will never belong to any other.
And every time you remember this, you'll ask for forgiveness.
Again and again. Because only those who want to see their names in the Book of the Forgiven...ever get written in.
He will forgive you too. One day.

—The smoke... I can't breathe this...
this burnt smell...I
... I think I'm...
I'm dying, Shakarim...
forgive me...

—Marisha! Close your eyes.
Keep walking with me. Don't stop.
Marisha ...

It was already too late.
The bastard knew exactly where to hit.
The burnt smoke had filled the whole space like poison gospel.

It wasn't choking me much, but Marisha—Marisha was fading.

Like someone drowning, collapsed on the floor, thrashing, gasping, trying to breathe.

Her lungs had stopped taking in air. Her blue eyes looked like they were about to shatter straight out of her skull.
Her heart was spitting out its final sparks—a body jerking on the edge of the cliff, half-spirit, half-flesh.
And ahead—the furnace kept burning. But behind it—only black.

And that was where she had to go.
I knew it.

Walking wouldn't cut it anymore.
I pulled her up—gathered what was left of my strength,
and as she thrashed like a drowning beast.

I ran.
Straight toward the dark.
And hurled her into it.

Feels like I did it right.
Within seconds, Marisha vanished into the dark.
With her, all light disappeared—and the entire space drowned in pitch-black. Perhaps my Lord will deliver her to the right place.
Let it be so.

—Now it's your turn, freak bird. Where are you?

!— Right here! All around you!
I must say Darius! Your execution was brilliant!
With the purity of that intent even the Lord of Light Himself must now hesitate! Whether to destroy the sinner child... or not!
Hyuk... whissssssssss!

—I have no doubt about His decision.
Or its execution. But that last bit—what the hell was it!?

!—That was me trying to laugh Darius! Whissss... sssuuu!
Why don't you step out of your shell now brother!
Fear is for mankind!
Not for you! Not for me!
Hyuk... whissss!

—Brother? How the fuck are you my brother?

!—All of creation can be brother and bastard to each other!
That's how I meant it!

—That logic belongs to the human race.
How do you even grasp such things!

!—The same way I understand the infinite Darkness inside you!

Impossible.
This thing—this entity—though it speaks like a spirit,
it's not incorporeal.
Not some ghost. Not an echo drifting on memory.
No.
It has substance.

Unbelievable—because I thought only the Lord Himself
had the right to command something like this.
Not even its own kind could leash it.

And yet, here it is—roaming freely through the material world,
as if it were born to breach it.

Worse—It's taken fragments of its own subconscious,
embedded them with precision, like sealed instruments,
triggered on cue—and used them.

Marisha didn't know. No one knew.
That Dark Weapon's reactor wasn't designed to detonate.
It was designed to preserve.
To protect the dormant essence of this thing.
This being.

Because once released into the physical world, it could,
under specific triggers, alter the nature of matter itself.
Like a patch update.
A live program dropped into a dead machine.
But now—that thing, it moves, acts, and infects on its own will.
It doesn't even need a power source. Neither the Lords own will.

!—Still thinking about tools and wires Darius!
This is no time for toys!

—Then come closer. Let me play with your head instead.

!—Head! What's that supposed to be!
Do we even have such things!
We are either Light or Darkness!
And your kind!
Those like you! Are both!
Nothing else exists Darius!!

—What exists and what doesn't...only the Lord decides.
But right now? I'm thinking what to do with you.

!—That's what I want to know too Darius!
What do you wish to do with me!
If destruction was your goal!
Then the Lord of Light would've done it already!
He still can! Why this endless crossing!
Back and forth! Through the paths of shade and shine!

I'd let wrath get the better of me.
Let it run wild.
Now I see—that was a mistake.

The question he asked... I do know the answer.
But is there any point in saying it?
The ones who believe...they don't need the words.
And the ones who don't?
Won't believe a thing—no matter how true it sounds.

!—Say it anyway! Maybe I'll find some use for it!

—Hmm... good to know—you can read my thoughts.

!—Even the patterns dancing in your brain!
I can trace them! But not all of them!
Not in you! Not fully!
Because you walk both worlds!
In the dark I can't see your light!
And when I light the ambient!
I can't see your shadows!

—Then strike a flicker. Something dim.

!—What's the point! Dim or bright it's still light!
And light hides the shadows not reveals them!
I tried it just now! You saw!

—Hmm... a good try. Now I understand you.
What a ridiculous thing—to call yourself The Naxivar.
One day, you'll be ashamed of it.
I never imagined something this twisted could happen to you.
Now I see why you roam like this.
The Lord never wanted your destruction.
He never wants anyone's.
Because He created it all.
He's been offering you a way back.
That's why He pulled me back, again and again.
You refused His hand—so He sent me again.
Had you taken it, He would've pulled you home once more.

!—Brilliant! Truly you are one of a kind Darius!
No one ever put it that way before!
I'm really honored to meet you! Brother!

—I'm honored too, to finally face you.
Didn't think we'd meet like this.
You thought you were punishing evil.
That you were balancing the scale.
Righting the wrong.
But all of it—was built on a mistake.
Now I see it clearly: you've severed completely from your own subconscious self.
Still—if you're willing... we can fix this.

!—Ohhh! Then tell me! Where was the mistake Darius!
I gave the tormented a path to justice! I gave them power!
And in time the tormented became tormentors themselves!
I gave the next wave of weak their chance to rise!
I showed them how to fight how to strike back!
That was my task! My truth!
Tell me Darius!
Where exactly did I go wrong!

—You pushed beyond a boundary your form was never built to sustain. That was your mistake.

!—Is that so!
And who set that boundary!
What defined it!
If we were created to stay within it
then why wasn't I stopped before I crossed it!
Why was I allowed to see the truth!
Why was I unleashed into the infinite!

I had come into this exchange with a flicker of hope.
But it died fast.
This being—cannot be destroyed by me.
That's clear now.
But there might still be a way...
to send him back to where he belongs.

To show him the path.
If I take the leap with him.
And that's what holds me.
Because if he's here...
then I was never meant to walk out.

!—What are you calculating Darius!
How to destroy me!

—There's nothing to calculate. Destruction isn't my mission. And it may not even be possible. But I can offer you something. I believe... that's why I was sent.

!—Ahhh! Now you have my attention Darius!
Maybe that's why it was you they chose to send!
Tell me more! About this dual-nature of yours!
Your strange ability to walk between both realms!
How did that come to be!
I want to see your inside! The darkness or the light!
Or if there is any fusion of it!
Maybe if I understood your secret...
I could finally perfect my own design!

Unthinkable.
Even this entity—has shown a flicker of desire.
A trace of greed.
That's not like him. That's never been like him.
And now I understand—why it's urgent to bring him back.
He's not beyond reach. Not yet.
And if he takes the bait—there may still be some way to fix it.
Because just like him—the same element lives inside me.
That's what's throwing him off.
He feels it. Wants it.
Wants to understand how it exists in me—and whether he can steal it for himself.

Idiot.
He doesn't get it.
Power that's given...comes with control.
But power that's seized? That turns.
It burns you. Breaks you.
That's why it destroys the sinners from within.

That's not my case.
I carry no confusion about who I am.
I know. I don't want anything.
Not the light. Not the dark.
That's why—with the weight of my force, comes the clarity of its burden.

But this fool—he can't handle that.

I'll bait him. Let him bite.
And if he does—if he dares to take it—
He'll be snapped back to where he actually belong.
And would take me with him.
That's fine.

I don't care how it ends. If the Lord decides I must be destroyed—then no one can stop it.
Not even me.

By now, Marisha's far enough.
I trust He'll carry her.
So let it come. Let it all come.
As it was always meant to.

!—Still calculating Darius! Just say it!
What do you want to do!

—I want to give you the chance.
That's the only reason I'm still standing here.

!—You speak truth Darius!
Though I can't understand why you'd agree so easily!
Maybe you think you're invincible now!
Merged between two realms! Honestly…
if you hadn't agreed I had something else planned for you!
But fine! You've saved me a step!
Now! Choose how shall we begin!

—There's nothing to choose. Try everything you want—
but unless the Lord wills it, you'll never see inside me.
You know that, don't you?

!—Yes… I was starting to understand that!
Once your mortal form breaks!
You'll flash back into the darkness at the speed of light!
And I won't get a second to act!
I was toying with you a little, brother!
Hyuukh… Whisssssshh!
But since you're the one offering now!
Tell me! How do we do it!

—Simple. You'll have to enter me—consciously.
Which means, you'll need to gather every piece of yourself,
and touch me—whole.

!—That's all it was! That simple!
Why haven't I done it before then!

—Because you couldn't.
Even if you tried,
my being would've rejected you on instinct.

!—Then why not now! What's changed!

—I changed. Now, I know where you should belong.
And I'm not here to stop you from going back.
If you want this chance—take it. If not—I'll walk away.
And the next time we meet...
there may be no second chance at all.

!—Wait! Don't go Darius!
Seeing you like this isn't something I can summon at will!
Once you vanish back into the Darkness!
Who knows when, where or how you'll rise again!
Come... merge with me!
Let the two of us... become one!

The sky split first.
A white surge climbing out of the Russo-Ukrainian ground, bright enough to feel like a newborn star forcing its way into daylight.

For a heartbeat, the world held still, balanced on the edge of annihilation.

Across the NATO grid, the signature hit like a nuclear event with its poison carved out.

UN reports labeled it a clean-yield phenomenon—something that detonated on the scale of a warhead but refused to leave a trace.

Moscow stayed quiet.
Just a silence heavy enough to bend global policy around it.

!—∞—!

Weight of the Quiet

Gurney Drive
Penang, Malaysia

Interior work was usually Macro's thing—she preferred doing it herself. Not just for control, though she did understand the cost lines better than most.

It was passion.
She loved the way space bent to color and shape, how contrast could make a room snap. But when the renovation started on the restaurant at Gurney Drive, she couldn't be there.

By the time she got her hands back on the project,
Tommy had already completed eighty percent.
Macro didn't bother jumping in just to nitpick.

What stood there now was sharp. A fine-dining Thai spot with clean architectural lines where rubble once sat.

Last time they'd built on this plot, there was an old structure they had to preserve—had to fold the new one into the bones of the old. But the blast had erased that burden. Nothing left to save.

This time, Tommy trimmed the footprint, left a green patch up front, threw down a lawn. The empty plot next door, used for parking back then—was still the same.

Today the finishing touches were done.

Tommy had cooked the full spread himself—signature Thai dishes—and invited three guests to christen the space:
Macro, Gobi, and Sahara.

Macro had come as a guest, but her mind wasn't idle.
She kept circling a silent question—If Tommy knew what was going to be happen with this place… would he still be smiling?

She shoved the thought under the table.
Not now.

Not while the plates were still warm.
Not while they were all pretending to celebrate.
They'd talk—later.

The air was thick with another issue.
Everyone felt it.
No one raised it.

Until Sahara blew the lid clean off.

—We're all pretending we're not thinking about the issue, right?

The question came mid-sip, half-buried in soup steam.
They'd been dancing around small talk for an hour,
but all of them—except Macro—had been waiting for someone to throw the match.

Sahara did, and the flame pointed straight at he.

Macro answered without flinching.

—It's not the first time, Sahara.
You know that. Boss didn't want us in the loop.
He pulled you, pulled everyone, for a reason.
I only got caught by accident—and the moment I was clear,
he yanked me too.

Sahara wasn't a boy anymore, but his mind still hadn't caught up to his shoulders.

He pressed again.

—I know why Dad kept us out.
He was afraid we'd get hurt. But are we that useless?
Dad is gone, and we're not even find out who hit him, or why?
Not going to hit back?

Macro didn't like the sound of that—not just the words,
but the way Sahara dropped them.

The boy was barely out of adolescence, but already flying loose like most of his generation. Worse—he'd started treating bluntness like a virtue. He needed a hard reset.

—If revenge is what he wanted, he would've left instructions.
For me. For you. For all of us.

She said, calm and exact.

—Instead of chasing what he didn't ask for,
why not focus on what he told you to do?

The man Sahara called "Dad" wasn't his blood.
Hadn't given him life, but had carried it anyway.
Long before Sahara and his sister Gobi had the words to name it, they'd seen that man do everything a real father should—except spend time. That part was missing.

They used to think he was working abroad, maybe had another family tucked somewhere else. They figured the money was his version of presence, and turned their freedom into indulgence without guilt. But when life started to fold around their shoulders, when the chaos started stacking higher—he brought them close.

And this time, he didn't repeat the mistakes.
He became a father in every way that mattered.
No bloodline, no paperwork—just care, constant and unpaid.

By the time they figured out the truth, they'd already seen enough of the world to understand: a man who loves without gain is rarer than the one who gives life.

For Gobi, that truth sat quiet.
She felt it, carried it—but had never found the courage to call him Dad out loud.

Sahara had no such brakes. He could turn a crime into a joke and still kiss a memory without shame.
But Macro's words had landed different.

Dad left something for him to do.
That... was new territory for Sahara.

—Really, Macro? he asked, eyes narrowing. —We've been talking for months. Not once did you mention Dad left me anything to handle.

Macro didn't blink. She'd outgrown the flutter and spark of Sahara's impulsive energy long ago.

Her voice stayed steady, spoon lifting to her lips.

—Because not every word is for every moment, *she said.*
—And the moment hadn't came then yet.

Sahara leaned forward, half impatient, half in challenge.

—Has the time come now?

Macro gave a slow shake of her head, the motion soft but final.

—Yes. We were all hot-headed back then.
That's why we didn't speak of this.
But there are things you need to know.

She placed her words with precision, like fitting glass into a broken frame.

—He was worried. About both of you—Gobi and you.
He said you'd been trained to fight for survival,
not to go charging into people.
Your growing aggression... it troubled him.
He saw you as his own, you know that.
And because of that, he didn't want you tangled in bloodshed.
He wanted you to build something better—for yourselves.
That's why he kept you at a distance, buried in safe assignments,
out of the worst of it. Even the last time we met,
he made sure to remind me of that—specifically.

Sahara didn't have the kind of heart that censors itself.
Not now. Maybe not ever.
His voice broke right through them, cracked and bleeding.

—You don't have a heart, Macro?
He was worried! He spoke! What does any of this mean?
Why are you saying it like he's gone forever?
He's disappeared before, you know that.
Last time—right here—after the bombing, six months passed and he came back, new face, new name, like nothing ever happened.

—So what makes this any different?
Why are you so sure he's not coming back?

Macro felt it too—same ache sitting in her chest like a stone.
But unlike Sahara, she'd learned how to carry it without collapse.
So had Tommy. So had Gobi.
But Sahara—he was still learning.

Which is why Macro didn't lie to him.
Didn't bother with hope-colored cushions.

She gave him the truth, flat and clean.

—What happened here—that was nothing.
There were two mapped escape routes, and the bomb didn't even take out the whole block.
But the Donetsk blast… that was different.
Almost two kilometers, Sahara.
Everything above and below ground—leveled.
You're allowed to hope. But I won't lie to you.

And Sahara—he didn't want to believe.
Didn't care how much logic she fed him.

He reached for another crack.

—But the girl—she made it out.
The one who was with Dad.
She survived. Why couldn't he?

Macro nodded once, then gave him what he was owed.

—Before the blast even started, your dad threw her into a water tunnel. She got flushed out—four kilometers downstream,
all the way to Nova Lake. Her escort team was waiting nearby.
They found her, figured out what was happening, and tried to launch a rescue party right away. That's when the explosion hit.
You've seen the satellite shots, haven't you?
The blast scale? It went everywhere—viral, all over the world
NATO even accused Russia of using a tactical nuke.
Turned out it wasn't nuclear—no fallout.

No radioactive trail. Lucky break for everyone, because if it was, we'd be neck-deep in a war zone by now.

She gave him the truth—nothing painted. Because the boy was growing up. And truth was what he'd need soon anyway.

But Sahara's voice still trembled with fire.

—So what? We don't even try to find out who killed my Dad? We just let them walk?

Macro knew the time had come—no way around it now.
She had to say it.

—For him, we never actually did anything, Sahara.
We wouldn't have. You were too young then.
Nobody wanted to put that weight on your shoulders.
But I think it's time you knew.

She kept her eyes on him, steady and unblinking.

—He wanted us to build something—a group that stood for truth and justice. Not one that picked fights, but one strong enough to defend itself when attacked. That's why he kept you with us.
He wanted us to lead it, run it, grow it—on our own.
But his own missions? His own cause?
He never passed that on.
He didn't want us to carry that burden.

Sahara's voice dropped.
He wasn't shouting now, just heavy.

—He tied our hands, left us drifting in the current.
What am I even supposed to tell myself now?

Before Macro could answer, Tommy stepped in—low and calm.

—Macro's right, Sahara. Every word.
He told me the same. When he saw what I built in Bangkok,
he said he was proud. Said he had dreams for you two—big ones.
If you see those through, that's the only thing that would've made him happy. But let's say you're right.
Let's say he comes back and finds you dead in a street war,

or rotting in prison for payback.
You think that would please him?

Sahara shook his head—quietly this time.

—No. He wouldn't want that.
But I still think it's because of that cursed girl.
That's why he's gone. And you know what?
I'd started calling her Mom.

There was no anger in that last line. Just innocence.
So pure and unguarded, none of them could help it—the laughter broke loose. Even Macro.

When the wave passed, she turned to Tommy.

—There's something you need to handle, too.
An order—meant for you.

Tommy nodded.

He wasn't Sahara.
He didn't break under weight—he absorbed it.

One long breath, and he was ready.

—Tell me, Macro.
Whatever it is, if Boss said it—I'll do it. Even if it kills me.

Macro didn't soften the blow.

—This restaurant—the land, the building,
everything tied to it—you're handing it all over to Antasia.
He told me. Told her, too.
There's something about this city, this place,
some connection she has. She's agreed to take it on.
And just like the rest of our ops, she'll funnel forty percent
of the net profits straight into the main fund.
But the legal transfer—that has to be complete.
In her name.

Macro had waited for the right moment to say it.
Now it was done.

She'd expected it wouldn't sit right with Tommy.

Still, the way he said it—raw, half pissed—landed heavy.

—This is insane, Macro.
Then why the hell did you make me bust my ass building this place? Why not tell Antasia to build her own damn spot?
I'd have wired her the funds. Still can.
But handing over the whole damn restaurant—just like that?

He pointed toward the tables like they were war medals.

—Every chair. Every table.
I stood there, picked each one.
I made this place mean something.

He shook his head.

—Boss might've been tough, but you?
You make it sound worse.
Shit, Macro—when does it end?

He didn't wait for an answer. Muttering under his breath, Tommy pushed back from the table and walked out.

Macro let a quiet laugh slip—just a breath through her nose.
That was Tommy.
He'd storm off. Swear under his breath.
Throw shade like it paid rent.
And still do exactly what he was told.
They all knew it.

Later, coffee in hand, they regrouped on the lawn.
Nobody spoke. No one really wanted to leave.
Tomorrow they'd split again—
Macro and Tommy back to Bangkok,
Gobi and Sahara returning to their base in Kazakhstan.
But for now, the air held them. No rush. No words.
Just a silence that felt like memory.

The street beyond had come back to life—loud again, busy again.
Vendors shouting. Laughter climbing like smoke through neon signs. The blast that tore through this place once?
Already folded into history.

Locals didn't just recover—they came back louder. Stronger.
But not these four.

Macro sat still, staring past the crowd.
A part of her wanted to leave, but the rest—the quiet parts—
stayed rooted in something she couldn't name.

She kept thinking of him.
The man who had lit the spark in each of them,
but never asked to be remembered like this.
Never wanted anything in return.
Never needed monuments.
He gave them direction, not legacy.

And now that he was gone,
everything around them felt...borrowed.

Tommy sipped slow, eyes low.
He wasn't mad anymore. Just... missing someone.

Sahara stared straight ahead, coffee untouched.
Even his rebellion had quieted.

Gobi, as always, carried her grief in stillness.
No tears. No tremble. Just presence.

They drank in silence.
Not mourning.
Just... remembering.

Outside, the world danced louder.
Inside, their cups emptied without celebration.

—*—

Encoded Silence

Roblox Mines, Seri Kembangan
Kuala Lumpur, Malaysia

The lights were blinding—just the way he liked it.
High-gloss floors, polished glass, ambient beams slicing the air
like capital's fever dream.

And in the center of it all, The Maker sat—admiring his kingdom.
Again.

The last time right after the soft lunch, there had been… a hiccup.
He'd handed security over to a team of walking liabilities,
a tactical error in hindsight.

Right after the soft launch, a nearby explosion had cracked
through the headlines. Technically, the blast went off in the
jungle just beyond the adjacent golf course.
The main structure hadn't taken a scratch.

But perception? That took the hit.
PR melted down.
Police froze operations for weeks.
The place was shuttered, sterile, dissected.
But like all good men who played God with data,
The Maker waited.

Let the world forget. Let time sponge it clean.
Now?
Now there was no soft launch.
This time it was fireworks and fanfare—an opening big enough
to give the world whiplash.

He'd invited everyone worth inviting.
Celebrities with blue ticks and hollow souls.
They danced, they dined, they took their selfies and left.
The Maker didn't meet a single one.
Why would he? That's what the PR director was for.
The man himself had better things to do.

Behind the curtain of glitz and champagne, he'd built something real, a cutting-edge tech lab masked as a luxury entertainment center.

Purpose: Big Data research and behavioral modeling for Southeast Asia's next leap.
Translation: surveillance, influence, and high-level blackmail.
But this time, no random strays would walk in and ruin it.
Security was airtight—this team didn't eat hay.

The celebrity circus was just for show.
The real party—the one happening right now—was private.
Invitation-only.
Attendees? Hand-picked by the Maker himself.
People who mattered. People who knew.
People who, above all, knew who he was.

Last time, the field ops fell apart in a heartbeat.
He could've recovered.
He would've, if not for one small surprise:
The Russians actually went to war.
And worse—everyone let them.

That wasn't supposed to happen.
He hadn't accounted for it.
Months of planning gone. Field teams vaporized.
Contacts ghosted. Models failed.
And yes—technically, that was his mistake.

The data said eighty percent probability.
He'd trusted the math.
But human nature?
That remained the glitch in every system.

He'd chosen operators based on credentials.
Trust metrics. Performance history.
And yet—on the ground, they were brittle.
Disconnected.
Soft.

Irony?
The one asset who ranked below fifty on trust,
the ex-Hamas fighter Rasheed Dameer—turned out
more effective than the rest combined.
And even then, the man had walked away.
Didn't even blink at the offer of power.
Didn't react to the coded nudge.
Didn't flinch at the unspoken gift.

The Maker misread him. Misread the soul.
That mistake still itched.
And it proved something—You can't run people like numbers.

It's why he'd made more of an effort this time—to mix with
the new team, play nice, pretend to "feel" things.
Music. Art. Abstract emotion.
All of it—fresh downloads he was still parsing.

Letting the new team plan the private party without oversight?
Part of the experiment.
Would he have approved it under older protocols?
Absolutely not.

"Color Bloom."
That was the theme. Color?
This kid they brought in had one shade
to his entire existence—Black.
Black hoodie. Black cap.
Black everything.
Even the posture screamed silhouette.
Hunched over like a dying emoji, rocking his shoulders to a beat
only irony could clap for.

If it were up to the old Maker,
he'd have had the kid muted at security.
King Cobra.
Yes, that's what he called him in the log files.

You're already a shadow, he thought.
Why double down with the hoodie?

And if you must wear one, at least use the hood properly.
But a hoodie and a cap? Overkill.
Functionally illogical. Aesthetically insulting.

Worse still, the whole venue had been dressed up like a bad acid trip.

Flames bursting into flowers,
visuals set to his song Love Addix.
Flowers? From fire?

The Maker tilted his head.
Fire destroys flora.
Fire doesn't fertilize.
This wasn't photosynthesis, this was bullshit.

They'd flown this guy in all the way
from England on a private jet.
For this.
And the lyrics? My god.

—Oooo I want you
But I still haven't finished the math
Oooo I want you
Like your father wants your mother
Oooo I want you
Like a bear wants honey...

That was the hook. And somehow, the crowd was losing their minds—hips swaying, drinks spilling.

The Maker understood joy.
He could simulate joy.
But this? If the kid had flipped the lyrics,
said the bear wanted to sleep with the mother
and the father wanted to eat the hive,
now that would've been art.
As it stood, the song was pure nonsense—but catchy nonsense.

He couldn't deny that.
The beats looped into slurred machine wails—dragging,
then snapping back with heat.

And those parts?

Oo-aiii… oo-aiii… oo-aiii… oo-aiii…

They hit something inside The Maker.
Not logic. Not rhythm. Something deeper.
Some hum of comfort buried in his signal chain.
He didn't understand it. But he liked it.

When the hook came around again, he found his shoulders swaying—just slightly—matching the crowd.

For once, the simulation felt real.
And the crowd?
Seeing him move sent them spinning harder.
Double-time grind. Drinks up.
Laughter like rain in a burning orchard.

Eventually, the song ended.
Applause flared.
Energy stayed high.

The Maker clapped once—then gestured.
His new team was dismissed to the control room.
They had a mission brief waiting—a full video deck.

He wouldn't speak to any of them directly.
That level of access? Earned only through success.
Only the one who delivered results in the field
would get a seat at his table.
The others? They'd dance. They'd burn.
And they'd never know they were just flowers in his fire.

Looked like the King Cobra was finally calling it a night.
He moved across the floor—all black-on-black flair, handshake to handshake—and headed straight toward The Maker.
A box in hand.

He didn't need to get close.
The Maker had already scanned it from a distance.
Fresh flowers.
What in the binary hell…?

Why was this shade-swathed songbird handing him flowers?
Even The Maker—flawless, composed, untouchable,
felt a flicker of curiosity.

—Good evening, Mr. Maker.
Never thought I'd actually meet you in person.

—The pleasure's mine, Mr. Eguel...

—Gambell. That's my last name.
If you don't mind me asking—did the show meet your expectations, sir?

—Very much so, Mr. Gambell.
My team's clearly quite taken with you.
You must've noticed they themed the entire venue around your track. Everyone enjoyed themselves.

—But not you, sir?

That line landed light, playful, but with an edge.

The Maker let it hang, just a moment longer than necessary.

—Enjoyment... outside the bounds of logic,
isn't something I'm easily capable of.
But I will admit—your beats had something.
A particular segment I found quite... enjoyable.

—The Ooo-aiii, ooo-aiii part?

—Exactly. I see you noticed too.

—That bit wasn't in the original, sir.
Once the team heard you'd be attending,
our beat composer added it just for this event.
She claims to know you,
actually—that's where the idea sparked.

The Maker's brow didn't move, but his neural threads tightened.

—Is that so? What's her name?

—She uses a stage name; you probably wouldn't recognize it.
But she did send this for you—a little token of appreciation.

Gambell placed the gift box on the nearby table.

One glance at the corner was enough.
A tiny owl insignia.
A clean monogram beneath it: B – C.

The Maker's fingers froze mid-air.
That wasn't a composer's signature.
That was a sigil.
His Highness had sent something.
And The Maker—his loyal projection, his intellectual envoy, understood the signal instantly.

The Owl was awake again.
Watching. Moving.
Of course. It was time.
Every cycle restarted eventually.
This was just the beginning of another.

King Cobra—blissfully ignorant, clearly—stood waiting for some response. But The Maker had no further use for the boy.

—Yes. I understand, Mr. Gambell.
She and I must share membership in...
a very exclusive social club.
There are many of those, all over the world.
You know how it is.
Some friend must've sent it.
I'll reach out later.

—That would be great, sir.
I have another event—early flight out.
Honestly, this whole night... wouldn't have happened without you. Thank you, again.

—Think nothing of it, Mr. Gambell.
Thank you—for keeping us entertained.

—The pleasure's all mine, sir.

And just like that, The King Cobra took his leave.

The other guests drifted out not long after—dinner done, mission briefs in hand.

Each one left lighter, smiling, unaware.
But The Maker?

Now it was time.
Time to unwrap the gift left behind.

The box opened without resistance.
Inside—exactly what he'd scanned earlier.
Fresh blood orchids.
Exquisite. Delicate.
Pointless.

He scanned it again.
Twice.
Three times.
Nothing.

Just a pretty floral arrangement.
Still, why did it feel like something was about to begin?
He kept the bouquet in hand—steel fingers brushing against soft petals.

And that's when it stirred.
The thin glass vial nestled at the base—meant to keep the flowers fresh—started to breathe.
A slow curl of black vapor teased upward.

Hello, old friend.

That smoke—he knew it.
The exact compound lost when the Ukrainian lab burned to ash.
Every last stock destroyed with the blast.
And yet—here it was again.
Delivered in silence.
By hand.
By his honored partner.
Of course.

The formula's delivery was microscopic.
But quantity wasn't the issue.
The Maker had already perfected the synthesis.
He just needed a single active sample.
And now he had it.

He smiled. Not the fake kind.
This one cut deeper—gratitude laced with triumph.

They weren't just working again.
They were winning again.
His neural processor surged—then stalled.
Once. Twice.
Then picked up double-speed.

Something fluttered inside his skull—rhythmic and wrong.
The signal felt... familiar.
Like the Ooo-aiii... ooo-aiii from the King Cobra's song.

A joke wrapped in bass.
Now echoing through his system like code that laughed back.

What was that line again?
Didn't matter.
He caught something glinting beneath the flowers.
A folded card.
He reached for it.

White paper. Black ink.
Clean handwriting.

Welcome to the Void.
—With compliments,
Count Amethyst Vega

He froze.
That name.
That name—why did it pull something?

He searched.
Internally. Globally.
Across all federated memory.

And that's when the edges began to melt.

The electronic boom hit inside his head first—or maybe it didn't. Maybe the smoke hit before the thought.

He'd never know which came first.

Neural detonation?
Or the black chemical bloom that rose from the bottle and devoured everything?

What he did know—
Was nothing.

Because in the next instant,
the blast consumed him and—
The Whole Roblox Mines.

Steel, glass, signal—all shredded in flame,
coded by silence, delivered with style.

—*—

The Botanical Guest

Defense Square
Rockchild Avenue, Tel Aviv, Israel

Defense Minister Dalat Zibram looked remarkably intact, especially compared to the wreck across the table.

Captain Daggan wore his failure like a dented helmet.
Permanent, public, and entirely earned.

Dalat, by contrast, stayed calm.
Daggan was young.
His mistakes? Monolithic.
But Dalat wasn't sure what weighed heavier on Daggan's mind, the catastrophic mission failure, or the fact that his reproductive system now looked like a collapsed tunnel.

He hadn't decided yet. He'd made worse mistakes at that age.
What mattered wasn't the failure—it was what you did next.

Dalat had told him as much, in language Daggan could digest.
The boy had made a permanent failure monument out of that hammer strike, a direct hit to his head.

The skull hadn't quite recovered.
Even after surgical restoration of internal trauma,
the bone structure decided to play abstract sculptor.

Doctors warned: it would heal, sure.
But not in any way nature intended.
Not symmetrically. Not politely.

And still—punishment was mandatory.
Symbolic or not, it had to hurt.
The bone would mend, but the message had to scar.

—No mission—small or large—is your excuse
to bring along your drinking buddies, Daggan.
You know that.
Every one of you does.

—But in practice? You turned it into a goddamn social—dragged half the Euro team in like you were hosting a launch party, pulled our best interrogator out of Tel Aviv without so much as a clearance form, because you owed someone a favor.

Dalat's tone was flat. Almost bored.

—Jamer Shavit was a legend.
He could extract truth from a corpse.
Now he's gone. So are half our finest operators in Europe.

Daggan leaned forward, seething. Still holding onto the one excuse he thought could buy him time.

—It was that whore's fault, sir.
She set the whole thing up.
She set it up.
I swear—I won't stop till I put her in the ground.

Dalat raised one brow.

—And I see your mouth, like your genitals,
suffers from a complete lack of discipline.
Let me remind you—continue talking like that,
and the next thing you lose will be above the neck.

—I'm not wrong, sir.
It all went to hell because of that bitch.

—You might have the facts right.
But your choice of words? Absolutely incorrect.
You're a captain, Daggan. Start acting like one.
And when you talk about a Lieutenant Colonel
from an allied nation—

His tone turned clinical.

—you say: 'Comrade Commander Zakharova.'
If you could manage that, maybe the op would've failed
anyway—but at least, you might still have your balls.

—Yes sir… I admit it—we got played.
Their combat tactics broke us.
We have the budget, why aren't we building a unit like that?

—Because, Daggan—your imagination, like your dick,
runs wild and unsupervised.
Every year, the Russians get maybe five,
six new Spets-grade operators.
Five or six, Daggan.
You know how many trained operators die
just trying to become one? At least fifty.
And ten times that walk away injured,
crippled, erased from combat. Now you tell me:
In a nation where we're already scraping
the bottom of the demographic barrel,
where most of the youth look like you:
Aroused by lust, and running on hormones,
what the fuck am I supposed to do with five Spets,
and no warfighters left to bury them?

Daggan winced. Swallowed hard.

—I'm... sorry, sir. I get it now. The constraints.

—Apologies for my words. *Dalat said, his voice calm again.*
—But if you and your team keep running field ops with your cocks instead of your brains, Israel won't fall. It'll evaporate.

Daggan had never seen him like this.
Dalat Zibram—known across the intelligence grid as
The Peacekeeper's Elegance—never raised his voice.
Never lost control. Not even when the stupid neighboring
countries mocked him, calling him the merchant of silence.
And not even when dogs around the world cheered on their
cruelty.

But now the smile was gone.
Only fire and pure field logic burned through.

And Daggan? He knew he'd earned it.
He'd felt it even before the hammer dropped.

They'd overplayed.
Let emotions and ego steer the op straight into the grinder.

And the analysts? They weren't off the hook either.
Not a single one of them predicted the Russian invasion will start from there. Not one.

An operation of that scale—troop movements, supply lines, encrypted chatter, months of prep—and yet...
radio silence from the entire analysis division.
The fuck were they doing—practicing jazz?

Daggan could've pinned the whole mess on them.
He should have.
If only, he hadn't been the ones who dragged half the Euro team into this disaster to begin with.

And then there was Uncle Shavit.
The legend.
They all called him "Vulture."
Even Daggan did admire him as the mentor.
Mossad's field king, the interrogator who could squeeze a confession out of a stone.
Dragged out of Tel Aviv on a last-minute favor.
Now? Shredded.
Gone.

All because Daggan wanted to show off. Because he himself treated real-world ops like a nightclub guest list.

If they'd kept it tight, stayed lean—not brought in so many extra bodies—the op would've failed, yes.
But only four people would've died.
And the survivors could've restructured.
Tried again.

Instead? Twenty-two dead.
Including Uncle Shavit.

The minister went silent, eyes drifting to the window, sipping his drink like he was tracking clouds—not a nation on the verge.
But everything he'd said was dead-on.

Daggan needed to burn off the old skin—all of it.
His thinking, his reflexes, that dog-brained libido.

They'd picked up the Spets girl from that disco, and the whole team—including him—had treated it like a strip show, already peeling her clothes off in their heads before she even made it to the safehouse.

Even after the first shots were fired—even when the mission was getting out of hand—half the team kept staring at her hips, her chest, like it was a goddamn bachelor party.

She used that.
Used it like a scalpel.
While they gawked, she butchered them—clean, precise.
Cattle. Goats.

And that image—goats and slaughter—triggered something in Daggan's fried circuits.

He snapped up, turned to the minister.

—Sir—that girl, she's the one. I'm sure of it now.

—What, Daggan? Your dick already twitching for honey again?

—N-no sir, I mean her kill pattern.
I'm certain she's the same one from Syria.
And the ambush that hit the local rebels in Iraq—the crew that were carrying the targeted payload—that was her.
We need to take her down.

The minister didn't even blink.
He cut in—cold, surgical.

—Take what down, exactly?
That ship's already sailed, hit a mine,
and blown itself into confetti, Daggan.
You're rusting my entire vocabulary with this teenage nonsense.
Do I need to remind you—
this isn't some Gaza strip schoolyard brawl.
You think a GRU Spetsnaz-class operator is just another Hezbollah dropout in a DIY vest?
The Russians launched one hypersonic missile,
just one—at Donetsk. Erased two kilometers off the map.

—If a shot like that ever landed in Tel Aviv—you, me, and our entire retaliation wishlist would be vapor.

—They wouldn't risk that in Tel Aviv, sir—

—Maybe not. But I'm not about to test the mood swings
of a unit that just leveled a Ukrainian province,
and casually erased an arms corridor in Africa. And neither
are our taxpayers would be happy to test their moods.
So forget the girl. If she crosses your path again—you salute.
Military posture. No smirk. That's an order.

—Yes sir.

Daggan's jaw twitched, but his voice stayed even.
Zibram noticed.

And for once, the minister softened the blow—just a little.
Because even broken tools sometimes learn the craft.

—You weren't wrong in your read, Daggan.
It's not that we don't have people inside the Russian military.
We do. And it's not impossible to buy influence in their ranks either. If it had been anyone else in her shoes, you and your team would've walked away clean.

He paused, tilted his glass slightly, watching the ice melt
like time he could afford to waste.

—But this one?
This girl—she's different.
Call it family ties.
The kind that money doesn't touch.
Just like us.

He locked eyes with Daggan.

—You could offer half our agents a suitcase of shekels,
and they'd still tear apart anyone who tried to lay a finger on you.
Same thing happened here.
Some Russian generals—the very same who'd sell out their own
for vodka and whores—went stone silent when it came to her.
And I get it.

A long sip. No emotion.

—Her father, the honored Ibroxim Samarovoski Zakharov,
Chechen war hero. A warrior. Martyr.
His legacy holds weight in Moscow even now.
And it means something to us, too.
If we'd known, this op would've looked different.

—Understood, sir. I won't step outside your orders again.
If I get decommissioned for this, I accept it.
No regrets. But I promise you, when I come back—
it'll be a new Daggan you see.

That earned a half nod.
Maybe even a flicker of respect.

Dalat Zibram didn't scream at people.
That wasn't his brand.
He was made of a different alloy altogether.

Back in his field years—he'd arrest Palestinian leaders with a prayer on his lips.
Wash for wudu, share meals with their families.
Smile over dates and lentils. Then escort them into custody like a dinner guest switching rooms.

Even when it came time to start the real work—
The ropes, The steel chair, crushing blood and bones,
He did not shout at them.
Never even cursed.

And when it ended? When the data was harvested,
the bodies still twitching?
He'd stand there, watching bodies dissolve in fire.
Smiling like it was policy.
That's the road he walked to get here.
Not slogans. Not by chance.
Results.

And Daggan—as reckless and idiotic as he'd been—hadn't quite crossed the line until today. If the boy hadn't poked the beast inside him, there'd be no need for fury at all.

Let Russia jump. Let them bark and bluster.
It wouldn't last.
Soon, they'd all calm down.
Iran. The entire Middle East.
Even America—their so-called eternal ally—

They'd be begging soon. Requesting aid with the same mouths they once used to lecture.

They'd be on their knees now,
if these imbeciles hadn't complicated things.
That's the problem with amateurs.
They don't know where the lines are.
Or who draws them.

They had no idea.
Inside this government—he was the real government.
The invisible hand.
The one even the Prime Minister never questioned.
The trust placed in him was absolute.
No briefings. No oversight.

Even after that incident in Eilat—where his own creation had turned the city into a graveyard—no one asked why.
No one asked who. They just handed him the investigation.

The Prime Minister was, of course, the more seasoned tactician.
And more evolved.

While the death toll in Eilat may have stirred something human in his chest, he wore it like an old bruise—felt, but never flinched.

He understood what it meant.
Just as 9/11 was needed to grip the Middle East,
Eilat's sacrifice was necessary to step into global control.

He knew. Because he'd helped design 9/11 himself.
And Zibram? He'd never forget that trust.
But before honoring it, he had a couple of idiots to deal with.

Daggan was nearly handled—a humiliation and a dismissal would do.
But the other one—Rasheed Dameer, aka Farish—the fool from Hamas who accidentally served Russia too well?
He wouldn't survive the sunrise.

Zibram leaned forward.

—Do you even remember how you made it out, Daggan?

—Not the whole thing, sir. I took a hit... blacked out.
When I woke, everyone was gone.
I ducked past a few soldiers on my way out.

—Hmm. And the damage to your precious balls—was that from the hammer?

—N-no sir. She... that bitch used her boot. Repeatedly.
I mean, Comrade Commander. The lady.

—Heh. Is that so? And the custom armor plate—the one specifically designed for that area—that didn't help?

—Actually made it worse, sir.
The impact folded the plate inward.
Internal damage was... severe.

—Ohh-ho-ho. Tragic.
Sorry to hear the next generation of Daggan
won't be joining us to the war.

He gave a dry, joyless chuckle.

—But since I'm in a generous mood—let me share something you don't know. You weren't the only one to slither out of that mess alive.

Daggan blinked, thrown.

—Seriously, sir?
But I heard Russia's handing over that Iranian bastard.
Forgive my tone, sir—calling him 'former commander' sticks in my throat.

—No offense taken, my boy.
When it comes to enemies, titles are optional.

He reclined slightly.

—And yes, you heard right.
Russia's playing the responsible ally now.
They'll turn him over—officially, through the courts.
And in return, they'll squeeze out...
let's say, favors from Iran.
But punishment's punishment.
We'll take it.

—Yes, sir. Even though the bastard was right under Iran's nose all these years, they claimed he couldn't be found.
Issued red notices, shrugged like fools.
Now, with a formal handover, they've run out of excuses.

He paused. Lowered his voice.

—But...
if it's not him—who else are you talking about, sir?

—I'm talking about your charming friend—Ex Hamas,
now Turkish civilian—Rasheed Farish.

Daggan's brows shot up like a rookie who just realized he missed the last five pages of the playbook.

—Rasheed? But sir... he was there with that bastard Kamran.
Why didn't the Russians bag him too?
Maybe he got the benefit of the doubt.
That Spets comrade met him in Prague, right?
Told us herself—Rasheed was freelance, no hard ties.

—We all have freelance contractors, Daggan.
Every side. Every flag.
You can't start a war over that—unless...

He let the word hang in the air like a gun waiting for someone to touch it.

—...Unless what, sir?

—Unless we catch him—with cargo in hand.

Daggan nearly bounced out of his seat.

—That would be incredible, sir. Is there anything I can do?

—Ha-ha, your enthusiasm is starting to qualify as a national treasure, Daggan. No need to waste it.
We already have him. Caught red-handed.

—You're a genius, sir! There's a reason you're called a national hero. My respect just went through the roof.
You actually tracked him through all this chaos?

Zibram shrugged, with the kind of smug restraint reserved for men who've orchestrated the fall of cities.

—It was nothing, my boy. Just keeping you trigger-happy youth from shooting yourselves out of shame.
War's chaos gave us all the cover we needed.
He was holed up in the Turkish sector of Cyprus.
We'd had eyes on the place for months.
When a certain package showed up—we closed the net.

—Package? Wait—sir...

—Yes, my boy. A sealed parcel.
Even with his shiny Turkish passport under Rasheed Dameer, the parcel was addressed to Rasheed Farish.
His real name.

Daggan blinked, gears spinning. Zibram continued.

—The courier service he used ran on software we designed.
The moment the data pinged—we knew.

—That's... brilliant, sir.
And... what was in the box?
Sorry, I mean—if it's classified, I completely understand.

—Oh, don't be coy, Daggan.
You carry the blood of Herz Daggan—what could I possibly hide?
It was something... botanical.

—Botanical?
Sir—what, is the Hamas bastard vegan now?
What's he doing with plants?

—That's exactly what we're trying to find out, Daggan.
We got to him just in time—before those Turkish bastards even caught a whiff. Apologies, by the way—my mouth's been slipping today. Hope you'll excuse the rough edges.

—Please, sir. I'm like a son to you.
You could kick my teeth in and I'd still call it discipline.

—Touching, my boy. Come on—let's go meet our botanical guest.

The Defense Square had its own ecosystem—full operational capacity with quarters, kitchen, private comms, and several secret basement levels built for everything no one talked about.
Black-site tech labs. Tactical extraction suites.
And rooms where men told the truth before they died.

By the time they got there, the hospitality department had already made full use of the facility.

Daggan noticed—slightly disappointed.

The detainee had been pre-treated.
Skin belts cut. Fingernails handled.
Most of the fun was already bagged and filed.

The one they were here for?
Rasheed Farish.
Once a Hamas foot soldier, now a state asset,
soon—nothing at all.

The same bastard who'd handed the hammer to her,
to that woman—when she crushed Uncle Shavit into memory.

Now, blood sprayed from his lips instead of spit.
The bastard deserved worse.
Daggan would've liked to deliver it himself.

Across the room, Rasheed blinked through the haze—eyes like smoke over a ruin.

When he saw Daggan, he didn't flinch. But when he spotted the man standing next to him—Dalat Zibram—his pupils widened.
Recognition. And fear.
Which made sense.

His tongue had a live current running through it.
Daggan spotted the blackened edges—burnt, curled, cooked.
Perfect voltage discipline.

Minister Zibram sat with the practiced calm of an absolute Peacekeeper's Elegance.

He pulled up a chair, settling with the ease of a man who'd never raised his voice to harm anyone.

His face stayed tranquil and perfectly composed as he looked across at the prisoner.

One flick of his fingers, and a hospitality tech stepped forward, disconnecting the current running through Rasheed's tongue.
Mercy in motion.

The prisoner didn't scream. Couldn't.
His tongue was scorched at the tip—charred black where the current had kissed it repeatedly.
Beautiful voltage work.
Clean. Focused.

Across the table,
the Minister began opening the parcel—the same botanical package that had delivered Rasheed into their net.

And then, in a voice dipped in silk and cyanide,
he offered the prisoner a deal.

—We won't make this too hard, son.
You're already dead; sentence is signed.
From here out—whatever we ask, you answer.
Nod for yes. Shake for no.
And you'll leave this world with the least pain we can offer.
Understood?

Rasheed nodded.
Once. Affirmative.

Even a Hamas war-dog could read the voice of peace.

Daggan watched the exchange like a disciple rediscovering faith.
This—this was the real power of peace:
Mercy delivered with perfect courtesy.

And Rasheed?
He just nodded his way into the final conversation of his life.
Which is why Daggan felt confident now.

The discussion would go well.

—Do you know who sent this parcel?

Rasheed shook his head—no.

Daggan didn't hold it against him.

If Rasheed had arranged the delivery himself, he sure as hell wouldn't have used his real name—and definitely not Rasheed Farish. Too sloppy, even for a man this cooked.

Zibram moved on.

—Do you know what was inside it?

Another slow, silent shake.
Negative.

This time, it irked. These types always played dumb just long enough to bleed the process dry.

Daggan watched him and felt it: that itch to bypass
the conversation and just start pulling out answers.
Organ by organ.

But the Minister had a method.
He handed the delivery box to Daggan, then calmly began inspecting the package himself.

What lay inside was deceptively polite.
A beautifully preserved bundle of blood orchids.

The packaging was high-grade—engineered for international transport. Hydrated glass vial sealed beneath the stems, perfect condition. Wouldn't wilt for days.

Minister Zibram frowned.
His age didn't align with flowers anymore.
Or sentiment.
They annoyed him.

Daggan, meanwhile,
spotted something beneath the petals—a card.
Small.
Tucked in with too much care to be harmless.

His mind clicked through protocols.
Hidden ink? Embedded code?
A grid coordinate wrapped in poetry?

He stepped forward just as the Minister's eyes narrowed on it.
Yes.
That caught his attention.

Zibram leaned in with visible interest—but age,
finally, threw in its card.
The lettering was too fine. And his glasses were upstairs.

So, with all the ceremony of a king passing a verdict,
he handed the card to Daggan.

—Read it out for us, my boy.

Daggan cleared his throat and read aloud, each syllable landing harder than the last:

In honor of Rasheed Farish,
for his sacrifice and struggle,
a token as promised.

With compliments,
—Count Amethyst Vega.

Silence. And then—

—What? Vega? That Romanian devil?

Zibram leaned back, tension sliding into place like a locked scope.

Vega's name had floated through too many black files.
Too many blown missions. Too many unexplained survivals.

They hadn't torched him yet—only because Brussels kept hiding the bastard's shadow. But now this?

Now Vega was sending floral tributes
to a washed-up Hamas tool?
That was personal.
That was a warning shot with a ribbon.
A leverage.

And Zibram—cold, calculating, clinically vicious—was already drafting the opening line of the report he'd hand to the U.S. Ambassador. A diplomatic kill shot.
One Vega wouldn't walk away from.

Daggan, standing nearby, was likely thinking the same.
Or something close.
But whatever they were thinking—it stalled.

Because laughter broke the air like a glass thrown at marble.

They turned—and saw Rasheed Farish.
Still cuffed. Still burned. Still bleeding.
Laughing. Howling.

The sound bent him sideways in the chair,
chains rattling as he shook.
Guttural. Hysterical. Unapologetic.

And no one in the room—not one of them—could figure out what the hell was funny.

Maybe—just maybe—if they had a few minutes more,
they could've opened Rasheed's chest and extracted the joke.
But fate, as always, had better timing.

Right beneath the orchids—from the tiny sealed glass vial tucked neatly at the base—a slow, dark coil began to rise.
Not smoke. Not gas. Something in between.

Minister Zibram was the first to notice.
Of course he was.

With all his years in conflict resolution, he'd developed an eye for what peace looked like right before it exploded.

He dropped the bouquet—quick, clean.
Tactical instinct, still sharp.

But the flowers never touched the ground.
They exploded in midair.

A low, throat-deep boom ripped through the room—not loud, not flashy, just enough to start peeling the edges off reality.

Then came the real sound—the kind that makes cement remember every body buried beneath it.

The ground shook like it was remembering every sin.
Steel screamed. Floor cracked.

And then, like a building realizing it was only bones—
Defense Square began to fold.
One slab at a time. Going down.
No warning. No escape plan.

Later, it was formally confirmed—in what officials described as a heartbreaking tragedy for peace-loving nations—that the explosion had tragically shattered and swallowed the entirety of Rockchild Avenue into the earth.

Among the casualties, National Hero Minister Dalat Zibram, and valiant young officer Daggan, alongside countless brave defenders of peace, were mourned worldwide.

The world, reportedly, remained in shock to the loss.

—*—

The Aquarium

Khoroshovskoye Shosse
Moscow, Russia

Alexander Moskovich Zakharov was studying the girl across from him with the kind of patience reserved for enemy tapes.

She sat still.
He didn't speak.
Just arranging words inside his mind.

Alexander's father had named him after the capital itself. A man who'd lived Lenin's scripture, bleed for the unity of the Soviet Union with the kind of madness only true believers possess.

Even on his deathbed, the old revolutionary passed on his torch with clenched fists—fight class division, preserve the Union, or die doing it.

His son tried. But history didn't care about bloodlines. In their generation, the torch passed straight into a storm.

The Soviet Union crumbled under its own contradictions, not because they lacked enemies—but because they couldn't stop eating themselves.

Alexander had accepted that.
Slowly. Painfully.
He'd rather have carved out his own mother's heart than watch Mother Russia break like that. But what's lost is lost.

Now he and his comrades fought on with the scraps.
A patchwork empire,
standing just tall enough to carry weight in the room.

And as it turns out, the ones carrying it weren't always the sons. Some victories were born from the inconvenient children.

This girl—the one sitting across from him, back straight, no apology in her eyes—had been one of them.

He hadn't expected much.
His hope had lived in his other two sons.

The younger had torched that hope early—burned it down with incompetence and ideology.

The elder? Promising on paper. Useless in reality.
And then, there was her.

The difficult one.
The one who refused rank, ignored compromise,
and flew into Death Valley like it was just another ops run.

He hadn't even wanted her deployed.
What she'd accomplished before that was more than enough to give the family a shine. He could've used his network, made the calls—landed her a comfortable FSB desk with zero resistance.
But of course, she refused.

Because she was stubborn. Because she was still mourning.
Because she never accepted the death of her older sister.
No matter how many state briefings or polite explanations were shoved down her throat—she wouldn't buy the party line that some sacrifices were "for unity."

She didn't care that Russia no longer persecuted religion.
Didn't care that her own father lived peacefully in another district under another doctrine.
Didn't care that the family had learned to adapt.
She only cared that her sister died.

That refusal, that disobedience—that was what made her dangerous. And ironically, that was what made her better than all of them.

Even Alexander couldn't deny it anymore.
She was the only one who carried the Zakharov name
with results, not sentiment.

This girl's father was Alexander's own younger brother.

Though they chose different gods, the elder never stopped loving the younger.

Alexander remained Orthodox, but his brother—
Ibroxim Samarovoski Zakharov—walked another path.
A Muslim, A Chechen by blood.
A Russian by loyalty.
And still a Zakharov by all means.

Then the wars came. Lines drawn in blood.
Moscow burned bridges. Chechnya burned back.
And so the brothers separated—not out of betrayal,
but out of survival.

Alexander moved to Moscow.
Ibroxim stayed rooted where he was born.
Their paths divided by ideology, but not by blood.

Even now, his name was spoken with respect—among allies, among enemies. And though his people had turned, he never had.

When the peace talks began, he accepted the condition of non-retaliation. He never took revenge for his elder daughter.

Alongside his valor in combat, this act of restraint was also remembered with high respect. But that respect was something this defiant girl rejected with disgust.

She hadn't used the family name for years.
Had lived with her mother alone since her teenage years.

Maybe from all that grief and isolation, Alexander's younger brother eventually broke—and took his own life.

To be honest, that's why he'd always partly blamed this girl's arrogance. Until today.

He'd always shown her politeness, but never warmth.
Not like he showed his own daughter, Polina.
Now he felt ashamed about that.

This girl had brought honor to the family name long ago, in many different ways. She'd even received a medal from the President himself—though that was for excellence in music.

Music and performance might be important to people of culture, but in the Zakharov family—born soldiers—it was little more than a punchline.

When the President learned her name and lineage, he said it was an honor to award someone from the Zakharov family.
But standing right next to him, he hadn't missed the sideways smirk aimed at Alexander Moskovich Zakharov.
That smile stung more than any silence.

And it burned deep—because he'd been carrying the weight of two failed sons on his back for years.

Still, he never gave in to despair.
His father, a true Leninist revolutionary,
never taught him how to break.
And now, while still alive, he was finally seeing someone in the family reach this rare height.

This defiant girl—today,
she had taken the Zakharov name to the edge of the sky.
Not just that—she had finally reclaimed the name,
now calling herself Marisha Samorovsky Zakharova.
Alexander Moskovich felt like dancing.

This coming June,
she would be awarded the title of Hero of the Federation
on National Day—the highest honor from the state.

And this time, he would stand beside his own daughter proudly, look the President in the eye, and accept that medal not as a formality—but as family.

Plenty had raised eyebrows about calling her his daughter.
Not niece.

Let them bark.
Pathetic little critics with empty mind and big opinions.
He'd adopted her from himself, thank you very much.

Turned a formidable niece into a full-blooded daughter.
Who exactly was supposed to object?

This time, he'd played it smart.
Didn't flinch when the rumors started—about her ties with that shady Romanian businessman.
Kept his face still. Stayed "supportive."
Didn't love it. But he played along.
Turns out, it worked.
Brilliantly.

She now saw him as a guardian.
Not just on paper—for real.

And he fully intended to cash in on that authority.
No more pretending.
He actually loved this defiant girl now.
Genuinely. Fully.
Not just for the state—but for the Zakharov name itself.

Three generations of men hadn't reached
where this one girl had landed.
Hero of the Federation.
At this age.
Unthinkable.

Moskovich was convinced his father and great-grandfather were somewhere in the afterlife, raising toasts to this win.

He hadn't rushed anything.
Had given her time—physically, mentally—to heal on her terms.
No more "niece nonsense."
Not a single soul would hear that word from his mouth again.
From now on, she'd be Mama—just like Polina.

He had so much to share with this daughter.
So much to ask. But no hurry.
None at all.

—Why didn't you finish your coffee, Mama?
Not good? I'll have them brew another.

—No sir, it's fine. I've just had too much already.

—Oh...
You've eaten, though, yes?
—There's lunch arrangement at home—you know that.
But if you want, we can have something nice brought up right here.

—Thank you, sir. But I promised Polina I'd have lunch with her after I get back.

—Good, very good, Mama.
But your voice—still sounds heavy.
Caught a cold?

—A little...
I drove back from Samara.
Long ride tore up my throat a bit.

—You drove?
Why would you do that, Mama?
I could have arranged a flight—any air force pilot would have flown you home with pride.

—I was looking for a place, sir.
And... it'd been a while since I'd really seen my own country.
Felt right to just drive. Gave me some peace, too.

—Ah... I see.
A little adventure. Very fitting for your age.
You know, you could have told Polina.
She'd have flown out to Samara and the two of you
could have turned it into a real road trip.

—I just needed a bit of time alone, sir.
Besides, Polina's going back with me anyway.
Didn't want to trouble her at that hour.

—Good... very good, Mama.
Keep her close. Teach her a thing or two.
There's a lot for a younger sister to learn.
The boys—well, they're brutes now.
Most days, they just drag the family name closer to the gutter.

—Please don't put it like that, sir.
They did their best—in their own way—for the country.
—And if lifting the Zakharov name is what matters,
you still have me.

—That we do, Mama.
You're the sun-child of this family.
We're all proud of you.

—That's my honor, sir.
And thank you—honestly—for holding off on the formal reporting. It helped.

—Come on, now. You deserved that much.
If you ask me, I don't see any reason
to dig into heavy talk today.
You've just come back to Moscow.
Take your sister, go out, see the city.
Drop the report before you leave,
one day is more than enough.

—Actually… I think it's better if we handle it now, sir.
That way, my head's clear for the rest.

—Hmm… fair enough. If that's your choice.
Sit tight—I'll call in my secretary.
She'll take the official notes, and if you need to be briefed on anything, she's got the clearance.

—Yes, sir. Of course.

Inside the unit, the name Mila Kruscheva
carried its own mythology.

Officially: Executive Secretary.
Unofficially: The bitch behind the briefings.
Some whispered it, most just said it out loud.
Nobody denied it.

She was hotter than a sunbeam in July and twice as volatile.
There wasn't a soul in the entire ops floor who hadn't been scorched by her temper at least once.

Even Marisha had been snapped at—more than once.
But today? Today was not a regular day.

The girl who had once been the boss's niece,
now officially stood as his daughter,
and more than that—she had crowned their entire unit
with a title no GRU operative at her age had ever worn:
Hero of the Federation.

Every tile, every brick in this HQ would carry that line like a war tattoo.

One of ours made it.
And not just made it—she crushed it.

When Mila Kruscheva walked in, she came carrying a chestful of pride, trying to push her 38D sized glory into something bigger her chest could hold.

A rare smile cut across her face like she'd rehearsed it for hours.

First thing Mila did was wrap Marisha in a hug that could've crushed steel.

—How's our favorite Mama doing?
Soon as I heard you were coming, I baked a cake myself.
You'll be in Moscow a few days, right?
Promise me you'll stop by Aunt Mila's place at least once, okay?

Marisha, half-stunned by the transformation,
smiled and said she'd try.
Sincerely.

Mila kissed her on both cheeks, then finally pulled out her laptop and slid into her designated chair.

—Shall we begin, Mila?

—Yes, Director General.
If I may say, though—was it really necessary
to push this sweet girl today? She's just arrived.

—I've already discussed it with her, Mila.
She wants to get it done now—her call.

—Ooooo… alright then, Mama.
But if it gets too heavy, you say the word.
We'll stop, anytime you want.

Marisha nodded once.
Silent green light.

The cameras in the room blinked to life.
Recording modules synced.
Laptop armed for state tags and entries.

Mila's tone shifted as the protocol kicked in.
Alexander Moscovich starts his Speech.

—We begin by honoring the memory of fallen heroes.
Even though this is a state debriefing, you're both young and direct bloodline—my own—so I'll keep calling you Mama.
Everything discussed here is under state-sealed classification.
Everyone present is duty-bound to provide full and truthful accounts. At this stage of reporting, you will be expected to disclose any operational errors committed on your part.
Other officers could face GRU discipline, but your status as a decorated national asset exempts you from such punitive review.
Unless the content is deemed contrary to state interest, you are fully shielded. In fact, on behalf of the President, I'm authorized to guarantee you formal clemency for any disclosed error—so long as it's stated in full.
What we need from you is the complete and unfiltered truth.
Have I made that clear, Mama?

—Yes, sir. I understand.
And I have no objections.
I've never engaged in anything counter to state interest.
I'm prepared to answer truthfully, in all matters.

—That's exactly what we expected, Mama.
These words are just protocol.
Your impact in the mission has already been acknowledged, those victories are yours. But before we review the wins, we need to start with the low-falls.

—There were quite a few low-falls, sir—large and small.
I'll note the minor ones in my written report.
Here, I'll go over the major issues.
First—our data analysts. The delay in intel delivery nearly compromised the mission before it even started.
We recovered, but just barely.
What's more serious—some of that intel leaked.
Mossad had proof-based awareness of nearly every tactical move we made. Fortunately, their own internal dysfunction kept them from acting on it in time. But think about it, sir—
if they'd passed that intel just two days earlier to Rasheed Farish or to the man operating in Count Vega's cover—before the mass interrogation theater even began—it could've destroyed my credibility entirely. And without that, we'd never have gotten near the dark weapons cache.

—Hmm...Yes, Mama. I had my eye on that issue too.
Mila, log a formal action note.
We'll start an internal review immediately.
And since it's come up—let's clear up Count Vega's issue as well.

—Thanks sir.
There were multiple gaps in analyst reporting about him.
To be transparent, I'm still not certain of his exact identity.
But yes—I was emotionally involved with him. At the start of the mission, he had no connection to my professional work.
The relationship began with family approval, and out of personal feeling. Though we hadn't the chance to move it toward a formal status.

—Yes, fully noted. Mila, log that.
I was informed in advance as Marisha's only male guardian.
We approved the relationship at the time. Go ahead, Mama.

—Whether he was Count Vega or not—he held direct influence within the organization. Despite not matching the behavior patterns or background of the real Vega, every staff member treated him as their superior. He had unrestricted access across their assets. Given that—I used the connection effectively.
I secured his cooperation in ensuring that—no weapon developed by Vega's would fall into the hands of any state hostile to Russia. This was part of my mission protocol—and he acknowledged, accepted, and honored it.

—Hmm...Were we able to secure their latest prototype, Mama?

—That wasn't part of my objective, sir. Attempting that would've risked compromising the entire op.

—Even if he wasn't Mr. Vega himself, your partner was undoubtedly high-ranking inside the organization.
That much is clear. If you had pushed further,
he might've let you field-test their prototypes.

—If he'd lived, I believe I could've convinced him, eventually.

—That was our assessment as well, Mama. Regardless—
we all mourn the loss of a man with that kind of potential.
You've already received the state's letter of condolence.
Shall we proceed?

—Y-yes, sir. My primary mission objective was the retrieval of the Dark Weapon. I was able to accomplish that—successfully delivered it to Russian control.
However, our technical teams failed to recognize its full merit.
They struggled to reconfigure and deploy it correctly.
Near the end of the mission, we were able to obtain key intel on how the system functions—how to operate and reconfigure it.
In addition to that, we successfully destroyed the full enemy stock and their capacity for re-production.

—You executed that stage flawlessly, Mama.

—Thank you, sir.

—Just one final point before I let you breathe.
The Donetsk blast—its magnitude was near-nuclear.
But with no trace of radiation. At first, it pinned us in diplomatically—then worked to our advantage.
The enemy now believes it was a new Russian super-sonic shell.
We did send an Su-57 through the airspace—but with no warhead. Pure intimidation. Now—your explanation of the blast?

—I can't be fully certain, sir.
No on-site faction had the materials for that scale of destruction.
If it wasn't our Su-57, my best guess is that it originated from some unaccounted material—possibly sourced from the banned Ukrainian factory lines.

—And you're fully confident
none of our tactical teams launched that shell?

—One thousand percent, sir. I led the rescue team myself.
Swept the entire zone. And this wasn't just state duty.

—It was personal. His life—was tied to that blast.
Later, I personally called the nearest air base, cross-checked with both military and private-sector command.
No launch orders were issued.
I...
I verified it all myself.

—Don't take it the wrong way, Mama.
Here—take these tissues.
We acknowledge, with full gratitude,
the sacrifice made by the man you loved.
He wasn't one of ours,
but he truly loved our girl—and our country.
The reason I bring him up again—is because
two more bombs have gone off.
One in Kuala Lumpur,
and the other in central Tel Aviv.
Both had smaller blast radii than what we saw
in Ukraine—but the signature matches. Same material.
Do you have any intel on this?

—No, sir. As you already know—since returning from Ukraine,
I've been in Samara. Alone.
I've had no contact or involvement with those cities,
and no awareness of the events.
But—there is something from the mission that may help you.

—Go on, Mama.
We want your read on this.

—Some Ukrainian manufacturers—anonymous throughout, supplied at least two confirmed shipments of that compound to Middle Eastern extremist cells. I learned it through indirect comms—via other units.

—Yes, we've confirmed that on our end too.
An SVR unit had been trailing them for a while.

—Understood, sir. The same group, as it turns out,
was being led by the Iranian commander I captured.
He's on the Red Notice list. Despite his arrest, his network blames Mossad and their local allies for the failure and exposure. If their remaining members retaliated with whatever stock they still had, it wouldn't surprise me.

—Hmm… That lines up with our own findings.
Your intel is clarifying things.
There's something I need to say, Mama.
And if it hurts, forgive me.

—Say it, sir. I'm ready.

—We trust your judgment. Completely.
And your courage has never failed us.
But men like Amethyst Vega—high-profile prospects,
are always vetted at the highest levels.
Especially after you flagged him in Malaysia.
I went back and checked everything myself.
The profile we sent you was accurate. There were no faults
in what we gave you about the man you loved.
And we never doubted your instincts, or your reasoning.
But since you're still uncertain—do you want us to run a final verification? Confirm his true identity, once and for all?

—Thank you, sir. But he's gone.
There's no need to exhume his past anymore.
If you can respect that, I'd appreciate it.

—Your request will be honored, Mama.
We won't dig. And with that—I won't trouble you any further.
Just hand your written report to Mila.
She'll also provide you with personnel profiles
from several collaborating departments.
They've asked for your assessment—specifically,
how effective their teams were, and what level of cooperation
they gave you in the field. No pressure.
Sit with Mila, walk through it while you talk.
It won't feel like work.

—Understood, sir.
And thank you—for standing by me.
For everything.

—Thank you, Mama.
For all of it.

—*—

Silence Is Ours to Keep

Samara City
The Russian Federation

This time of year, Samara waits for snow like a lover waits for a letter that stopped coming years ago.

Temperatures had dropped past minus ten, but the sky hadn't cracked open in two winters. This year didn't look any more promising. Until just before dusk, that was the talk of the town.

To the west: the Volga River.
To the east: the Samara, the city's namesake.

At the heart of their meeting point lies the Seven Roads Circle. A junction where streets fork into markets, municipal offices, and the roads that feed the city's malls.

And right in the middle of that swirl of commerce and movement: a round concrete island crowned with a fountain. It's massive. Glorious in summer.

On official days, the Russian flag rises from the center shaft, flanked by jets of water and lights.
But no one, not even the weather gods, expected that fountain to be turned on in mid-January. Not in this brutal cold.

And yet, tonight—it was.
Not for a national holiday. Not for a visiting dignitary.
But in honor of one of the city's own.
A daughter. A fighter.
A name spoken with reverence, fear, and love.

And she—
She wasn't at the city hall where the ceremony had happened.
She was where the road splits toward the night market, where the steam from grilled meats meets the cries of vendors.

She was behind a bread stall.
Selling Tabani.
They weren't very good. Didn't need to be.
No one was really buying them to eat.

Teenage girls queued just to snag a selfie.
They wanted to look like her. Be like her.

Their parents stood in line too—asking for a photo,
a story, a scrap of her smile.

And she gave it. Every time. Polite. Quiet.
But her eyes kept drifting back to the fountain.

She'd seen it a thousand times.
From the pram. From the school bus. From a speeding SUV.
But never like this.

No one had ever promised her a playdate with that fountain.
Only one man had.

With a warning:
—Promises are made to be broken, you know.
But her heart—
Her heart refused to believe he meant it.

By 9PM, the last of the tabani were gone.
The night market was still winding down, but her part was over.
She crossed the street and sat down on the nearest bench,
eyes still on the fountain.

The mayor had issued standing orders:
That fountain doesn't turn off until she leaves.

The water was kept warm to fight the frost, jets steaming into the air.

Which is probably why no one noticed when warmer water slid down her cheek. Steam was everywhere tonight.
But the mist rising from her eyes wasn't water vapor.

And no one—no one in this proud city—saw that their infamous rebel daughter was breaking.

She'd taken a vow.
She would come back to this bench every winter evening,
until her body failed or her heart gave up.

Waiting.

Even though she didn't know if the man who made the promise would ever walk out of the silence again.

—*—

www.ingramcontent.com/pod-product-compliance
Lightning Source LLC
LaVergne TN
LVHW090545110826
845146LV00001B/22

* 9 7 8 9 8 4 3 5 8 9 1 8 7 *